THE HEAVENLY HORSE FROM THE OUTERMOST WEST

'You always want to know too much, El Arat,' said Cissy. 'Let's get on with it, the Oath.'

'Yes,' said Fancy. 'Back to business.'

'I won't take the Oath, I tell you!' shouted Duchess.

'I don't need any of you. I'll bide my time. I won't be here forever. Nothing is forever. The only thing that never changes is that you have to fight. Alone. It's that or be beaten, and I won't be beaten. I haven't been yet and I never will be. So forget about the Oath. Forget about the herd. The only thing I have is myself.'

'We can wait for you,' said Fancy. 'There's no Law about when the Oath has to be taken. It can be now – or it can be later. We'll wait, Duchess, until you see for yourself what life is like here. You've only just arrived. You haven't had time to forget. But we have time.'

Duchess stood with her nose to the back wall, refusing to think. She would just get through tomorrow, and that would be enough.

About the Author

Mary Stanton is president of a marketing communications firm in Rochester, New York, which numbers Eastman Kodak Company, Xerox Corporation, and Goldome Bank among its clients.

Her fiction, articles, and short stories have appeared in a wide variety of national and regional magazines, including *Isaac Asimov's Science Fiction Magazine*, *Horse Lover's National Magazine*, and her short stories have been anthologised in LAUGHING SPACE HORSE TALES.

Mary Stanton's early years were spent abroad in Japan and Hawaii. She is a graduate in philosophy from the University of Minnesota; she is also a former law student, claims adjuster, PR writer, and newspaper reporter.

Mary Stanton now lives on a farm in upstate New York with some of the horses who appear in *The Heavenly Horse from the Outermost West*. *Piper at the Gates of Dawn*, the sequel is also published by New English Library.

The Heavenly Horse from the Outermost West

Mary Stanton

NEW ENGLISH LIBRARY
Hodder and Stoughton

Copyright © 1988 by Mary Stanton

First published in the United States
of America in 1988 by Baen
Publishing Enterprises

First published in Great Britain in
1988 by New English Library
hardbacks

First New English Library paperback
edition 1989

British Library C.I.P.

Stanton, Mary
    The heavenly horse from the
    outermost west
    I. Title
    813'.54 [F]

ISBN 0-450-50812-9

Printed and bound in Great Britain
for Hodder and Stoughton
paperbacks, a division of Hodder and
Stoughton Ltd, Mill Road,
Dunton Green, Sevenoaks, Kent
TN13 2YA (Editorial Office:
47 Bedford Square, London
WC1B 3DP) by Cox & Wyman

For Robert J. Stanton
  who brought Duchess home
and
For Julie Jane Stanton
  who helped with her care

ACKNOWLEDGMENTS

Nancy Kress: writer, mentor and friend

Marilyn DeWispalaere: who owns the real
Bishop Farm

Manuel Brontmann: who gave me the key to the
gate

Duchess

BOOK
ONE

1

A New Arrival

Bishop Farm lay a mile northeast of Litchfield in a long, slow valley easy with oaks and meadows. Of the Farm's two hundred acres, most were in oats, corn, and hay. At the Farm's heart were thirty acres of barns, paddocks and pasture for the Bishop Farm bloodstock. The horses that Emmanuel Bishop and his son David raised there were known all over the county for their quality.

The stone farmhouse, white wood trim neatly painted every year, had lain on the hillside for a century or more. On one wet afternoon in June, the farm collie waited on its porch for the Bishops to return from a visit to the other side of town.

It had rained steadily all that summer's day. The small brook that wound through the brood mare pasture was swollen with water and the stream tapped at the gravel banks with an uneven slap. The rain had swept some of the petals from the flowering cherry that shaded the Big Barn and flattened them against the walls, where they showed bright pink against the dark brown wood.

Some hours before the rain, after sponging down an empty horse stall with disinfectant, Emmanuel and his son had left the Farm in the blue horse van. The pungent scent of the cleanser used to prepare stalls for new stock reached the dog even through the rain. The Bishops would be returning with a new horse, and the dog waited with some curiosity. His afternoon rounds were finished.

He had checked the five brood mares in their pasture next to the Small Barn; circled the weanling pasture where the Paint mare watched over this year's crop of foals; then paced through the Big Barn, with its arena, tack rooms and feed bins.

He was wet, and the rain had dulled his gold coat to brown. He lay stretched nose-to-forepaw, eyes on the gravel drive, occasionally scratching to relieve the itch from his drying hair.

He was alert to the small movements and activities of the Farm's routine: the barn cat stalking field mice in the grain bins, the goslings murmuring in a futile attempt at escape from their wire pen. But he was also patient, as dogs always are, suspended in a state of mind where time meant little.

The afternoon drew on. The rain stopped. Blue edged the rain clouds from the West and summer sunshine washed over the field of wheat.

The dog shifted and yawned. The slant of the sun told him it was getting close to time for afternoon chores, and Emmanuel wasn't back. The five brood mares in their paddock gathered at their gate as feeding time grew nearer, splashing in the puddles in the hollow made by mares who had gathered there for generations.

'They're late,' a chestnut mare called to the dog. A Quarterhorse, she carried a white blaze and a furrow between her eyes that gave her an intelligent, inquiring expression. Her name was Fancy. She was Lead Mare, and she moved with authority.

'They've disinfected a stall,' said the collie, Cory.

'What?'

The dog leaped down from the porch and crossed the drive to the paddock.

'I say they've disinfected a stall. Can't you smell it? And they've taken the horse van. There'll be a new horse coming in.'

'A new horse,' said a big, clumsy-looking Thorough-bred mare. Her name was Snip, and she was unranked in

14

the herd hierarchy. Horses, by instinct and their own
Laws, are herd animals, and have a strictly observed
order of precedence: Lead Mare, Second-in-Command,
Story-Teller, Caretaker, and unranked. Some herds, such
as Bishop Farm's, have Dreamspeakers – mares blessed
with dreams from the mouth of Equus, the horse god.

Snip, bumping Fancy's withers to get her attention, said
again, 'A new horse. Will it be a new mare, Fancy? Are
we goin' to be one-two-three-four-five-six instead of one-
two-three-four-five? Are we?'

Cissy, a liver chustnut, and like Snip unranked, said
irritably, 'I wish you'd learn to count like a matron,
instead of a weanling, Snip. You're forgetting Susie. You
always forget somebody, and since Susie went to take
care of the babies, you've decided she isn't part of the
herd anymore. That's dumb. There are six of us in this
herd, Snip, and if this new mare joins us, we'll be seven.'

'How are we seven?' said Snip anxiously. 'We are
Fancy, that's one. And Feather, who's Second-in-Com-
mand, that's two. And El Arat, who's Story-Teller and
Dreamspeaker, that's three. . . .'

'She's going to go on and on,' said Cissy to Fancy. 'Like
she always does.'

'Let her be,' said El Arat. The Bishop Farm's Story-
Teller and Dreamspeaker was finely made, a coal-black
Egyptian Arabian. She had the distant, liquid look char-
acteristic of her rank.

'. . . and me, that's four,' said Snip, 'and you, Cissy,
that's five. So how are we six?'

'Susie!' shouted Cissy in frustration. 'The Caretaker!
She's right over there with the weanlings. With *your* baby,
and mine, and El Arat's, and Fancy's, and . . .'

'Quiet,' said Cory. He stood at full alert in the drive,
ears tuliped forward, testing the wind. 'They're back.'

'I hear 'em, I hear 'em!' Snip jigged up and down in the
mud. A great splash of it hit Cissy's flank. Cissy snapped
at Snip, then whirled and cow-kicked, a kick intended for

15

small stinging insects like gnats and flies. Snip ignored the insult.

'Seven,' said Snip, with a sudden air of enlightenment. 'Seven with the new mare.'

'We don't know that it's a mare,' said Fancy mildly. 'It might be a gelding, for the riding students.'

The van came jouncing over the gravel drive. Cory inhaled sharply. 'It's a mare.' He stood for a moment, sniffing intently. 'She's come from the vet.'

'I hope she isn't sick,' said Cissy. 'That's all we need – an attack of stealsbreath or nose-runs-water.'

'You know the Bishops wouldn't bring sickness to the Farm, Cissy,' said Feather, the bay Second-in-Command.

The van came to a halt in front of the Great Barn. This barn, directly opposite the brood mare's own quarters, had been built with the narrowed planking and thick-timbered joists of a more extravagantly wooded age. In Emmanuel's father's time, it had held discs, harrows and plows. Emmanuel had expanded it to include a riding arena, tack rooms, and stalls for visiting horses, or horses who had to be in the three-week quarantine necessary to keep traveling sickness from resident animals.

Emmanuel jumped down from the van cab, and Cory dashed forward, barking in welcome. The brood mares craned their necks over the paddock fence.

Emmanuel and David walked to the rear of the van. Together, they let down the ramp. David disappeared inside the horse box. There was a thump, a scrape, and David backed a buckskin mare down the ramp. Emmanuel snapped a lead line to her ragged halter.

The mare was young and thin and had once been beautiful. What she was now could be seen in her frightened eyes, rolled to white half-moons. What she had been lay in her graceful head, finely carved muscle, and slender legs. She was a buckskin, the color of corn in late summer, with black mane, legs and tail.

As she stood in the drive, the sun broke through the last of the rain clouds and bathed her in sunshine.

El Arat, the Dreamspeaker, drew in her breath sharply, let it out in an explosive sound and backed away from the fence. The sun glanced off her coal-colored neck in rippling, fiery shadows. 'I see,' El Arat trembled, 'I see an Appaloosa. She is splashed with color, as though a rainbow shattered. O, Jehanna! Do you see the gold, the blue, the red?'

Fancy, the Lead Mare, looked at the Dreamspeaker curiously. 'She's a buckskin, El Arat. She's as pale as wheat, except for her points, and they're as black as crows.'

El Arat's eyes clouded and her neck stiffened.

'Perhaps you see a rainbow – a reflection from the sky and rain,' said Feather.

'The Rainbow Horse exists,' said El Arat, barely above a whisper. 'He is all the colors splintered. Red, Green, Blue, and Violet.'

'Indeed he does,' said Cissy, snidely. 'But he's a god, isn't he? Second only to Equus himself? The Rainbow Horse, Dancer, the Lead Stallion of the Army of One Hundred and Five? Breedmaster to the Appaloosa, too, as I recall. Not even your own Breedmaster, Hakimer the Arabian, outranks him. But he's not standing in our barnyard, El Arat. And anyway – that's a *mare*.'

'Look at her,' said Feather, in a gentle attempt at diplomacy. 'It's so sad, El Arat. She's been starved – anyone can see that; and beaten, too. Maybe you mistook her scars for Appaloosa color.'

'Appaloosas fade,' said Snip. 'I don't know why I know it but I do. At my home farm they thought they had a colored colt, and it turned dun its second year. They gelded it because it wasn't an Appaloosa anymore.'

'The color doesn't come back, though,' said Fancy. 'Does it?'

'No,' said El Arat. 'Not on the outside, at any rate.'

The buckskin mare in the drive pulled sharply back on the lead line, dragging Emmanuel across the gravel. Cory danced at her feet, his bark a warning. Suddenly, the mare kicked out with a vicious snort, a kick to maim and kill. The brood mares stiffened in shock.

'Did you see that?' demanded Snip. 'She kicked at Cory, she meant to hurt him bad!' Snip raised her voice in an indignant whinny. 'You! You there! Don't you kick at Cory.'

'Duchess,' said Emmanuel softly. 'Sa, saa, Duchess.' He reached up to pat her neck. The mare snaked her head, teeth bared. Emmanuel tugged sharply on the lead line, and she reared. The underside of her belly was scabbed with healing wounds.

'You, Duchess!' shouted Snip. 'You cut it OUT!'

'Be quiet, Snip,' said Fancy, glancing at El Arat. The Dreamspeaker stood with her great liquid eyes fastened on the struggle in the drive.

David grabbed the buckskin's halter from one side, and Emmanuel wound the lead line closer about his wrist. 'Sa, saa,' Emmanuel said. Duchess reared again. From the beginning, she had made no sound, and she struggled with the men in that same unnatural silence. Emmanuel pulled her forward with a sharp jerk, and she planted all four feet in the drive. The man pulled her head to one side and then the other, back and forth. The mare took one step forward, then another. Slowly holding her head from either side, the men walked her into the darkness of the small barn.

'Well,' said Cissy, 'well.'

'Are you all right, Cory?' asked Fancy.

The collie shook himself free of the grit that had been kicked up in the scuffle and trotted over to the fence. 'Wherever she's from, she's had a bad time,' he said briefly. 'You can tell just from looking at her.'

'The question is what El Arat can tell from looking at her,' said Feather.

The collie cocked his head inquiringly.

'El Arat says she's a funny-color – a what dy'call it: Appaloosa,' said Snip. 'She's not a funny-color, she's a

18

buckskin. Unless you think buckskin's a funny color, El Arat, do you?'

El Arat began to whicker to herself, barely audible sounds that could have been prayers, or imprecations.

'Stop that,' said Fancy.

The Arabian looked into the drive with an eerie farsightedness.

'Somebody do something,' said Cissy.

Cory wriggled under the fence and took a sharp nip at El Arat's fetlock. The Dreamspeaker jumped. Her eyes cleared, and she shook herself. She looked calmly from mare to mare, 'Tell me if there will be a full moon tonight.'

'Yes,' said Cory. 'But it'll be late. We're near Longlight.'

'I must get to the pond when the moon is rising. And you, Cory, shall help me.'

'We're in the barn tonight,' said Fancy. 'We won't be out for evening pasture until it's too hot to be out during the day. You know that.'

'Cory will draw the bolt on my stall, and then open the gate to the duck pond,' said El Arat.

There was a very long silence. Finally, Fancy said, 'This would be wrong, El Arat. There's no reason for disobedience. The men here have kept their bargain with the horse. They create the breeds, and for that we serve them, nothing more. There is a Balance, just as the One has ordained. We are sheltered and fed, and in return, we bear our foals for them to train and sell. I can see no reason to break this bargain.'

'*You* can see no reason. I can. And I must get to the pond – tonight.'

'Why tonight?' asked Fancy. 'And why the duck pond, of all places? The only reason you'd need the pond is if . . .' She broke off; a genuine horror shook her. 'You can't be serious!'

El Arat nodded. 'Yes. The Path to the Courts will be

open then. I must walk the Path to the Moon, and consult with Equus.'

'But that's a *legend*!' said Fancy. 'It's not true. It's a story . . . like the Tale of the Alamain, or the Tale of Alindar and the Eight Immortals.'

'This is not your business, it is mine, and it might not work, anyway.' A gleam of amusement flashed in her eyes, and she whickered comfortingly. 'All that will happen, I am sure, is that you will look out your stall window and see a black mare standing belly-deep in a duck pond, singing to an indifferent moon. But it is very important that I try.' She narrowed her eyes and directed a sharp look at Cory. 'You must help me, Cory.'

'There'd better be a good reason,' said the dog. 'My job's to guard you and keep you safe. What kind of herd guardian would I be if I helped you get out? They'd send me to the stinking city if they found out.' He snapped bad-temperedly at a fly. 'I'm needed in the barn.'

El Arat bent her head over the paddock gate. 'She is not what she seems, Cory,' she whispered. 'And you sense it too, do you not?'

'Maybe,' said Cory grudgingly. 'There was something.' Then as he walked away, he glanced back at El Arat. 'I'll check your stall tonight,' he said. 'We'll see.'

'Mares that aren't what they seem,' said Feather. 'What're they doing in there, anyway?'

In the depth of the barn, Duchess stood dead center in the deep piled straw and looked carefully around her. Horses have wide-angle vision, and from her spot in the center, Duchess could see all four sides of the stall; the stout oak planks that rose withers-high, the mesh that stretched from the planks to the roof, and the two double doors, barred shut, that led to what must be small in-and-out paddocks on the outer wall of the barn.

The water bucket smelled full; underneath it was a pile of alfalfa. Duchess was hungry. It was a familiar sensation; she couldn't remember a time when she hadn't been. She ignored it. In her struggles with Emmanuel and

David, she had slipped on the concrete aisle in the barn, and her left hock was scraped. She ignored that, too.

The daylight at the end of the aisle darkened with shapes. The men were coming back, and with them was another horse. Duchess backed to the farthest corner of her stall. The horse was a Paint mare, not young, who dished slightly when she moved.

Duchess rolled her eyes to get a better look. The Paint had a coarse, kindly head and soft eyes. Duchess caught her smell – of rain, and another, stronger odor. Weanlings. She was a Caretaker then. Duchess remembered that she had glimpsed the Paint in one of the far paddocks, standing guard over three or four youngsters. She had been pulled from her duties with the weanlings . . . to do what?

The men rolled open the stall door next to Duchess, and the Paint walked in. She pushed her brown-and-white muzzle to the mesh that separated the two stalls and blew out once in a friendly greeting.

'Howdy.'

Duchess backed into her corner and didn't reply.

'My herd name is Susie,' said the Paint. 'I'm the farm welcomer, like.'

Duchess' proper response was to blow out in a repeated sequence that indicated degrees of warmth or enmity. The range was from the soft, feather-light puffs of air with which matron mares greet their foals, to the harsh, explosive burst which means a stallion is ready for battle. Duchess settled for a greeting somewhere in the middle: I'm neutral, it said, ready to go either way.

There was a clink of a metal bucket outside Duchess' stall.

'David's going to clean the blood off your leg,' said Susie.

Duchess trembled. The door rolled open the the men stepped in. Duchess smelled their sweat, but no fear. She blew out once sharply, and charged. David sidestepped neatly, grabbed her halter, and clamped a metal twitch

21

Susie

over her muzzle. No fool, Duchess stopped in mid-stride. She knew about twitches. David tightened the twitch to a soft pinch. Emmanuel, metal bucket in one hand and a swab in the other, bent to her hind leg. She clenched her hindquarters, ready to kick again, but the twitch held her firmly, forcing her to stand still.

'Scrape's not too bad,' said Susie, moving to get a better look through the mesh. 'And they're very gentle, the Bishops, don't you think?'

Emmanuel cleaned the wound with hydrogen peroxide, then smoothed green paste on it.

'That's bag balm, that is,' said Susie. 'Good for the teats, too, when they're tight with milk and the foal's been weaned. But you probably know that already.'

Emmanuel straightened up, picked the cotton swab off the stall floor, and left. David, pulling gently on the twitch so that Duchess followed him to the door, released the metal clamp in one smooth motion and slid out after his father.

'Not so bad after all,' said Susie. 'They'll be back in a while to feed, but there's a little hay by your water bucket already. Why don't you have some? I'm always hungry after a trailer ride. I don't know how it is, but I am.'

An almost uncontrollable need to move pushed Duchess into a walk, and she began to circle the stall in a regular, unnatural rhythm. Her hindquarters hit the water bucket and the contents splashed into Susie's face. She walked faster and faster, her breath harsh and explosive.

Susie backed away, then took a bite of her own hay. This kind of dangerous restlessness was rare. It was a kind of madness, this circling. Horses were meant to walk, graze, and run over large stretches of territory. Confining them to a single small space could lead to this circling madness.

The buckskin's flanks were thin, and each rib was visible. Faint white scars crossed her neck. It was an unusual place for them – perhaps Duchess had been tangled in barbed wire.

23

Susie cleared her throat with a slight cough. 'Let me tell you about the barn routine. We get fed twice a day here, Duchess – once in the morning and once at night. Turn out is during the day until Longlight, then we get turned out at night, because it's too hot. Now, the blacksmith . . .'

'Why are you telling me all this?'

'I'm supposed to,' said Susie. 'It's part of my job. Now, the blacksmith . . .'

'I'm not going to be here long enough to worry about barn routine. Just tell me about the fences.'

'The fences?' Susie's forehead wrinkled in bewilderment.

'I can get out of anything as long as I'm not locked in.'

'You mean you want to leave the Farm? Why? Where would you go? This is our home, and it's yours now, too. We get fed twice a day, like I said, and the vet comes when you need him, and the pasture's good.'

'Now, maybe,' Duchess hissed. She stopped, and thrust her muzzle close to Susie's ear, whispering through the mesh, 'but what about winter? What happens when the cold white snow covers these good pastures of yours, and all you have to eat are leaves and branches rotting with the damp?' She began to move around the stall again, her breath harsh and heavy.

'Well, that won't happen here,' said Susie cheerfully. 'The Bishops are good men.'

'Good men,' said Duchess. 'There are no good men. And you're a fool or worse if you think so. Tell me about the fences.'

'I'll tell you about the fences. But you've got to stop that movin' around and listen to me. I can't talk to you if you move around like that. It makes me dizzy.'

She waited. Duchess circled the stall once, twice, then stopped.

'Now, the brood mares have the ten-acre pasture near their own barn. This pasture has a stream and timothy grass and clover. I can show you when we get turned out.'

24

Duchess bobbed her head impatiently, and Susie went on quickly.

'The fence there is like all our pasture fences – four boards and a post.'

'What about wire?'

Susie wrinkled her nose in distaste. 'No wire. Not here.'

'What about wire with points?'

'Barbed wire? On this Farm? Never.'

'How high is this board fence?'

'Um – maybe up to your shoulders. I can just get my head over to look around. It's awful high to jump, if that's what you're thinking.'

'Oh, I can jump it.'

'You can?' said Susie. 'Well, how about that. Maybe that's what you'll be doing here. Experienced jumpers are highly thought of at our Farm, very highly. You've been in shows, like? You're not a hunter, are you? That would be wonderful. The mares will be impressed. Now,' said Susie cautiously, 'why don't you eat some of that hay and tell me about it.'

Duchess turned with a startled look at the hay. She had forgotten it was there. She took a huge mouthful, chewed it hastily and swallowed.

'Good,' said Susie. 'So you're a jumper, are you? And your herd, what about them?'

The buckskin turned to her with a stricken look that made Susie's heart go cold. 'Oh, Equus,' said Susie softly. 'I'm sorry – I didn't mean . . . I won't ask anymore. Until you want to tell me. I won't ask anymore. We'll eat. The others will be in soon.'

Duchess finished the hay in great, tearing gulps. She drank a little, and Susie couldn't help a grunt of satisfaction. She finished her own hay except for a twist of dried alfalfa blossoms, her favorite, which she always saved for last. 'Here,' she said to Duchess. She pushed the twist through the wire mesh. 'I'm full. Do you want to finish this?'

Duchess, uncertain, glared at her. 'Save it. We're

25

locked in here and we can't get out. And I'm not going to share my straw. It's all I have and I have to make it last.'

'We don't need to eat straw. See, I've had so much hay I can't eat any more. Take it.'

Duchess lunged forward, grabbed the hay and worked it through the mesh. She ate and drank a little again. Despite herself, she relaxed a little, although her ears rotated back and forth, listening. Outside, she could hear the faint hoof falls of the others in the pasture and the scrabble of the collie's claws on the drive, punctuated by an occasional bark. Gradually, she dozed in the warmth, in the clean scent of the straw. Then, a faint smell of oats drifted toward her and she jerked her head up.

'The others are coming in now for evening feed,' said Susie.

There was a murmuring sound of horses and men and the scrape of hooves against gravel. One by one the brood mares filed into the barn. Emmanuel led Fancy with a lead line looped carelessly around her neck. The others followed in order of their rank: El Arat, Feather, Snip and Cissy. Fancy was in the stall directly across from Duchess; on either side of the Lead Mare were Feather and Cissy. Snip took the stall on Susie's far side and El Arat was placed on Duchess' near side.

Duchess shifted uneasily on her feet. The other mares were quiet; there were no whickerings of formal greeting. Only El Arat looked directly at her, and her gaze was strangely unfocused. Even more distracting was the intensity of her stare. Horses maintain eye contact with each other for brief moments, but El Arat's eye didn't waver.

Susie broke the prolonged silence. 'This is Duchess, Fancy. Duchess, here is Fancy, our Lead Mare. And this is the rest of our herd. Feather, that bay Thoroughbred there, is Second-in-Command. On Fancy's near side is Cissy. She's unranked. A Thoroughbred too. And this is Snip, here on my other side. Also a Thoroughbred. And on your near side is El Arat, our Dreamspeaker. El Arat's an Egyptian Arabian. They're very rare.'

26

'Yes,' said Duchess.

David Bishop wheeled a cart of grain down the aisle and filled the stall buckets with scoops of oats. The amount of grain given to each mare varied. Emmanuel followed with a long, narrow hay cart. Cory wriggled between the men and came up to Susie's stall.

'Everything all right?' he asked.

'Oh, yes. Duchess was a little nervous at first. But she ate her hay and she relaxed a little, I think. The others haven't formally greeted her yet, but they will after they've finished their oats.' David opened her stall door and put two scoops of grain in Susie's bucket, and she nudged him affectionately. Duchess' door slid open then, and the buckskin backed warily into the corner. The oats in the scoop he carried smelled fresh and filled with sun. Duchess lunged at the grain. Her shoulder struck David's chest, and the boy fell backwards. Cory barked, dashed forward and nipped at her ankles. Most of the grain landed in the bucket and Duchess lunged again. David backed out of the stall, pulling Cory with him.

There was a shocked pause. Fancy lifted her head and said mildly, 'We don't push here, you know. Please take things a little more calmly.'

Duchess ignored her and ate her oats as rapidly as she could without choking. Cissy clicked her tongue in disgust at the discourtesy. Susie made a murmur of protest. It caught in her throat and she coughed harshly, then turned to her own grain.

Duchess finished her grain and snatched at her hay, slowing only when her belly protested the sudden ingestion of food. She raised her head a little dazedly and encountered Fancy's grave and questioning gaze.

'Welcome to the herd, Duchess,' said Fancy. She blew out politely, and Duchess nodded her head.

'Oink, oink,' said Cissy, by way of greeting.

'What is your color, anyways?' said Snip. 'El Arat sees you funny. She's says you're more than one color. Are you, Duchess?'

27

'Be quiet, Snip,' said El Arat. 'I forbid this talk. I forbid it. Fancy, you must keep Snip silent.'

'Tell us,' said Cissy, 'what Farm were you stabled at before, Duchess? Anyplace we might know? It wasn't from around here, was it? We haven't seen you at any of the local shows.'

'I've never been to a show,' said Duchess.

'Oh. Are you a brood mare, then? How many foals have you had?'

'I haven't had any.'

'No foals? You're not a maiden mare, surely. Not at your age. You must be four or five at least . . .'

'Six,' said Duchess shortly.

'Six. And never been to a show,' said Cissy. 'Or had a foal. What have you been doing, then?'

'That's enough, Cissy,' Fancy said. 'She's barely had time to settle in. The barn lights will be turned out soon and we'll all get some sleep. We can talk in the morning, out at pasture.'

'I just wanted to find out if she's ranked.'

'I said that's enough for tonight.'

'Your word's law around here, is it?' said Duchess.

'Not law, exactly,' said Susie. 'But Fancy is our Lead Mare. Elected every year, just like we're supposed to. And she makes final decisions, of course. But not without asking us about things. Fancy believes in discussing things, don't you, Fance?'

Fancy nodded.

'Final decisions?' said Duchess. 'Discussions? What happens when the herd's in danger? What kind of discussions do you have then? Where I come from, any Lead Mare that lets the herd make up its own mind doesn't have any business being a leader.'

'Danger?' said Susie, bewildered. 'What kind of danger, like?'

'Dogs. No food. Men with chains. I don't know,' said Duchess impatiently. 'All kinds of things.'

28

'We don't have danger here,' said Feather. 'Not that kind, at least.'

Duchess snorted. David pushed a large broom down the concrete aisle, and the mares fell silent. Cory ticked along behind his master and paused in front of Fancy's door. 'We'll be turning out the lights soon,' he said. 'How's the new mare settling in?'

'Just fine,' said Fancy. 'A little uneasy, but it's the first day here, after all, and all of us find change a little unsettling.'

'Um. Well, you'd better let her know that we run a quiet barn,' said Cory. 'I don't want to have any more rearing or lunging, especially at feeding time.'

'She must be pretty valuable, for the Bishops to put up with that kind of behavior,' said Cissy. 'An Arabian, is she?'

'A Grade,' said Cory. 'She was a giveaway, taken from a place on the other side of the village. She hasn't been treated well, as you can see. She's going to be used as a lesson horse for new students.' David called to the dog from the other end of the barn, and the collie gave Duchess a friendly little nod. 'Good night, then. Sleep well, mares.' As he trotted off, he paused for a moment at El Arat's stall. 'I'll be on guard tonight,' he said. David turned the lights off, and the barn was plunged into darkness.

'A Grade,' said Cissy. 'I should have guessed.'

Fancy sighed and pressed her nose against the wire mesh. 'Cissy's stuck on some very unimportant things, Duchess. I ignore her. Take some time to settle in. Have a good rest.'

One by one the mares knelt and rolled into sleep. Susie settled peacefully onto her side, her coarse, kindly head stretched out in the rough straw. Eventually, a slow snoring came from her throat, undercut by a slight, unnatural rasp to her breathing. The silence was almost complete.

'Fools,' said Duchess loudly. Susie blinked in her sleep,

and rolled slightly. Duchess pawed angrily at the straw, exposing the hard clay floor. She nosed at the double doors to the outside.

Except for Duchess' own, the double doors at the back of each mare's stall were open, and faint moonlight flooded the barn. Duchess grunted, striking at her latch, but it refused to move. After a time, sleep stole up like a cat, carrying whimpering images of chestnut-colored men pouring an endless stream of oats into a bucket with a hole in the bottom. Duchess locked her knees and slept.

And as she slept, she dreamed:

She was walking in the dark. A pale moon was rising with a thick greenish cast to its sullen circle. She was walking, and the way was rough, uphill, filled with holes to catch unwary feet and trap them. She was walking, and the shed where she had spent those last weeks was above her, and she walked, walked, walked into its open door. Pride was there, his great sides sunken, ribs shining high and bony-white. His muzzle was torn, the lips spotted dark with dried and drying blood, his eyes wide open, staring. Duchess walked in the moonlight, the air around her heavy as water. She bent her head to the remembered face and blew gently on his cheek. A snarl. Whine. Low-pitched and eerie. A thick snake of a sound that made her whirl and rise to her hind legs, sharp hooves ready. But the shed was empty except for the slow dead air, and Pride. The whine rose and fell, and the floor of the shed, piled high with feces and splintered wood, heaved and cracked. Duchess reared again. A Hound's body exploded from the shed's floor, red as bloody death. On the dog-like frame, was a skull's head: hideous, grinning, sharp-fanged. The floor heaved. The Hound/Horse crawled. The whinning rose, and Duchess screamed . . .

'Duchess!'

The Hound/Horse crawled nearer, dead eyes looming, cutting off Pride's body, blotting out the shed.

'Duchess!'

And she sprang away, hindquarters bunched, and fell

30

against the wooden sides of the stall at Bishop Farm. Susie's homely head, outlined in the grave-grey night, was just beyond the mesh. 'Oh,' said the Paint. 'That sound was terrible, Duchess. You screamed like nothing I heard before in my life. Are you all right? If I call, Cory will come, and he can help. He'll bring David, and he'll bring Emmanuel, Duchess.'

Duchess trembled. Sweat dampened her chest and withers, and her breath came harsh and short. She swallowed hard and Susie, pressed tight against the mesh that divided the two stalls, called her name again. On the other side of the stall, Fancy stirred awake, and farther down she heard the sleepy mutterings of Feather and Snip, and then Cissy's sharply querulous tone.

'What's going on?' Fancy asked quietly.

'I . . . had a bad dream. That's all. Go back to sleep.' The night was alive now, and the whole herd awake, bringing with the questions a sense of community and protection.

Duchess put her head to her bucket and drank some water. 'Steady. Steady,' said Susie, as she would to a young foal. 'Just a bad dream, like. We all have 'em. Even Stillmeadow himself.'

'Not strictly true,' said El Arat, from her stall beside Susie. 'But well enough to say in the dark. Tell me, Duchess, what was this dream you had?'

'El Arat can interpret dreams,' said Susie in an undertone. 'And she tells the best Stories. Maybe you could tell us one now, El Arat. Put us back to sleep.'

'I can fall asleep just fine if you all shut up,' said Cissy.

'Yes. Let's settle down again,' said Fancy. 'That is, Duchess, if you're all right now.'

'I'm fine. Go back to sleep.'

'I'll stay up a little while,' whispered Susie. 'The babies sometimes need a little company, like, if they've had a dream in the night. Maybe El Arat will tell the Tale of the Second Law tomorrow – you know – "The Least Shall be Best."' Susie arched her neck in shy pride and said humbly, 'She says I'm just like that there mare in the Story, what's her name . . .'

'Shadow,' supplied Duchess wearily.

'Yeah. Just like Shadow. Not really, though. I expect El Arat says that just to be nice. But I am of the Caretakers, you know. That's my job.'

The two mares stood together in the dark, and Duchess could feel Susie's warm breath as they stood nose to nose. Susie started to hum the 'Horse in the Moon' song, and as she sang, Duchess' eyelids dropped.

'Come down, the beech trees whispered with a dry leaf rattle and hiss. Come down, they sang with a breezy snarl, come down for a beech tree's kiss . . .' Susie's voice faded. Duchess slept. And she dreamed no dreams.

2

The Path to the Moon

El Arat waited until the moon rose like a silver apple over the fields and pastures of Bishop Farm. The night was very still, the barn quiet. She walked out to the little paddock attached to her stall and raised her muzzle to the breeze. A sweet scent came from the roses under the windows of the big house, and a cool, fishy odor marked the presence of the duck pond. She stepped back into her stall for a moment. The strange mare was soundly asleep after her bad dream; Susie was snoring comfortably beside her. El Arat rather thought Fancy was awake; she could sense the chestnut's breathing. She also knew the Lead Mare wouldn't interfere.

It was time. She moved purposefully down the length of her paddock and nosed at the gate. The gravity latch, set too low for her teeth, was snugged tightly against the oak cross board. She would need Cory, after all.

The big dog should be making nighttime rounds; El Arat waited, stamping a little with impatience. The moon was high and full, and she was anxious not to miss its peak. Finally, she glimpsed his shaggy outline on the hill near Stillmeadow's shed, his white ruff tipped with silver moonlight. The silver disappeared for a long moment as he went down the hill, then reappeared as he approached the brood mare's barn. He stopped to sniff intently at the abandoned fox den under the Russian olive hedge, then headed toward her.

33

'I thought you wouldn't get here in time,' said El Arat. 'Help me with the latch.'

The big dog was uneasy.

'Cory,' said El Arat. 'You saw what I saw. I know it. The mare is not what she seems. I don't believe that she knows it herself.'

'I saw a trick of the light – an aftereffect of the rain.'

'Cory.' El Arat dropped to an urgent whisper, sweet for all its insistence. 'Cory, when I see and hear the shapes and signs Lord Equus sends, I know you see them too.'

Cory shrugged a little angrily. 'All dogs are the same. It's a keener sense, a gift from the One, like my nose, my coat, my speed. I am no more and no less than any other dog.' He raised his eyes to hers. 'And I didn't really see what you did, you know. I saw just enough to know that you are not a liar or a faker, El Arat. But I don't know what it means. And I don't know what you intend to do now.' He paused expectantly, but El Arat looked past his shoulder, and said merely, 'Open the gate for me, please, before the moon dips, and the Path is closed.'

'Can't it wait? The new mare will be turned out with you tomorrow. You can ask her . . .'

'I tell you, she knows no more than I, and probably less. It is I who am Dreamspeaker here. I who am Story-Teller. And Jehanna, my Goddess-Patron, has a Tale to send to me tonight. This is a task meant for me alone. Is it mere chance that I, a mare whose lineage goes back to the time when all the earth was grass, was the only one to see that this mare is an Appaloosa, although she appears to be a Grade mare to all others? Events are in motion that you cannot stop, and they concern me and that mare.'

Cory looked gravely. El Arat ducked her head, 'I know. I sound as much a boaster as that gander that you drive out of the roadway every week. But I only speak the truth. And if the truth sounds vain, Cory, so be it.'

Cory grunted and raised himself on his hind legs. He

34

worked at the latch with both teeth and paws, and finally the gate swung free.

El Arat stepped quietly through the long grass, barely disturbing the air as she moved. The pond, fed by the streams that snaked through the meadows, lay past a rise to the side of the farmhouse.

Cory followed El Arat at a steady lope, nose to the ground, alert for any unnatural sounds. Once he felt the snick of wings, as of a great bird passing. He leaped into the air and snapped at it futilely. There was no sight, no scent of any real presence other than his own and the black mare's.

At the pond, the moon shone straight into its own reflection, so that a silvery arc passed from water to sky and back again. El Arat paused at the edge, then waded slowly to the center. Her mane floated like shadowy silk on the water. She raised her muzzle to the moon and from under the water her left fore rose and fell, three times. The splashing sounded like a rising fish.

Cory jumped suddenly. The great wings were just over his head again. But this time, the wings were real.

Slowly, like a rising planet, a great white Owl flew over the waters of the pond. His wings spread from one edge to the other. His eyes were great with a shining light. The snow white of his head, chest and back feathered into wings, one tipped with the black, the other white.

El Arat called, 'Jehanna. Goddess. Patron Mare of Dreamspeakers. Open the Path.'

The Owl swept his wings down and up again. He floated over the pond, over El Arat's gleaming head.

Cory growled and his hackles rose. El Arat lifted her left fore once and once again. On the third strike her hoof seemed to catch and hold, and she reared, a splendid ebony arc, streaming jet-dark water. The moonlight brightened to a painful intensity, and Cory shut his eyes. He heard the clarion call of stallions, a hundred or more. A trick of the night wind he told himself, or perhaps he mistook the low croaking of the frogs.

Time passed. The light dimmed. He opened his eyes against the glare. The bird was gone. El Arat was in the center of the pond, a black shape springing out of the water. She turned, came slowly out and stood dripping at the pond's edge.

Her eyes were glowing and she was touched with starlight. El Arat seemed a stranger to him. Even her odor had changed.

'I will tell you,' she said softly, 'what it was I saw, and where I have been.'

'You haven't moved from the pond,' said Cory. 'I closed my eyes because it's a clear night, and too bright to look directly at the moon. But you haven't been anywhere, El Arat. You were there all the time in the water.'

'Oh, no. I have crossed into Summer, and from there through the white gate to the Courts themselves. I have a new Tale now. It is a true Tale, Cory. And you will stand with me while I tell it . . . just to you, and to no other. Do you promise? For you will have a part in this, I think. They told me you must know.'

Cory nodded in startled agreement.

'You must know, Cory, that we horses are part of the whole, just as you dogs are – one of many under the One Who Rules Us All.

'Our own gods, the horse gods, are both good and evil – both kind and cruel. And, like many gods, your own, perhaps, among them, some are more one than the other. There is Equus, our good Lord, and his Army of One Hundred and Five, who live in the Courts of the Outermost West. Each stallion in the Army of One Hundred and Five is a Breedmaster; each a foundation sire for the breeds in the world of men. And the Army is ranked, as all herds are ranked – according to duty and function. The Breeds themselves are numbered: the oldest god is Equus the First. The Dancer, Breedmaster of the Appaloosa, is Second; El Hakimer, Breedmaster to the Arabians, is Third – and so on down to the youngest breed, the Palomino, One Hundred and Fifth.'

'With Equus in the Courts live a band of Mares. As each stallion is Breedmaster, so each mare is Breedmistress. My own goddess-mare, Jehanna, is Dreamspeaker to these mares, and indeed, to Lord Equus himself. She is a Watcher at the Pool. She is Jehanna, the Arabian, my Dreamspeaker.'

'Well, then, there must be a Breedmistrees for Dancer, the Appaloosa,' said Cory. 'Didn't you say that the Dancer came after Equus himself? And if the Arabian is Third – and the Breedmistress is a Dreamspeaker . . .'

'*The* Dreamspeaker,' said El Arat.

'. . . Sorry, *The* Dreamspeaker, then the Appaloosa Breedmistress must be Lead Mare. Who is she?'

El Arat paused, and looked at the horizon. Dawn was curling around the edges of the night. She drew a breath and went on. 'It grows lighter and the dark recedes. I have told you our gods are both good and evil. I have told you of the good. I will tell you now of the evil.'

She said, 'The Dark Lord lives in the Black Barns guarded by Three Gates.

'He is the Lord of the Final Death – the Death that is the end of all life; the Death that is nothingness, complete, total, and absolute. He is called the Black Horse, the Horse with the Twisted Horn, and the path to his kingdom is guarded by three gates.

'The first gate bars the den of the Harrier Hounds – hounds that follow and never lose the scent.

'The second imprisons Sycha – a name so despised by mares that it has been cursed forever.

'The last gate binds Anor – the Destroyer, the Executioner – whose jaws rend the flesh of horses the Black Horse has condemned to the nothingness of the pit.

'These creatures are called forth when the Balance is broken. When good takes steps to evil, the Dark Lord's creatures are let loose.

'And his creatures are these: The Harrier Hounds – skull-headed, fire-eyed – who chivvy and course to his bidding. The pack leader's name is Scant, and he serves his Master, the Dark Lord, well. Scant is the Voice of Anor the Red.

'Sycha, the Soul-Taker . . . and no goddess-mare to me, or mine. Once Breedmistress to the Appoloosa, Sycha betrayed her kind to follow the Dark Lord and call horses to the Final Death.

'Anor, the Destroyer, the Executioner, whose teeth, they say, are as sharp as a lion's, who drinks blood and eats meat, whose hooves are like swords. Anor kills for his Lord, destroys at his Lord's bidding.

'You asked me, Cory, about the Appaloosa Breedmistress. The Lead Mare. For Equus, there is no Lead Mare,' said El Arat. 'There hasn't been a Lead Mare, an Appaloosa Breedmistress to partner the Rainbow Horse, since the Palouse Wars. This war was, to begin with, a war of men upon men, until the horse was drawn in, nose over tail, unwilling.'

Cory settled himself more comfortably on the pond path.

'Long ago, the spotted horse lived with men by a river. The river was called Palouse, and from its name came the name of the spotted horse, the Appaloosa. These men were of the far past, for they had hair the color of my coat and as long as my tail. They wore the feathers of birds on their chests, and the skins of predators on their shoulders.

'There were other men, men of the present, who coveted the horses, the lands, the river, the very sky that watched over the men from the past. These men warred upon each other. The men from the past, their women, their children, and their horses, lost this war.

'A madness came over the victors, and they slaughtered all, the men, the women, the children – and the horses, Cory, the horses. They cut the throats of the foals as they nursed from their dams. They shot the stallions and left them to die on the mountainside. The mares they stole to haul coal in their cities. Only a few escaped the killing.

'Sycha the Cursed was the Lead Mare of Equus then.

She, the Appaloosa Breedmistress and partner to Dancer, watched her children killed, her sisters scattered into slavery, her brothers bleeding on the mountainside. She herself was trapped and tortured by men – escaping only through the blackest bargain that has ever been made. She lost faith, heart and love. And then, Cory, she betrayed her own kind, out of grief and rage, and to save her life. The bargain she made, Cory, was that the Appaloosa could only exist at the hands of man – that breeding an Appaloosa stallion to an Appaloosa mare may not give an Appaloosa foal. That two times out of three, the foal that is born is not spotted, but solid. The spotted horse is the only true Appaloosa, Cory – and they are dying, dying. Until the Appaloosa line breeds true – every time – Sycha's black bargain is the cause. And there is more, Cory. More. For every three spotted foals that are born, one loses its color by its breeding age. The colors die as green dies from leaves in autumn, and only grey remains. And the Appaloosas are lost.'

'And the Tale you say you heard tonight?'

'The Tale I heard tonight? The Dark Lord's Hounds hunt again to remove forever the last of the Appaloosa breed. And this time, they hunt their quarry here.' El Arat dropped her head, went still, and began to speak her dream.

The Tale of El Arat's Dream

I passed through Summer's Meadow, the place of Judgment, and from there to the Courts themselves. I saw Jehanna, Dreamspeaker and Story-Teller to the Courts of Equus. It was evening, and Jehenna stood by the Watching Pool that lies in a grove of lindens at the heart of the Heavenly Courts. Not even Equus knows the origins of the Watching Pool; just that it has been there, perhaps since before the time of the One, so that the Army may Watch the Pool and there guard the welfare of horses in

39

the world of men. There are Visions here, and it is such a Vision that I, El Arat saw, and will tell to you.

There was a Vision in the Pool as Jehanna watched, and I saw it over her shoulder.

In the Vision, it was earth-night, and the earth's moon shone on a garbage-strewn shack. From the shack came an odor of despair, of death and near-death.

In the shed revealed in the Watching Pool was Duchess, the last true mare of the Appaloosa line. The Black Horse, bent on evil, had set his Harrier Hounds questing for Duchess. Tonight, near the shed in the Vision, they were very close.

'No time,' Jehanna murmured. 'We must be ready.' For Jehanna herself was prepared to plunge into the Watching Pool and follow the Path of the Moon to save the mare that lay dying in the shed. Much would depend on the Black Horse and his Executioner, Anor the Red. If the Red placed so much as a forefoot in the yard surrounding the hovel, the Balance would be overset, and the agreement of Light and Dark not to mix in the affairs of mortals well and truly broken. But the Black Horse had been wily, as is his custom, and we could see no trace of evil, other than the evil of men. But we sensed it. We knew it must be there.

Jehanna raised her head and called, 'Sentinel!'

'Dreamspeaker?' A sturdily built chestnut stallion appeared from the grove of trees surrounding the Pool and stepped to her side. It was Miler, the Quarterhorse.

'Find Lord Equus. The Army of One Hundred and Five must be assembled.'

'It's come then,' said Miler gravely. 'The Dancer's fate is to be decided. The last true mare of his line is dying.'

'Soon. Perhaps. Equus must Watch with me. I may be called to the Path of the Moon to save her.'

Miler glanced quickly at the Vision in the Pool. The Moon was full over the garbage-strewn shed and yard; a scum-filled pond nearby reflected moonshine with a sickly yellow-green light. He pivoted on his hind legs, calling

aloud. In moments Flyer, the Standardbred, the Eighty-
fifth, appeared through the trees.

'Trouble?' asked Flyer.

'Yes,' said Miler. 'Take Watch for me. I must find
Equus.' Flyer's ears swiveled forward in surprise. 'The
Dreamspeaker's here. Has the time come then?'

'Yes. The Moon is full. The Path's open. The Hounds
draw closer to the Appaloosa mare. Jehanna must be
guarded. I'll call the others – the Dancer, too. And I'll
call Equus.'

Flyer stood protecting Jehanna at the Pool. We heard
Miler's rallying cry echoing high and fierce.

One by one the cry was answered until the starred sky
echoed with the whinnies of the stallions responding to
the call. In twos and threes, the great horses of the Army
raced through the trees and formed ranks around the
Watching Pool. They drew together with a restless stamping, hindquarters bunched and ready to spring into battle.

Then – alone through the trees – came the Dancer, the
Appaloosa, known as the Rainbow Horse. He was swept
with all the colors of a splintered rainbow. His hindquarters were full and powerful, his eye was large and dark,
and his head and neck crested with power. Of all the
breeds on earth and above it, his was the oldest. In times
when the earth itself was new, the rivers few, and all
earth's land was grass, the Dancer's mares and stallions
had been the first to lend their minds and bodies to the
will of men.

And now, it seemed, they would be the first to
disappear.

And then, a white shining like a banked and glowing
moon moved among the Army. The stallions parted like
a wave, great necks arched in respect. Equus, glowing
more brightly silver than the Moon itself, stepped to
Jehanna's side.

'The gelding with Duchess is dead.' Jehanna groaned
as she spoke, as though she were in labor. 'A Harrier

The Dancer

Hound is near. I am sure of it. But he hasn't shown himself – and I must wait.'

Equus nodded, silver eyes grave. The Dancer stopped to Equus' side. The light from his god threw his colors into bright relief and he shone like a rainbow over a waterfall.

'We will Watch together,' said Equus.

The images in the Pool fanned into a large circle, and the stallions crowded close together to Watch:

The Vision in the Pool

'This is the kind of call we gonna be gettin' out here?' said the recruit. 'Animal abuse don't seem like much of a police matter.' His winter uniform was sharply creased, stiff-collared, and the back of his neck was pink, unlined, and vulnerable.

His partner was older; his uniform, and the belly beneath it, had settled like an old foundation. Belly, jowls, the corners of his eyelids all fell in a downward march from age and experience.

They were parked curbside, at night, in a part of their village that spoke of poverty and neglect in equal parts. The older cop spat out the passenger window of the cruiser and squinted at the house beyond the curb. The moon was full, and he could see more than he wanted to. The shack was two rooms slapped together, encased in asphalt siding that peeled like a split sausage casing in the cold. Snow covered the garbage-strewn ground in front: the broken half of a rusted bicycle; a stained toilet base; a faded maroon couch, seat springs gaping wide.

'Animal abuse don't seem like much of a police matter,' repeated the old cop matter-of-factly. 'We'll go take a look.'

As they got out of the car, the door to the shack opened and a pool of sickly yellow light flooded the darkened yard. The owner – skinny, middle-aged, perhaps younger,

chest concave in an undershirt – leaned against the door
jamb, his truculent gaze directed carefully down the
street. A yellow dog whined at his feet.

The old cop ignored the easy insolence with an indiffer-
ence born of larger wars. The recruit stopped, looked, a
cautionary hand at his holstered gun.

'C'mon,' his partner said. They eased over a wire fence
and walked through the snow to the back of the house. A
rusted windbreak made of tin and wooden board shouldered into a rise in the backyard. Melted snow runneled
from the roof and fell in large drops on the two horses
below.

'Jesus.' The recruit swallowed hard and wiped his
mouth with one hand.

A spotted gelding, an Appaloosa, who must have stood
over 16 hands, was lying dead in the muddied snow.
Muzzle blood-spotted, teeth broken, his ribs sprang high
and wide through his feces-covered coat. A buckskin
mare stood beside him. She raised her head as the men
came up the rise.

'Look at her mouth,' said the recruit.

'You gonna be sick?'

'No. I . . . why is her mouth tore like that? She's got
blood all over.'

'They was trying to eat the walls down. For food.'

The buckskin shifted her weight, awareness stirring.

'We gotta do something. Food – water.'

'Little late for that. Ain't no vet in the county goin' to
save that mare. It's a damn shame. She's young and
pretty, even with all that shit she's been laying in.'

The mare's head dropped, and it seemed from her
hopeless stance that she understood and would welcome
a single shot. An end to it. 'Hell with that,' the recruit
muttered, then jumped at a slight shifting in the snow.
The yellow dog, skinny and silent, crept through a broken
slat in the fence and licked at the gelding's face. Flies
hung at the corners of his yellow-green eyes, and a
curiously shaped black crescent, the size of a horse's hoof,

44

marked his yellow chest. 'Gaah!' said the recruit, and moved to shove the dog away.

The mare's emaciated frame jerked. She screamed and kicked. The hound crouched and dodged, snarling. She reared, the underside of her belly pitifully thin, her hooves cracked and peeling. She struck. The dog howled, bellied in the snow, then rolled down the rise. The mare shivered and nosed the gelding's body.

The old cop unbuttoned his jacket with quick snaps and drew his pistol, clasping his left hand over his right wrist. He shook slightly – perhaps from the cold. 'Put her out of her misery,' he said, and steadied himself in the snow.

Suddenly, the buckskin mare raised her head, eyes wide, ears swiveled forward. She looked intently past the old cop's shoulder. The cop whirled. Something faintly gold shimmered in the snow bank, a reflection, he said aloud, of the dying mare behind him.

The yellow dog howled, a cry that made the hair stand up on the old cop's neck, then leaped at the shadow with a snarl to freeze the air. Without pausing to think, the old cop squeezed off a shot. The dog dropped in mid-air, twisted once and lay still.

'That's my dog,' screamed the man from the shack. 'You lousy bastards shot my dog.'

The old cop holstered his gun. 'Well, now,' he said slowly. 'I'll tell you what. You call the vet. Now. And if you do, we just might forget about those charges. We just might. If we can save that mare.'

The Vision faded.

Jehanna rose from the Pool. A dark red trickle ran from her neck in a slow-moving stream. She knuckled slowly forward and rinsed the wound in the Pool's Waters until the trickle stopped. She stood then and looked at Equus, golden eyes calm.

'So,' said Equus, 'we have a little time.' He looked at the Dancer. 'The Agreement has been broken. It was a Harrier Hound that attacked the Dreamspeaker.

45

Jehanna, you're certain that this is the last mare of the Dancer's line?'

The Dancer quivered and seemed about to speak.

Jehanna nodded. 'She is the six times great granddaughter of the cursed Breedmistress Sycha. Surely you can see that, Lord.'

'And you, Dancer, you know her?'

'I have Watched,' said the Dancer, 'ever since Duchess was born. When she was young, no higher than my chest, her head, withers and flanks were as gold as Jehanna's, and a white blanket covered her quarters.'

'This mare,' said Equus, 'this great-granddaughter of Sycha the Betrayer, could she be Tested for the rank of Lead Mare to my mares? A new Breedmistress would save the Appaloosa line. Does she know who she is?'

'No, her own dam died early of stealsbreath. She herself was passed from hand to hand.'

'With as rare a color as this gold and white that the Dancer has described?' said Equus in surprise, 'why didn't men keep her?'

'She lost her color before she attained maiden status,' said Jehanna. 'Sycha's curse.'

'Her colors died,' said the Dancer. 'I could do nothing. I have Watched the Pool these years past as the colts and fillies of my breed lose their color, one by one. And you have kept me, Lord, from action.'

'Duchess carries the true color within her,' said Jehanna. 'If she's mated with an Appaloosa stallion, the foals should be as brightly marked as in the old days, when the breed was at its height, and the colors will remain. Men can breed the Appaloosa true once again. And we shall have victory over Sycha's foul bargain with the Black Horse.'

'She must mate with me,' said the Dancer.

Equus looked at the Rainbow Horse. 'The Balance,' he said gravely. 'It cannot be lightly broken.'

'I must go,' said the Dancer. 'I must leave and save her.'

'The Balance,' repeated Equus sharply. 'We can't disturb the natural Balance unless the Black Horse moves first. Otherwise, Sycha's betrayal stands.'

'The agreement *has* been broken,' shouted the Dancer. 'You said yourself that a Harrier Hound stalks the buckskin mare. See how the Black Horse keeps the Balance!' He reared and his hooves flashed in the starlight. 'I will find the man who starved her and I will break his back.'

'Yes,' Jehanna nodded, flicking her tail impatiently. 'We have the right to make the Balance equal once again, after this attack.'

'We should have moved first,' the Dancer shouted. 'Why wait on his pleasure?'

'You know that as well as I do,' said Equus. 'We upset the Balance – and there may be war. Would you be responsible for bringing evil on some other creature?'

'The agreement,' snarled the Dancer. 'Am I to stand by while my breed is attacked and slaughtered? First, my brothers at the Palouse River. Then, Sycha's betrayal. And now this mare nearly dead and her brother murdered!' He pawed furiously at the pond's edge, and the bank crumbled a little under the thrust of his weight. The Stallions in the Army stirred, and the Percheron reared and screamed the battle cry.

'You're impetuous,' said Equus. 'A good trait in war – but the Courts are at peace.' He paused. 'What would you do, Dancer?'

'I would hunt the Black Horse and kill him.'

Equus blew out once, sharply, and the Dancer subsided a little. 'Then let me force Anor the Executioner to the Final Death. I'll meet him here, or on his own ground or on the earth itself. I'll tear his throat from jaw to chest.' The Dancer, in a fury, struck at the Waters of the Pool. The blow left a crescent-shaped hole. From its depths spat a gout of fire.

Jehanna screamed.

A Vision came of death: a horse – red, massive in his build, clawed talons glinting where solid hoof should be.

Anor the Executioner, Killer for the Black Horse. Anor's muzzle opened wide to show the fanged teeth found in carnivores. An Appaloosa stallion, black and white, lay before him, its spotted belly gutted. From Anor's wolf-like teeth ran gouts of blood and flesh, and his eyes were closed in a terrible ecstasy of feeding.

Then, the massive head turned slowly, slowly, and the eyelids rose with the laziness of maggots.

Teeth bared, head snaked low, the Dancer plunged straight at the Vision. Jehanna leaped between them. The Dancer struck her full in the side and fell back.

The Pool went dark.

The Army shouted: 'Anor! Anor! Anor!'

Equus moved slowly to the Pool and looked down in the quiet water.

'A challenge has been issued,' he said, 'and we may answer it.' He looked at the Dancer. The Appaloosa flung his head up. His chest was taut with muscle, his legs long, hard, and clean, and his hindquarters were swept with all the rainbow colors, full and powerful. 'Let me go!' he cried. 'I must!'

'It's not your courage that I doubt,' said Equus quietly, 'or your ability as a warrior. You move too quickly, Dancer. Your senses make your decisions before you have time to think. I will consult the Owl. If the One Who Rules Us All allows you to leave the Courts, you shall go. I shall ask three things to right the Balance.

'First, because the Black Horse even now seeks this mare, that you get her in foal. We ask this so that the Appaloosa line will have a chance of surviving, since the foal – a true son of Appaloosas – will breed true.'

The stallions stamped their hooves in unison, and the trees shook with their power.

'Second, that the mare be Tested for the rank of Breedmistress to the Dancer. As the great-granddaughter of Sycha, she is the heir to the Dancer's line. If she passes the Tests of Courage, in War and the Games of War; of Wisdom as Lead Mare; of Knowledge as Dreamspeaker;

48

of Heart as Caretaker, then she is the worthy successor of her line.'

The stallions raised their voices in a shout that made waves upon the Pool.

'Third, that the Dancer answers Anor's challenge – and that they fight to the Final Death.'

The stallions reared as one, and screamed the battle cry – and the sky trembled.

The Dancer shook with eagerness.

Equus raised his head. 'So you would go, would you?' he said. 'Do you understand what it would mean? You'd have no powers there. When you follow the Path of the Moon, you leave your color here. You shine in the Courts with the colors of your name, the Rainbow Horse. But your coat will be black and white in the pastures and fields of men. And your power lies with the Rainbow, Dancer. You'd be left with nothing but your hooves, teeth and speed. You'd go as a mortal stallion, and not a god.'

'For his time with the mare only,' said Jehanna. 'When Anor comes, the Dancer will be allowed his power.'

'True enough,' said Equus. 'But consider what that means, Jehanna. When the Dancer's powers return to him, it will be because he must fight Anor. Are we prepared to stand more death? More blood?'

'Peace, despite the cost?' said the Dancer.

Equus looked at him sharply. 'I think of the welfare of all, Dancer. And so must you. Do you realize what you risk? What this task means to you and the future of your breed? You must consent to the rule of men – a rule that may be harsh or kind. You will not be one of the One Hundred and Five to them. You must keep your allegiance to me – and to the One who rules us all, and do nothing that would tip the Balance in the Black Horse's favor. You may not act for yourself alone. You must remain at Bishop Farm, and obey the men there. You will get the buckskin mare in foal. You will not let her know who you are, or why you are there. She will be Tested for the rank of Breedmistress, and she must pass the Test

49

without hope or knowledge of reward, if the Tests are to be true. And finally,' Equus leaned close to the Dancer, his voice compelling, 'you may *not seek out* Anor. He must come to you, or the Balance will be well and truly overset. There are temptations below, Dancer. You are one of the oldest members of the Army. You may not recall the feel of earth beneath your hooves, the exhilaration of an autumn breeze, the feel of a mare's loins beneath your own on a summer's morning. Although you will be vulnerable to mortal pleasures, you must not forget who you are and why you have been sent. You must resist, for to follow these pleasures and forget your task is fatal. You will lose your right to Breedmaster. *You will lose your breed itself*. Redemption is a slow and painful path, Dancer. The greater the sin you commit, the greater the sacrifice if you are to be forgiven. And Dancer, there is no return from the Final Death. Not for you. Not for any of us.'

'I will go, Lord,' shouted the Dancer. 'And I will not fail you or my breed.'

Equus stamped his feet, and a sheet of white light rose from the rocks around the Pool.

'Hear me, Black Horse! We have been challenged. We will ask for the right to the destiny of the Appaloosa.

'He paused, and I believe that I alone saw the grief in his silver eyes.

'He turned then,' said El Arat, 'and I think he went to consult the Owl.'

El Arat paused. Sweat patched her withers. A breeze had sprung up, carrying breakfast odors from the farmhouse. Cory shivered, glad it was daylight.

'We've got to get back,' he said. 'There'll be trouble if you're found loose. I'd guess that the others in the barn already know you're gone and are wondering where we are. Come on. I can't latch your gate again, but you can at least be in your stall.' He hesitated. 'El Arat, how true are these things?'

'They're true.'

'What is going to happen?'

'I don't know.'

'If these things begin to happen – and I say if – what would happen first?'

'The Testing of the Mare.'

'When?'

El Arat gazed behind him. She was remote, unapproachable. 'Soon,' she said. 'Very soon.'

3

The Tale of Alamain

After morning chores, which included abashed wriggling when Emmanuel found El Arat's gate unlatched, Cory went up to the porch and slept heavily. He was jolted awake by squeals and angry drummings from the brood mare pasture. He raced down the broad front steps, through the front yard and stopped at the pasture fence.

Duchess held a squealing Cissy by the nape of the neck. Cory watched them for a moment; Cissy tore free, whirled, and kicked out with both hind legs, catching Duchess in the chest. The dog slipped under the fence and dashed towards them, plumed tail waving. He cut Duchess from the herd, nipping lightly at her ankles, forcing her to the corner of the fence. He watched her warily and addressed the mares.

'What's going on here?'

'Duchess done it!' said Snip. 'She tried to beat up on Fance! She tried to wallop her and wallop her, and then Cissy passed some remark like she does, you know, and then Feather tried to tell Duchess she couldn't thump Fance unless she was trying to be Lead Mare. And then Cissy passed another remark. And,' Snip took a deep breath, 'Cissy kept passin' remarks until Duchess thumped her.'

'Where I come from,' said Duchess, 'I was Lead Mare.'

'Where *do* you come from?' jeered Cissy. 'A pony ride? A mule train?'

'See?' said Snip. 'See?'

'I know,' said Cory. 'Passin' remarks. Look, Duchess, take it easy, will you?'

El Arat, moving like a delicate cat, picked her way through the meadow. The black stopped in front of Duchess, her eyes liquid with wisdom. 'What is happening here, Cory, is that Duchess is issuing a call for a new Lead Mare.'

Duchess, doubtful, pawed the ground.

'There are four Tests for a Lead Mare, Duchess,' said El Arat. 'I will tell them to you.'

'There are?' said Feather. 'I thought we all voted, and that was it. I've never heard of any tests.'

'A dressage test?' asked Snip. 'Will she have to do a half pass and a side pass? I don't think she knows how to do those things. I could show her, I guess.'

'I don't want to be Lead Mare,' said Duchess. 'I just want to be left alone. I was Lead Mare in my old herd. I didn't say I wanted to be Lead Mare here. I don't.'

'How many were in your herd?' asked Fancy. 'If the herd was larger than ours, we really should consider it, Duchess.'

Duchess drew back her lips in a terrible grin. Fancy jerked back at the mare's sudden odor of fear and despair. 'Just one,' said Duchees softly. 'Just one.'

'Easy,' said Cory. He nosed the buckskin's flank and she backed away from him.

'There are four Tests for Lead Mare,' El Arat said again. Her eyes were glowing. Cory cocked his head at her, then sat down at Duchess' feet. 'Perhaps you better tell them what they are, El Arat.'

'I think so,' said Fancy, 'because I've never heard of them. Is this something new, Dreamspeaker? Is there a new Law? Will I have to pass this test?'

'It is very old, Fancy. Duchess will have to pass this test. Not you.' El Arat's voice was light and sweet. She stood squared up, her mane and tail waving a little in the morning breeze. She looked very dark against the sun.

53

'The First Test is of Pride. It is Pride of Place. And you must set no other beneath you.

'The Second Test is of Courage. In War and in the Games of War.

'The Third is of Heart, in concern for those in your care.

'The Last is the Test of Knowledge. You must know and obey the Laws.

'These tests mean the Lead Mare has the pride of a stallion for her herd, the courage of a Second-in-Command in war, the heart of a Caretaker in the matter of foals, and the knowledge of a Dreamspeaker. These tests you must pass Duchess, if you are to become Lead Mare.'

'All those things in one Lead Mare?' said Snip. 'My.'

'I told you. I don't want to be Lead Mare. I don't even want to be a member of the herd. I don't want your Laws. I don't want your rules. I want to be left alone.'

'You cannot deny the Balance of Existence, Duchess,' said El Arat. 'You cannot reject the Law.'

Duchess lowered her voice to a fierce whisper and leaned to the black mare's ear. 'I,' she hissed, 'reject everything. The world is out of Balance. Evil rises. Good falls before it. Strength is necessary to combat the tide. Independence, quick decision, are needed to save us all. The horse who lives under Laws is doomed, not me.'

'What else can you expect from a Grade?' said Cissy. 'Lead Mare of a herd of one, eh, Duchess. What happened to your herd anyway, sold to a circus?'

Duchess rushed Cissy, and kicked her hard before Cory could move to stop her. There were shouts from the farmhouse, and Emmanuel ran to the fence, a lead rope in his hand.

'Sorry,' said the collie. 'But I've got to bring you in.'

He sprang to a gallop and shouldered Duchess to the gate, first one flank, then the other. 'You're going to work off some of that hotheadedness in the arena. Come on, right up to the gate. Now stand, dammit. Good. Behave yourself, or you'll find a piece of skin out of your hide quicker than you might think.'

Emmanuel snapped the lead line to her halter, and led Duchess from the pasture.

'Take it easy,' said the dog. 'We're going to take you into the arena, saddle you up, put you on the longe line and see how you do. You're here to give lessons, so we have to school you a little beforehand, you know.' He grinned a little. 'Think of it as a Test of Courage. Schooling is one of the games of war. Take it slow and quiet.'

Emmanuel handed her over to David in the brood mare barn and David brushed her down, working with a stiff curry comb, then a brush, and finally a damp rag. He slipped a bridle over her ears, and Duchess flung her head high, clamping her teeth shut against the bit. David's fingers slipped into the corner of her mouth and, involuntarily, she unclenched her teeth. The bit slid into place with a soft bump. She worked it around her tongue. It was a type she hadn't encountered before, and she was briefly surprised. She tossed her head high, pulling her lips back from her teeth.

'It's rubber,' said the dog. 'And if I were you, I wouldn't take it into your head to fight it. The next step is the metal one, you know. The rubber is much kinder.'

'I know all about metal bits,' said Duchess.

David led Duchess down the concrete aisle, through the wooden half-gate that separated the arena from the stalls. She stiffened when he placed the saddle high on her withers, her muscles tensing when David moved it down into place. When he tightened the girth snugly against her stomach, she turned her head sharply to bite him, then backed up, panicked and waited for the whip.

'Sa, sa, sa,' said David. He laced the reins under the stirrups, attached a longe line under the chinstrap of the bridle, then walked away from her to the center of the ring. Cory sat beside him.

'Walk,' he said.

Duchess waited, one eye on the dog.

'Walk,' said the boy.

Duchess walked, her legs moving in a tight, nervous tattoo on the cedar-chip floor. She walked in a wide circle, over and over again, until her muscles relaxed in sheer boredom.

'Trot,' said the boy. 'Sa, sa. Trot.'

Duchess stopped short, and felt the imperative jerk of the longe line under her chin. She began a slow, wary trot, circle after circle.

'Extend.'

Duchess stepped out, lengthening her stride until she was moving freely around the arena. She could wait, she thought, she could wait, she could wait . . .

'Canter.'

Now.

Duchess struck out with her left foreleg, squealed, bucked, and jerked the line from David's hands. He shouted 'Whoa!' as she bucked around the arena, squealing, hind legs slamming into the arena walls whenever she came too close, stepping on the longe line trailing behind her, squealing when the bit jammed up against the bars of her mouth. She ran until she couldn't run anymore, then stopped by the bales of straw, heaving, with her head down and her flanks sweaty.

The boy stood in the middle of the arena, waiting, the dog alert at his feet.

Slowly, he moved toward her, hand outstretched. No whip, thought Duchess, no whip.

'Sa, sa, sa.' The calming hand at her withers made her shiver. David picked up the longe line and drew her again to the center of the ring.

'Walk,' he said.

Duchess walked and trotted on command, waiting for the call to canter. When it came, she was ready. She backed and reared to loosen the boy's grip, but he held on and she bucked in place.

'It's wasted effort, you know,' called the dog. 'Just canter in a circle, and you can go back to your stall.'

Duchess flattened her ears and bucked again, until she was taking in great gasps of air.

'Whoa,' said the boy.

Duchess stopped, out of exhaustion.

'Walk.' Duchess walked, walked, and stopped again.

'Sa, sa. Walk.'

Duchess exhaled, sighing, and moved her weary legs.

'Canter.'

She put her head down and bucked, the saddle jouncing painfully on her back.

'Duchess, Duchess!' said the boy. He walked up to her, unclipped the longe line, loosened the girth of the saddle, unbuckled the bridle, and snapped her halter into place. He put his soft, warm palm beneath her lips, and she sniffed at the apple in his hand.

Duchess ate the apple, then walked up and down the arena, the boy at her head, until the sweat cooled from her chest and her breathing slowed.

'It's going to take longer than I thought,' said Cory. 'We'll see you at evening feed.'

David led her back to her stall and opened the double doors to the attached paddock. The paddock was nailed directly to Duchess' stall, bound on one side by a similar paddock for El Arat, on the other by Fancy's. Her view was the pasture, bright green with spring grass, dotted with a few yellow dandelions. Duchess pressed close to the top rail of the fence and raised her nose to the wind. The mares were nowhere in sight. Probably, she guessed, they were on back of the hill where the oak tree grew. To her near side was the barricaded weanling meadow where Susie had been sent back to the four gangly foals.

Duchess chewed angrily at the top rail of her fence. The barn cat sauntered by, tail at an arrogant angle. It was going to be a long, warm afternoon.

By evening, Duchess had cropped most of the grass in her paddock short. As the sun slipped over the hill, David went to the long iron gate of the pasture and banged the feed bucket against the latch. Fancy came first, Feather just behind her, Snip and Cissy bringing up the rear. El Arat moved lightly a few paces away from the group. Arabian, Thoroughbred, Quarterhorse, thought Duchess. Perhaps you could tell – even Snip, bumbling as she was, had a certain elegance of bone. And I, thought Duchess. Where do I fit in?

There were large stones mixed in Duchess' grain bucket that evening, and she drew back in indignant surprise. 'It's so you won't bolt your food,' said Susie. 'Snip's got them too, don't you, Snip?'

'Mmhm. One of these days I'll eat them stones right up,' said Snip. 'I *know* I'm not gettin' as much as you guys.'

'You're an easy keeper,' said Cory as he made his way down the concrete aisle. 'That's a compliment, Snip. That big gelding in the boarders' barn gets sixteen quarts a day and still doesn't keep weight on.'

'Now that'd be somethin',' said Snip wistfully. 'Sixteen quarts a day and no fat to worry about. It's not fair, you know.'

'Life's not fair,' said Feather. 'Look, if everyone's finished, we should get this business of herd membership over. I take it that Duchess is *not* challenging Fancy for Lead Mare?'

'You take it right,' muttered Duchess.

'For now,' said El Arat. 'Well, as you all know, we must vote Duchess into the herd. This vote confirms allegiance to the First Law: A Horse Is a Member of a Company. A Horse Is One with Her Fellows. So. Cissy. How do you decide? I must remind you that this is herd business – serious business – and that your whims and caprices have no place here. You must decide fairly if Duchess is to be a member of the herd.'

Cissy looked from Duchess to Fancy and back again. 'If she takes the herd oath, I guess she'll behave. Agreed.'

'Snip?' asked El Arat.

The stout brown mare moved uneasily. One hip still ached from the sharp kick Duchess had given her. 'Ummm. Well . . . the question is, can Fancy keep order? Can she keep Duchess from kicking me and kicking me? I don't like to be kicked. I'm not especially good at kicking – I never have been. And I don't like running around all the time. I like to stand and eat. I like to feel the sun on me and not be running around all the time like we had black flies after us.' She stopped.

'Well?' asked El Arat after a moment.

'That's not a vote,' said Cissy. 'Do you want Duchess in the herd?'

'I don't like to be kicked; I'm not good at kicking.'

'Just vote, will you?' said Cissy. 'Honestly, Snip, some-times I think your tail is where your head should be.'

'That's my vote,' said Snip stubbornly. 'My vote is for no kicking.'

'Well, I change my vote to put *you* in with the chickens,' said Cissy. 'I vote we stand and take turns giving you kicks where it counts . . .'

'I vote we get on with it,' said Fancy dryly.

El Arat, unmoved, said, 'Feather?'

Feather sighed and gave Fancy an affectionate look. 'She has to abide by the rules, but if she takes the Oath, she's bound. Agreed.'

'Susie?' said El Arat.

The Paint cleared her throat several times. 'Duchess is a fighter. I've seen this in some of the babies, this fight. They don't like to be held down. They're the ones that have the most trouble learning about fences – the ones that take the most time to be green-broke. But if they're green-broke the right way, they're some of the best horses ever to come off this Farm.

'I think Duchess has bad memories, and that maybe she was broke the hard way, by punishing instead of kindness. We're lucky here, I think, because none of us has ever had to worry about getting whipped, or being scared, or having enough food to eat – or anything else. It takes a special kind of horse to get through those things without turning into a plug. We've all seen plugs – the ones with their heads hanging and the white scars on their hides. Duchess isn't a plug. She's got stubbornness and spunk. Duchess' way could be good for us if it were someplace different, and we needed the things she has, the things she can do. Being brave. Not lettin' bad things take the hope out of us. So, I agree.'

'I agree, too,' said Fancy.

'And I,' said El Arat. 'Welcome, Duchess.'

Duchess said nothing.

Fancy waited a moment and said, 'The Oath, then. I'll begin it and you all can follow me. I, Fancy . . .'

'Forget it,' said Duchess. 'I'm not taking it.'

'You must,' said El Arat. 'If you don't . . . why, we would have to invoke the Silence. You'd be cast out. Here, but not here. Never to be recognized by the herd.'

'So what?'

'I think El Arat should tell a Story,' said Susie firmly. 'The First Law, El Arat. Please.'

'No,' said Duchess flatly. 'I'm not standing around to hear Stories.'

'You'll listen,' said Fancy. 'Because I say so. El Arat, may we have the First Law?'

El Arat, standing slightly aloof, began to recite the Tale of Alamain in a soft, melodious voice:

The Tale of the First Law

'Many seasons ago . . . a time from winters past counting, from summers past remembering . . . Alamain roamed dry pastures with her brand of mares. The world was different then – lakes were scarce, rivers few and all the earth was grass. Equus himself roamed the earth, four-footed.'

'Equus,' chanted Feather, Snip and Cissy. 'Oh, Equus,

with mane and tail shining like the moon. Oh, Equus, with eyes like stars on nights when there is no moon.'

'Equus roamed the earth for love of Alamain. Alamain. Men prized her for high bravery in war. Equus loved her beauty. All mares loved her foals of courage. And Alamain grew proud. She gloried in her shining coat, her floating mane, her lion's heart. Alamain grew proud, so that she walked as though her head touched the sun where it rose and set over the dry-sand pastures of her home. She would bow to no one, nor let men ride upon her back, nor listen to the wisdom of the herd at grazing time, nor help guard the foals against the terrors of the night. Alamain grew proud, that she was one with Equus Himself. Equus the Just, Equus the Wise, Equus (grieving) knew Alamain was doomed; for this is the First Law:

> *A horse is a member of a company*
> *A horse is one with her fellows*
> *A horse cannot live without the herd*
> *That is the Law and has been*
> *Since the world itself was born.*

'So, Equus the Just, Equus the Wise, Equus (grieving) sent lions to the desert, where Alamain walked alone and proud. Sent wolves and cougars, sent birds with carrion beaks to Alamain. And no horse came to help her. She was set upon, by claws and teeth, and no horse came to help her. Wounded past recall, past the medicine of men to heal her, past Equus' own reclaiming, Alamain lay bleeding, and no horse came to help her – but one. The Black Horse. The Dark Horse. The Horse with the Twisted Horn. Now Alamain lies beneath the moon, beneath the stars, beneath the Sun. Alamain lies and died alone, in the field of the Horse with the Twisted Horn. Alamain lies at the Black Barn's gate. Remember, mares, what pride forgot:

> *A horse is a member of a company*
> *A horse is one with her fellows*

61

A horse cannot live without the herd
That is the Law and has been
Since the world itself was born.'

'I have always wondered,' said El Arat a little dreamily, 'why the Tale of Alamain does not tell of a judgment in Summer. I thought that all – no matter how good or bad a life – were judged before a final decision was made. Were given a chance to plead in Summer before set on the path to glory in the Courts of the Outermost West – or to the Black Barns, whose name we fear. Was she unable to redeem her sin, do you suppose?'

'You always want to know too much, El Arat,' said Cissy. 'Let's get on with it, the Oath.'

'Yes,' said Fancy. 'Back to business.'

'I won't take the Oath, I tell you!' shouted Duchess. 'I don't need any of you. I'll bide my time. I won't be here forever. Nothing is forever. The only thing that never changes is that you have to fight. Alone. It's that or be beaten, and I won't be beaten. I haven't been yet and I never will be. So forget about the Oath. Forget about the herd. The only thing I have is myself.'

'We can wait for you,' said Fancy. 'There's no Law about when the Oath has to be taken. It can be now – or it can be later. We'll wait, Duchess, until you see for yourself what life is like here. You've only just arrived. You haven't had time to forget. But we have time.'

Duchess stood with her nose to the back wall, refusing to think. She would just get through tomorrow, and that would be enough.

For a week or two, the days swung in a simple rhythm. Susie returned to the weanlings and El Arat moved one stall closer. Duchess fell, almost without thinking, into the barn's routine: water, hay, grain in the morning; pasture during the day; an hour's work in the arena. And slowly, spring eased into summer with graceful, ordered steps. She let the memories of who she was and where she had been, drift. And she dreamed no dreams.

4

A Settling Tale

'Not that I'm interested,' said Duchess one evening a few weeks later, 'but where is Feather going?' Emmanuel had wrapped Feather's tail with gauze, and slipped her halter over her head.

The mares were settled for the night. The barn lights softened the wood to bark-brown, and grey shadows pooled in the stall corners. Fancy was stretched out at the back of her stall. El Arat dozed on the other side of Duchess' stall. Cissy munched hay. Feather's hooves echoed hollowly on the concrete aisle as Emmanuel led her into the evening darkness.

'She's going to Stillmeadow,' said El Arat, waking soundlessly, 'our farm stallion. Feather is going off to be bred.'

'Feather's an every-other-year mare,' said Cissy. 'And even every other *year* she never seems to catch. She should be retired to lesson work, if you ask me.'

'Nobody has,' said Fancy, getting to her feet. 'Besides, when Feather does catch and bear a foal, they're some of the best the Farm has ever had. Cory told me her three-year-old took two firsts in Green Hunter Over Fences at the last show.'

'So? All of us visited Stillmeadow for breeding before the snow melted, and you don't see me going back to him every three weeks,' said Cissy. 'Of course, I suppose it isn't her fault, is it? Or is it?'

63

'Keep your bit between your teeth,' advised Fancy.

'Are you all brood mares?' asked Duchess.

'Oh, yes,' said El Arat, 'although most of us do – how would you express it? – double duty. The Farm has horse shows every year, and when times are a little hard, lessons are given. And we all help. Fancy is excellent at the Western Style of equitation. I myself am a gaited Arabian. I do three gaits – the rack, the pace and the saddle-seat walk. And of course there's Cissy. How would you characterize your contribution, Cissy?'

Fancy chuckled, 'Yes, Cissy, describe yourself to Duchess.'

'I'm a brood mare,' said Cissy, 'and I drop a healthy foal every year. And I'm a hunting mare.'

'When she feels like it,' said Fancy wickedly. 'Now, when Cissy feels like it, she pops over fences pretty well. And when she *doesn't*, oh, she jumps hay bales, judges . . .'

'Very funny,' said Cissy. 'A brood mare's function is babies, isn't it? And that's what I do best. The rest is ridiculous.

'Ridiculous,' said Snip suddenly. 'That's the word I couldn't remember. Ridiculous. I saw Stillmeadow a few days before you did this winter, and he said, "Thank Equus you aren't that ridiculous Cissy. All she does is squeal and act ridiculous."' Snip chewed a bit of hay in satisfaction. 'I *knew* I'd remember that word. I've been trying to think of it for months.'

'You just wait until I get you alone in the pasture,' said Cissy furiously. 'I'll show *you* ridiculous.'

'All right, all right,' said Fancy. 'That wasn't kind, Snip. I'm sure Stillmeadow said no such thing.'

'He did, *too*,' said Snip. 'He said it to me, didn't he, not to nobody else. "Thank Equus you aren't that ridiculous . . ."'

Cissy kicked the side of her stall violently and Snip jumped and squealed.

'I've never had a foal,' said Duchess.

'Well, don't worry, you won't,' sniffed Cissy. 'Now, *there's* a ridiculous idea for you.'

'What do you mean?' Duchess demanded.

'You think you're here to have foals? You're a lesson horse,' said Cissy. The other mares were silent, and Duchess looked from one to the other.

'Wait a moment, now,' said Fancy. 'We don't know if that's true, Cissy. Tell us, Duchess, where are you from? What's your breeding?'

A brief memory flooded Duchess: Pride, blood on his lips, chewing at the wall of the shed, his ribs sprung from his sides like barrel staves. 'None of your business.'

'I mean your sire, your dam,' said Fancy gently. 'Your lineage.'

'Your ancestors,' said Snip. 'My sire was Walk-Don't-Run. My dam was Molly-Be-Good. My grandsire was Runaway. My granddam . . .'

'Oh, shut up, Snip,' said Cissy.

'I'm a Thoroughbred,' Snip explained to Duchess. 'El Arat's an Arabian, Fancy's a Quarterhorse. And Cissy's a Thoroughbred, too. A ridic . . .'

'Stop,' said Fancy.

'. . . Ha. Susie's a Paint. And even Cory's a registered Collie. And you, Duchess, what are you? A Grade, that's what.'

'Maybe she isn't,' said Fancy.

'There's definitely Arabian in her,' said Feather. 'Look at her head, it's very fine. And her ears are small and almost perfect.'

'I'd say Quarterhorse,' said Fancy. 'Look at the length of her leg and the muscle in her hindquarters.'

'Who ever heard of a buckskin Arabian? Or a buckskin Quarterhorse?' said Cissy.

'There are buckskin Quarterhorses,' said Fancy. 'I'm sure of it.'

'If my stall door were open, I'd be delighted to step outside so you could see better,' said Duchess sarcastically.

65

'Definitely Grade manners,' said Cissy. 'So, to answer your question, Duchess, no, you won't be getting a chance to kick or bite Stillmeadow, the way you did us. Don't bother your Arab-type head about it.'

'What's wrong with being a Grade?' Duchess was dangerously quiet.

'Not a thing,' said Fancy. 'But this is a bloodstock farm, and your value here . . . it could very well be different somewhere else . . . lies in teaching students to ride.'

'It isn't worth the expense to bring up a foal that can't be registered,' said Cissy.

'Not strictly true.' El Arat arched her neck a little and gave Duchess a small wink. 'Many fine horses have been bred from Grades, and registered, too.'

'Sure. Right,' said Cissy. 'What shows would this marvelous son or daughter of Duchess be able to enter? We can register the Stillmeadow half as a Half-Bred, but we haven't the faintest idea of what the Duchess-half would turn out like. Equus knows what would turn up.'

'It's custom more than anything, Duchess,' said Fancy. 'This Farm, like many others, is interested in registered stock. It has nothing whatever to do with your worth.'

'None at all,' said Cissy. 'Of course, I can trace my ancestry back to where it joins El Arat's. That doesn't make a difference.'

'That's enough out of you, Cissy,' said Fancy sharply. 'Look, here's Feather back. David will turn the barn lights out now and we'll get some sleep.'

Emmanuel Bishop turned Feather into the stall beside Cissy.

'How is Stillmeadow?' said El Arat. 'Well, I hope.'

'Mm hm,' Feather yawned. 'He sends his regards.'

'Anything else?' asked Cissy.

'Yeah, anything ridiculous else?' Giggling, Snip plunged her nose into her grain bucket and began to stamp her feet in hilarity.

'No,' said Feather, surprised. 'Should there be? I just

hope I caught this time. The foal's going to be late enough as it is.' She edged over to Snip. 'What happened?'

Snip shook her head helplessly.

'C'mon Snip, tell. I tell *you* things.'

Cissy, pushed past the point of mere irritation, started running her teeth up and down the wire mesh that enclosed her stall, and Fancy shouted. 'Stop! That's enough. This jumping and stamping isn't good for the foals we're carrying. El Arat, tell us a story – something to settle everyone down. Once Snip starts her foolishness . . .' She cast an exasperated look at the brown mare.

El Arat lowered her head in thought, then glanced sidelong at Duchess out of her liquid eyes. 'A Settling Tale? To stop the laughter?

'A Tale that will accomplish that, and,' she gazed thoughtfully at Duchess, 'a Tale to make us all reflect on the futility of certain attitudes. Very well. This is a Tale of Pride. You remember, Duchess, the First Test. I shall recite the Tale of Sycha, the Soul-Taker, the Betrayer.'

'Ooo, ridic . . .' Snip chortled.

'The Soul-Taker and the Black Bargain,' El Arat announced.

And the barn fell silent.

The Tale of the Soul-Taker and the Black Bargain

Sycha was once the greatest of all Lead Mares, second only to Jehanna the Dreamspeaker in beauty, for she shone with radiant color like clouds before sunrise.

She was the Breedmistress of the Appaloosa, Lead Mare to the Rainbow Horse himself, and before the earth was made for mortal mares to roam, she lived with Equus and the Army of One Hundred and Five in the Heavenly Courts.

In the time of the Palouse Wars, she Watched at the Pool as her brothers and sisters fell under the swords and guns of men. She had grieved with the Rainbow Horse at the sight of their bodies on the banks of the Palouse River – lying there for wolves and carrion birds to feed on. So she walked the Path to the Moon to save them and she was captured by men who tried to destroy her. Who cut her silvery coat with knives. Who threatened her eyes with fire. Who beat her with knife-bladed whips.

'Why did you not prevent this?' she cried to the Rainbow Horse. 'Your power is worth nothing!'

'Why did you not prevent this?' she challenged Equus, their god. 'Your power is worth nothing!'

She wept. And she prayed to the Dark Lord, the Black Horse. And she raged for deliverance.

Now, there is a time between moonset and sunrise, when the Gates to the Black Barns ease open and foul things slip through to taint the air. At such a time, and on such a night, Scant, chief of the Harrier Hounds and the Voice of Anor the Executioner, slipped through the gates on this dark errand for his Master, the Black Horse. Scant was no more than a foul odor, a shadow passing in the night.

Scant, alone in the brush and silent, heard Sycha's prayers and grinned. He crept away before the sun rose, to sit in evil with his Master.

And the next night, when the Black Gates eased open, He slipped through with Scant.

'Sycha,' He said. 'Oh, Sycha.' For there she was by the river, torn and bleeding – approaching the Final Death.

And as Scant watched, the Black Horse himself paced beside her in the half-light, His deadly shadow blotting the radiance of her coat, His horned head bent.

'Sycha!' He whispered. 'Is it right for a mare with your beauty and grace? That you suffer at the hands of those who should worship you? Did Equus save your mares and stallions? Or did he let them die – through cowardice. Through fear. And who is it, Sycha, that they fear? They fear me. The Dark Lord. Ruler of victories. Soon to be, my Sycha, *your* Lord, if you will have me. I promise you

the power. I promise you the art. For if you follow me –
all, all, Sycha, must needs follow you. You will be
Appaloosa no longer. You will be mine.'

Who shall know what else He said to Sycha, pacing
beside her in the predawn gloom? Who shall know why
the Black Bargain was struck?'

Then, suddenly, Sycha reared, and screaming, shrilled
to the darkness that walked at her side. Her colors turned
from stippled dawn to grey. The river she stood by rose
in a tidal wave. The earth she stood on turned in upon
itself, heaved inside out, and made a bleak desert of the
former meadow. Burred bushes rose from the ground.
Swollen green fruit hung from their branches – not fruit,
but sentient things, fly-covered. Under each buzzing cloud
sat a Hound with red eyes and a tongue rotten with a
carrion stink. Their high keening filled the air, then
thickened to a yawling wail – a sound to open wounds.
The Hounds twitched, moved, and formed a circle, clouds
of flies humming overhead. The wail became a chant and
Sycha, her radiance dimmed, stood there, the crowd of
her worshippers howling: 'Sycha. Sycha. Sycha.'

A rhythmic thunder came. The grey mare began to
dance, her colors gone forever. And like a lightning strike
the Black Horse danced with her, and with each circle
they wove a mare died somewhere, a horse fell somewhere, and their souls joined the circle and the chant rose
higher:

'Sycha! Sycha! Sycha!'

She was lost.

She had become the Soul-Taker.

Sycha, the Ghost Mare. The Taker of Souls.

Now, in the nighttime, after the moon has set and
before the sun has risen, she snatches the souls of the
living, while the Hounds call, 'Sycha!'

Horses die the Final Death to swell the chant of 'Sycha!'

El Arat paused. Suddenly, the barn lights snapped out,
and the mares were plunged into the dark. Snip squealed.

Cory's claws ticked on the concrete, and he called out, 'Everything all right? I'm making one last round before I go up to the house for the night.'

'Umm. It's fine,' said Fancy.

'I heard somebody yelp. Was it Snip?'

'Scary story,' admitted Snip. 'Those hounds, El Arat. What about those hounds? They're not fox hounds are they? Should I be scared when I go huntin'? I'm goin' huntin' soon. I always do, after the foal's dropped. I don't want those hounds to follow me.'

'The Dark Lord is a master of illusion, Snip,' said Cissy. 'Who knows if the fox hounds are really what they seem? Who knows if a red-eyed skull lies underneath those dog-faces?'

Snip's eyes rolled back in her head, and Fancy kicked out sharply, her hoof hitting the stall door with a crack. 'That's quite enough, Cissy!'

'You'll know when the hounds follow you,' said El Arat. 'There is a howling in the sky, and black flies out of season. You'll hear them long before you see them – and when you hear them, Snip, you cannot hide. Once the Harriers follow, they never lose the scent.'

'It's all legend, after all,' said Fancy firmly. 'Good night.'

'I'm goin' to sleep now, I hope,' said Snip.

'Good,' said the dog. 'Fancy, tomorrow is Longlight. We make the Change. It's Turn Around Time. It's getting too hot to be outside during the day, so we'll reverse. You'll be in your stalls during the day and out in the pastures at night. And the blacksmith is coming, too. Everyone gets a trim. And Duchess gets shod.'

'We'll remember,' said Fancy. 'Good night, Cory.'

'Good night.' the dog left.

'So your work in the arena is going well, Duchess,' said El Arat. 'This is good.'

'What does getting shod have to do with it?' said Duchess angrily.

'Shoes will protect your hooves from chipping,' said

70

Fancy. 'Cory says you're a talented jumper and that the Bishops are pleased with your progress. If they're going to be shoeing you, it means that you'll be doing more work.'

'For men?' said Duchess. 'Never. What does that dog know, anyway?'

'I don't believe she's ever been shod before,' said Cissy. 'Donkeys don't need shoes. Maybe Duchess doesn't need shoes, either.'

'Stop it, Cissy,' said Fancy.

'Stop what?' The liver chestnut looked innocently at Duchess. 'Cory was the one who told me about donkeys. I'm just . . .'

'Passing remarks, as usual,' said Snip. 'I'm going to sleep.'

'We all should,' said Fancy. 'Good night, Duchess.'

Duchess slept and dreamed of men with whips, giving her Tests she didn't understand.

5

Blacksmith Day

El Arat dreamed no dreams, and she woke with a jerk just before dawn. The moon was not quite full and it hung low on the horizon, a weak and pale echo of its nighttime glory. The air was still and soundless. She pawed the grass in her paddock, and turned up a clod of earth. Underneath, a nest of fleshy worms writhed naked in the half light. She snorted in disgust and stamped at the pink coils. A red gout of blood spurted from the bodies and she leaped back, shivering. When she looked again, the blood and worms were gone.

The blacksmith arrived just after morning feed. El Arat had not eaten, and when David came to her stall to take her out to get her hooves trimmed, he ran his hands over her belly and rubbed her ears.

'Sa, saa, El Arat,' he said.

She tossed her head.

'Are you all right?' Fancy called.

'Yes. Of course,' El Arat said. The concrete aisle felt cold and she stepped high. David led her past Duchess' stall, and El Arat glanced sideways at the buckskin. She stood with her nose to the back doors, hindquarters insolently presented to the barn.

'Duchess,' said El Arat, stopping. David tugged at her halter, but she refused to move. 'Duchess, something is not right.' She hesitated. Duchess flicked one ear back;

you matter less than flies, her posture said. El Arat snorted and moved on.

The farrier trimmed and hammered at his anvil, the smell of singed hoof and hot iron hanging in the air like a solid weight. He reset El Arat's shoes and she resumed her place in her stall.

David took Feather, Fancy, and Susie to the farrier in turn, and the morning wore on. It grew hot, and the odors of man sweat and manure overlay the sweet scent of hay. The flies grew thick. David sprayed the air with fly killer, and sprayed again.

Each of the weanlings was presented for a trim, their high pitched squeals sounding at irregular intervals.

David pulled Duchess from her stall. She walked heavily down the aisle, ears flattened against her skull. Cory weaved in and out of the way. He brushed up against her and she aimed a half-hearted cow-kick in his direction.

David spoke to her sharply and jerked her halter.

El Arat watched, nostrils wide, ears pricked forward. A cloud of flies circled the blacksmith's head and he grunted, sweeping them from around his face with the rasp. As he swung, Duchess backed up, alarmed perhaps by the motion, and the rasp caught her over the ear.

The buckskin screamed and reared, swinging toward the open door. Cory barked twice, a warning, and she dropped to all fours, then suddenly kicked back with her right hind, a killing kick.

She caught Cory squarely over the heart. The dog made an odd chuffing sound, then dropped like a stone to the concrete.

El Arat froze. David shouted, and dropped the lead line to kneel by his dog.

Duchess bolted out the open door and headed for the open.

'Oh, Equus!' breathed El Arat. 'That stupid mare. That infernal mare.'

David shifted Cory's body onto an empty grain sack and made a sling with the long handles of two pitchforks.

He and Emmanuel carried the dog to the house. The blacksmith packed up and left.

Time passed, and the mares stood quietly in their stalls.

'Vet's here,' said Fancy briefly, as a long red car pulled past the open door.

'Where is she?' said Feather, a little while later. 'I smelled her out by the oak tree for a while, but now she's gone.'

'Isolation stall, I expect,' said Cissy.

'Do you suppose Cory's dead, El Arat?' asked Fancy.

'If he is, there will be great trouble,' said the black mare. 'I fear to think that it could be so.'

'Psst!' A slim glitter of grey slipped through El Arat's paddock door and jumped to the barn beam over her head. 'Psst, you, mare!' The barn cat, grey fur washed with an undercurrent of cocoa brown, picked her careful way across the beam. Her name, El Arat recalled, was Bunkie.

'*This* is a fine mess,' Bunkie said with satisfaction. 'Half-killed that dog, she did. Everyone's all a twit and a twitter. "Where did she go?" they asked after her crime – after her attempt at murder. Find her. Bring her back. She ought to be whipped. Starved. Locked in a shed.'

The cat gave El Arat a long yellow look through half-closed eyes. 'Just kidding,' she drawled. 'They put her in the sick stall. She's all alone.'

'What about Cory?' said Snip. 'Is Cory dead? Is he?'

'No. He ain't dead yet.' The cat stretched and worked her claws into the beam. 'As far as I'm concerned, I'd just as soon she killed that dog. Gives me fits, he does.'

'Is he badly hurt?' asked El Arat.

'Bad enough. But not too bad,' said the cat in a considering way. 'I got a good look before they pushed me out of the house. Got him up on the kitchen table, stretched out on the grain bag. Not enough blood, I'd say, but some. Boss is mad enough. They were going to an auction up to town, and now they can't. Got a bunch of wild horses in and they were looking to buy a couple.'

'Wild horses?' said El Arat, an absurd hope springing in her breast. 'What breed, Bunkie, do you know?'

The cat shrugged and yawned, showing her sharp white teeth. 'Nope, I don't suppose we'll find out. No one's goin' anywhere now.'

It didn't matter, Duchess told herself. She was glad. She didn't need the herd, or David either. No beatings, no whips . . . and they thought putting her alone in this stall was punishment. Her food was regular, the stall was airy, and she could crop the grass in her small paddock short. From her paddock, she could see almost the entire front of the house, and she began to wonder if the dog was dead. The refrain of the First Law echoed in her head. 'A horse cannot live without the herd . . .' and she shook her head as if to get rid of flies. The red car came and left. Then Cory himself, a shaved patch of hair on his side grotesque in the luxuriant gold and snow of his coat, made his shaky way down the steps of the front porch.

She thrust her head over the fence and called, 'Cory?' It was a low-voiced call, almost inaudible. The dog swung his head around in a puzzled way, tail wagging slowly. Duchess pulled her head back and walked quickly into her stall, so he couldn't tell she was there. The faint scrabble of his paws sounded outside, and then a bark, 'Duchess?'

She stood quietly. A fly stung her flank, and she automatically switched her tail. 'You *are* there,' said Cory. 'Come out for a moment. I want to talk to you.'

Duchess walked out. The dog sat on the other side of the fence. 'Are you all right?' she asked unwillingly.

'A cracked rib or two. But I'll be fine.'

'Does it hurt?'

'Some. I almost missed going to an auction because of you, you know.'

'I'm sorry,' said Duchess. 'I didn't mean to hurt you. When that rasp hit me on the ear – I don't know what I thought. And the flies were so bad!' She shook her head. 'I could have killed you.'

'Well, I'll be around a long time yet. But watch it next time, will you?'

'Oh, I don't think there'll be a next time,' said Duchess.

'Why not?'

'They'll sell me, won't they? Or send me back to where I was before?'

'They thought of selling you, of course. But David said no. He thinks you might have a future as a jumper. Emmanuel doesn't agree. It all depends on how well you behave this summer. How well you get along with the herd – and with the Bishops. I understand you haven't taken the Oath yet.'

'It doesn't look like I have much choice.'

The dog shrugged. 'No one's forcing you to do anything. But you'll have to choose, one way or the other. Sometime.'

Duchess stared at the fence, then said, 'Look, I'm sorry about what happened.'

'It's done. We'll forget it.' The dog raised himself on his hind legs. Duchess bent her muzzle to his and his tongue briefly caressed her cheek. 'I've got rounds to do,' he said. 'I won't see you until late tomorrow. The auction's a way from here – and Emmanuel's taking his bags. He always takes his bags when we aren't going to be back.' Without a backward glance, he left, and Duchess was alone.

Duchess dreamed again that night. She was back in the shed that stank of old manure and of water buckets filled with green slime. Pride was there, his great sides sunken so the ribs showed through, his lips clotted with blood from chewing at the walls of the shed that caged them.

'Fight!' she screamed. 'Stand up, Pride! Stand up!'

Moonlight flowed like water around their feet, and Pride looked at her with great misted eyes. Dogs howled in the sky. There was a strange scent of wild thyme. A thundering came, a drumming, and the walls of the shed split open. A stallion screamed and she reared in the flood of the moonlight, the walls of the shed flat around her.

A spotted horse danced on the hillside, then plunged down the hill to a meadow bright with flowers, and divided by a river. The stallion's body was black, flecked with white like trailing ivy leaves. Duchess called out. The stallion screamed again.

She woke with a start, her heart pounding, and walked outside into the quiet night. The moon swam high and serene, mirrored in the duck pond, and the night was clean. No strange scent, no hound-like cry slipped among the stars like an evil spirit. She concentrated on familiar shapes: the arch of the barn roof, the twisted roots of the miniature willow at pond's edge, the reflection of the moon in the water. Susie had once hummed the Moon Song to her, Duchess recalled, a lullaby for very young foals. She watched the moon in the pond and shook off the terror of the dream, and sang the song under her breath: 'Joachim the silver, the Horse in the Moon looked down from a nighttime sky . . .'

And the moon's shape swirled in the water.

'To a ribbon of dark that was forest . . .'

The moon swirled and spun, faster, faster, the moonshine bubbling up from the water's surface. 'No,' said Duchess, and then, like a charm against the spinning, whirling moon that seemed to be rising from the water, she gabbled, '. . . with his moon's unwinking eye. Come down, the beech trees whispered . . .'

The moon rose from the pond.

Duchess stepped back.

A new terror shook her, and she was barely aware of a fine sweat breaking out on her flanks. 'No dream . . .' she whispered. 'No. Dream.' Within the circle of moonlight, time stopped.

Slowly, a Great White Owl came from the waters of the pond. Wings spread from pond's edge to pond's edge, eyes great with a shining light, the snow white of his head,

77

back, chest feathered into colors as shadowy and mysterious as the dark side of the moon. He rose noiselessly, circling the pond once, twice, and once again. Duchess froze, pinned by terror. Then, the fear that had sickened and wakened her from her dream was gone . . . replaced by the feeling of being a very small thing, a mouse perhaps, caught up in the great beating of the bird's wings.

'Watch and wait. The Test of War will come.' The Owl's voice filled the circle of light. He swept his wings up, the tips reaching to the real moon, sailing high and white.

Duchess backed, backed, eyes rolling in fear.

The Owl raised his wings once more. Then he, the whirling reflection of the moon, and the mists of the duck pond's waters went out like the blink of an eyelid.

Duchess was alone.

She stood at the fence, eyes straining in the sudden dark, blackness deep around her from the cessation of the light. Senses returned slowly; she felt her heart beating, the grass beneath her feet, the way her breath came and went in rapid, bewildered rhythm.

Ordinary night sounds returned, reassuring in their homeliness – the creak of the paddock gates in the night wind; the rustle of sleepy barn swallows; the 'cut-cup' of curious frogs. The duck pond held an ordinary moon's reflection; the stars were their usual sizes. Trembling, she hid in her stall, her thoughts dark and fearful. And when the light grew white again, outside the paddock fence, she closed her eyes and prayed.

6

The Dancer Comes down the Mountain

The mares were at pasture, under the nighttime sky, and El Arat dreamed under the oak tree. She dreamed, fearfully, of her ancestors, and the places of honor they had held. She dreamed that Duchess wasn't worthy.

And then she snapped awake. The Owl was here. She could feel it. And he had not come to her, but to Duchess. The Arabian stepped out from under the oak tree quietly so as not to wake the others. The moon rose high and white over the pond and she shook a little at the sight of the moonshine on the water. She trotted up and down the length of the pasture fence, over and over, until finally, with no more than a swift apology to her gods, she moved from a trot to a tight, collected canter and, every muscle straining upward, leaped up and over. The top rail caught her belly and she scrambled, hindquarters working, until her left hind caught the middle rail. Her hoof held. She pushed. And she was over. She forced herself to walk calmly to the pond, rippling quietly now in the moonlight. The cool water stung the flesh made raw by her jump. She walked into the water, rose to her hind legs, and called upon Jehanna.

While the buckskin mare trembled in her stall, El Arat walked the Path to the Moon once more, and stood before the Watching Pool, the Army all around her. . . .

The Vision in the Pool

Mountains lay two hundred leagues north of Bishop Farm
– steep, sharp-shouldered granite shaded with clumps of
pine, veined with streams. Near the highest peak sat an
owl, lamplit eyes unblinking. The air was still and quiet.
The moon passed slowly overhead, then hung suspended
at the mountaintop. All forest sounds stopped.

A ribbon of light came from the Outermost West and
formed a Path. At the Path's head stood The Dancer.

Formed of all the colors splintered, made of rainbow
light, he raced down the Path in a soundless rush of wind
and landed upright on a peak. He stood in crystalline
splendor, scarlet, blue and green, his mane and tail
plumed out by the celestial wind. The Owl blinked once.

The Dancer turned to the sky and bowed with arrogant
grace.

Equus spoke. The Dancer paused to listen.

'You know the risks? You are mortal once again.
Vulnerable to all that earthbound creatures are.

'The Dark Lord is filled with tricks. Your task is this:
to find the buckskin mare, and get her with foal. If she
has passed the Tests, she may return with you, if she
wishes, but you may not reveal who you are.

'Anor remains locked behind his gate. You'll fight only
if you must, you shall not seek him out.

'Find the mare. Remain with her. Obey the laws of
men. And, Dancer, watch for traps. The Dark Horse has
many followers, some in strange guises.

'Be careful in your choices.'

The voice of Equus died. The Dancer stared silently
down the mountain, then gave voice to a challenging
scream, a big-bellied, awesome, trumpeting sound that
bounced off the sheer-muscled rock walls like a golden
hammer.

Running. He raced down the mountain, and the rainbow colors of his coat merged into black and white, like ivy leaves in shadow. Running. The celestial Path behind him faded, as rainbows will when the light is lost.

The Owl spun lazily from his perch and disappeared.

He was running, and the Dancer forgot everything but that. Wind slid through his mane with a touch like rolling water, cupping his flanks with tender blows of mountain air. Skidding, his hooves struck sparks from the rock-littered trail and a pebble, thrown up by his downward plunge, glanced stinging off his withers. The Dancer jerked a little in surprise.

The mountain was moonlit, the air sharp with the scent of pine. Ash-green brush; silver birch; the solid trunks of oak, maple; the scarlet shine of bittersweet and evergreen flashed by him. This was unfamiliar and far different from the honeyed green of his former Courts. This was real earth beneath his hooves: solid, thick and weighty.

Running, the Dancer plunged down the mountainside, to a creek that twisted through the gorge. Sweat darkened his flanks, patched his long, curved neck and muscled withers.

He reached the creek and wading deep he drank, and snorted at wet-feathered water rising around him.

The Dancer swung his head in a half-circle, nostrils wide, searching. A scent of fox and squirrel – a clean, cold taste from the river. But no large animal, no Hound, no Red Executioner had passed this way. He would stay the night and move on down the mountain in the morning.

A patch of wild thyme grew on the riverbanks. He rolled and stretched, the scent rising all around him, and when the night wind came, he slept until the sky began to lighten, then ran along the river in the rising light sliding to sudden, coltish stops in the thickets by the water. As the sun rose he ate, drank, and met the morning with a chant:

'I am the Dancer
and the scent of wild thyme floats from my mane.

I am the Rainbow, on a journey to right the Balance.
I am the rivers, rising with the floods of spring.
I am the Dancer
and the scent of wild thyme floats from my mane.'

He moved out and down the mountain. It had been a long time since he had moved on the earth, heard the cry of mockingbirds, the crow's sly call . . . and he paused, distracted by the memories of his earlier time here, before he had joined his gods.

Halfway down the mountain, he passed a family of coyotes on a rock, sand-beige fur blending into the stone. They were tearing at a deer carcass, at the soft throat of a doe, the body fawn and red. He would have passed them by except for the smell – faint, fetid – and the pale-green glow in the dogs' opaque eyes. The female yipped and slid behind the rocks, two pups scurrying after; the male pinned back his ears, flattened his belly to the ground: 'Good morning, grass-eater.'

The Dancer paused in his easy canter, flicked one ear and said, 'Rather a large kill for one your size, meat-eater. You accomplish that alone?'

The coyote slid across the entrance to the small hole beneath the rocks; the sharp whimper of a pup was cut off by a maternal growl. 'As you see. But I admit, the taste of deer is rare for me and mine.' He licked his lips.

'You will help me. I am looking for a Farm – near here, I think. A buckskin mare is there.'

'A buckskin on a farm,' said the coyote thoughtfully. 'No, I can't say that I've seen such as you describe.' The coyote advanced a few paces, grinning. 'Is this mare a member of your herd?'

'Not yet. She's been lost, but I'll find her.' Then he said with cheerful courtesy, 'With your help.'

'I could try,' said the coyote, rolling in the dust. 'A mare you say? Buckskin?'

'You have seen her, then? She is colored like wild

82

wheat at the end of summer. Her mane is as black as a crow's wing, and she is mine.' He reared, and shouted.

'Tcah!' said the coyote. 'If I were you I would spend some time gathering my forces together, I would. It could be dangerous, seeking this mare.'

The coyote bitch crawled from the hold in the rocks and hissed like a snake. The dog whined, 'We have seen two mares pass this way but one suntime ago. Would they be the ones you are seeking?'

'And where do I find these mares?'

'At the foot of the mountain. Where the pine trees grow thick.'

'Is the buckskin mare with them?' The Dancer snaked his head low to the ground, his eyes fierce and glowing.

'I don't know. Lift your nose to the wind. When the breeze blows up from the valley you can tell for yourself.'

The Dancer whirled, head up, and trotted to the edge of the trail. Below it lay an untracked mass of shrub and underbrush, and the breeze carried a faint female scent. Gathering himself into a clenched and compact mass, he leaped forward and disappeared over the edge.

'Well?' demanded the female. She stuck her head out of the den and glared.

'Gone.'

'And what did you tell him?'

'What I was told to tell him. I sent him to where the mares wait.' He snarled, 'Your payment's there. Eat!'

The coyote's mate lifted her muzzle in a peculiar, yowling laugh, and laughing, bit into the deer carcass, the blood staining her snout.

The Dancer plunged down the mountainside to the meadow, where the pine trees grew thick at the mountain's edge. The female scent grew stronger, and a kind of crazy exultation possessed him. He stopped among the pine trees facing a small clearing. Two mares stood in the meadow, one grey, one brown. 'You, there!' he shouted. 'I am looking for a buckskin mare. Have you seen her?'

The grey jumped and squealed, backing around until

she faced him. Pinning his ears back, shaking his head from side to side, the Dancer moved through the pines and stepped on the short spring grass. Through the thunder in his head came the scent of the mares and the rich odor of grass crushed underfoot.

He stopped.

'Help us!' said the grey. 'Please.' She was colored like the clouds before sunrise, the grey shading to a dappled silver. She looked familiar, but the Dancer, in the confusion of his senses, couldn't recall where he had seen her before.

The Dancer laid his ears flat against his skull. A disturbing odor was underneath the breeze – an odor of meat, fresh-killed. A black fly buzzed in the sunshine near the brush at the clearing's edge, and then another. The Dancer's ears swiveled forward: There was a rustle in the bushes – a movement too slight for horse or hound.

'Oh, stallion,' said the grey. 'You are kind, and you know what will happen if you leave us here. There are men about – I see that you have discovered that one there – how many there are we cannot tell. Have you mares of your own that we could join? Will you take us with you?'

Still the Dancer hesitated.

'We are young. And desperate. And there is something else that chases us, besides the men. Something dark.'

'Dark. Dark. Dark,' said the brown mare slowly. She was half-dazed. Her breath came unevenly.

He took a slow step forward.

'No!' said the brown mare.

The grey turned, snarling, and laid the brown mare's ear open with a flick of her yellowing teeth. 'She doesn't know, as I do,' the grey said. 'She doesn't know what lies ahead for us. We would be safe with you. Safe from the dark.'

'The dark . . .' echoed her companion, in the same dead tone.

The Dancer turned to the figure crouching in the bushes – a man, thin-chested, skinny. 'We can give you fine

84

colts,' the grey whispered. 'We'll be the start of a new line, and stand with you on the mountain peaks in the light of the setting sun. We're mares. And we are yours. All it takes is a rush to free us. What's a creature like that man against the likes of you?'

The Dancer snorted in amused agreement. Then the brown mare looked at him, appeal in her eyes, and his heart melted. His gait certain, purposeful, he crossed the meadow.

'We're bait!' screamed the brown mare. 'No!'

A sting – on his neck, just behind the ears. A wasp? The smell of closed-in places, of trapped grief, hit him like a blow. He tried to run, but a buzzing filled his head. A mist hid the sun. A sound like sliding rock roared in his ears.

He dropped to the ground and lay still.

He became aware of a rhythmic 'thwack-thwack-thwack,' a sound like wind at a broken branch, creeping through the grey cloudiness in his head. He shook himself, feeling that he had somehow fallen into water and couldn't get out again.

He was in a trailer, the wheels slapping against the roadway. He was haltered and tied with a thick rope to an iron bar. He made a convulsive leap and fell heavily against the trailer's side, wrenching his neck.

'Trapped,' he thought. And the taste of blood was in his mouth like a bit.

'Don't struggle.' The grey mare stood next to him, unbound, untied, and there was a strange green-yellow glow in her eyes. 'You'll break your neck if you struggle,' she said, 'and if you try to bite through the bars, you'll break your teeth on the metal. It's no use. But then, I never could give you advice, could I?'

'Sycha,' said the Dancer. 'Damn you. How did you do this?'

Sycha simply looked at him, and he remembered the

wasp-sting of the tranquilizing needle. Men and Sycha: betrayers.

'Where are we going?'

She laughed – and the Dancer's flesh prickled. 'We're going,' she said, 'to an auction.'

The trailer slowed, and the floor swayed beneath the Dancer's feet.

'We're pulling into the pens right now,' said Sycha, glancing over her shoulder to the rear of the trailer. 'You've been unconscious for a long time.' She stopped, then said, 'We don't usually get your kind here. It was easier then we thought.'

The Dancer jerked his head high and kicked.

'Don't fight. It'll just be worse for you. Sometimes I think they like it better when you fight. Those that fight are beaten. First. Last. And they never escape.'

'You are as I remember you,' the Dancer snarled. 'And I wept to find you gone. I wouldn't believe you'd done it, not even when I Watched and saw you there, in the Barns, with those meat-eaters, with that filth you worship now. Tell me, Sycha, was it worth it? Are you indeed Sycha, flawless as the Moon? Have you regained the colors that you lost when you gave up our line to join the Dead? Or do you shine more brightly still?' He quivered with contempt; if he were free he would have gone for her throat and bitten deep.

There was grief in her eyes – and a helpless viciousness, kin to the look of tied and beaten jackals. He drew his lips over his teeth and shrilled his rage.

She stepped forward, lightly, and he backed away, quivering with disgust. She blew out once, softly. 'You still smell of thyme, Dancer.'

The rear door of the trailer was pulled open with a rattle; moonlight flooded in. In a confusion of dust and pungent odors he heard the crowded voices of many horses, squealing, and the undertones of men. The Dancer kicked again. 'Take my advice,' said Sycha, backing out of the trailer and melting into the dark.

'There's nothing you can do to save yourself now. And you'll get hurt if you try.'

Men came, accompanied by shouts and whistles. The Dancer crouched like a cat, shoulders and hindquarters quivering, his eyes blood-rimmed. A foul-smelling cloth was bound roughly over his eyes. His other senses sharpened, and he held himself in readiness, waiting for a chance to attack. Metal pinched his muzzle with a searing pain, like a cat's claws, and he whistled in outrage. 'Follow along, please,' Sycha whispered. 'You've felt a twitch before . . . yes?'

They backed him out of the trailer in a slow, hate-filled waltz; he thrashed forward two steps for every backward three. His hindquarters shifted (ONE!) first from one side, then (TWO – THREE) to the other, rocking the trailer bed. The wooden floor ended abruptly, and he stumbled and fell into the thick, dusty earth. His feet on the ground, he plunged forward to escape.

The steel twitch bit into the soft cartilage of his muzzle, and involuntarily he took a few stumbling steps, following the lead ropes. He shouted, 'I will not have this!' He relaxed, stopped, pulled sharply back, then lunged forward, and the rope's taut length suddenly slackened. He shook his muzzle free of the twitch and plunged over the insubstantial chest of the man on the ground before him, landing on soft, yielding men's bones. He ran and scarcely noticed the wasp-sharp sting in his neck, for the second time that day.

This time was different. This time he didn't pass into that realm of underwater sleep. This time he heard, and dimly felt what was being done to him. The moon seemed to stop in its path across the night sky. The wind moved with the heated blows in languid, unnatural eddies. And the whips rose and fell, rose and fell, with the inevitability of scarlet flowers blooming.

They dragged him to a boxed-in pen, and left him to wait.

He spit his hatred and tried to kick out the walls to

freedom. Sweat dimmed the fierce white of his coat, quarters and belly. Finally, he stood with his head down, flanks heaving, and passed into a state where time meant nothing at all.

He was roused by his thirst, and the distant smell of water.

From the pen next to him came a whisper. 'Are you all right?' It was the brown mare, the one that had tried to warn him of the trap. The blood from Sycha's teeth had crusted on her muzzle, and she spoke thickly through the scab.

'She told you not to struggle. What are you going to do now?'

He heard the clank of the water pail being carried down the concrete aisle of the barn.

'Wait and see.'

He heard the rusty rolling sound of opening stall doors. And then the slosh of the water and the slow, weight-laden footsteps of someone carrying the pail. He slumped in pretended exhaustion, nose to the farthest corner of the pen. The water boy paused outside his stall door, hesitating, and the Dancer could smell his fear. The door opened a cautious crack and the Dancer kept his head down until he heard the clank of the pail on the floor. He whirled and struck. A human shriek filled the air. The door shivered and buckled under the Dancer's kicks, and he burst into the aisle of the barn, and galloped, sliding and scrambling, to the smell and the sight of the outdoor air. Shouts came behind him, and the Dancer ran, his hooves sending up gouts of earth. He barely noticed the sting of the night air on the open wounds of his flanks.

He raced for a wide, tarry path with a surface stinking of man-made fumes. He dodged yellow-eyed metal beings, choking with the smoke, and ran for the dark beyond the road. He paused at the edge, ears questing, and gathering himself in, he leapt.

Pebbles and gravel caught his feet. The path smoked with an evil scent and he struck angrily at the murmuring surface. A tiny light of yellow-green fire flickered at his left shoulder, then shone again at his right.

He stopped.

The light harried him from behind now, and he moved forward with short, high steps to keep his feet from the foulness. He was being herded – toward what, he didn't know – and in baffled rage, he lunged and galloped straight ahead, into the hands of those who waited.

Wooden slats were driven home behind him, in front of him. The yellow light shimmered and grew, illuminating sharp-clawed hands that pulled at his mane and clawed his neck. The light intensified, and he saw his prison.

He was in a slaughtering chute.

The Dancer knew a moment of fear so keen, so intense, that death itself might have been a release. Hands steadied his head, a rope clamped his muzzle shut. The killing tool hung before him.

Harrier Hounds crouched in a circle around the chute; clouds of flies buzzed overhead. The wail became a chant as they crouched there, the one word that was never spoken by the living except in the dead of night: A-NOR. A-NOR. A-NOR.

The Dancer thought, with despair, of the quest that might have been, of the Courts and his shining god, and screamed out his rage at the trick, vowing vengeance. 'A-a-a-nor!' And with a great tearing sigh, he lowered his head for the blow.

'Well, Dancer.' Sycha stepped lightly through the darkness surrounding the killing chute. 'So you'll join us soon, after all.'

The Dancer flattened his ears in contempt, and Sycha drew her lips back over her teeth. 'Are you thinking that I might redeem myself and set you free?' she whispered. 'I've missed you, Dancer. I want you with me. Together, we can roam the pastures of His Land.' She leaned closer. 'Together, we may . . .' She snapped to attention, her eyes a sudden yellow-green. 'Who is that! Who's there!

89

Who dares to spring my trap! I CANNOT SEE! Who comes!'

In the Courts, the Pool boiled fountain high and the Watchers whinnied in alarm. . . .

Driving the pickup truck with one hand, Emmanuel Bishop fished the newspaper clipping from the pocket of his tweed jacket. The fading afternoon light made reading difficult, and he smoothed it on his knee, trying to keep one eye on the road. 'Left on Slocum,' he said, 'and is that a one or a two? Second left. It's a two.'

The big collie curled in the passenger seat beside him thumped his tail and yawned. Suddenly, the dog scrambled to his feet, and his massive shoulder nudged the wheel.

'Down, Cory!' Emmanuel pushed the dog, and the newspaper clipping drifted to the floor. 'Damn. Down, I said!' Cory sat obediently, a low whine in his throat. Emmanuel, swearing softly, groped for the clipping.

Cory barked, and barked again, filling the truck cab with a rolling volley of noise. A stallion came hurtling across the road, out of the dusk and into the headlights. 'Sit!' roared Emmanuel. He jumped on the brakes, and the truck squealed to a yawning halt, the dog pitching forward into the windshield.

The stallion leaped aside. 'An Appaloosa!' Emmanuel thought. The biggest he'd ever seen, standing seventeen hands or more, and in the glare of the headlights, brilliantly marked: coal-black head and neck, with white spots blanketing the heavily muscled hindquarters, and a head as fine as he'd seen anywhere, with a deep-set eye and broad forehead.

'God! Quiet, Cory!' He cupped the dog's tawny nape, and Cory, intent on the horse, thrust his head from under Emmanuel's hand and out the window.

The Appaloosa galloped straight across the field, harried by something Emmanuel couldn't see in the failing light, spinning left, then right, with a steady, baffled purpose in which Emmanuel saw no panic.

Emmanuel gunned the accelerator and swung onto the dirt road that bound the nearly grassless field where the auction tents sat. A sign appeared in his headlights: STAFFENBACK'S SLAUGHTERHOUSE: DEAD AND DYING ANIMALS HAULED FREE, and across the sign, in red, 'Auction Today.'

The stallion thundered past the tents. Two shabbily dressed workers leaped, hands outstretched. The horse swerved . . .

'No!' said Emmanuel aloud.

. . . into the slautering chute.

Emmanuel wheeled into the graveled parking lot. Ancient tractor-trailers jammed one end and from the filled vans came the scream of frightened horses. Emmanuel braked and turned the motor off.

'Here for the wild horse auction?' A grizzled face thrust itself into the opened driver's window and Emmanuel drew back. 'Gotta buy now, or else them animals'll keep that fine-lookin' dog in feed for a year or two.' Emmanuel, his attention on the Appaloosa imprisoned in the chute, opened the door to shove past.

'That'll be a dollar to park,' said the attendant. 'Hey! A dollar. One buck.' Emmanuel snapped Cory's leash to the dog's collar with one hand, thrust a crumpled bill at the attendant with the other. Cory lunged to the end of the chain, snarling

The Appaloosa reared in the chute, his scream cresting above the shouts of the surrounding crowd. Emmanuel dropped the dog's leash and began to run, Cory racing ahead.

'Hold on.' Emmanuel's deep bass cut through the noise of the crowd around the chute, and there was a moment of startled silence. He jumped up to the edge of the chute's wall, balancing on the concrete blocks that held it, and looked the Appaloosa in the eye.

The giant horse was trapped between the narrow walls.

Two burly men bent over the chest-high sides, each maintaining a precarious hold on the stallion's halter. A third, skinny, with a concave chest and eyes that failed to meet Emmanuel's level gaze, held a killing tool in his left hand, a mallet in his right.

'This horse scheduled for auction?' said Emmanuel. 'I called . . . someone said there was an App in the stock you brought in from the mountains. . . .'

'That'd be this mother, for sure.' The executioner shrugged, spat. 'You crazy enough to take him on, it's okay by me.'

The sun was almost gone, and the last faint light fell on the stallion. Sweat covered his withers; foam flecked his muzzle. Emmanuel saw the fresh whip cuts, welling blood. Emmanuel looked into his eye and something caught in his chest.

'How much?'

The executioner grinned. His teeth were yellow, faintly pointed. Cory growled and snapped his jaws together – click-click-click – as he did when hunting fox.

'How much?' Emmanuel said again.

'Hunnert dollars.'

Emmanuel counted out the bills and the executioner folded them twice over. 'All yours,' he said, and the three men walked away grinning.

The stallion kicked furiously at the sides of the chute, and the oak boards shook. Emmanuel reached out a hand, and the stallion snapped like a striking snake.

'How the hell are we going to get him in the trailer?' said Emmanuel aloud. 'And what's the vet going to say when we bring him in for the three weeks' observation – if we *do* get him in the trailer?'

The dog, uncomprehending, scratched at a flea, and Emmanuel ruffled his tawny ears. He walked twice around the chute, noticing the stallion's muscled chest and shoulders, the concentrated power in the heavy hindquarters.

He made a decision. 'Stay,' he ordered the dog. 'Guard.'

Cory's ears came up alertly at the command and he barked. Emmanuel returned to the truck for the tranquilizer.

And for the third time that day, the Dancer passed into that dim, underwater world of sleep that was not sleep.

7

An Exchange of Information

Duchess woke before sunrise, and stood quietly in her paddock while the morning routine went on around her. Emmanuel and Cory had not returned from the auction, and David did chores alone.

She could run, if she wanted to. There was nothing to stop her from leaving, no stablemate dying as Pride had been in that shed. She was bewildered and afraid. She thought of the spotted horse with excitement and with terror. She thought of Fancy, Susie and the others. There was safety with the herd, danger without them.

And there was this Test, this unknown Test.

The piping call of a weanling floated across the air; Duchess heard Susie's maternal chuckle in response. She didn't remember her own dam, just a sour-tempered Caretaker who had grudgingly let her nurse with the Caretaker's own bony foal. Her ears rotated forward; she heard David's footsteps on the grass.

She would decide – soon – but until then, she would be patient.

When David opened her stall door with the morning grain, she greeted him with an affectionate whicker before she moved to her bucket to eat. She ate slowly but steadily, and when she finished, she again stood quietly, watching the boy as he cleaned her stall and bedded it with fresh straw. Cory slipped into the stall at David's side. Duchess leaned over and gently nuzzled his shorn side.

'You're back then?' she said. The dog looked at her steadily, then said, 'We're back, yes.'

David groomed her down, the curry comb moving in a circular pattern over her back, bringing out the shine to her coat. She lowered her head obediently as he brushed her ears and forehead with a soft cloth. She jumped a little when she heard the buzz of the clippers, but stood gamely still as her ears, bridle path, and muzzle were shorn clean.

'Fly spray, next,' warned Cory. And Duchess, who hated the stink of the liquid spray, backed up a little, snorting as the fine mist settled in her ears and nose.

David slipped the bridle over her head, loosely buckled the saddle and led her into the arena. She stayed the correct two paces at his left without pulling or jigging. She turned her head reflexively as he tightened the girth, but recalled herself in time and simply nosed his shoulder.

Cory crouched on his haunches in the corner.

David shook the line out, and Duchess kept the proper length between them – loose, but not sagging. She circled twice at the walk, the trot, and the canter, then smoothly reversed. David signalled a halt. He tightened the girth and settled into the saddle. They began to work in earnest, in circles, half-circles, and finally, figure eights.

Duchess started the right-hand loop of the figure eight at a canter. She moved into the crossover and executed a lead change in stride. At the moment of suspension, with all four feet off the ground, she changed from striking out with her left foreleg to her right, maintaining the canter without breaking into the trot.

'We didn't know you could do a flying 'change,' said Cory, sitting up.

Duchess circled into the left hand of the loop, and made the flying 'change at the crossover from left to right without faltering. David dismounted, looped the reins under the stirrup leathers and said, 'Stand.' Duchess

95

squared up, all four feet positioned as though she were in a show ring, her neck slightly arched and her ears forward.

'Beautiful!' said the collie.

David set up the jump standards, then mounted again and walked her once through the course so she could see where the jumps were placed. There were nine – four in each loop of the figure eight, one at a slant in the center. He pushed her into a trot and she headed confidently into the right loop. She hesitated at the crossover, and as she took the center jump, came down with her right fore extended, ready to break into a canter. David squeezed her slightly with the calves of both legs, lightly flexing the reins. Duchess pushed on at a slightly uneven trot, jarring the boy in the saddle so that he bumped ber backbone uncomfortably. She regained her rhythm at the seventh jump and finished the round in stride. She trotted to the center of the ring, turned and faced the open door to the arena, squared up. Cory danced up to her.

The collie cocked his head and looked eagerly up at David. His tail began to wag furiously and he leaped in the air. 'Hey! We're going for a ride!'

'What have we been doing?'

'No. I mean outside on the trail.'

Duchess felt a flash of excitement. 'Really?' she said. 'Well. That's . . . pleasant.'

'And a privilege.'

David signalled a walk and they headed for the open overhead door. Outside, the breeze ruffled the treetops on the hill, and the air was fresh and clear. Duchess headed down the dirt road by the brood mare pasture at an easy trot, her head up, breathing in the taste of honeysuckle and phlox. David squeezed with his right leg, lifting slightly on the rein, and they broke into a relaxed, distance-eating canter. Fancy and Snip were standing in their paddocks and they raised their heads in greeting as Duchess and David rode by, Cory at the mare's heels.

'Hello,' called Duchess.

'Duchess?' said Snip. 'Is that Duchess, Fancy? But

Cory's with her. See that? Cory and David and Duchess are out for an outside ride. Now I seen it all.'

They headed down the gently rolling path, green pastures and white fences on either side. David tapped her side with his right heel, and Duchess lengthened her canter to a hard gallop. The stream that fed the duck pond wandered through the meadows here, crossing the trail about three furlongs ahead. Duchess' ears swiveled forward. She checked her stride as she felt the reins flex left, right, left, right, and shifted her weight to her hindquarters as David settled in the cantle. They jumped, the boy rising out of the saddle, knees gripping the knee rolls, hands low and steady at her neck. She cleared the running water in an arc, landing just before the rise of the bank on the other side, and continued her even canter across the field to the four-railed fence enclosing the large pasture.

''Ware!' shouted Cory, dropping behind.

The top rail was breast high. David checked the reins and pushed forward, squeezing hard. Duchess put all her power into the leap and they rose, David's cheek on her neck, his hands holding the reins close to her jaw, clearing the top rail with inches to spare.

Duchess stumbled heavily as she landed. David overbalanced and slid onto her neck. She stopped and waited while the boy regained his seat. Cory caught up with them, panting heavily.

Sweat streamed from her withers and neck and she blew dust out of her nose with a snort. David rubbed her neck and shoulders and scratched between her ears. 'Duchess!' he said. 'Duchess.'

'Well,' said Cory.

Duchess looked back at the fence in modest pride. 'Five feet, about?' she said. 'First time I've taken a jump that high.'

They walked back to the Big Barn so that Duchess could cool off. When the heat left her chest and legs,

David put her in her old stall, between Fancy and El Arat, directly across from Cissy and Snip.

'We saw you,' said Fancy by way of greeting. 'And Cory's already told us about that second fence. He said you stopped when David slipped.'

'Yeah. *We* thought you'd get shipped off,' said Cissy. 'Bunkie told me they talked it over yesterday at the House. It doesn't do to have a bad-mannered horse in the barn, they said. Certainly wouldn't help the Farm reputation any . . . and how can you trust a horse like that with new riders? If a Grade can't behave in the ring or on the hunt field, what possible good is it? I mean, it isn't as though you can retire them as brood mares.'

'Cissy, I don't care what you think about Grades, or anything else,' said Duchess. 'All I want to do is to get along. You understand? So it doesn't matter what you say to me. I'm ready to take my place in the herd. I'm sorry for my behavior when I first came. Things were just – too new. Now, if you don't mind, I'd like a word with El Arat.' She turned politely to Fancy, 'If it's all right with you, that is.'

'Of course,' said Fancy. 'Cissy – you heard her. Duchess is a member of the herd. Tonight, when we're out at pasture, we'll have the Oath-Taking.'

Duchess turned to El Arat. 'Dreamspeaker?'

'Yes, Duchess.'

'Cory said that you can interpret dreams.'

'Yes, that is so.'

'Then may I speak to you? I need your help.'

El Arat looked at her distantly. 'It is not good for a horse to be alone. Strange dreams may come just from that. Wait for a moment, until the others sleep.'

The barn quieted. Outside, the sun shone with an afternoon fierceness. The bees sounded in the roses and the faint cool/fish odor of the duck pond undercut the flower scent. Finally, Feather, Snip, Cissy, Fancy and Susie slept soundly in the heat.

El Arat said, 'Don't talk too loudly now, or you may

wake the others. Tell me about it. Some dreams are sent by Equus as a message. And it is well to speak about them immediately, when the memory is clear. What did you see?'

'It started with the old dream. I was back in the shed, with Pride. We were hungry. We were always hungry in that shed. And then . . . the walls of the shed fell away . . . and there was a horse, a stallion, running. He was running down a mountainside, with the green grass rising all around him.'

El Arat shifted restlessly. 'A stallion? Not our Stillmeadow?'

'No, this was a wild horse, a horse colored different colors, black and white. It wasn't Stillmeadow.'

Duchess looked out her stall window. The sun hung in the sky like a gold apple, reflecting off the duck pond with a shimmer/shimmer/shimmer that recalled the mists of light in her dream.

'And then?'

'The Owl,' said Duchess. 'The Owl came out of the duck pond.'

El Arat nodded, 'You had a visit from the Owl?'

'Yes.'

'And what happened?'

'He said I was to wait for the Test of War.'

'And then?'

'The Owl winked out, like lights in the barn when David throws the switch. He was just gone.'

El Arat waited, 'That is all?'

'That was all,' said Duchess rapidly. 'Yes. Yes. I can't . . . I stayed awake until morning when Cory came. And I stood and thought, alone. El Arat, is what I saw a true thing? Who is this stallion? I must know. You must tell me. And what is this Test? Is it like those tests you told me about before?' She trembled.

'I don't know. The Owl is a messenger, from Equus. And he is a symbol of the Balance.' She stopped, hesitating, then said slowly, almost reluctantly, 'You must do what you are asked to do – and perform it well.'

'If you two would stop hissing in that corner, some of us could get some sleep,' said Cissy peevishly. 'What's going on, anyway?'

'Nothing for you to concern yourself with, Cissy,' said El Arat.

'Nothing at all . . .' came a sibilant comment from the barn beams about the mares' heads. 'So, you're back, buckskin. Didn't get yourself shipped off after all.'

'Bunkie,' said Duchess. 'How long have you been sitting up there?'

'Long enough.' The cat grinned and lashed her tail. 'You folks surely do go on, though, about birds and such.' She licked her lips with a sharp pink tongue. 'Owls, heh? Now, I never tasted owl. Like to, though.'

Duchess reared and snorted; Bunkie jerked upright as the mare's head reached her perch, clinging to the beam with needle claws. 'You *watch* it,' she hissed. 'And here I came down from the Big Barn just to give you folks some news.'

'What news?' asked Snip.

'Now everyone's awake,' said Duchess.

'Wait a moment,' said El Arat. 'What news, Bunkie? Something of interest?'

The cat peered down at both of them with steady yellow eyes.

'Maybe. Maybe not.' Bunkie began to groom her paws with quick delicate movements of her head.

'Maybe, maybe not,' echoed Snip. 'Maybe, maybe not.'

'Snip!' said El Arat. 'Please, be quiet. Do you have something to say, or not, Bunkie? Or were you just boasting?'

'Boasting, am I?' The cat stopped her bath and looked sharply down at them.

'If she won't tell us, Cory will,' said Fancy.

'What does that stupid dog know? He's not a house pet.'

'Neither are you,' reminded Cissy. 'You're a barn cat. Not that you're a particularly good one. I must have heard

100

a whole family of field mice in the granary the other day. Why don't you do the job you're supposed to do?'

'You should talk,' sneered the cat. 'If we're talking about sitting down on the job, what about *you* . . . what a waste of valuable farm labor you are, Ridiculous.'

'Go about your business, Bunkie,' said Fancy. 'I doubt that you have anything that would be of interest to us.'

'Oh, no? Not even if I had information about a certain stallion?' The cat blinked at Duchess.

'Stillmeadow?' asked Fancy anxiously. 'He's all right, isn't he? Nothing's happened to him?'

'You mares aren't interested.' Bunkie began picking her way gracefully across the beams.

'Maybe, maybe not,' sang out Snip, suddenly.

'What stallion?' Duchess called out.

'Wild one.' Bunkie proceeded to the end of the beam and leaped to the top of a tack box sitting on the floor. 'Bye.'

'Bunkie,' said El Arat. 'Would you like to pick the corn out of my feed for the next few days?'

'She does like it,' muttered Feather. 'Silly animal picks the corn out of your grain bucket if you give her half a chance. Dumbest thing I've ever heard of. Cats are supposed to be meat-eaters.'

'I might,' said Bunkie, strolling back to the front door of El Arat's stall.

'I'm sure you can have Duchess' too,' said El Arat.

'Yes,' said Duchess. 'And my oats, if you want them.'

'Won't eat oats,' said Feather. 'Why are you two so anxious to hear about this stallion, anyway? We'll find out eventually.'

'So,' said El Arat to the cat. 'Tell us what you know.'

Bunkie sat down and curled her tail around her feet. 'The Bishops have taken in a wild stallion. An Appaloosa. They got him from this wild horse auction.' Bunkie leveled a considering look at Duchess. 'This horse has been taken away from the mountains up north. He's been running free, no men to own him, no barn to sleep in.

101

Goodness knows where he gets his meals. This stallion, and other horses like him, are gathered up and sold to farms who can tame them or whatever. Otherwise, they are destroyed. They're a menace.'

'A menace? Why?' asked Fancy.

'I don't know. Destroy crops, or steal mares, or something. Anyhow, the Bishops have taken this one. A big App.'

'What's a App?' asked Snip.

'An Appaloosa,' said El Arat.

'Where's he from?' asked Fancy. 'Emmanuel got him at an auction? We don't buy auction horses here. It can't be true, Bunkie.'

'It's true all right. Emmanuel rescued him from the slaughterhouse at the auction. He'll be in isolation at the vet's for a week, then he's comin' here.'

'Slotterhouse?' said Snip. 'Fancy, what's a slotterhouse?'

'I'm not sure,' said Fancy.

'I know,' said Duchess, 'and the rest of you better hope you never find out. A week, you said, Bunkie. At the vet's.'

'Yeah. So if he carries any diseases, they'll come out there, not here.'

'Is he going to be a Farm stud?' asked Cissy. 'What's he like?'

'For me to know and you to find out,' said the cat. 'Give me the grain now.'

A week, thought Duchess. A lot could happen in a week. Too much. She looked at El Arat and then quickly away.

102

8

Clear Round, No Faults

As the week passed, the winds grew soft and humid with the scent of growing corn and hay and the grass took on a deep, lazy green.

Duchess, for whom the arrival of the spotted horse was a certainty, possessed herself in patience. She avoided El Arat, for El Arat had begun to spend most of her time by herself, standing under the oak tree or wandering down to the stream to stare silently at the water. Occasionally, Duchess would hear the black mare chanting to herself, and she waited, hoping for a word or two, but the Egyptian mare was silent, almost furtive. Twice Duchess almost yielded to Fancy's gentle proddings to take the herd Oath, and twice she drew back. The image of the spotted horse came between her and a final commitment to the herd.

The good times were with David and the collie. Twice that week they went out on the trails and she flew over the brooks and fences like a bird: willing, responsive, taking conscious joy in the fluid ease of muscle and bone.

And then, five days from the time that the Dancer had been rescued from the killing chute and sent to the veterinarian's barn, Cory turned up at noon feed, dripping wet and out of sorts.

'You been in the duck pond, Cory?' asked Snip. 'Were you too hot and jumped in to swim? I don't like swimming much, but I do like to stand in the water up to my stomach on a hot day and swish my tail in the water. It keeps the black flies off.'

'Those goslings got out of the pen again,' said Cory. 'I had a job getting them all back again. We can't have them running loose tomorrow – they'll get stepped on.'

'Little cheepies,' said Snip. 'Can't let them get stepped on.' She thought for a moment. 'Who'll step on 'em, Cory? I won't. Fancy wouldn't. Duchess wouldn't. Ah ha! Cissy probably would, that's who.'

'Shut up, Snip,' said Cissy. 'There'll be a crowd here tomorrow. Don't you know what day of the week this is?'

'Of course I do,' said Snip indignantly. 'What week is it?'

'You remember from last year, Snip,' said Cory.

'Snip doesn't remember what she ate for breakfast, much less what happened last year,' said Cissy.

'Well, I wasn't here last year,' said Duchess. 'What's going on?'

'The Bishop Farm Horse Show.' El Arat shifted on her feet and snorted pleasurably. 'We'll have almost a thousand people here from all over. Judges to judge the classes. Music in the parking lot. Blue ribbons for the talented.'

'The horse show!' exclaimed Snip. 'Of course I remember. Will we all be in it this year?'

'Most of us,' said Cissy, with a sidelong glance at Duchess. 'Same as last year.'

'What about Duchess?' said Snip. 'Duchess wasn't here last year. How can she? She doesn't have any babies to show. Oh, maybe she'll be in a jump class. I'll bet that's it.'

'Beginning jumping. Maybe,' said Cissy kindly. 'She wouldn't be in anything like Equitation Over Fences or Open Jumping. That's for bloodstock. Not Grades.'

'We'll get a bath, then,' said Snip gloomily. 'And have our manes and tails braided. And have the clippers on our necks. Ugh.'

'Settle down, please,' said Fancy. 'Here come David with the buckets and sponges for our baths.'

One of the stalls at the far end of the barn had never had a proper door, and the floor was concrete instead of wood. Duchess had wondered about its use, and she saw now, as the others were led into it one by one, that streams of water came from the ceiling. When Duchess herself stood under the glittering flow, she discovered it was warm. David dried her with a towel, and took her outside to the hot walker, where he hooked her up to the overhead wooden wheel with the others. They walked patiently in the sun until they were dry.

The breeze was cool against her wet skin, and she addressed Fancy's glossy hindquarters in a pleasant, dozy kind of way.

'What exactly will happen tomorrow?'

'You've never seen a show?'

'I've heard about them, of course.'

'Of course. Well, it's a little different every year. This year the five of us brood mares will be in a class called Mares with Foals at Side. Mares will come with their weanlings from all over the county, and even farther than that, to be judged on the quality of their breeding. It's very important to the future of the Farm. It's where our reputation is established. Men who comne to watch make a decision on what foals to buy from here, and what will be done with them.'

'Snip said something about jumping classes. What's that?'

Fancy turned her head a little. 'Nothing, much,' she said casually. 'Stillmeadow is a Thoroughbred stallion, and we've made quite a reputation for breeding some of the best Hunter-Jumper horses in the area. The classes are a kind of competition to see who can do the best over jumps. That's all.'

Duchess thought of the brooks, and her rides with David in the woods. 'What sort of jumps? Will the class be in the woods?'

'No. You see where the Bishops have put up those giant steps at the side of the boarder's barn? That big paddock is the show ring. Men will sit on those steps and watch the show in the ring. Fences and such are put in the middle of that ring, and that's where the class is held. Everyone goes over the same set of jumps. Sometimes the class is a race – that means you have to go over the jumps faster than anyone else. And sometimes the jumps are high and wide. That's to judge how well you can jump rather than how fast. Ah, here's David come to take us off the hot walker. Are you dry?'

'Do you think . . .'

'What?' asked Fancy, her gaze again deliberately casual. 'Look.' She stopped, then began tentatively, 'You might be in a Green Hunter Over Fences class.'

'Green Hunter Over Fences,' said Duchess. 'What's that?'

'For ponies,' Cissy offered over her shoulder. 'Kids' horses.'

'It could be the start of a career as a jumper,' said Feather. 'Don't be such a donkey, Cissy.'

'Start of your career,' echoed El Arat, with a strange kind of laughter. 'Yes. Indeed.' David, taking the mares one by one off the hot walker, stopped to look at El Arat for a moment, then clipped a led line to her halter and led her into the barn before the others.

David put them all back into their stalls, and beginning with Snip, began to groom them. The afternoon wore on, and by evening feed, all of the mares had braided manes and tails. Their hooves were shiny with hoof blacking and their coats gleamed with the oil sheen of show gloss. Duchess stood carefully in her stall, lifting her feet occasionally with high, mincing steps. Her neck was cool and unaccustomedly bare from the braiding, and her tail, bound up in colorful bandages, didn't have quite the effectiveness brushing off flies that it did before.

The mares were kept inside that night. Duchess was careful to sleep standing up, so that her coat remained supple and glossy. And then, early in the morning, before the sun rose, they all heard the sound of trucks and trailers pulling into the long driveway at the front of the Farm, then the stamping of strange hooves, the shrill whinny of foreigners.

David fed them early. Duchess noticed that the rations were smaller, and she felt the old, accustomed fear in her heart. Then Feather, with deceptive vagueness, remarked that the feeds always were smaller before shows, and for her part that was fine, since she was too excited to eat anyway.

'There's Susie with the weanlings,' said Fancy. 'It'll be quite a job getting them brushed up in time. The mare's class is one of the first.'

Duchess poked her head out of the stall window and saw that brightly colored flags decorated the outdoor arena. 'That large structure near the end of the arena is the judges' stand,' said Fancy. 'That's where you face when you finish your rounds.'

'You don't think the Bishops really intend to show her,' said Cissy.

'Be quiet, Cissy!' said El Arat. The Arabian's eyes clouded. 'Duchess must do what the gods intend. Fulfill what the Balance has ordained. This show today is to Test her ability in War and Games of War.' Her eyes cleared and she looked toward the open end of the barn. 'Ah! Here is my foal from this year. I don't believe you have met him, Duchess. He was turned out with Susie before you joined us this Spring, and of course, I have seen little of him since he was weaned. His name is El Riadam. It looks as though the mare's class is starting, so I will leave you now. You watch from the window and see how we do, eh?'

David and Emmanuel began taking the mares from the stalls, brushing their coats a final time. The weanlings squealed as they were marched up to their mothers, and the barn was filled with the soft nickering of the mares. El Riadam had his mother's eyes and coal-black coat and his tiny hooves beat a nervous tattoo on the concrete. David brushed El Arat down a final time, and walked the mare and foal down the aisle, striding between them. 'Come now,' said El Arat to the foal. 'Goodbye, Duchess.' She paused, then said, 'The Games of War, Duchess. Do you understand?' El Arat moved briskly onto the field. Duchess was left alone, gazing out of the window, bewildered.

The five mares and their foals, led by Emmanuel, David and three farmhands, joined perhaps a dozen mares and foals in the arena. One of the farmhands stopped at the weanling paddock, then raced back into the barn, pulling Susie behind her. She shoved the Paint hastily into El Arat's stall, then ran out again to the arena. 'Howdy!' said Susie. 'I haven't seen you all spring. My, you do look nice, Duchess. How have you been?'

Duchess blew out in warm welcome. Susie poked her head out her own window and asked, 'How do the babies look? We practiced what would happen in the ring out in the pasture, but I don't know if they were listening. They're nervous, like. Lucky, that's Fancy's foal, there, is the only one who really understands about squaring up. He leads pretty well, too. And that's Skimmer – he's Cissy's weanling. I don't know *what* he's going to do out there. He won't even stand still, much less . . . Oh, there he goes.' Skimmer, a smaller version of his dam, except for a white blaze on his forehead, jibbed backwards, pulling against the lead. He backed into Cissy, who squealed angrily and cowkicked.

'There goes *that* ribbon,' said Duchess.

'Oh, no, it's not on behavior, this class. At least, only a little. It's more on how they look, like. How they're shaped and how much they take after Stillmeadow – the best parts of him, that is.' Susie, her eyes fixed on the ring, continued, 'It's very important for the future of our line, this class. The best stallion colt and the best fillies will be selected out. And if it's some of ours that get chosen, why, the Farm will be known all over for the fine horses we have. Look, there's the judge.'

'Just on looks alone?' asked Duchess, scornfully.

Susie turned and gazed at her. 'Yes. It doesn't seem quite right, I know. And Cory says that Mr Bishop is more concerned with performance. What a horse can do instead of what a horse should look like. See the judge? He marks down stuff about the babies and the mares on that board in his hand.'

'Who do you think will win?'

'Oh, El Arat and her colt, for sure. But what's important is that we take as many ribbons as we can. Hooray! There's one!'

The judge pinned a green ribbon to Snip's halter. Pink, yellow and white ribbons followed in quick succession to horses Duchess didn't know. 'Look! Second!' shouted Susie. 'Fancy and Lucky second! And there's El Arat.' She stopped, bewildered. 'That dun mare and her foal got a first! See that blue? That means first. And El Arat lost. That's never happened before.' Susie raised her head and gave a shrill whinny, answered by three of the weanlings in the ring. 'This is *very* strange, Duchess. Unheard of! Why – El Riadam may not be sold to the best Farm.'

The mares and foals were led out of the arena, and Susie turned to Duchess. 'You see? You can never tell with men,' she sighed. 'I'll be turned out with the babies again, so we can watch the rest of the show, and I'll be able to watch you especially, Duchess.'

'What do you mean?'

'Why, they wouldn't have taken all the time with you if you weren't going to be in the show . . . you'll be in the jumping, like.'

'How do you know? Are you sure?'

'I heard it around, like,' said Susie. 'I'm sure I did. Oh, here they are. Come on, guys. That was very good. Lucky, you looked very nice. He did a great job, Fance.'

'Thanks to you,' said Fancy. Duchess stood in the middle of the confusion, her heart beating slightly faster,

109

annoyed with herself for the hope that sprang in her breast.

El Arat replaced Susie in the stall next to her, and Duchess said, 'I'm sorry.'

'It was meant, you see,' said El Arat. 'I can do nothing about it. My little son's future had been assured until now. He *must* go to a Farm that will take good care of him. He should occupy a position as great as Stillmeadow's. This is not right. The gods work in mysterious ways.' Her eyes were dark and angry.

'Duchess! Can you see this? My ribbon. My green ribbon. I never done that before.' Snip stood with her head held carefully high. 'Fancy, see this? My ribbon? It'll go on the wall with all the others and everyone will be able to see it. Cissy, you didn't get a ribbon, not like this one. Not like Fancy's. Not like mine. And even El Arat didn't get one.'

'Quiet, Snip,' said Fancy. She turned to Duchess. 'They're setting up the junior jumps, Duchess,' said Fancy. 'Good luck to you.'

The first class of riders came and went. Duchess remained in her stall. Then the second, third and fourth were held without her. Duchess watched with slowly dying hope.

'It doesn't matter,' said Fancy as the afternoon wore on.

'They're setting up for the big jump classes now,' observed Cissy. 'Look at that course. It's a killer! And look at the bloodstock lining up. Is that a Trakhener in the corner? Good looking, isn't he? Too bad he's a gelding.'

The barn door slid open and David, dressed in breeches, black coat, white stock shirt, and a velvet hunt cap, walked down the aisle and opened the door to Duchess' stall.

The mares stood in amazed silence.

'Duchess,' he said. And Duchess, bewildered with

sudden excitement, found herself equipped with a flat saddle and double bridle.

'You get a ribbon, just like mine,' said Snip. 'And then we'll all have ribbons. Except for Cissy and El Arat.'

'We're proud of you,' said Fancy. 'This is an extraordinary honor – and so soon after you decided to work well, Duchess! I can't see that anyone else from the Farm is entered in this class. It's Open Jumping and it's very challenging. Take care.'

Duchess paraded past the bleachers with David on her back. The air was strange with unfamiliar smells – a smoky odor and a scent of sweetened fruit. Papers and wrappings of all kinds lay on the ground, and the grass was flattened by the tramp of many feet and hooves; dust rose in small puffs from bare spots of the lawn. A number of horses and riders milled at the gate to the arena. Duchess felt very small.

A metallic voice came from a lily-shaped cone on a pole and David pressed her to the gate. She quivered in sudden apprehension. Foam sprayed out from her muzzle as she chewed nervously at the bit.

David's hands were at her neck, and she thought, 'It's the same as being out in the woods; just like the woods,' and for a moment she convinced herself that the hot sky overhead was the cool, leafy green of the forest behind the Bishop Farm, and that the murmur of the crowd was the rustle of the stream.

She turned to the arena, stopped, and looked at the jumps with a kind of bemused horror. There was a water hazard, with a man-made puddle and a pine board fence. A series of triple upright poles followed the water hazard. Duchess knew from looking at the three that there was no room for more than a stride in between. In the middle of the arena was a tall hill, with a steep vertical drop going down the far side, ending in a post and rail.

A tall, rangy grey hunter cantered into the arena with an easy stride. The grey took the water jump in stride, but stumbled coming into the curve of the triple, knocking

111

off the top rail of the final vertical. He took the brick wall, the coop, and the in-and-out, then swung into the middle of the arena and faced the hill. He scrambled up to the top where a low rail waited, and jumped it, then skidded down the far side on his haunches, in a cloud of dirt and stones. The crowd groaned. The grey left the arena, limping, to the sound of polite applause.

'No. No. No.' A Quarterhorse gelding next to her began to rear and plunge as his rider urged him forward.

The rider's whip rose and descended with a crack that was almost lost in the noise of the crowd. The gelding screamed, and Duchess saw that he was young, and more frightened than she was. The gelding's rider forced him to the gate with sharp digs of his spurs, and they were in the arena.

Duchess called out in reassurance. The gelding sidled, withers foamy with sweat. His rider raised the whip again, and with a scrambled rush, the gelding took the first fence offsides, landing with an awkward stumble. He faltered through the two vertical jumps that led to the triple combination and then, quarters bulging, scrambled at the triple and pitched his rider forward. The gelding fell against the middle bar and his right foreleg cracked like an explosion.

The crowd was quiet. The only sound was the gelding's harsh and heavy breathing. The rider, pinned under the body of the horse, cried out. The gelding lurched up and stood with his right fore dangling at a hideous, unnatural angle. Duchess heard the motor of a pickup truck rumble into life and men drove it into the arena. A ramp was lowered, the gelding urged carefully onto the truck bed and driven out again. Duchess caught a glimpse of the gelding's eyes, pain-filled, and a stench of fear and blood. She gave a half-desperate whinny.

'Stupid,' said the grey hunter at her shoulder. 'He was too new, too young. It was his first season. I've seen it happen before.'

Duchess shook her head up and down, the bit jingling

in her mouth, and felt David's hand at her shoulder in a slow, circular movement. 'He was forced,' she said. 'They should have let him be.'

It was their turn. They were up.

The eyes of the crowd were like tiny patting hands. She faltered into a trot on her first circle; David's leg urged her back into a canter.

David held her head steady between the reins, shifting his weight forward, and she was up and over the first fence. She landed on her right fore, then took off on her left lead, knowing that she'd take the second fence dead on, knowing that the fences that lay just ahead were easy, dreading the triple to come. But David held her true, and she took the triple like a buckskin snake, going up-and-over, up-and-over, up-and-over, as easy as water falling.

She managed the brick wall, the coop, and even the spread, although trembling overtook her once, and her hindquarters shifted out from underneath her rounding a corner.

She circled into the center of the ring and raced to the bank. The crowd was dead quiet. The grey had fumbled here. The gelding hadn't even reached it. She could hear David's even breathing above the drum of her hoofbeats. He settled firmly into the cantle, laid his right hand on her neck in a brief caress, and she was up the bank, the ground giving way beneath her feet. She took the post and rail at the top like a young bird soaring, slid upright to the bottom, then heaved up and over the small jump at the base of the hill.

Her hind legs ticked the rail behind her. The rail teetered and fell.

She finished the rest of the round to the startling sound of applause.

'Bad luck, that,' said the grey. 'I was convinced the rail was going to stay in place. But you have an excellent chance to place, still.'

'Thank you,' said Duchess. David dismounted and walked her out, and when she entered the ring again it

113

was to receive a red ribbon on her halter, and she trotted second in line of six horses in the winner's circle. As she stood there, she heard the Quarterhorse gelding scream from the Great Barn.

9

Duchess and The Dancer

'It isn't right,' said Duchess fiercely. 'And there's nothing you can say to convince me that it is. That gelding never should have been forced into the ring.'

'It is the way of man, Duchess,' El Arat shrugged. 'These things happen. And you've done well. More than well.'

The last rig had left the Farm, the evening feed was long past, and the mares were out at pasture, under a cloudy moon.

'You did it!' said Snip. 'We all saw you, even Cissy, although she pretended she was bored and wasn't looking.'

Duchess, troubled, grabbed at a mouthful of orchard grass and mumbled, 'I did what I did because . . .'

'. . . because you wanted to?' asked Fancy. 'Tcha! A fine life we'd all have if we did just what we wanted to. You did it because it was right.'

'Right,' mused El Arat. 'What is right, after all, but a mere version of the truth?'

Fancy moved uneasily in the darkness. 'I don't think that's precisely it, El Arat. It's more a matter of taking responsibility for the law.'

'It's not that at all,' spat Duchess. 'It's a matter of choice.'

'What's a matter of choice?' Cory loomed up in the darkness, the moonshine making a silver pattern at his throat. 'Would you have chosen not to win today, Duchess? You did it extremely well, you know. The Bishops are pleased.'

'Tell me what happened to the gelding,' said Duchess.

Cory was quiet, then said, 'The gelding was put down.'

'Shot,' said Duchess.

'No, it was a peaceful death. The leg was shattered. There was nothing they could do. It was . . .'

'It was wrong,' Duchess shouted. 'He had no choice!'

'He had a choice!' said Cory in surprise. 'All the time he was in training, he had a choice. He performed those jumps before, you know. perhaps not at the same form, but in the same height and width. He had a choice. And it looks as though he chose fear. How can we be responsible for that?'

'None of us can,' said Fancy. 'Cory, perhaps we'd better not discuss this anymore. It's been a long day, we're all tired. We've had enough excitement.'

'Well, there's going to be a little more excitement,' said the dog.

'More excitement!' Snip exclaimed. 'I like it better when it's quiet. That's part of my ugh list. Black flies is on it. Clippers is on it. Baths is on it. And excitement is on it.'

'What is it, Cory?' said Fancy.

'The new stallion is coming tomorrow. The Apaloosa.'

Duchess raised her head suddenly and encountered El Arat's somber gaze.

'Why? said Cissy. 'We've got a Farm stud.'

'It's not for us to wonder why he's here, said Cory shortly. 'Perhaps they'll start an Appaloosa line at the Farm. That's why you horses have an agreement, isn't it? They create the breeds, and you serve them in return.'

'No matter how they treat us?' said Duchess bitterly.

'There's a Balance,' said Cory. 'That's more in your line, El Arat – you tell her.'

'She may believe what she wishes,' El Arat shrugged.

116

'Well,' said Cory uncertainly, 'I'll be off on my rounds now. Is everything quiet?'

'All's quiet,' said El Arat. 'Good night.'

'Yes,' said Duchess. 'All's quiet.' The dog trotted swiftly away and the mares dropped their heads to the pasture one by one. Duchess stood alone, her head up, ears forward, facing the east, where the sun would rise. And the night passed slowly, the stars wheeling overhead.

The sun was well over the horizon and the dew had burned off the grass before the mares came in from pasture the next morning. 'Thought we'd never get the morning feed,' grumbled Cissy, as they waited for David and Cory at the gate. 'Look – you can see the fence around the isolation stall in the Big Barn. They've made it higher.'

Long rows of squared wire had been fastened between the boards, and a large chain padlocked the gate.

'I hear a truck,' said Duchess tensely.

The mares clustered together. Pulled by Emmanuel's pickup, the Farm trailer came rattling down the lane. A scream of tremendous power came from its depths.

Duchess leaped against the fence, her heart alive in her chest like a caged bird. The pickup came to a halt. A series of powerful thumps shook the trailer back and forth. Feather, Cissy, and Snip bolted down the pasture to the safety of the oak tree. Fancy flinched, but stood her ground. El Arat, her eyes on Duchess' eager face, gave a long, low whinny like a sound of chains rattling.

Emmanuel jumped down from the cab, Cory dancing at his feet. The scream from the trailer split the air a third time, like an omen. Emmanuel, a stout longe line in his hand, disappeared into the trailer back.

The trailer swayed back and forth. A large, powerfully muscled stallion backed out. Emmanuel held a chain twisted against the stallion's muzzle.

The stallion reared and bared his teeth. His chest, neck and withers were as black as a crow's wing, and white trailed across his quarters like ivy leaves.

117

'Who are you?' cried Duchess, ignoring Fancy's aston-ished stare. 'Tell me your name!'

The stallion's cry rang deep and it cut through the summer air like the blows of a blacksmith's hammer.

The Dancer reared again, plunged to all four feet, and stood rock still. His eyes on Duchess, he shouted:

Running over rock pastures
Under an autumn moon,
I seek the mare that was lost.
I stand on cliffs that peak at cloud's point,
I stand under the winter's pale sun,
And under the rains of spring
And the scent of wild thyme floats from my mane.
I am the Dancer!
I look for the mare that was lost.
From the stalking of the Dark Horse,
I guard the mare that was lost.
And the scent of wild thyme floats from my mane.'

The stallion's ears were pinned back flat against his head, and his muscles quivered under his dappled hide.

'What's going on here?' demanded Fancy.

'An injustice is going on here!' cried El Arat. 'This is not right. Not fair!' Cory heard her and stopped in astonishment.

Duchess, blind to Cory's look and to El Arat's rage, shouldered past the black mare and plunged at the fence. El Arat whirled and sank her teeth into her shoulder and the sudden pain made the buckskin squeal. 'You fool!' hissed El Arat. 'Who do you think you are? What do you think *he* is? Do you think he is for the likes of you?'

'I'm sorry,' she whispered. 'You're jealous, and I'm sorry. Sorry that it's not you. But the moon has come down out of the sky! There is nothing you can do to stop it.' She bucked in an ecstasy of feeling, and raced along the fence as Emmanuel pulled the Dancer into the barn. 'There is a choice!' she cried.

El Arat, furious, raced over the top of the hill and disappeared. It took Cory and David the better part of the morning to find her, and when they did, she was covered with sweat, as though she had been running to the moon and back again.

The next morning, Emmanuel brought Duchess to the Dancer. Duchess stood trembling inside the paddock gate. The ground in front of her had been trampled flat by the Dancer's hooves. Hoof-shaped depressions scored the dust, as though the Dancer had cantered over and over again restlessly, seeking a way out. Duchess snorted, a small shy sound that barely disturbed the air. She noticed details that hadn't caught her attention before: how the grain of the oak boards of the fence snaked like a river; how the dandelions sprang green and vital from the trampled dirt around the fence posts, their yellow heads mirroring the color of the sun.

Her sky darkened with a shadow.

'Well,' said the Dancer.

His voice was deep, rumbling from his great chest with a sound that filled her ears so that she heard nothing else. She backed against the fence, hindquarters pressed against the oak.

'Welcome,' said the Dancer, 'to my . . . prison.' He had a strange, wild scent. His chest and back were coal-black, like raven's wings, and spots of white trailed across his hindquarters like drops of snow. Suddenly, he reared and blotted out the sun, then raced around the paddock fence, the great muscles of his hindquarters clenching and unclenching, hooves drumming until the dust rose about him like a windstorm. A small, high-pitched sound escaped Duchess' throat, and suddenly she ran with him.

The Dancer stopped, blowing softly, sweat darkening the white on his withers. 'Duchess,' he said, 'come here. You are beautiful. You are the color of corn in autumn, after the sun has bleached it almost white. your eye is as dark as a wild doe's in spring.' He spoke close to her ear. 'If we were in the mountains, we would run together, down the rocky slides, faster then the hawks that spin

119

above the hilltops. Faster than the fish leaping upstream in the rivers.' He stopped, and there was a deep and tender grief in his eyes. 'But I'm not among my mountains. I am here,' and he struck the ground with a savage blow. 'And instead of freedom, there is this fence. And these men, with halters, ropes. I had forgotten what it was like.' He leaned close, and nipped the nape of her neck gently.

Duchess backed up uneasily, and the Dancer jerked his head up.

'Stand still!' he commanded.

'You must give me a little time,' said Duchess. 'This is new to me. You are new to me.'

'A choice?' said the Dancer, amused. 'You demand a choice?'

'Yes. I thought . . .'

'Thought what?'

'That you would be different. From the the way things are here. That *I* would choose.'

'Not your choice,' roared the Dancer. 'My choice!' Suddenly, he was everywhere at once, biting, striking, his head snaking low to the ground, his teeth bared and his lips drawn back. He grabbed the nape of her neck in a brutal grip and Duchess struggled in fury, kicking with all the strength she had.

The Dancer trumpeted, a new note in his voice, a killing note, and Duchess felt a sharp nip at her fetlock. 'Cory!'

'Back to the gate!' commanded the dog. The collie ducked, and whirled and slipped between the Dancer's lethal hooves.

'Back! Back!' the dog shouted. 'Duchess, get to the gate!'

Duchess hesitated, confused, drawn to the gate where Emmanuel stood, a halter in his hand, drawn to the Dancer, who chased the collie with single-minded rage. Her nerve broke, and she ran to the gate, ducking her head impatiently for the halter. Emmanuel closed the

120

gate behind her, whistled to the dog, and the collie wriggled out from beneath the fence, grinning. Behind them the Dancer stormed, his eyes red, teeth bared, screams splitting the still morning air.

'Sa, sa, sa,' said Emmanuel. She felt his hand on her withers, and she butted her head against his shirt, shaking.

The Dancer flung himself against the oak boards, and they creaked under his massive weight.

He glared at them. 'I see!' he shouted. 'Men can take you from me whenever they wish? They may pen me in and take you where they will?' He pawed at the ground, sending up great gouts of dirt.

'Duchess,' he said softly, between clenched teeth. 'You will choose, mare. Soon.'

10

Duchess Makes a Choice

'Well,' said Bunkie the next morning. 'You fixed yourself good and proper, you did.' She settled onto the barn beam over Duchess' head and contemplated the mare with a cynical eye. 'Kicked him a couple of good ones, I hear. Lucky you didn't stick around to find out what he can do when he's really mad. I hear he's a terror.'

Duchess flattened her ears against her skull.

'What's the matter . . . cat got your tongue?' Bunkie closed her eyes and grinned in appreciation of her own wit. 'I say, *cat got your tongue*?' She flexed, then boxed at her shadow, her tail lashing back and forth on the barn beam.

'You'll see him again this morning,' said Fancy. 'Have you decided what you're going to do?'

'It's ridiculous, the whole thing,' said Cissy. 'Bad manners. Pigs behave better than you did.'

Snip looked somewhat disconsolately into her grain bucket. It was empty. 'Duchess didn't mean to kick the stallion, did you, Duchess?'

'Possibly not,' said Fancy. She lowered her tones and said, 'Duchess, it *is* very wrong to kick the stallion.'

'I don't believe this,' said Duchess. 'I get all this talk about becoming a member of the herd. All this fool's jabber about "a horse is a member of a company." "A horse is one with her fellows." He left me with *this*,' she bent her head furiously, and the mares closest to her stall could see the teeth marks on the nape of her neck.

'I had no choice!' Her tones rose to a scream. 'I had no choice in the matter at all!'

Fancy responded as though Duchess had commented on the state of the pasture. 'You know as well as the rest of us – or you should – that stallions have their Rights. Granted by Law. There is a penalty for disobedience to the herd stallion, Duchess.'

'*Your* Laws maybe. Not mine. Who made him herd stallion? Who decided that? I didn't hear of the herd taking a vote. I didn't see any ritual or rule which was invoked to put him in his place. Who decided for us? Who forced me into this? There's nothing left for me to choose. There never has been!'

The barn doors at the far end of the aisle swung open and David walked in. He pulled a lead line from the wall hook and approached Duchess' stall. She backed into a corner and swerved her head as David tried to put the halter over her ears.

'Oh, my!' said Bunkie. 'Aren't *we* all het up this morning!' Duchess reared and pushed at the cat. With a yowl, Bunkie fell into the straw in Fancy's stall, and while Duchess looked to see if she was hurt, David forced the halter over her ears, buckled it closed, and snapped the lead line under her chin. 'Sa sa sa,' he said, and pulled her into the aisle. She shook her head back and forth. David slapped her smartly on the withers. She took two steps forward.

She followed David through the sanded arena to the Dancer's stall and stopped, ignoring David's patient tugs on the line. Raging, she bucked in place.

David hit her with his open palm, and she settled. As she reached the Dancer's door, she shook her head violently from side to side, trying to loosen David's grip. He opened the stall door with one hand, pulled her head around, and shouted 'Back!' She responded instinctively,

123

stepping backward into the stall. David slid the door closed.

'Duchess.'

He spoke from semi-darkness, from the farthest corner of the stall. He moved into the sunlit patch under the window and arched his neck, blowing softly.

'Come out to the grass. The air is fresh and clean there, and the wind carries a scent of far-off pine. There's a pile of fresh hay. We can share it.'

Her skin felt tight, as though exposed to a hot summer sun. She walked out of the back door of the stall and into the fenced paddock without looking at him. He followed quietly and they both bent their heads to the alfalfa. 'Tell me where you are from,' he said. 'Have you always lived in this place?'

'No.' Duchess began to search the hay with particular attention to the purple-green blossoms, which were the best.

'How long have you been here? Through the rains of spring? The snows of last winter? The frosts of autumn?'

Duchess pulled her head up sharply and looked directly at him for the first time. 'Why are you asking me these things? Everyone has made it very clear to me that I have no choice in this matter. That their precious Laws mean slavery for someone like me. Especially someone like me.'

'What do you mean – especially for someone like me? What are you that you should not be free to choose?'

'I don't understand. You yourself said I had no choice.'

'I was wrong. I'm not used to this . . . life . . . yet. To the sights and sounds of living things like yourself. To the scent of mares. I forgot that we all have the right to choose.'

'That's not what *they* say.'

'And who are *they*?'

'The mares in this herd.'

'*This* herd? Not *your* herd?'

'Not mine. No. There are too many rules. There are

124

too many Laws. And they are wrong Laws, bad Laws. Laws that can kill.' She thought of the gelding and his broken leg; she thought of Pride in the shed; and if she could have, she would have wept in the sudden wave of confusion and emotion that swept over her.

'Perhaps your mares are wrong. Or perhaps – like many of the messages that come from our gods, and from the One – the true laws have been lost, or misunderstood.' He moved close to her side, grazing as he talked, and his breath was sweet on her face. 'We choose every day of our lives,' he said. 'And the Laws themselves allow it. That's why they were made, you know. Because if we weren't able to choose, why would we need our gods at all? The Laws are there so the consequences of our choices are clear.'

Duchess stood in silence.

'You have chosen to listen to me – here,' he said. 'When you could have fought, as we did the day before.' He looked at her then, and Duchess raised her head and breathed out softly, twice. 'Shall we walk together, you and I? I'll give you time to choose.'

And as the summer sun turned toward the west, as the night shadows pooled in the paddock corners and the moon pulled the early evening over Bishop Farm, Duchess chose the Dancer.

Later, they stood together at the paddock fence, watching Fancy and the others turn out to evening pasture. El Arat turned and raised her head to them for a moment on her way through the pasture gate, and Duchess felt a chill. She shivered, and the Dancer moved to protect her from the evening air. 'You haven't told me where you have come from,' he said. 'Where you were before this Farm brought us together.'

'It was a bad place,' she said. 'I lived in a shed with a stablemate. His name was Pride. A gelding. Big, almost as tall as you are – but not as strong. In the summertime, it wasn't bad, that shed. There was a little grass enclosed by a rusty wire fence – the kind with barbs. We had a

125

wooden pool, a trough, that held water most of the time, but not all. When it was very hot, green scum formed on the top and in the corners, and sometimes the trough dried up. But the rains would come to fill it, and we managed.'

'And when the snows came. In the wintertime?'

Duchess closed her eyes.

'Tell me.' His muzzle brushed her shoulder.

'In the wintertime, snow covered the grass the turned it brown and damp. There wasn't enough to eat, although sometimes we could find a fallen branch or some leaves which still carried a bit of green. Men would come with stacks of hay once in a while – never enough, it seemed, but Pride and I shared for all of that. He was bigger, you see, and needed a bigger share, so sometimes I would eat more slowly, so that he could get a chance. But it was hard, when I was so hungry, not to eat it all as fast as I could.

'There came a time when the snows were so deep that we could barely see over the roof of the shed. I told Pride we should jump the fence, get out, find somewhere where there was food and water. But by then, he was too weak to go far, much less take the fence, and I couldn't leave him there. I still believed, you see. I still believed in the Laws of the herd. I believed all those things that El Arat has to say about being a member of a company.

'The water in the trough was long dried up and we had only the snow to eat and drink. I started to chew the walls of the shed. The wood was tough, and it hurt to chew it. I saw the blood on Pride's muzzle and I thought, if night would only come! A permanent night and a permanent sleep could drop on us forever, and I wouldn't care.

'We chewed down the walls of the shed, all but the big oak timbers. Pride broke his teeth on them, and one morning he just gave up. He lay down his head, stretched out in the snow, with blood around his nose like a soft rain. "Get up!" I shouted. I bit him, kicked him. "We must fight!" I said. "Get up. Get up. Get up."'

In the meadow a bobwhite whistled. Duchess looked blindly at the pile of hay.

'He didn't get up, of course. He never got up again. Just before . . . just before he passed into Summer he opened his eyes and looked at me. "Men will come with food," he said. "I dreamed it and it was a true dream . . ."'

'But they didn't. Not in time. Not until he had lain there two days and two nights, and the flies buzzed around his head. Then men came up over the hill. Men I hadn't seen before. They fed me. Put me in a trailer. And then I came here.'

Duchess bent her head to the pile of hay and began to eat in huge, tearing gulps, mouthfuls that she barely stopped to chew. The Dancer stood quietly. She sensed his rage, suppressed but violent, and she was surprised to feel protected.

'Duchess,' said the Dancer. 'Bishop Farm is a prison for you. Are the men here evil? Do they serve the Dark Lord?'

'Oh, no! They are good men. They feed us well, take care of us. And they take care with the future of the breeds here. I think they're kind and good.'

The Dancer gouged at the ground. 'They can take you from me at their will. And we are both imprisoned. *I* am imprisoned.'

'But that's the way things are,' said Duchess doubtfully.

'Why?' demanded the Dancer. 'Did you see how I was brought here? Did you see how I was trapped? I no more arrived than I was tied, bound, dragged into a killing chute. AND I COULD NOT GET OUT!'

'Where did you come from?' asked Duchess timidly. 'And how did you escape from the chute?'

'Never mind where I'm from. But this humiliation I was forced to endure. . . .' He struck the ground once more. 'Never! Never again!' He swung his head and looked deep into her eyes. 'Tell me. What would prevent this Bishop from taking me to the killing chute again?'

'Nothing,' said Duchess in a whisper. 'But I don't think he would.'

'But you don't know,' said the Dancer. 'And you – with the way men have dared to treat you, you think this is a good place?'

Duchess hesitated. 'I thought perhaps it might be. Yes, the first few days I was here – with Fancy and the others – I thought it seemed as though the world had gone right again. And then . . .' and she echoed the words she had spoken to El Arat, '. . . the Owl came.'

'The Owl.' The Dancer didn't seem surprised. If anything, it was as though a suspicion he had held had been confirmed. 'Yes. And what did the Owl carry underneath his wing?'

'You know about the Owl?'

The Dancer may have nodded, or it could have been the shifting of the nighttime air. 'There is a legend about the Owl. I'm sure that – El Arat, her name is – your Dreamspeaker would have let you know.'

'She said that the Owl carried two paths under his wings. That he could show me choices. But she wouldn't tell me more.' She shook her head. 'These are strange times. I don't understand,' she whispered, in a sudden burst of trust. 'Sometimes, sometimes I dream of Harrier Hounds. Of the Legend they call Scant, and of the horse whose voice he is.'

'Anor,' said the Dancer. And in that single word there seemed to rise an echo of a larger war, and the smell of hot-copper blood. 'Anor.' The Dancer turned, and became remote, as though he had passed into another time. Duchess called out anxiously. To have him and now lose him seemed a worse evil than her dream.

'To fight Anor at last. No traps to catch me this time. No tricks. No distraction from my purpose. I will have him. Aaaaanor!'

The Dancer's shriek was sudden, and made the night seem small. From the pasture came an answer, shrill and thin. 'El Arat,' said Duchess, under her breath.

'Your Dreamspeaker,' said the Dancer. 'Perhaps she can tell me more of what I need to know.' He turned abruptly to Duchess. 'I must see her, I think. Will you come with me, or stay?'

'You can't,' said Duchess in surprise.

'*I* can't?' said the Dancer, amused. 'What do you mean?'

'You can't just go. How will you get over the fence? And stallions just can't visit mares whenever they feel like it – it's wrong. Even I know that.' Duchess fought back her exasperation. 'No one would be able to tell what the foals were, for one thing, if stallions could get to mares at the wrong time, and besides – ' she stopped and whickered. 'I'm beginning to sound like Cissy. But I've felt like you have, you know. I understand – at least I think I do. When I'm afraid, I want to run away, break the Law of Fences and the bargain we have with men. But I've never known what I'll run to, or what will happen when I get there. But when I want to run, to escape, it's because it would be better to die than to stay.'

'And you have to be that desperate before you'll seek freedom? Tell me,' he said abruptly, 'whether this fence keeps you in, or keeps things out.'

'Both, I guess,' said Duchess.

'And tell me when they will bring you to me.'

'The men? When I'm in season, as now.'

'And if we conceive a foal? Will I see you then?'

Duchess dropped her head. 'Not at all then, I suppose.'

'And they could decide to breed you to this Farm stallion here. Oh, yes, I know there's another here; I can smell him.'

'They could, yes.'

The Dancer moved restlessly around the paddock. 'There is too much in the power of men. They took me from the killing chute; they can put me back again. They can keep you from me. They can sell you. They have us both in prison. And if Anor comes – can they keep me from that task, as well?'

Duchess said nothing, but she was afraid.

'I can see no way out. No way out. We must leave, and soon.' He began to move, and a thought came to Duchess: 'He is going mad from being penned in!' She trotted behind him moving to a canter as his pace increased, and then they were both racing around the paddock. The Dancer came to a sudden halt, and Duchess stopped as well, her eyes wide and fearful.

'Will you go with me, now?' A breeze had sprung up, the Dancer's coally mane blew wild, and a fire seemed all about him. 'You will come with me now!' There was a sound underneath the wind, a howling, and Duchess' heart caught in her throat.

'What?' she cried. 'Where? Where will we go?'

The fire which seemed to play around the Dancer's head dimmed. The eerie howling died. Something huge, gigantic, was holding its breath – and Duchess had never been more afraid. The Dancer stood without speaking, and the scent from his body rose like crushed wild grasses.

'How can we get out? This fence is too high to jump,' said Duchess, a desperate practicality in her voice. 'It's better, isn't it, to stay here? The men here treat us well.'

The Dancer cocked his head listening. 'Do you hear it?' he said softly. 'The howling in the sky?'

Her knees trembled. 'I hear nothing,' she whispered. The faint touch of a clawed hand brushed the sensitive skin at her muzzle. 'I see nothing,' she whispered, her eyes shut. Whatever it was suddenly seemed to exhale, and a hot breath passed her cheek.

The night grew sane again.

'I'm frightening you, aren't I?' the Dancer said. 'Come close to me and lean against my side. You need to sleep. You're safe now. You're with me. Safe.' His voice seemed to wash the scent of fear away. And Duchess slept, a little.

Night stole over Bishop Farm like a fox on soft, careful feet. Duchess woke suddenly and stood very still acutely aware of night sounds; the whispery rustle of leaves in the giant oak; the scrabble of some small creatures's claws outside the paddock gate. She had been dreaming of a golden mare, with a kind eye and sweet breath. The lights in the farmhouse were out, and the moonlight softened the hills and hummocks of the pastures. The farm seemed turned in upon itself, like a cat curled in sleep; and amid these small, secret settlings, the Dancer moved, massive and discreet.

'I am ready, now. I have thought of the Path my lord would wish me to choose – and I have chosen. There is evil here. I feel it. And I can't, *won't* fight when imprisoned as I am.' He cocked his head, as if waiting for an answer that never came. 'They are so far away,' he murmured, 'my herd and my home. Just as you must choose, Duchess, so must I. And I choose freedom!' he said. Beyond the farm lay the dark lines of the hills, and beyond those, the Dancer's mountain, at a distance unimaginable to Duchess. 'Will you come with me, Duchess? To my mountains, where the river waits? It will be a long journey, and a hard one. And when we arrive, the danger will be great. I have a task to do, a war to wage, a battle to fight. I want you with me, Duchess, to stand at my shoulder on the granite peaks. To raise our foal among the grasses of a free and unfenced meadow.'

'There is a story I must tell you,' said Duchess, surprising herself. 'I believe I dreamed it.'

He looked at her intently, and nuzzled her ear. 'Yes?'

'Don't,' she said sharply. 'You must listen. There once was a yearling colt, the tallest and strongest of his herd, and he was chosen by his stallion to go out from the herd and find water, for the herd's pool was running dry.

'The colt soon came to a place in his journey where the path divided in two. On the left was a meadow thick with grasses, tall with feed corn ripe in the husk, shaded by trees of an ancient age. Through the meadow wound a trail twisting like a snake's back, soft and springy with no holes to catch the hooves of the unwary.

'On the right, the way was stony and the grass grew

131

sparse. But in the distance, more a scent then a vision, the yearling colt sensed the presence of a river.

'The colt thought: If I take the right-hand path, I may soon find water. But if I take the left, I may discover a place where the herd can forage for the winter. My stallion may be pleased with me. The mares will sing my praises. I may even be allowed to form a herd of my own. And surely, a place as green and lush as this will be filled with pools of water, rivers of water.

'The colt turned from the stony field and ran into the meadow. He lost himself among the shade trees, was distracted by the clover and the corn, forgot his quest for the river. And lost as he was among this plenty, he soon died of thirst.'

'Is that the end?' said the Dancer.

'Yes. I'm sorry. I'm not sure what it means, or even why I told it to you.'

'You tell Jehanna, if she comes to you again, that I am much more than a yearling.

'What?'

'Never mind.'

The Dancer lifted his head. His nostrils wide, he inhaled the night, his gaze directed at the brood mare pasture, where Fancy and the others grazed unseen. 'There are six fine mares out there. Six mares to form a herd – with you the seventh. And my mountain has shelter from the changing seasons, deep pockets of grass to carry you over winters. I can form a whole new herd. Re-establish our line. Bring back the breed that was almost destroyed by betrayal. We could do that, Duchess.' The timbre of his voice deepened, changed, and the eagerness and longing in it pulled at Duchess' heart.

'Then I'll go with you,' she said softly. 'And we can ask the others, too, if they'll join us. We'll form our own herd in the mountains.'

With a glad shout, the Dancer gathered himself together and leaped over the paddock fence, a leap – it

132

seemed to Duchess – that no mortal horse could have made.

'Come with me, Duchess!' he called, and she thought the joy and triumph in his tones would wake the house. 'Jump!'

She made a rush at the fence, faltered, stopped. 'I can't – the rail's too high!'

'There's a weak spot in the fence, here, lean against it.' Her heart pounding, Duchess leaned against the top rail of the fence, the wood creaking in protest. The Dancer pushed from the outside and said, 'The top rail's loosening. Feel it?' Duchess threw her weight into her hindquarters and pushed. The board splintered, sagged, and the Dancer struck it aside. 'Now, jump!'

Duchess gathered her hindquarters in and leaped into the air. The boards of the fence brushed the underside of her belly, and she felt the sharp sting of a splinter on one hock. For a moment, she jumped through a blackness more intense than she had ever known – dense, hot, unnatural. Her hooves brushed fire and a bladed rush of air swept her face like teeth. She heard an eerie wailing, and a voice cried 'Yes!' She landed hard and stumbled. 'Did you hear it?' she cried. 'Did you hear it? Somewhere a gate has burst. Something's been let loose!'

The Dancer was beside her in an instant. 'The summer's drawing to a close!' he shouted. 'Autumn is in the air. Can you smell the falling leaves, the drying grass? Can you taste the end of summer's flowers and hear the fall of acorns? Come with me, Duchess! To the mountains!'

He sprang into the darkness with a single, powerful lunge, and Duchess followed him across the damp and silvery grass to the top of the hill.

'There they are, the mares!' said the Dancer. It seemed to Duchess that he had hurtled more than the fence. His breath came rapidly, and the massive chest glowed with sweat in the moonlight. At the foot of the hill, Duchess could make out the dim forms of the brood mares. The

133

Dancer reared, then plunged down the hill, calling. Duchess raced after him, feeling the wind in her mane with a sudden rush of exultation. He knew what was right. And if not, she didn't care.

Suddenly, El Arat appeared out of the dark, the moon mirrored in the whites of her eyes and the gloss of her hooves.

'I know who you are, Spotted One.' Her voice was flat, unaccented. 'I know why you're here. And you're making a mistake, taking these mares with you. A mistake that will lead to the Final Death. You'll be followed. By those who never lose a scent.'

The Dancer reared and poised immobile against the sky, limned against the moon as he had appeared to Duchess in her dream. El Arat backed away from his raised hooves, her voice rising. 'Leave them here! I see nothing ahead of you but the dark!'

'And who will come with me?' The Dancer came to all four feet with a crash that shook the hillside.

'They are all in foal. To Stillmeadow,' said El Arat, flatly. 'They belong to another herd. You know you cannot steal bred mares away – it's a sin. Although,' she said in a lowered tone, 'not as great as the one you are committing now.'

'Susie isn't!' said Duchess eagerly. 'Susie, you would come with us, wouldn't you? To have your own babies, instead of caretaking others? To run free in the mountains, instead of between men's fences?'

The mares huddled together in the dark. Fancy, a faint tremble in her voice, said, 'We have no wish to brook the will of a stallion, but El Arat is right – we have all been bred back to Stillmeadow, and we can't follow you, even if . . .' She broke off. 'Duchess,' she said in an urgent whisper, 'you cannot do this thing. El Arat has been telling of such visions that she's seen – you must stay here!'

But Duchess, her eyes on the giant stallion at her side, merely shook her head.

134

'You, Paint,' said the Dancer gravely. He approached Susie, standing with her head bowed, and blew softly on her neck. 'You will come with me – you will be the second in my herd of mares. Will you not?'

'Your *own* foal, Susie!' said Duchess. 'And the mountains to be free in.' El Arat screamed suddenly – a warning call that seemed purposeless to Duchess. Her cries filled the air with a cascading volley of noise that seemed to shake the heavens. The lights of the farmhouse snapped on and she realized they were betrayed. Dancer sprang into action.

'Move!' he shouted. He whirled, head low, ears pinned back, and raced around the bewildered Susie, nipping at her legs and hindquarters. 'Move! Move! And jump again, both of you!'

Duchess jumped the pasture wire with Susie at her heels. The Dancer paused for a breathless moment, and then cried, 'This way!' Duchess sensed the farmhouse door bang open, and Cory bounded out onto the lawn. The dog's warning barks pushed Susie into an involuntary canter. 'This way!' The Dancer's voice seemed to ricochet from all sides. 'Behind me, now. Come!'

'Tell them,' shouted El Arat from the pasture. 'Tell them who you are and why you are here!'

'It is no concern of yours what I choose to do, seer.' The Dancer snorted, surrounded by white fire. 'I will take them with me, away from this Farm of men. If the Dark is anywhere, it is here. Out of my way.' And he plunged at the ground, the dirt flying up between his hooves.

El Arat jumped the wire and ran between them, swift and oddly ungraceful.

'If you take anyone at all . . .'

The Dancer snorted again, in contempt. His massive shoulder knocked El Arat aside, and he gave Susie a fierce nudge. Cory's barks sounded closer. 'Run!' he shouted. 'Run before me, now!' And the two mares, buckskin and Paint, raced before him like leaves on a

135

falling wind. They raced from the hills and valleys surrounding Bishop Farm, the night turning familiar trees and brush to menacing shapes in the dark. Cory's barks faded, died in the distance, until only a faint echo rimmed the night. They ran for hours, while the moon sailed overhead and the night deepened to its nadir. The sound of their running filled Duchess' ears and mind, and she galloped without thinking.

When morning came, all familiar landmarks had disappeared, and they were in a wilderness.

11

In the Wilderness

Duchess stood on the crest of a hill and looked at freedom under a rising sun. Wilderness lay before her: wild laurel, birch and poplars grew thick and tangled under a sun-filled sky. Blue mountains lay in the distance, mere shadows in the clear air. She looked over her withers at where they'd been: behind were the fields of men, the hedgerows neat and symmetrical. Late corn stubbled the fields and the meadows were shorn of hay. They carried the oily scent of men and their machines.

Susie lay half-dozing in thick brush. Her cough had forced them to stop well before dawn. While she rested, the Dancer had gone ahead to scout for water.

Home, at Bishop Farm, David would be feeding oats right now. Duchess' stomach grumbled. The meadow behind her had just been mown, and she trotted back to graze. She'd taken no more than a few mouthfuls when she heard the buzzing of many flies, then an alarmed grunt from Susie. She ran to the brush where Susie had been lying. A dense cloud of black flies buzzed furiously around the Paint's head. She was standing in their midst, shaking her head and switching her tail.

'Come out!' Duchess called. 'Susie! Over here!'

Susie grunted again. As if commanded by a single, unheard voice, the flies suddenly clustered on Susie's face, burrowing into her eyes, buzzing furiously into her nose and mouth.

Duchess ran forward and butted Susie in the ribs. 'Come *away* from there, Suze!'

Susie opened her mouth, took a deep breath and coughed as though she would never stop. The flies attacked Duchess with the same sudden fury. They filled her ears and clung to her eyeballs with sticky, stinging legs.

'Suze! Susie, follow me up the hill!' Pushing the Paint forward, Duchess forced her up the hill. At the top, the breeze sprang to welcome life, and the flies disappeared as quickly as they came.

'Ugh,' said Susie. 'Ugh! I *hate* those things.'

'Where did they come from?'

Susie peered at her through swollen eyelids. 'I don't know. I was sleeping, and not too good a sleep, Duchess, I have to say, when they were just there.'

'Well, stay out of that kind of brush from now on, all right? We don't know what might be in there. Snakes, bees, anything.'

'Sure,' said Susie comfortably. 'I'm glad you know about such things, Duchess. Maybe you could tell me ahead of time so I don't get into trouble.'

'Yes. Well. I'll try.'

Susie look around. 'My. This is a wild place, isn't it? What do we do now?'

Duchess didn't know. She thought a moment. 'Wait for the Dancer, because he's gone to find water. Meantime, eat some of that alfalfa. It may be a while before we find another field like it.'

They moved back to the field and Susie cropped quietly, then said, 'I sure didn't like those flies. I've never seen them like that. Where did they come from?'

'I don't know. But we probably won't run into them again. It must have been a – a nest of some kind. They probably won't be where we're going.'

Susie cleared her throat and blinked mildly. 'Where *would* we be going, like?'

138

Duchess raised her head. 'He's back,' she said with quiet joy. 'We'll ask him.'

The Dancer, trotting swiftly, came expertly through the trees and brush. He greeted the mares with a brief snort. 'There's a small pond up ahead, about a furlong. Follow me!'

Susie cleared her throat. 'Just a moment, please. Where are we going, Dancer?'

The Dancer swung his head to the West. 'There. To the mountain.' A black fly rose lazily from the brush at his feet. It buzzed around his neck and ears, and he snapped at it angrily.

'Will it take long? I mean, I'm very glad to be part of this herd, sir. If Duchess meant what she said about havin' my own foal – why, that would be a great thing. I just had the one, you know, a long time ago, and then I was retired, like, to be with the babies. But I would like to know where we're goin' and how long it'll take. And,' she said firmly, with an air of daring, 'when we'll be back.'

'Back? We won't be going back,' said the Dancer.

Susie shifted uncomfortably on her feet, and said miserably, 'I see.'

'Don't you say "I see" as though you didn't have the right to stay or go,' said Duchess. 'You can choose, Susie, it's up to you. But think of the freedom we'll have! Dancer, tell her of the mountains, so she'll see, as I have seen.'

'There is a large river running down the mountainsides that twists and turns like a new-hatched snake. There are deep pockets of grass in the spring and summer, so when winter comes, the snow buries it, and keeps it safe for feed. There are places among the rocks to hide from the rain and wind.'

'Yes,' said Susie. And then, with a glance at Duchess, who nodded encouragingly, she asked, 'Will there be grain and hay? And a blacksmith to trim our feet? And will the vet come if we have a hard time birthing?'

'The grass and leaves of the mountain are all we need

to eat. The rocks and sand will keep our hooves trimmed as no farrier ever could. And the other mares will help you with the birthing.' The Dancer moved restlessly in the grass.

'Other mares?' said Susie hopefully. 'We'll have our own herd, like?'

The Dancer snorted and reared a little. 'We will find others and form a herd. A new line of horse to replace what was stolen from me and mine. And now, Susie, choose! We must be off.'

'If there are other mares there'll be other babies,' said Susie to Duchess. She looked at the Dancer shyly. 'I can really decide on my own, like? It's really up to me?'

The Dancer trotted out into the waiting field, and looked impatiently over his shoulder. 'Choose!' he shouted.

'Yes, it's up to you, Susie,' said Duchess. 'Please – come with us. Come with me. We'll be the very first in Dancer's herd.'

'The very first. A baby of my own, and others to watch,' said Susie. 'Well. I have to think about this.'

'When we have our own foals in the spring, Susie, they'll never leave us,' Duchess said. 'They'll become part of the herd, and we can watch them grow up in front of us and have foals of their own. They won't be sold off, to go away in some trailer, never to be seen again.'

'I saw my colt once,' said Susie, mildly objecting. 'Year before last, or maybe it was longer than that, he came to the Bishop Farm Horse Show. Enrolled in Western Pleasure class, he did, and took a third-place ribbon.'

Duchess, remembering the wash of applause as she trotted down the winners' lane at Open Jumping Class, said nothing.

Susie said cheerfully, 'Never have to say good-bye to any of them? They'll be right there all along?'

'The fillies will grow up to be brood mares of the herd. The colts will grow up to be stallions, to form herds of their own. And he told us, didn't he, that we're to start a

140

whole new breed of spotted horses, to live in glory in the mountains.'

'Live in glory,' said Susie. 'And, just think of it, Duchess, you and me the start of it all.'

'And him, of course.'

'And him. That's something, isn't it,' Susie chuckled. 'That'll put a burr under Cissy's saddle. And all that talk she had about you being a Grade, with no proper learning, or dam to teach you.'

'Well, she was right in a way. I don't remember much of my dam,' Duchess admitted. 'She did tell me that my ancestors had been great once, like yours and El Arat's. That men valued our line for – let's see, how did she put it: "Sturdiness of heart. Sturdiness of purpose." But something happened to us, she never told me what. Maybe she didn't know.'

'Maybe it was too terrible to tell,' said Susie wisely. 'We Paints have had some bad times in our line. And you know what happened to the Morgans.'

'Yes. The foundation sire pulling a rock wagon all his life. But look what happened to him after! He's one of the One Hundred and Five now. And his line is at every big show, or so I've heard.'

'As proud as anything,' said Susie. 'And the Morgans started out modest. What d'ya suppose they'll call our line, Duchess? Dancer, who are we?'

'We are Appaloosas,' said the Dancer, who had apparently resigned himself to wait.

'Appaloosas,' said Susie in disappointment. 'But I've seen them. They're not too many, but they're around. And how can I be an Appaloosa? I'm a Paint. And Duchess is . . . um . . .'

'You are foundation mares,' said the Dancer. 'And if you wish to know the Story of our line, I will tell you and you will pass it along to new mares as the herd increases, and then to the foals in spring.' The sun shone on the Dancer's neck as he told them the story:

141

'When all was mist and stone – before the earth was grass and rivers, before wild time itself was harnessed – the One created light to see by.

'He cupped it in his hands and shaped it and set it in the sky.

'As he did, the light shone through his palm, and fell to earth in all the colors, splintered.

'How beautiful,' he said. And breathed into the colors and set them dancing. But as he withdrew his hand, to work again, the colors flickered and died. So he took the merest sliver of his fingernail, and set it for the light to shine through. And with all these colors, splintered, he brought the Rainbow Horse to life and dance.

'That is how the Rainbow Horse was made, from the light of the sun falling through the crystal nail of what is called the Moon.

'The Horse in the Moon,' said Susie.

'Actually, it's the Horse *from* the Moon,' said the Dancer, with what Duchess thought was an unwarranted assumption of authority, 'but no matter. That is why our line will have all the colors of the Rainbow in it. That is why I am the Dancer.' He reared on his hind legs, his black and white stippled mane cresting in the wind. He circled, his forefeet curved in a graceful arc, hind legs moving delicately in the grass. He plunged to the earth and flung his hind legs to the sky, then turned and ran in a sweeping arc up the slight rise of the hill. Duchess followed, leaping over the hollows, her body in time with his.

'Dance with me!' she cried. He turned and shouted, and they ran together, the rusty black of her mane mingling with his own contrary colors. The Dancer chanted, and Duchess spun to his song.

'The wind is filled with music,
New breezes chase the night.
Away we run beneath the sun, whirling, feather light.'

'Whirling feather light,' said Duchess, spinning.

'Come with me!' the Dancer cried. 'We'll find the water, and begin our journey!'

With hearts filled with hope, the three set off for the mountains.

'The hardest thing is to get used to this space,' said Susie one late afternoon. 'Don't you get nervous like, without fences and stalls? Nobody to brush us, either.' She bent her head and peered at her forelegs, splashed with the dust of travel.

The sun was going down, and they were travelling through a stand of trees that edged a grassy meadow. The night dropped more quickly these days.

'I like the space,' said Duchess. 'No fences anywhere. Endless room to run. We can sleep where we like, graze where we want to.'

'It's getting foggy,' Duchess observed a little while later. 'I can't see the Dancer too well. We'd better move out a little.'

They quickened their walk to a half trot, following the Dancer's stippled hindquarters in the gloom. He came to a sudden halt and raised his head, ears forward, nose to the wind. Susie stumbled heavily over a log hidden in the mist rising from the earth and squealed. A hot-copper scent of blood made Duchess sneeze.

'Are you all right, Susie?'

'Bumped my leg,' the Paint muttered. 'Why'd he stop like that?'

The Dancer loomed out of the fog. 'I want you out from under these trees,' he ordered. 'Quickly, now.'

'I think we should stop until this fog lifts a little,' said Duchess. 'Susie scraped her coronet band.'

'All the more reason to get into the open,' said the

Dancer. 'The smell of blood may have attracted . . .' He stopped short and inhaled sharply. Duchess strained her ears into the silent night. A faint rustling came from the brush. She stepped protectively in front of Susie, her heart thudding painfully. She wanted to run, crashing through the trees.

'Quiet. And follow me.' the Dancer inhaled with a long sigh, and then stepped carefully through a scrubby hedgerow. There was a slight, scrabbling movement in the short pine trees, and Duchess jumped, ready to run.

'Welcome,' said Dancer.

A pony shoved her head from around the trunk of a thick birch, and just as suddenly withdrew it and disappeared. The Dancer moved forward with a slow, deliberate walk, his head close to the ground. Duchess whickered.

'Come out from behind the tree,' said the Dancer. There was a short pause, and the pony emerged, a little defiantly, Duchess thought, and jerked her chin up in the air.

'What d'ya want?'

'Are you alone?' asked Duchess politely.

The pony eyed the Dancer warily. 'Might be.'

The stallion extended his head low to the ground, sideways, like a snake, and lipped at the pony's muzzle. She jumped backwards and planted her stubby forelegs in the earth.

'Take Susie to the meadow, Duchess,' said the Dancer. 'I will be with you in a short while.'

'Yes, but Dancer, ponies are . . .'

He pulled his head up, and his eye was fierce. 'Move! I don't need to repeat it.'

'No. You don't.' Duchess hesitated, then turned and trotted through the trees to the meadow, Susie obediently following. When they reached the thick grass, they stopped and bent their heads to graze. Duchess flicked one ear back, listening for sounds from the woods. 'Another mare,' she said.

Susie's eyes were bright. 'So we're starting to build the herd!' she said. 'I knew it all along. He keeps his promises, doesn't he?'

'It's a pony, Susie.'

'A pony!' Susie said. 'What do you suppose a pony's doing all the way out here?'

'Up to no good,' said Duchess. 'You ever had much to do with ponies, Susie? They're nasty, deceitful, tricky little things, and I don't like them.'

'Liars, too, I'll bet,' said the pony. 'Can't trust one of 'em.' Duchess sprang forward in surprise. The pony had come up behind her without any kind of warning.

'This is Pony,' said the Dancer, joining them. 'And she'll be part of the herd from now on. You are to welcome her to the herd.'

'Howdy,' said Susie.

'Welcome,' said Duchess, sourly. 'Where are you from?'

'Around.' Pony glanced a little carelessly over her shoulder. 'Where are you from?'

'Bishop Farm,' said Susie. 'We're . . .'

'We're free horses,' Duchess interrupted with a warning frown, 'and we have a free herd. We're going to live in the mountains.'

'Well, it suits me to travel with you just fine, for now,' said Pony. She looked at them from under her thick fringe of forelock.

'A Shetland, are you?' asked Susie. 'I've seen some of your line at shows and such. Are you a wild pony, or did you come from a farm, like we . . .' she fumbled to a stop under Duchess' warning glare. 'Did you come from a barn?'

Pony threw out her chest, and glanced again at the Dancer, who had moved away from them and was grazing. 'Actually, I'm a show horse. I was with a circus, and kind of got, a-um, sidetracked, so to speak. This stallion here seems to think I've got a pretty good future with your herd, so we talked, and I decided that maybe I

Pony

wouldn't go back to the circus, but that I'd join you.' She grinned slyly. 'He's a pretty persuasive fellow.'

'A circus horse,' said Susie. 'That sounds elegant. Was it like the Horse Shows we used to have at home? With blue ribbons for the winner? I was in one of them once. I had a saddle with silver flowers on it.'

'Huh,' said Pony. 'No. I was a circus horse. A star. I had a red leather saddle with gold and silver trim. I did this act, in a ring, under a tent, with bright lights shining all the time. I was a bigger star than the Lippizaners. A bigger star than the Liberty horses . . .'

'And a bigger mouth than the donkeys,' muttered Duchess.

'Did you say something?'

'Nothing. Look, I guess it's a good thing that the herd is growing, and we're glad to have you with us. Did he tell you what the herd rules are?'

'Travel by day. Sleep by night,' said Pony. 'Don't sleep under trees, 'cause predators can be there. Walk toe to heel, so you don't trip. Yes, he told me all that.'

'He didn't tell *us* all that,' said Susie in honest surprise. 'Did he tell you all that? Duchess . . .'

'Yes, yes. It's common sense, anyway,' she said.

'Didn't tell you, did he?' said Pony shrewdly. 'Well, he's probably got plans for me. You have a Lead Mare? I thought not. Well, that's why he mentioned it to me, the rules. So I could tell you. Like a Lead Mare would.'

'We haven't actually voted on a Lead Mare, yet,' said Susie. 'We should vote, I guess.'

'I suppose we should,' said Duchess.

'I vote *you* to be Lead Mare, Duchess,' said Susie.

'I think that's a donkey idea,' said Pony. 'Maybe you should think about voting in someone who's smarter than the average, so to speak.'

'You mean you?' asked Susie. 'We could discuss it, I guess. Fancy was always big on discussion.'

Duchess turned her hindquarters to both of them in an abrupt and angry movement. She felt the Dancer's dark gaze; after a moment, he moved close to her side. Susie chattered on, telling Pony about the Bishop Farm herd.

'You must decide, you know,' he said.

He was anxious, she could feel it in the tensing of his muscles and the faint odor that rose from his hide.

'I don't want to be Lead Mare.'

'One of you must,' he said. 'It is the way of the herd. You've been making choices for Susie. She turns to you when she's in need. Choose.'

'Why should it matter to you?' she snapped. 'It's mare's business.'

'You're thinking of Pride,' he said. 'And how you failed him, perhaps?'

Duchess wanted to run, to plunge through the night which pressed around her like the walls of an immense, confining barn.

The Dancer waited. Out of the corner of her eye, Duchess caught a glimpse of shimmering gold. Something brushed her withers. She turned back to the waiting mares.

Pony challenged her with a look. Duchess looked Pony in the eye, drew back her lips and showed her teeth. Then she flattened her ears close to her head and kicked out sharply with her right leg. Susie looked around at the whistle of the kick and Duchess straightened up.

'Well, Pony,' said Susie, 'are you considering? Do you need more time?'

'Changed my mind. Who wants to be Lead Mare of this bunch anyway? I guess it's okay to have Duchess as Lead Mare. For now.'

'Good!' Susie said. 'I think we should let the Dancer know. He'll be proud of us. Now, which one of us should tell him?' She looked anxiously from Pony to Duchess.

'You go ahead and do it, Susie. I'll have a word with Pony while you're gone.'

Susie trotted up to the the Dancer. Once she was out of earshot, Duchess leaned forward and said into Pony's ear, 'You listen to me, you squat little flea-bitten pony.

148

I'll be Lead Mare – for now, at least. And one bit of trouble out of you, and I'll kick like you've never been kicked before. Understand?'

'Oh, I got it,' said Pony. 'You won't get a bit of trouble out of me. Sure's I'm a circus star.'

They moved steadily westward. Duchess felt the hardening of her muscles, the expansion of her chest with the long hours of work. Even Pony began to lose a little of her fat, and took on, as Susie commented, at least the look of a respectable mare.

'She's driving me crazy, though,' the Paint mare confided to Duchess one afternoon. 'Sneaks up on you, and bites when you aren't looking.'

'I know.'

'And those stories she tells! Do you believe them, Duchess? Do you think she did all those things in the circus? I don't. I think she's as full of it as last year's hay.'

'I've never met a pony that wasn't,' said Duchess.

'Well, you're Lead Mare. You should do something about it. Fancy would. Have a talk with her. A horse is a member of a Company. A horse cannot live without a herd. We all know that.'

'I don't know if that applies to ponies,' said Duchess.

'Ask her if her dam ever told her the Stories,' said Susie. 'I don't know much about ponies, but they are members of the Company after all, aren't they?'

'Of course they are,' snapped Duchess. 'I'll move back and talk to her.'

Pony was plodding steadily along and rolled her eyes as Duchess came up to her. 'I'm moving as fast as I can.'

Duchess nodded.

'Pony, we have an unusual opportunity, you know. It's not many horses that can run free.'

'I don't see what's so great about it,' said Pony. 'We walk and run all day, and at night, do we get a nice bucket of grain and a soft place to sleep? We do not. We get kicks from *him* if we don't move fast enough, and rocks to sleep on, and trees to stand under, and rain on our heads. I don't see what the big deal is, anyway.'

'We're free,' said Duchess.

'Doesn't make any difference to me,' said Pony. 'Looks like we're in a different kind of prison, is all. And it's safer at home.'

'Who wants to be safe?'

'Me,' said Pony.

'The reason that I stopped to talk to you is to see if you have any Stories you can tell us.' Duchess began to feel more in control of the situation. Maybe being Lead Mare wasn't as difficult as she thought. She continued, 'We don't have a herd Storyteller yet, and we need someone to tell stories to the foals in the spring. Did you . . . um . . . learn much from your dam? I assume that ponies are told the Stories, just as horses are.'

'Well, sure,' said Pony indignantly. 'What d'ya think we are, chickens? Ponies aren't any different, just shorter.'

'So, have you heard the Tale of Alamain?'

'Yeah,' said Pony, suspiciously.

'Then you know we mut all pull together and work as one.'

'Um.'

'So, perhaps you have a Story to tell us tonight, after evening feed.'

'Maybe.'

'And you'll remember not to sneak up on Susie and bite her when she isn't looking. That's not proper herd behavior.'

'Ah,' said Pony. 'I see.'

'Well?' said Duchess, suppressing irritation.

'I'll think about it,' promised Pony.

Pony behaved fairly well all the rest of the day. And when night came, when the sun plunged beneath the low-lying mountain and dark crept up like a cat, she even had a Story.

'This Story is how Ponies came into the world,' she said

150

as the three mares huddled close together in the chill night air.

'Back in the days when horses were the size of foxes, and ran on three toes instead of one,' began Pony.

'Oh, they did *not*!' exclaimed Susie ignorantly.

'Back in those days,' said Pony stubbornly, 'Equus himself went to the Council of All Animals, to ask permission for a bigger place in life for Horses.'

'Oh, Equus, with mane and tail shining like the moon . . .' Susie sang.

'That isn't part of this Story,' said Pony. 'So, where was I – "Hmmm!" said Lion, who was Keeper of the Peace and had the right to speak first. "What are your reasons, Equus?"

'"Yes," said Monkey, who is the Law Giver, the Changer, "we'll listen to what you have to say, Equus, and if by reason and by thought, you have a case, why, indeed we will vote to grant you Horses a bigger size and shape."

'"Very well," said Equus, whose shape and style were glorious even then.

'"We . . . the Horse, have no claws with which to rend, no teeth with which to bite and tear.

'We . . . the Horse, have only our cunning, have only our running, to protect us from those who would hunt and kill us.

'We . . . the Horse, need size and strength so that we may flourish, like the grass in an eternal spring."

'"I see," said Monkey. "What you say may be true, Oh, Equus. But after all, I am not too large myself. Isn't your wish to be larger a vain one? Out of pride?"

'"You, Monkey, have hands and feet to clutch and climb. Owl has wings to fly and eyes like the horned moon. We horses can only run . . . and not fast enough at that, and hide. The law is unjust."

'Monkey sat and thought for a minute.

'"Very well. I will present your wish to the One, and it will be granted. The Horse shall grow larger in size and strength. Your legs shall lengthen, and the hoof grow strong and single, so that you may have strength to run faster and farther. Your chests shall widen and your noses grow long, so that you may drink the wind.

'"But . . . because the One makes no changes without penalty, because the One keeps a Balance in the universe, you must give something up."'

At this point in the story, Pony began to back around a very large boulder, so that only her voice floated through the air.

'"But . . ." said Monkey, "Your skulls shall narrow as you grow, and your brain grow smaller, and as Horses you shall lose your shrewdness. Some among you shall remain small . . . to remind you of what was lost in the counting. And these horses . . . small, clever beasts . . . shall be called . . . PONIES."'

'Oh!!' said Susie.

Duchess made a quick dive for Pony, but she was too late.

Pony crowed, wedged safely behind her rock.

'I told him, didn't I?' snorted Duchess, 'Ponies! Ugh!'

The journey continued, the days growing shorter, the sunlight paling as autumn moved slowly into winter. Duchess found the business of being Lead Mare exasperating. Pony never directly challenged her decisions, but would glance sidelong at her out of one brown eye. Duchess wasn't certain if this new responsibility caused her uneasy sleep, or if it was something else. Occasionally, she'd catch the faint foul odor of what she thought was decaying flesh.

Once or twice, the clouds of flies reappeared, stronger now than ever, as winter came closer. She heard strange calls in her dreams, and she'd jerk out of an easy doze with the meaning just out of reach.

They carefully skirted the villages and towns. One day, they circled furlongs out of the way to avoid a city belching scum and smoke into a polluted sky. 'Looks like a stall that hasn't been cleaned for months,' said Duchess,

152

as they paused on a hilltop and looked at grimy streets and buildings. The Dancer curled his lip and nudged them on. They stopped that night at the edge of a haylot guarded by a barbed wire fence.

The Dancer jumped first, followed by Duchess and Susie. Pony hung back. 'Come on, Pony,' said Duchess. 'This is good grass, clover and alfalfa, mixed.'

'Too high,' said Pony. 'Let's go around. This wire is sharp.'

'Just jump, will you?' said Duchess. 'Jump or starve, one of the two, but stop complaining.'

'I'll bet it's hot,' said Pony. 'I'll bet it's electric.' She shoved her nose against the wire. 'It *is*! I'm not coming in.'

The Dancer raised his head. 'Do I have to come and get you?'

Pony trotted back and forth. She put one foreleg through the two strands of wire and snatched it back.

'Pony!' shouted the Dancer. With a gasp, Pony squeezed her eyes shut and wriggled through, shrieking.

'Be quiet,' snapped Duchess. 'We're too near that farmhouse as it is. We don't want men down on us.'

'Maybe *you* don't,' grumbled Pony. Positioning herself by Susie, she said quietly, 'Getting enough to eat?'

'Oh, yes, thank you.'

'There's a barn up there,' said Pony. 'See the lights?' Susie blinked and raised her head, 'Yes.'

Pony snorted. 'I smell oats in that barn. Give a good sniff. You want to go get some?'

Susie looked at her for a long moment. 'No. And you'd better not.'

Pony, exasperated, grabbed at a large clump of timothy.

The moon rose late and full. Pony grazed closer and closer to the darkened barn. She heard one heavy thump, then another, as Susie and then Duchess settled into the grass to sleep.

Then the Dancer himelf seemed to doze off in the

moonlight. Pony moved cautiously up to the gate. She sniffed: cows, the faint odor of a dog, and underneath, the scent of oats. Pony shoved at the gate, and it swung open with a loud creak. The cows rustled in the barn as she moved quietly to the barn door.

Pony shoved at the door latch, and found a handle in the center. She thought for a moment, then grabbed the cold metal with her teeth and twisted her head. The latch slipped and stuck, so she tried again, until the latch slid over and the door swung free. Pony shoved her way into the warm darkness.

'What's that?' asked a startled heifer.

'Just me!' said Pony. 'A passing visitor. I thought maybe I could borrow some oats. I have a sick friend travelin' with me. Gonna bring her some. Go back to sleep, this'll just take a moment.'

'You're stealing oats?' asked the heifer.

'Not stealing – borrowing, for my friend.'

'How are you going to get them to your friend?' asked the heifer practically.

'Never mind,' said Pony.

The grain bin stood inside the door. A piece of rope was knotted through the ring. Pony, who had a long acquaintance with ropes, untied it, and stuffed her muzzle deep into the bin.

'I think I hear your friend,' said the heifer, as the Dancer's muscular bulk appeared at the open door.

'Get out of there!' he hissed. Pony squealed and jumped.

Slipping on the concrete floor, her hindquarters crashing into the garbage cans next to the bin, she scrambled for the door.

'Move!' bellowed the Dancer. Pony squeezed past him with a squeal.

The lights in the farmhouse snapped on. '*Now* you've done it,' the Dancer raged. 'Back to the herd!'

Pony broke into a rocking canter.

Footsteps raced over the gravel and the Dancer drove Pony before him with furious nips.

'Whoa!' A man's furious voice. 'Whoa! Whoa!' The night became alive with light. Susie and Duchess jumped up as the Dancer galloped toward them. They leaped the fence and raced into the darkness, the wind flying past their flattened ears. They stopped, finally, when the lights and the shouts faded into the setting moon.

'I hope you *colic*!' said Duchess. 'You hopeless, miserable pony. You . . . oat stealer!'

'Is that what she did?' asked Susie. 'Stole oats?'

'We could have been captured. Brought back,' said Duchess. 'You ought to be locked up!'

'Easy,' said the Dancer. 'We're safe now. But your greediness is going to get you in trouble one of these days, Pony.'

'Leave me alone. I don't feel good.'

'She *is* going to colic,' said Duchess. 'I hope it teaches you something.' Pony rolled an eye at Susie in uncomfortable appeal.

'Let me take care of her, Duchess,' said Susie. 'Come on, Pony, you have to keep walking, you know.'

'I'm really thirsty,' said Pony plaintively. 'Any water around here?'

'Worst thing for you,' said Susie. 'Whenever you get colic, you've got to remember, no water. At least, not until you pass those oats.'

'I want a drink!'

'We'll keep on moving tonight,' said the Dancer. 'If I'm not mistaken, you'll have water enough in the morning, Pony. Tomorrow we reach the river.'

12

Dancer's Mountain

At midday, the Dancer sensed the river. He stopped in midstride, quivering, and wheeled to face the mares, nostrils wide. 'We're close, now. Move carefully.'

They stepped cautiously, broke through a stand of brush, and there before them was the river.

Beyond was the Dancer's mountain.

The river was twice the length of the arena at Bishop Farm, the water running a clear, sky-like green. Underneath the rushing water was a hint of sharp rocks and the occasional silver strike of a fish. The Dancer cantered carefully along the bank, then stood and gazed at the mountain. It rose in a series of granite hills, the highest peak disappearing into thick clouds that swirled and ducked like lazy birds.

Duchess felt a sudden stab of loneliness and a faint, tugging fear.

Susie and Pony stood beside her, and Pony shivered suddenly, as though a rough hand lay on her neck. The three mares moved close to the Dancer. He whistled, a long, drawn-out note that bounced from the mountainside and came back thinned and bloodless.

A black and green fly rose lazily from the brush at the Dancer's feet, and he twitched impatiently. 'We'll cross the river and go up.'

'How are we going to cross that?' said Pony indignantly.

'Ssssst!' A noise like flies in deep summer came from

the brush. The three mares pressed together. The Dancer whirled.

'Good afternoon, stallion.' The brush parted and a dog crept out, belly close to the earth. Duchess shrank from the odor of its fur. The dog's eyes were yellow-green in the narrow skull, and a crescent-shaped hoof mark was on its chest.

'Tribute!' said the dog. 'All who pass this way must pay my master tribute.' The scabby nose twitched, and he eyed the mares sidelong. 'A gift, before you pass this way.'

The Dancer drew back his lips in a terrible grin. 'We meet so soon?' he said with deceptive calm. 'And you ask a gift.' He charged, clamped his teeth around the matted neck and whirled the dog in the air. The hound's cry rose in an eerie wail. Duchess jumped in sudden recognition.

The Dancer spun and dropped the dog at the river's edge.

'There's a gift,' the Dancer shouted. 'A gift for your Master. Tell him that we will meet soon, and that I pass along more such gifts.'

The dog snarled. His fur rippled with an oily sheen. The yellow eyes narrowed and he grinned, opening his mouth wide. The teeth were sharp, the carrion tongue pointed.

Then, like a shadow passing over the sun, the dog's frame stretched and pulled taut. Its face enlarged, shedding fur like a snake its skin. A death's head skull formed where his head had been. His body arched like a malformed bow. His hind legs lengthened to clawed feet.

Before them in the daylight stood a Harrier Hound.

Pony screamed high and thin, like knives on granite. Susie drew in her breath with a sharp gasp and quivered with a tearing cough. Duchess stood frozen, the hauntings of her dreams made flesh in the ordinary light of day. Only the Dancer seemed unmoved.

'Mares.' The Hound extended his foreclaws and bent his skull to the ground in a hideous parody of a canine

157

invitation to play. 'Walk with me. Talk to me. I have ssssuch things to tell you, sssssuch wonders to show you. I must introduce you to my Master. He is fond of mares like you. He would delight in your company.'

'What is it?' whispered Duchess. 'Oh, what is it? I am afraid. I've heard this voice before.'

The Dancer watched the Hound with a terrible stillness. When he spoke, he was calm, almost indifferent.

'This is Scant, Pack Leader of the Harrier Hounds.' He raised his voice a little. 'I didn't think to see you here, Pack Leader. Have you slipped your Master's leash?'

'I wear no leash!' the Hound spat. 'I ssserve my Master out of love, as all his sssubjects do. As you, ssstallion, ssserve that piece of dung you call a god.'

The Dancer's hindquarters tightened and he showed his teeth. The Hound cowered in the dirt, lipless skull's head grinning. 'No offense. I meant no offense. You do not ssserve from love? You did not ignore your god's commands for love? You did not forsake your sssacred task . . . break your sssilly Laws for love?' He rolled a sly red eye at Duchess. 'Perhaps it is you I have to thank for this, Breedmistress. Were it not for you, this ssspotted one might have remained where he should have . . . out of the way of my Master. Upon reflection, though, upon sssincere consideration, *I* would not be here if *you* were not. Your precious stallion has opened the Gate for me and mine. For that I thank you.'

'Silence!' roared the Dancer. He struck the ground in warning, driving his left fore against the stony ground. 'You forget to whom you speak, Scant.' He struck the ground again, and then a third time.

'I sssee no rainbow arc of light,' Scant gasped a little with suppressed laughter. 'I SSSEE NO LIGHT!' His laughter grew, and beneath it came a hollow booming, as of a giant horse moving under the earth. 'WAS YOUR IDYLL WORTH THIS?' he shrieked. 'DANCER, WAS IT? WAS IT? WAS IT . . . ?'

A wind rolled down the mountain and flattened the mares' manes and tails against their flanks.

'You have lost much, Dancer,' cried the Hound. 'Tell us, what have you gained?' He howled then, a rallying cry that ululated across the river. The Dancer spun and kicked, with a blow that hit like a lightning strike. His hind feet caught Scant in the ribs, and the Hound rolled down the dirt, back to the water. He rose on all four clawed feet, red eyes gleaming.

'You dare,' said the Hound. 'You've lost the battle before the war's begun. You've behaved as any moon-struck weanling would. Paah!' He spat in the Dancer's face.

The Dancer screamed. 'Hear me, Scant, and your Master, too!' He crashed to the earth and began to gouge great rifts in the bank with his forefoot. 'Your Master's doomed for what he took from me. I have a score to settle for Sycha's loss. We shall meet up there on the mountain. I shall destroy Anor there. And I will start my line anew. Anor! Do you hear me, Anor?! You say I've tipped the Balance and allowed this scum to roam? I'll do better than that. I'll kill him, here. Now! And if this *bursts* the damned Gate, so much the better. I need nothing to destroy you but my own four hooves and teeth! And my rage, Anor, my rage!'

The killing note was in the Dancer's voice, and Duchess felt as though her breath was torn from her body, that she would never breathe again. The hound's whimpering filled the air, and she flattened her ears against it. She moved quickly, pressing Susie far back into the brush.

The Dancer picked his way down the bank with terrifying deliberation. Scant scrabbled with his hind feet, hunching toward the water. The Dancer reached the Hound, rose high in the air and came down, burying both forefeet in the Hound's body. Scant squealed with a sound like slaughtering pigs. The Dancer grabbed Scant's neck and flung him into the river. The Hound moved feebly, his head above the water. In moments, the river had carried him from sight.

Duchess, fear and agony in her chest, began to ask the Dancer how the terror of her dream could appear here, at the threshold of their goal, and why the Dancer seemed to know him. But the stallion sprang into a hard gallop, circling the three mares. 'Swim!' he shouted. Prodding, nipping, he pushed them to the river's edge. Duchess and Susie plunged into the water, paddling desperately for the shore, their noses held high. Pony held back, running frantically back along the trail that led to the wilderness. The Dancer pushed her forward.

'No!' she screamed. 'I won't.'

'Move! Move! Move!'

Pony closed her eyes, jumped, and barreled into the water, swimming in a circle that took her back to the bank where the Dancer stood waiting.

The stallion jumped in beside her, sheets of water curving over his powerful chest, churning the water with swift strokes of his forelegs. He herded Pony toward Duchess and Susie.

Susie took a deep breath and choked. Her cough came back, tearing at her throat with the ferocity of a trapped weasel. She had no breath to cry for help. Like a stone she went down, the waters closing over her head, the roar of the river cut off in eerie silence as she sank. One of Duchess' hooves struck her ear, and she gasped in pain, the water filling her eyes, her nose, pushing into her lungs. The river turned red in front of Susie's eyes. A thrumming filled her ears. The world grew dark. 'The babies!' she thought.

Duchess reached the opposite side of the river and scrambled up, bruising her legs as she lunged toward safety. She turned to look at the river and shook the water from her ears and eyes. She saw Pony, and the black and white shoulders of the Dancer.

'Susie!' she cried. 'Where's Susie?'

Pony reached the shore and clambered, grumbling, to

safety. 'This is stupid,' she muttered. 'I say. This is dangerous.'

'Shut up!' said Duchess. 'Where is she? I can't see her.' She called desperately to the Dancer.

'Come back and help!' he roared.

Duchess leaped into the river. The Dancer plunged his head beneath the surface and brought Susie with him, her mane clenched securely between his teeth. Duchess swam to Susie's side and pushed against her withers. They headed to shore.

The Dancer pulled himself out of the water, tugging Susie's head and shoulders out onto the bank, where she lay, eyes closed, scarcely breathing.

'Susie!' said Duchess. 'Wake up. Get up. Oh, get up.'

She bit her, drawing blood from one shoulder, and nipped again at her poll and cheek. Susie twitched, groaned and began to cough.

Duchess pushed her nose close to Susie's cheek and whickered. 'Are you all right?' she whispered.

Susie opened one eye and began to pull herself up the river bank.

'Here, you, Pony. Come and help,' said Duchess. 'Don't stand around like the fat little snail that you are.'

'What d'ya want me to do?' asked Pony reasonably. 'She's making it.'

Susie rolled and heaved herself to her feet. Water gushed from her muzzle, and she coughed again and again.

'The sun's dropping and it's getting colder,' said Duchess to Pony. 'We have to find a more sheltered place to rest. Go tell him.'

'Who, me?'

'That's right. Go on!'

Pony trotted off to where the Dancer stood in the trees, and Duchess turned to Susie.

'Susie, I thought you were drowned.'

'So did I.' Her voice was hoarse from the water and the coughing. She shook in the chill nighttime breeze.

Duchess nibbled at Susie's neck, her breath warming the Paint mare's shoulders and back. 'Can you make it to the trees? Can you rest in the brush? It will be warmer there.'

'I'm shaky, like,' said Susie in mild surprise. 'I'll follow you, though.'

Susie's stride reminded Duchess of a foal's first steps. She put her nose to Susie's side and pushed her gently in the direction of the forest. The Dancer galloped up to them.

'No!' said the Dancer. 'Wait.'

'For what?' snapped Duchess. 'Can't you see that she's half dead? You've been pushing us too hard. She's not used to this.'

'We're going to move on up the mountain,' he said. 'And we're going now.'

'We can't travel with Susie so weak. We'll have to wait.'

'I just need a few moments,' Susie said apologetically. 'I'll be fine soon.'

'Moving will keep her warm,' said Pony, one eye on the Dancer.

'Moving might kill her!' snapped Duchess. She began to groom Susie's damp coat with her tongue.

The Dancer looked at Duchess for a long moment. 'Very well,' he said grudgingly. 'We'll stop. But we move on at first sunrise.'

Susie spent the night alternating between shivering and a stuporous half-sleep. Duchess lay down beside her but the warmth of her own body didn't seem to be enough. She woke Pony with a sharp nip. 'Get on Susie's other side, Pony. We have to protect her from this wind.' Grumbling, Pony rolled over and promptly fell asleep again, her mouth slightly open, snoring.

When the sun rose in the morning, glancing off the early frost with a fresh clear shine, flooding the river water and the mountain in front of them with welcome light, Susie seemed fit to travel. The grass under the trees was thick and green, and the river water held the taste of apples. The whole band was in high spirits. When the sun cleared the tops of the pines, they set off on the first furlong to the Dancer's valley.

They came upon it at midday, after scrambling over rock-topped ridges that chipped their hooves and bruised their fetlocks. The Dancer gained the last ridge top first, and stood gazing down the other side as the mares struggled up the path. Duchess, looking up, saw him limned against the sky, his thick mane lifted by the wind. She climbed beside him.

'We're home,' he said.

The valley below was deep and green, sheltered from the world by three sides of the mountain. Here, the beginning of the river snaked its way through the meadows in a wide rush. There were thick stands of trees already gold with autumn among grass knolls and glades. Duchess lifted her head and called out with a fierce, guilty joy. It was here that the foals would be born, to grow up healthy, long-legged, free of the scent and hand of man. It was here she would walk with the Dancer.

'Doesn't look too bad,' said Pony, coming up beside her. 'How are we going to get down?'

'Follow me!' said the Dancer.

'Follow him!' shouted Susie. She kicked up her heels, and was first behind the stallion as they picked their way down the rock-strewn path.

'There's a cave beyond that stand of rocks,' said the Dancer. 'That's one of the reasons I chose this spot. It'll provide protection through the winter and a place to shelter the foals in the spring. And the river becomes a stream here, for watering.'

The cave was wide and only faintly dark, its wide mouth letting in the sunshine. Pony made a cursory exploration, noting that it was just big enough, without too much crowding – not as good as the circus, but good enough. She wandered out under the trees and began to eat the grass.

Duchess circled the cave, and finally Susie said, 'You ought to settle down and graze, Duchess. This is going to be here for a while, like.'

The first day in the mountains passed in peace.

As the shadows of the evening began to pool in the cave, the Dancer scented trouble.

'Gather into a circle,' he said, 'and be ready to kick.'

'What is it?' demanded Duchess. Fear rose in her throat, and she choked. 'Is that Thing back? It's . . .'

'Quiet!' The Dancer moved cautiously, his head strained high. 'Dog. I smell that wretched dog.' Duchess' knees trembled. She pushed Pony and Susie into a half-circle, their hindquarters poised and ready to strike. The Dancer screamed a sudden challenge. Duchess whirled. There, at the crest of the granite peak that led into the valley, loped a familiar collie shape.

'Cory!' shouted Susie. 'It's Cory!'

Cory barked and barked again, running back and forth along the ridge. He scrambled down the mountainside, and disappeared into the trees. Soon they heard the dog's labored breathing, and the soft pad of his running feet. He broke through the pines and ran toward them.

The feathered hair of his legs was matted with burrs and dirty, but the golden color of his coat glimmered in the rays of the setting sun. He slowed to a trot as he neared the cave, and broke into a broad grin. 'So!' he said. 'I've caught up with you at last.'

'How did you find us, Cory?' asked Susie. 'We've been gone for such a long time! How did you come here?'

The collie eyed the Dancer, who was watching him with lowered head and bared teeth. 'I'm not a bad tracker, you know, and the forests and meadows provided small game to catch. And wherever you all have been, there's been water.' He glanced at Pony. 'I got a little confused when you picked her up, but I figured he just added her on to the herd in the same way that he stole you.' He glanced at the Dancer, then said to the mares, 'I've come to bring you back.'

164

The Dancer rushed him, teeth bared and eyes rolling. Cory ducked and slipped away.

'Cory!' said Susie. 'You didn't follow us all the way here – you couldn't have.'

The dog grinned again, tongue lolling. 'Well, I did. And now we can start back.'

'Start back?' said Duchess. 'What makes you think we'd start back?'

'He has come to reclaim his master's property,' said the Dancer grimly. 'Isn't that so, dog?'

The collie flattened his ears. His uncombed gold-and-white coat didn't quite conceal his gaunt ribs; his paws were splayed with long months of travel. Dried and crusted blood edged his feet.

'You belong at home,' said the dog. 'Not out here in the wilderness. Dancer, how are you going to survive the winter? These are domestic mares, who've always been cared for. Where will they be stabled? What will they eat? Who's going to protect them from the wild? They must go back if they are to live.'

The Dancer didn't respond.

Cory settled onto the ground with a grunt of relief. 'I'll rest up for a day or two, and then we'll start back. If we hurry, we can get fairly far south before the first snow comes.'

The Dancer snorted, then sprang like a diving hawk. He caught Cory by his ruff and lifted him high in the air. Cory snapped, struggling, his snarls half-strangled by the pressure of the stallion's teeth. The mares plunged in terror.

'Let him go,' said Susie, 'please! He's just doing his job, Dancer, like we all have to. Put him down.' The Dancer glared at the mares over the dog's furious, jerking body, then dropped him. The collie rolled and regained his feet, his snarls transformed into barks that echoed off the mountainsides.

Duchess stepped between them. 'Please don't fight.

Susie's right, you know, he is just doing his job. Can't we just let him go in peace?'

'Certainly,' said the Dancer. 'Get out, dog, while I'm in a charitable mood.'

The collie stopped his barking. 'I can't,' he said, reasonably. 'You know I can't. You took two of the most valuable mares on the Farm. There's no one to stay with the weanlings now. And no one to enter the jumping classes. It's my duty to bring you back to where you belong.'

The Dancer advanced, ears pinned back, head snaked low to the ground.

'And besides,' he said, 'I have a message. From El Arat, Dreamspeaker.'

'What is this message?' said the Dancer, low-voiced. He hesitated, uncertain.

'Wait,' said Duchess. 'Dancer, I have an idea.' The stallion hesitated, then nodded, and they moved a short distance away.

'Well?' The Dancer's tone was imperative. The dog had dropped to the ground in exhaustion; he watched him carefully.

'There must be something we can work out,' said Duchess, nervously. 'He won't go without us. I know him. And we certainly don't want to go back with him.' The Dancer looked at Susie, who had ambled over to the dog and was in an animated discussion about 'home.' 'We won't go back with him,' Duchess repeated stubbornly, 'but as Lead Mare, I can't have any fighting.' The Dancer's look was now directed at her, incredulous. 'I know that it's part of your task as Herd Stallion to protect us. But what are we being protected from? Cory can't make us go if we don't want to. And you can certainly hurt him – even kill him, if you have to. I understand that. But to what end? I think we should compromise.'

'Compromise,' said the Dancer rigidly.

'And he said he had a message from El Arat.'

'A message.' The Dancer looked at the sky uneasily. 'From your Dreamspeaker.'

Abruptly, he relaxed. He rubbed Duchess' nose affectionately. 'Your world is becoming Balanced, Duchess,' he said. 'Compromise, indeed. Well, tell me of your compromise.'

Duchess continued with a little more confidence. 'Why don't we make him a member of the herd?'

'A dog?'

'Why not? He could be very useful, taking turns watching over us all. He could be of help there, couldn't he?'

The Dancer was quiet. Then he said, 'There is a – possibility. A possibility that he might be needed. For several reasons. You may be right.' The Dancer's eye clouded, and he gazed into the setting sun. 'If there were to come a time when you would be without me . . .'

'No.' Duchess felt her heart jump in her chest, and her breath came short. 'That's not what I meant.'

The Dancer struck at the ground, absently, and a small spurt of rainbow light seemed to glance off the polished black of his hoof. 'Yes. Invite the dog to join the herd. The trick will be to get him to abandon his duty. And that will not be easy. But you're right, he will be a loyal member of our band if he agrees.' The Dancer moved restlessly, as though something were calling him in a voice only he could hear. 'Settle it among yourselves. I'll return shortly.' He wheeled and trotted into the pines, and Duchess turned to where Cory and Susie were deep in conversation.

'Cory,' she said as she approached, 'I've discussed this with the Dancer and I believe we have a solution.' Pony, she noticed, had wandered off somewhere, but it was no time to wonder what mischief she was getting into.

'Cory says that everyone was very upset when they found we were gone,' said Susie. 'They had search parties out, with dogs. They looked and looked, and Cory says he and David went out camping on the trail with Biz, that big gelding, looking for us. David turned back after a while, but Cory took off without telling him and he finally picked up the scent, and here he is. He says Fancy was very upset, and that El Arat's been acting strange like, not telling Stories, not singing songs. It's very upsetting.' Susie took a deep breath and her cough sounded harsh and rasping. 'It's terrible! The weanlings are all asking for me. What are we going to do, Duchess. Did the Dancer say we could go back?'

'You don't really want to go back,' said Duchess. 'You shouldn't talk to Susie, Cory; you know how she is. It isn't fair. And you can't make us go back with you. You ought to know that. He wouldn't let you.'

'Then I'll just have to go and bring David here,' said the dog.

'Well, I've thought about that,' said Duchess. 'By the time you get anywhere near home, the snows will have come. And you'll never find us in these mountains. We can hide from you.'

'I can try,' said the dog stubbornly. 'I have to try.'

'You should at least wait until spring,' said Duchess. 'Then the foals will have come, and it will be harder for us to move on. Why don't you stay with us for the winter? And become a member of the herd.'

'A dog?' said Susie. 'Now, that's a grand idea, Cory. I like it. We can teach you lots of things about being a horse.'

'Not as a horse, Susie. As a dog. As a special member of the herd.'

'I like it,' said Susie. 'What do you think, Cory?'

'I don't like it,' said the dog bluntly. 'I can't do it. I belong to David and the Farm.'

'You could at least stay with us until spring. Until it's safe to leave,' said Duchess. 'The snow may make it difficult to get back.'

'Yes, Cory. Become a member of the herd.' Susie nibbled gently at the dog's coat. 'That would make us special all right.'

'And we really could use your help,' said Duchess.

'Isn't it your basic duty to guard us, after all? If the Dancer . . . if the Dancer has to be away, we'll need you more than ever. And if you've gone back to the Farm without us, you've lost that job. If you stay here, you're doing it. Don't make a decision yet. Stay here until you get your strength back, and then we'll talk about it some more.'

Cory, his entire body expressing his reluctance, agreed. 'But,' he said, 'I'm going to do my best to talk you into coming home.'

'You can talk all you like!' said Duchess cheerfully. 'There's just one more thing. When the Dancer returns, you must take a herd oath. Just a temporary one,' she said hastily, seeing the dog's expression of dismay. 'Nothing that would bind you to us more than you want to be bound. But he needs your word of loyalty. And, as Lead Mare, so do I.'

'Which Oath would he take?' asked Susie anxiously. 'Not the same one we take to become herd mares. Can we use a horse oath for a dog?'

'We should think about that,' said Duchess. 'I'll try and come up with something that everyone can agree to – you, me, the Dancer, and of course Cory himself.'

'And Pony,' said Susie firmly.

'Of course. Where is she, by the way?'

Susie looked around a little vaguely. 'She isn't here? Wait, here she comes!' Pony, stumbling a little, came through the strand of pine trees, and joined the circle furtively. 'Pony!' said Susie. 'You know what? Cory's going to become a member of the herd. He's going to take the herd oath and all. Is that something?'

'Is that so,' said Pony, looking nervously over her shoulder.

'Where have you been, Pony?' asked Duchess.

'Out.' She blinked her little eyes at the dog. 'So, you're going to join us? Who are you, anyway?'

'This is Cory,' said Duchess. 'Cory, this is Pony. She joined our herd a while back.'

169

'I've seen dogs like you before,' said Pony. 'In the circus, where I was part of a star act. Center ring in a three-ring circus. They had a dog act that came off and on that had collies in it. Folks didn't take to it much.'

Cory's ears tuliped forward. 'You're a Shetland, aren't you? You wouldn't happen to be from down south of here?

Pony shifted a little uneasily. 'That's right. What's it to you?'

'I came across a German Shepherd bitch in my travels,' said Cory. 'She had much the same problem I did – her master had lost a Shetland. What kind of place did you say you came from?'

'Circus act,' said Pony with suspicious belligerence. 'I walked around and around in a ring with a gold saddle on my back and a diamond bridle and plumes of feathers on my head. The crowd loved it. I was a star.'

'I thought it was a scarlet leather saddle,' said Duchess, 'with a patent leather bridle, wasn't it, Pony? Or was that another show you were in?'

'Might have been. They changed our fittings pretty often, come to think of it. I had . . .'

'The Shepherd bitch told me the pony had escaped from a pony ride,' said Cory. 'She asked me to keep an eye out, and to bring the pony back if I happened to come across her.'

'Pony ride,' said Duchess politely. 'You mean one of those grubby little acts that go around the country in a rusty truck? The kind that never takes care of their animals and have half of them drop dead of worms or heat stroke in the summers? The kind that . . .'

'Shut up,' said Pony. 'What do you know about the circus, anyway? So what if it was a pony ride. I still had a silver – gold, I mean, saddle, and a snappy bridle. And I was the pony all the kids chose to ride. What's this stupid junkyard dog know, anyway?'

'I know that the pony was about to be sold at a meat auction,' said Cory. 'That's what this stupid dog knows. I

170

also know that the pony bucked a kid off and hurt him. That's what this junkyard dog knows.'

'It doesn't sound like your circus, Pony,' said Susie anxiously. 'Maybe it was another pony, Duchess. There's lots of them around, you know.'

'Sounds like our Pony to me,' said Duchess. 'What did this pony look like, Cory?'

Cory said carelessly, 'Just a Shetland. And there are lots of them, you know.'

'Two Shetlands with mouths bigger than their pea brains?' asked Duchess. 'Maybe.' She glared at Pony. 'And maybe you should think twice about those stories you make up, Pony. And maybe we should let the Dancer know that you're . . .'

'Shut *up*,' said Pony furiously. 'Here he comes now. You aren't going to tell him a thing.'

'What thing?' said the Dancer. He looked tired, weary, and Duchess nickered in concern. 'Well, have you settled accounts with the dog?'

'Cory's decided to stay for the winter,' said Duchess. 'And he's agreed to take an Oath – not a horse Oath, but a modified one. I've even thought of an Oath that would work. Would you like to hear it?'

'This is grand,' said Susie with excitement. 'The first time a dog has ever become a member of a horse herd – at least, that I know of. It's just like being in a Story. Tell it, Duchess.'

'All right. It's like the one we all take when we join a herd for the first time, but because he's a dog, and because his first allegiance is to David and the Farm, I've added a few bits.'

'This *is* exciting,' said Susie. 'I've never known any horse to make up an Oath before. Cory, if you go back to the Farm in the spring be sure and tell El Arat. She'll be amazed.'

'I could make up something if you don't like *hers*,' said Pony. 'I used to . . .'

'What,' said Duchess, 'make up songs in your red

171

leather saddle? Chant in your silver bridle? What did you used to do, Pony?'

'Nothing,' she muttered. 'Let's hear it, for oat's sake.'

Duchess straightened up a little and said in a formal, Story-telling tone: 'I a Dog – Cory by name/ agree to live/ by laws the same/ for dog and horse/ by paw and hoof/ I swear to this/ by both gods' truth.'

Cory considered this a moment, then said, 'It's all right, as far as it goes, but I want to add something.'

Duchess said a little irritably, 'Tell us, then.'

Cory cocked his head to one side and said: 'My duty first/ the laws of man/ My heart and soul for man's command/ My duty next, by Canis' truth/ to Dancer's herd/ by paw and hoof.'

'Welcome, Cory,' said the Dancer.

'Welcome,' echoed Duchess.

'Welcome, Cory, welcome,' said Susie. 'This'll be so nice: We can talk of ho . . .' She glanced at the Dancer and said, 'I mean *things* together.'

'Pony?' said the Dancer sternly.

'Yeah, welcome,' said Pony sourly. 'Craziest thing I ever heard of. Things are getting more mucked up every day.' Look at those clouds. Winter's coming, and there's a def-i-nite chill in the air. A def-i-nite chill.' Pony flattened her ears in satisfaction and switched her tail.

'Nonsense,' said Duchess briskly. 'The cave will provide shelter for us, and as the Dancer said, there's plenty of grass here. Snow acts as an excellent ground cover, you know. It'll protect the food for us.'

'And you should know, Duchess,' said Susie cheerfully. 'You've been through hard winters before. She *does* know,' she said to Pony. 'So don't you worry. We're going to have a fine life here in the mountains. We can sleep in the cave at night and eat grass by day. In the spring, before you know it, the foals will be here. It's a fine life we're headed for, Pony, a fine life.'

Suddenly, the Dancer planted both feet in the ground

and kicked his heels to the sky. 'We'll race!' he cried. 'Come! To the top of the mountain!'

Susie squealed. Duchess reared, then plunged after the stallion. Cory leaped into a springing gallop. Pony, her short legs pumping hard, followed them.

The setting sun shone with unnatural brilliance on the horses travelling up the mountain.

They came back to feed and rest in the cave as night came. The dark came quickly to the mountains. In less time than it took to cross from the stream back to the cave, the heavy gold of the afternoon sunlight was replaced by deep blue evening. The moon shone three-quarters full, suspended over the spiky pines. Susie and Pony lay down in the cave to sleep, and Duchess walked with the Dancer.

'You're tired,' he said. He rested his muzzle briefly in her mane. 'You should sleep, too.'

'I can't, not yet. I want to ask you about that thing by the river.'

'I may not answer.'

'I think you must,' said Duchess. 'I dreamed of you, before you came to Bishop Farm, and what I saw was a true dream. You came to me, as El Arat said you would. But she wouldn't tell me who you were, or why you appeared, and neither would you. All you would say is that I would know in time. It's time.'

'The Testing isn't over,' said the Dancer. 'Until it is, I may not tell you. El Arat may not. No one may.'

'What testing? I don't understand. What am I being tested for? And who has the right to test me? No one has the right.'

'Life is a test, Duchess. And all our choices weighed on the Balance scales of the One. You've always known this. I have always known this. My lord was right – I think I may have been found wanting in my own test.'

'Does it have to do with that Thing by the river?' asked Duchess, softly. There was a great grief in the Dancer's eyes, and she nipped his shoulder gently. 'You were all

173

that I've ever dreamed of. You protected us. Where I would have fled, you stayed and fought. That thing frightened me more than anything I've ever known.'

'There are worse things in this world and beyond,' said the Dancer. He looked at her tenderly. 'He is mostly boastful talk.'

'Then what did his talk mean? And who is his master?'

The Dancer didn't reply immediately. Duchess could see the black and white of his flank moving faintly with his breath.

'His master is my enemy, and yours, and chief of all, of our foal.' He rubbed his cheek along Duchess' belly. She blew softly in his mane, feather-light breaths for reassurance.

'If what the Hound says is true, then I may have destroyed us all, through my arrogance.' He raised his head to the Moon, once more. 'The moon's three-quarters, and a week or more until the Path is open.' He turned to Duchess. 'I won't know what his talk may mean until I discover how much, if any, of what the Hound says is truth. He is,' the Dancer struck the ground in sudden violence, 'a liar, as were his ancestors before him.'

'Well,' said Duchess in a high, foal-like voice, 'I'm tired. I don't want to think about this anymore.' She ignored the great upwelling of sorrow in her heart and said a little roughly, 'That dog was a loathsome creature and not quite . . . not quite natural. I mean, I've never seen a dog change into such an ugly thing in my life, have you?' She went on, rapidly, before the Dancer could answer. 'The only thing I can compare it to is butterflies. Except that they start out ugly and end up beautiful. Do you suppose this thing is a new sort of dog? I could ask Cory. Maybe he knows.' She started at a rustling in the brush. 'What's that? What's that?'

'It's Cory,' said the Dancer. 'He went out to find something to eat. He may be a member of the herd, but he still can't live on grass.'

'Dancer, Duchess,' said Cory by way of greeting. His

tail stopped in mid-wag. 'What's the matter, Duchess? Are you all right? Dancer, she has a look . . .'

'She's tired,' said the Dancer angrily. 'She's been pushed too hard. Duchess, into the cave with the others and sleep. I'll stand watch. Move, now.'

'Maybe Cory knows what kind of dog that thing is and how we can get rid of it. It's terrible to say so, and Susie would be very unhappy if she heard me, but I think you ought to kill it.'

'Yes,' said the Dancer, 'I'll try to do that.'

'Do more than try,' said Duchess, a little sharply. 'Good night.'

'Sleep well, Lead Mare. And dream no dreams.'

'What dog thing?' said Cory.

'Wait,' said the Dancer. He stood with his ears pricked forward. They heard Duchess settle heavily on her side in the cave, then he turned to the dog.

'You've agreed to join the herd. Do I count you as enemy or friend?'

The dog cocked his head. 'That depends on you. My job is to protect these mares. And my duty is to take them home.'

'My job is to protect these mares. And to begin my breed anew.'

'Then we can travel down the same path at least partway together. Until the time comes in the spring when I must take them back, I'll count you friend.'

'And until the time comes in the spring when I must keep the foals and their dams with me, I will count you friend.'

'It is agreed, then,' said Cory.

'Agreed. Now, what news do you really bring?'

'Not good. El Arat is frantic. She says that you tipped the Balance when you left the Farm. That you were supposed to stay there. She sent me to bring you back. And I think, Dancer, that you should come with me.'

The Dancer walked a little way under the pines, and the dog followed him. 'Look here,' said the stallion. 'Do

175

you see how the ash leaves are dying? And when the sun sets, do you feel how quickly the light falls, and how the sharpness of the air makes the stars seem clear? Winter is close upon our heels, Cory. I, and perhaps Pony could make it back to the Farm, but I don't believe that Duchess, as strong as she is, could do it. And I know that Susie would be lost.

'They are in foal to me, these two, and they carry the future of my breed.'

'What about that Pony?'

'Her season has not come upon her yet. I must wait a short while, and then she, too, will carry a spotted foal. Three foals to begin my line, Cory. And three mares, one not young and certainly not strong. I will need your help, I think, to see them through this winter.'

'We can try,' said Cory. 'El Arat told me a dream she had, just after your escape, and I am to tell it to you. Would you hear it now? Or do you wish to wait until sunrise?'

The Dancer cocked a grimly humorous eye at the dog. 'There isn't much that I haven't seen in my life, dog, as you should know.'

'Not easily frightened?' said the dog. 'Well, I'm not either, but this will frighten even you, Dancer, the Tale I have to tell. Stand and listen. This is the Dream of El Arat, who stood in water when the Moon was full.'

'It is a true dream, she says, and she speaks now, through me.'

The Dream of El Arat

'I passed through Summer, and stood before the Gates, as I have each time the Path has been open to me.

At one end of Summer's meadow is the white gate to the Courts; at the other, the Black Gate to the Barns of He who should not be named in the Dark.

176

The goddess mare Jehanna guided my steps, and I passed through the Black Gate, and to what lay beyond.

I saw Sycha, the Soul-Taker, on the path to the Dark Barns. She picked her way along the rotting path. The ground beneath her hooves was split and broken, a suppurating length patched by holes, hoof-shaped, that steamed in the murky air. Beyond the path, on each side of the path, lay darkness, held back by the yellow-green glow she carries with her like a banner.

She passed the Watching Pool, its oily surface rocked by the Visions from above, and bared her teeth in greeting at the Watcher. No word passed between them, but the Watcher's whisper followed as she passed and the air shifted with the call of "Sycha."

The Hound Scant sat before the path at Gate's end, the perpetual grin of the Harrier skull meeting her first. Her left hind leg clenched in an involuntary kick.

'So, you're back.' Scant rose from his crouch and it seemed that the skull-grin widened. 'Your task has failed. The Dancer arrived at Bishop Farm, and met the new Breedmistress of his herd. And she herself has passed the Test of Courage in wars and games of war, and the Test of the Lead Mare. The Dark Lord won't be pleased. Your bargain is falling apart, SSSycha. The Final Death may be near for you, after all.' He licked his lips.

'It's merely incomplete.' She shrugged. 'He broke his vow and stole them from the Farm. A resolution's near.'

'Resolution,' sneered the Hound. 'In that black hole of your heart, Sycha, what feeling lurks there for this spotted horse? And what would the Dark Lord say if he knew? Would you lose your place, Sycha? Would there be another Soul-Taker?'

Sycha snarled, 'You, hound? Never!'

The Hound laughed. 'Then perhaps you'll be turned over to me and mine, Sycha. For sport.'

The Black Barn rose before them both.

The Second Gate swung open and horse and hound passed through. They walked onto the aisle and waited.

177

Something skittered on the darkness beyond, and bubbled with a drowning call.

Sycha bent her head and called out, 'Lord.'

There was a sound of immense stall doors rolling open, a grating, steely noise, and an unnatural reddish glow suffused the Barn.

He moved beyond the shadows, a gigantic pool of black which no sun could lighten, which could swallow any moon. A spear of iron sprang from the place where the brow would have been. The Black shaped itself into a vaguely equine form. Sycha fixed her gaze on the Twisted Horn and didn't speak. Scant, wriggling and whining on the stone floor, crawled on his belly toward his Master.

'That piece of dung has escaped from Bishop Farm,' the Hound said eagerly. 'You know, Lord, that she,' he flung a skinny claw toward Sycha, 'freed him from the sword, and the spotted horse has found his way to the Mare who can start the breed anew. And it is her fault.'

'The spotted horse chose the path we wished him to choose,' said Sycha quietly. 'He has fallen, but the downward spiral's slow. He has left his place of refuge, and taken the mare with him. This is against the wishes of the god of the White Courts. I believe that we may move now. This crime he has committed is one of pride. My bargain will hold. The One will decide in our favor. There will be no more Appaloosas.'

The Twisted Horn rose. The Dark Lord hissed. Scant bellied to the floor and whined, his eyes rolled back. Sycha raised her head, and the look in her eyes was terrible.

'I believe you are right, grey mare,' said the Black shape before her. 'Yes, O Sycha, I believe you may be right.'

'Now,' said the Dark Lord, 'it is my turn.' His voice rose and thundered, It is MY Turn. I may choose, And I choose . . . . THIS!'

Somewhere in the Black Barn's depths an iron gate

Anor

burst and a thunderclap split the air. A lightning strike split the ground before the Dark Lord's hooves.

Then, silence.

And a slow, dull booming.

ONE!

As of a weight, immeasurable.

TWO!

A slow rolling of destruction.

THREE!

'Anor,' said the Dark Lord. 'Anor is let loose.'

FOUR!

And the Third Gate sprang open and swung wide.'

The collie shivered as he finished the recitation of El Arat's dream.

'And you have seen Scant, Dancer, haven't you?'

'This afternoon, at the river, yes.'

The hackles rose on Cory's ruff, and he growled.

'Then the Executioner is not far behind?'

'Not far, no.'

'Then what will you do? You can't go home without loss. You can't stay here without loss, and El Arat says that the Army has abandoned you, because you abandoned your task. What are you going to do?'

The Dancer lifted his muzzle to the Moon. The sky was empty, and the light from the Moon seemed very far away. The air was cold, and there was a taste of snow in the night breeze.

'We will stay here,' said the Dancer. 'And we will wait.'

BOOK
TWO

1

A Gathering Storm

Pony emerged from the mouth of the cave into a weak winter sun, and began to nose a little pettishly into the snow. The air was cold, edged with frost, and the bare branches of the oaks and maples poked among the pines like skeletal fingers.

Snow had come early to the mountains, and in this, the second month of the new year, it was a torment to the horses. Ice crystals formed under their fetlocks in hard grey balls, and packed into their hooves. The cave allowed them some relief at night. Although it was small, it sheltered them from the dark and cold, and the combined heat of their bodies chased the bone-deep chill. But in the mornings, when they came out to eat and to break the thick ice of the stream for water, the snow and cold were waiting like a trap.

Cory, an anxious eye on the changing position of the sun, was the only member of the herd who really noticed the passage of time. For the others, the days wheeled forward in an unchanging rhythm: sleep, at night, and in the daytime, a patterned roaming to the creek and a slow, patient pawing through the snow to find dried grass and withered leaves.

The scarce forage caused them all to lose condition; even the Dancer had faint hollows behind his withers. Susie and Duchess walked a little splay-footed, their bellies showing the first slight moundings of early pregnancy. Pony had come into season late, and it was too early for the others to know if she had caught. Pony's thick coat and hardy constitution seemed to protect her better than the others. She travelled the farthest on her quest for food; her short legs and wide, flat hooves gave her excellent purchase on the mountain slopes. Susie and Duchess tended to stay in the valley, the warmth of their bodies giving each other comfort as they grazed together.

The Dancer left them early each morning to pace off a wide, guardian circle he had established around the mountain. At night, he walked the whitened meadow in front of the cave, his bulk now and again dimming the moon's reflection on the sleeping mares. Cory was with him frequently.

Their muscles were hard and lean from digging through the snow to the buried grass, and, except for Susie's cough, which was more persistent now in the frozen air, their eyes were bright. Despite the hardships, they were, as Susie put it happily, 'Gettin' by. Gettin' by.'

This morning, like all the other mornings since the snow had come, Dancer and Cory left the cave just before dawn. The mares rose late, waiting for the sunshine to reach its pallid morning height. Pony, first out, blinked to adjust her vision to the brightness outside, and began to paw through the snow for grass. Suddenly, a long grey shape slipped out of a snow drift and flattened against the shadow cast by a large pine. She yelled and jumped back, slamming her hindquarters into the rough arch of the cave entrance. Susie and Duchess came out at a run and Cory dashed out from a copse of trees.

'What is it now?' Duchess demanded.

'Wolf,' gasped Pony. 'I saw it through the trees.'

Cory circled the clearing, sniffing hard. 'She's right, Duchess. I wonder why they waited this long?' He sat for a moment and thought, then said reluctantly, 'They've probably hunted out their territory and they're moving on up here.'

'What're we going to do?' said Pony.

'There's another cave – up the east side of the mountain by the falls. We could move,' said the dog. 'I think I'll find the Dancer, though, and let him know what happened.'

'While you do that, why don't we go look at that place,' said Susie. 'It's pretty cramped in where we are now. Every time Pony rolls over, she bumps into somebody.'

'Duchess?' asked Cory. 'What do you think?'

'We can take a look,' said Duchess. 'Susie and I are just going to get bigger, as spring comes. And the Dancer will breed Pony again, if she hasn't caught. When the foals arrive we'll certainly need more room.'

'Then I'll come with you,' said Cory. 'We'll talk with the Dancer tonight.'

They walked through the woods single file. The footing was treacherous and hidden rocks underneath the snow made their progress slow. A buried twig snapped under Duchess' hoof and Pony squealed and jumped.

'What's the matter with you?' asked Duchess irritably. 'You're as jumpy as a barn cat.'

'Nothing. Just wonder where *he* is, and why he leaves us alone all the time. What if those wolves move farther up and get us? The woods are full of creepy things. I just don't like travelling like this, all bunched together. We ought to spread out, so one of us can get away if we get jumped on.'

'Cory's here,' said Susie comfortingly. 'I'm not worried a bit.'

'There's the cave,' said Duchess.

The falls were frozen, the live and flashing water of the autumn reduced to a trickle that wandered through the bumps and whorls of ice. Heavy brush half-concealed the dark mouth of a cave at the back of the falls. The mountains on the north protected the entrance from the wind, and thick pines provided a windbreak from the south and west. A long slide of bare rocks and snow exposed the cave to the east.

'The exposure's not too good if we get a storm from the east,' said Cory. 'It might be all right in the spring . . . but for right now, I'm not so sure.'

Susie picked her way through the snow to the entrance and thrust her head inside. 'Come and see how big it is!'

'Let me see,' said Cory. Susie backed out and the dog disappeared, reemerging a few moments later.

'It should take all of us, plus foals, quite comfortably. And it seems deserted.'

The mares crowded into the cave; it was spacious, as Cory had said. The floor was covered with twigs, dried leaves, pebbles, and pockets of gravel. A musty odor pervaded the place. Duchess examined the walls carefully. The ceiling was high, dropping in back to a ledge partly concealed by boulders. The ledge was difficult to see in the darkness and Duchess brushed the crumbling shelf with her muzzle. 'Cory might be able to curl up here,' she said. 'Then Pony wouldn't step on him all the time. What's that smell?'

'Bear,' said the collie matter-of-factly. 'At least, I think so. Some wild-meat eater, at any rate.'

'Well, isn't *that* great,' said Pony. 'Move right in with a bear. *Good* idea!'

'The scent's old, Pony, even I can tell that,' said Susie. They moved out of the cave and into the pale sunshine. Duchess pawed automatically at the snow and uncovered a clump of autumn grass, still faintly green in places. 'Susie, look. Pony, come. There's enough here for all of us.'

'No. I'm going to move on out the mountain,' said Pony. She shifted uneasily. 'You eat it. You look like you need it.'

Duchess raised her head in surprise. 'Why, thanks, Pony, but you've had just as hard a time as we have. Although . . .' She stopped and walked closer to the Shetland, who edged back defiantly. 'Pony, you're not thin at all. Cory, look at her.' Duchess curled her lip over her teeth. 'You're just as round as when we came here,

186

when the grass was thick!' she said. 'Pony, if you've found food you're keeping to yourself, you're in real trouble.'

Susie raised her head from the grass patch Duchess had uncovered and protested, 'No, Duchess. She would have let us know.'

'Would she?' said Duchess. She pinned her ears back. 'If you've found green grass, you'd better tell us now, before the Dancer gets back.'

There was an embarrassed quiet. An occasional crow call sounded in the lonely pines, and the wind rose softly and died again. Pony hesitated. Suddenly, she broke for the pines at a trot.

'Stop!' Duchess charged into a run and shouldered Pony to a halt. 'Look, you little . . .' She bit the words back, and continued with forced calm. 'Pony, I know you're not used to herd life but you know we're supposed to share. You show us where you've been feeding. Now.'

Pony looked at her hooves, and rubbed her nose thoughtfully along one foreleg. She raised her head to the grey clouds rolling in from the rim of the mountains and shrugged. 'Hey, if there were green grass to be found, the Dancer would've found it, right? I mean, he's supposed to do that kind of thing. Protect us, feed us.'

'Answer me!' snarled Duchess. She pushed the Shetland back toward the waterfall. 'And what are those marks on your neck? Fly bites? In winter?'

'So? You don't like the flies around here, complain to him. He picked this place, after all.'

'Pony, there aren't any flies in winter,' said Susie.

Pony looked nervously over Duchess' shoulder, her gaze flickering from the buckskin, to the pines, and back again.

'Leave me alone.'

'And teeth marks,' said Duchess, examining Pony's neck. 'Pony, something very strange is going on.'

Pony stiffened. 'Hear that?' she whispered. 'Smell that?'

187

Duchess spun around. 'Cory! What is it? Susie, get behind me.'

The dog stood at full alert, his body stiff with the effort of scenting the air. 'There's a funny odor . . .'

Duchess stood braced for a long moment. When Cory didn't move, she let her breath out and snapped, 'Another one of your tricks, Pony.'

'Hold hard,' said Cory.

A red fox stumbled out of the pines, white-tipped brush held low, the black mask cupping narrow golden eyes that squinted against the sunshine. His mouth was held open at an unnatural angle, and from the ivory teeth ran bloody spittle. An odor came from the matted, vulpine fur that every living animal recognized with astonished panic.

Duchess backed, backed, her heart as icy as the frozen water. 'Mad fox,' she whispered.

'Mad fox!' screamed Pony. 'Mad!' She galloped for the pines. The sudden movement attracted the fox. He crouched, distempered snarls rising from the fixed jaws. Duchess swung to protect Susie.

'Get out of the way, Susie. Don't startle him. Cory, are you all right?'

'I think so. He's upwind of me, and I don't think he smells me.'

The fox hesitated. Swinging his head like a heavy sack, he fumbled through the drifts toward Susie.

'Susie, turn and run,' said Duchess.

The fox swung its head back and forth, back and forth.

'No. Stand still, Susie,' ordered Cory. 'I'm going to get the Dancer.' The dog moved quietly to the woods, and they could hear the swift rustle of his cautious running.

Susie, breath whistling through her muzzle, made a careful circle behind the fox.

'Make a noise, Duchess. Whinny, stamp your feet,' she whispered. 'But not too loud. It'll hurt his ears and he'll charge. Do as I say.'

Duchess whinnied, a low-pitched sound that barely

188

disturbed the air. The fox jerked, his paws working in the snow like a cat about to spring. An agonized whining came from his swollen throat.

'Again,' urged Susie.

Duchess snorted. The fox sprang with a tangled snarl. Susie reared and struck. Her right fore, razor sharp, hit the fox's skull and crushed it like a plastic bucket.

The red body twisted convulsively and lay still. The Paint leaped away, her neck patched with sweat.

The mares stood immobile. No whimper moved the matted flanks of the fox.

'I think he's dead,' said Duchess very quietly. 'There's no blood, nothing. You killed him, Susie, with one strike.'

Susie bent her head, her lips curled over her teeth in unfamiliar ferocity.

Cory and the Dancer raced into the clearing, the dog panting excitedly, the stallion quiet and deadly.

'What's happened here!' the Dancer demanded. He slid to a halt at the sight of the red body. 'What's this?'

'A mad fox,' said Duchess. 'A mad fox, and Susie killed it with one blow.'

'Don't touch it, Cory,' warned the Paint. 'The madness comes through touching.'

Cory gave the body a wide berth, growling in little worried spasms. 'Why this time of year?' he said to the Dancer. 'It's all wrong. This sickness comes in deep summer, from the hot weather with neither rain nor breeze to cool it. How could this happen now?'

The Dancer shook his head, troubled. Cory began to scratch at the snow beside the body, and as he dug, the white snow turned to black dirt. The body began to disappear under a mound of snow and earth.

Shivering from reaction, Duchess moved to Susie's side. The Dancer moved to them, his breath warm on their flanks.

'Brave work, Susie. All animals fear the madness. I would have hesitated to do what you did. And you did it so neatly! One blow to the head, in the precise spot.'

Susie shuddered and he nuzzled her gently. 'And no blood. You should be pleased. But you aren't, I can smell it. Why?'

Susie looked at him sadly, 'I've never killed anything before. I never thought that'd be my job. I don't like it much, Dancer.'

'We'll have to make up a Story about this, Susie,' said Duchess with forced cheerfulness. 'You're a true hero, and we can't forget it. Perhaps we can call it "The Tale of the Mad Fox," or "Susie's Bravery," or something like that. I'll think of something, as I did with the Oath for Cory, you know. And I'm sure Pony will have something to contribute . . . she always does. Where did she go, by the way? Ran off, I suppose. The little sneak. Cory, did you pass her in the woods?'

Cory, busy cleaning himself of dirt and packed snow, licked his right forepaw carefully, then said with his head down, 'Yes, I saw her. She was headed east, as she does every day. She doesn't stay around much anymore.'

The Dancer blew out with a troubled, angry sound. 'She's been leaving the herd?'

'Yes,' said Duchess. 'That is, I was trying to find out what she's been up to and where she goes, when that fox attacked. I think she may have found some green grass under the snow that she didn't want to share. You know how she is, Dancer. She hasn't got a bad heart – just a selfish one. I haven't been paying attention to her as I should. She makes me lose my temper, so I avoid her.'

'None of us have bad hearts,' said Susie, 'Perhaps she's doing what she has to do. This life's so different – let her alone, Duchess.'

'Can you pick up the trail, dog?' said the Dancer. A vertical line had appeared between his eyes and he looked at the sky with uneasiness. 'There's been a storm brewing all day. There's something strange in the wind, black crows in the woods. I've found carcasses of animals killed for sport, not food. And now the fox, with a summer sickness in deep winter. I'm uneasy. Track her down,

190

Cory, and bring her back. I want her with the others, where I can keep an eye on her.'

Cory, with a backward look at the fox's grave, trotted swiftly to the eastward path and disappeared among the pines.

'We'd better look, too,' said Duchess. 'We'll find her faster if we spread out. Susie, you take the southern path and I'll go west.'

'That leaves north for me, my Duchess,' said the Dancer with amusement. 'Lead Mare, indeed. We'll meet at the old cave – at sunset.'

They went their separate ways, and the wind rose in the treetops with a groaning howl.

They searched, severally, all afternoon, while the sun sank low with a sullen light, and the afternoon sky turned an ominous yellow. Duchess returned to the familiar cave at twilight, just as the Dancer came through the trees on the opposite side of the clearing.

'No luck,' said Duchess. 'She seems to have disappeared completely.'

The Dancer scanned the sky and said, 'Storm,' in the tone of one who has had long experience. 'Cory should be along soon.'

'Dancer,' said Duchess as they waited. 'You remember that hound at the river? The day we arrived in the mountain?'

The stallion swung his coal-black head and looked at Duchess gravely.

'Yes. Do you regret that we've come here?'

'I? No! Never! But something you said to me then, actually a lot of what you said, has been troubling me. I haven't liked to ask, especially with the others around. You said . . .'

'There are things you aren't to know,' he said calmly. 'I couldn't tell you of them then, and I can't now. It has been forbidden. And it wouldn't be right for mares to know stallions' business.'

'A stallion's business is his own,' said Duchess,

191

impatiently. 'That's what all the mares say, although I've never understood *why*. It's our welfare at stake. It's all herd business, anyway.'

'It's not herd business. It's mine. And there lies the difference.' Duchess, taken aback, thought briefly ahead to spring, when the woods would be soft with green and growing things and the air filled with the gentle stirrings of new life. Perhaps she would wait until then, when his mood would be more receptive.

'Well, not the dream then, or the battle we talked about . . . or rather *didn't* talk about. But . . .'

The Dancer jerked in surprise. 'I mentioned the battle?'

'Some. Not much. And you said you may have . . .' She stopped, and went on steadily, 'You may have destroyed us. Ever since then, you've been waiting for something. What is it? I just want to know. I won't say anything to the others. Tell me. What's wrong?' She looked deep into his eyes. The scent of wild thyme rose from his body like a mist. 'What are you, then?' she said, simply. 'Should I be afraid of you?'

The Dancer made an involuntary movement, as if wakened from a dream too suddenly. A pad-pad-pad came from the woods.

'Cory!' Duchess braced herself, 'Did you find her? Where's Susie?'

Cory trotted up, silent, with a terrible fear in his eyes. He pressed close to Duchess and then, amazingly, went to the Dancer and whined, curling into a tight ball at the stallion's feet. He was shaking, breathing shallowly, as though he had been running for miles.

The Dancer broke the silence with a deep rumble.

'Have you found Pony?'

Cory nodded.

'Is she coming back?'

'Yes, Dancer,' said Cory. 'She isn't alone.'

The storm, with the night gathering behind it, broke with a sibilant rush of snow mixed with evil-smelling rain.

'Is Susie with her?' demanded Duchess.

Cory shook his head. 'I don't know where Susie is. But I tracked Pony. To the east . . .' A glance passed between him and the Dancer that chilled Duchess far more than the snow beating at her flanks.

'It's come then,' the Dancer said. The stallion bent his head. It seemed to Duchess that a small bright light flickered and died in him. 'We must find the Paint,' he said softly. 'Stay in the cave, Duchess. Cory, guard Duchess well. And come out for no one but me.'

The Dancer trotted into the rising dark. His trot swelled to a canter, a gallop, then a flat-out run, veiled by the gusting storm.

2

A Challenge Delivered

The wind rose, spiraling thick gouts of snow in Duchess' face and turning Cory's leaf-gold coat to white. The mare blinked the ice from her eyelashes and peered futilely into the depths of the storm.

'We'd better get out of this, into the cave,' said Cory. 'Come on. It isn't going to do us any good to stand here and wait. We might as well be warm.'

They fought their way into the darkness, huddling together for reassurance.

'What did you mean when you said that Pony isn't alone?' said Duchess. 'You were afraid, weren't you? I've never seen you afraid before.'

Cory gazed out into the swirling white, then began in a low voice.

'Pony's trail wasn't hard to follow. She was headed in a straight line to the east over the wash of grass and rocks where we used to take our morning runs, before the snow came. She made no attempt to hide her trail.'

'Why should she?'

'Let me finish,' said the dog. 'Just let me finish. I followed her trail. She was moving quickly, at a canter. After a while, she slowed to a trot. Then a slow walk. She seemed reluctant. More than once she turned to look back from where she came. I had to belly low so she wouldn't see me.'

'Why didn't you just stop her, tell her to come back?'

'I had to know for sure where she was going, you see. I suspected. And I think the Dancer knows. But anyhow, she would stand for moments at a time, shuffling her feet, then she'd turn and head east again. I caught up with her just as she disappeared over the ridge . . . the one that backs the waterfall where I first came into the valley.

'There was a strange scent in the air – foul, black-tasting. And then,' the collie shook himself all over, as if to rid himself of an unpleasant touch, 'clouds of black flies, August flies, only they buzzed like hornets, and they were marked with a yellow spot, like no flies I've ever seen before.

'They flew around me in a big cloud, but I wasn't stung. My coat's pretty thick, and I shut my eyes and crawled close to the earth. They went away finally, and I got up and picked up her trail again. I got to the top of the ridge.

'The valley below was terrible. The sky held a yellowish overcast, tinged with green, and the snow was melting. Underneath the puddling, I could see blasted earth – not regular withered grass, but earth blackened by fire, or worse. Pony picked her way through the craters, through the piles of dirty snow, with that ugly sky overhead, and somewhere, there was the sound of black flies.

'She stopped.

'And the earth opened in front of her, like a slow tear in a blanket.

'A long, sloping path appeared in the very belly of the earth, and on it walked a Hound. Not one of my race, Duchess, for his scent and way of moving were foreign to me and my kind. It had rotting teeth, and eyes of a color that is talked about in Tales of Evil among us Dogs. It spoke, in a sniveling, creeping voice. Then Pony followed it down the path, into the earth.'

Duchess, trembling, whispered, 'And was there a sound? A sound of wailing, of a chase in the sky? Did the air around this Thing whirl like an oily pool?'

'Yes,' said Cory, and, ears flattened in shame, he tried to hide his shaking.

'I'm the one who's brought us to all this!' cried Duchess. 'I have dreamed of this Hound – and of the Dancer too. And then, just before we crossed the river . . . the Hound met us in the flesh.' She hung her head. 'I should have turned back then. This is my fault.'

'Nonsense,' said Cory briskly. 'We'll both get hold of ourselves, and wait for the Dancer to bring Susie back.'

The blinding white darkened outside the cave mouth and the long, slow night crept by. They slept a little, waking suddenly at the smallest sound – a shift in the wind, a slide of snow, the click of the pebbles as one or the other moved restlessly in sleep. And still the Dancer had not returned.

The white wall outside lightened with the dawn, and Duchess paced back and forth, pawing at the earth.

'They're lost,' she said. 'We'll have to go out and find them.'

'Where would we look?' said Cory. 'The Dancer knows these mountains like I know Bishop Farm. If she can be found, he'll find her. It's no use you getting lost in the storm, too.'

A shadow appeared on the cave wall, and Duchess leaped for the entrance. 'Susie!'

'I couldn't find her.' The Dancer entered the cave with a weary stagger. The tops of his ears were grey with cold, and Duchess warmed them with her breath.

'No trace?' she said. 'No trace at all?'

'This storm makes it almost impossible to see or smell anything,' said the Dancer. 'I decided to come back after I circled the same stand of trees three times. I was just bumping into myself.' He stood at the farthest corner of the cave and closed his eyes. 'The storm's lessening a little. I'll wait until the wind dies down, then go out again.'

Cory settled onto the floor, forepaws outstretched. His steady brown eyes held the Dancer's.

'You haven't asked me about Pony,' he said.

'No. I'm reasonably sure what's happened to Pony. She has met up with an old enemy of mine.'

The air in the cave grew briefly hot, as though a sigh had come from the walls.

The Dancer opened his eyes, and their white shining drove Cory to his feet. The stallion said, 'She was with the Hound.'

'Yes. Not a dog-hound. Something else.'

The Dancer nodded, thoughtfully. 'Scant.'

'I dreamed,' began Duchess, quavering.

'I know your dreams – and your visions,' said the Dancer.

'But why!' she demanded. 'I don't understand. And it's time that I did. What's going on? The herd is split up! Susie's out there, alone and lost and sick. Pony is Equus knows where. I'm Lead Mare. And my herd is gone! I don't care if it's *your* business or not. I have a right to know!'

'Duchess,' said the Dancer sadly. 'Duchess, you are the last mare of my line. The last true Appaloosa mare. The foal you're carrying will be as brightly colored as I – perhaps even brighter. And so will all its get.'

'That's ridiculous,' snapped Duchess. 'I'm a Grade mare. Everyone knows that. Just ask that fool Cissy.' She turned, partly in humiliation, partly in anger, and faced the wall. 'How would you know anything about it? A brightly colored foal. The last mare of the Appaloosas. Who do you think you are, anyway?' She began to shake in anger. 'You've lost Susie. Pony's gone – and she never should have come with us anyway. The foals are endangered. They may never see the spring. These Things are following us, and are you doing anything about it? You are not!

'You just stand there and sigh and say, "I know your dreams." What do you know of my dreams. You're nothing more than a charlatan, a trickster!' She whirled and struck out at him, her hoof just missing his shoulder.

197

The Dancer reared in place, his voice a thunder in that small space.

'I AM THE DANCER!'

Cory, rather prudently, stared out into the blizzard.

'I know you are!' shrieked Duchess in frustration.

'I AM THE RAINBOW HORSE!'

Cory swung his head around at the sudden silence. Duchess stared at the Dancer with wide and frightened eyes.

'That,' the dog said dryly, 'is true, Duchess.'

The Dancer twitched impatiently. 'I am the Dancer, the Rainbow Horse, chief of the Appaloosas, and a member of the Army of One Hundred and Five.'

'You can't be,' said Duchess, angry, rejecting, as though a fear had been confirmed. 'Why, that means you're a god.'

'No, no. Not a god. A half-god, maybe. We – all of us in the Army – exist at the whim of the One, and only when the Balance is in order. That's why I came from the Courts – to restore the Balance, regain what is mine. Sycha had destroyed my line, or almost . . .' A dreaming filmed his eyes, and he spoke softly, from a great distance. 'I remember that time of destruction myself. I remember watching as my brothers were torn from the herd – and a long, confused struggle to reach this mountain and safety. I remember how we hid, for those of our kind, the spotted horses, were chased, slaughtered for meat in the packing houses of men.

'I remember farther back than that. Of men who rode me, and my dam, too, without saddle or bit. Men with hair a glossy black like raven's wings, with the feathers of forest birds on their chest and wrists.

'I remember the hunts for great hump-backed creatures they called buffalo, and the races between us horses on the grass plains on an autumn afternoon.

'I remember all of this: the beginning and now, it seems, the end.'

'And what has the Hound to do with all this?' asked Duchess.

'I can't tell you more. I shouldn't have told you what I did, but . . .' he glanced ruefully at her standing meekly in his shadow. 'My Duchess has a temper still, it seems. Now you know what you should not know . . . or part of it, at any rate.' He shook himself. 'The storm is dying down, and I must bring Susie back. Stay here, both of you. Cory? Guard.'

He went out into the storm again, the wind whipping his mane and tail.

'I think it's letting up a little,' said Cory, peering after the stallion. He yawned too casually, shook himself and settled on the cave floor with ostentatious comfort. After a moment he said carelessly, 'Do you understand what's going on?'

'I don't want to think about it,' replied Duchess.

Cory said nothing, noticing her rigid stance, the way her ears rotated back and forth, alert for the slightest sound, the tight muscles beneath her rough winter coat. If his thoughts were of a coal stove, the warmth of the kitchen at Bishop Farm, and the security of David's knee against his collie coat, he didn't voice them. His fears for their safety were swallowed, too.

But, as if in answer to the dog's unspoken thought, Duchess raised her head and said fiercely, 'If I die here, it doesn't matter. I don't care, I tell you. And that Pony can go straight to the Black Barn's Third Gate. It's just that Susie . . . and you . . .' she trailed off miserably.

'I'll take what comes down the road,' said Cory, 'and as for Susie, I have a feeling that he'll find her this time. Get some sleep. I'll keep watch.'

But sleep remained elusive, and Duchess strained her ears foward, waiting for the sound of Dancer's return.

Susie was dreaming.

It was spring at Bishop Farm and she was teaching the new crop of weanlings about fences. The sun was warm on her back, and an errant cabbage fly soared among the dandelions, wings frantic, dizzy with the scent of flowers.

'It tickles!' said the smallest foal, Lucky. He was Fancy's latest colt, the product of the chestnut mare and a visiting Paint stallion, and he was marked with definite splotches of chestnut and white, like shadows splashed in clear water. 'Almost like me!' Susie said to herself. Although she'd rather have her teeth floated than admit it, the Paint weanlings were her favorites, reminding her of her own colt sired by Stillmeadow years before.

'This, babies, is the fence,' Susie said. 'Follow me. In order, now, and no biting or kicking. We're to follow the fence.'

She lined the babies up, nose to tail, inhaling their sweet, new scent with soft whickerings of pleasure. They trotted around the perimeter of the pasture in an uneven parade.

'Don't stick your legs through the boards. Yes, I mean no, like that, Pippin.' The little bay, Feather's filly, poked one foreleg through the bottom boards and Susie gently nosed her free.

'Now, this is smooth electric wire,' she explained. 'It buzzes you when you touch it. It's hard to see when it's strung between these posts, so be careful.'

Lucky pushed an inquisitive nose toward the wire, then squealed 'Eeeeyah! It *bit* me!' In a cascade of awkward, knuckly legs, the weanlings broke formation and raced for the far end of the pasture.

'Old bones,' thought Susie ruefully, as she trotted in pursuit. 'It's getting harder and harder every year to chase them.'

She waded, panting, through the grass, which seemed oddly thick and cold for this time of year, more like – what – she couldn't think. She rounded up the sprawling little herd again, and began to organize a game of Tag-Tail, but somehow, the grass kept getting in her way, thick, slippery, strangling cold, and the small piping voices and the murmur of a gentle summer mingled, swirled together. She fell into the grass, rolling, tangled, and the babies faded into a cold white wall.

She woke up.

She was backed against a tree, wedged between the slender trunk and a huge drift of snow, and she was not at Bishop Farm at all, but . . . where? The Dancer's mountain. That was it, and what surrounded her was not summer grass, but snow. And she was very, very tired.

Susie snorted, taking a deep breath of air. The cough came like a sharp-clawed cat, tearing at her throat, leaving her weak and shaking, frightening her a little, as it always did. She looked in dismay at the storm around her.

'Duchess?' she called timidly.

The sound was taken up and whirled away by the winds. Susie was afraid to call out again – it sounded lonesome, and why wasn't she home, where she ought to be? She would think about home, the babies, the way yellow straw piled thick and warm in her stall, the way the sunshine would slant through the door to her own paddock.

The white snow glared, making her eyes water, and she closed them tight, to see the sunshine, to hear the call of the yearlings playing in the duck pond, to smell . . .

She opened her eyes cautiously. Meat-eaters . . . here?

A wolf, gaunt-grey, haggard with the long winter behind him, eyes sunken with the knowledge of the long winter before him, stood poised on the snowbank over her head.

A warning sounded in the back of her mind. 'Don't sleep under trees, predators can lurk there,' and here she was, under a tree, and wasn't that just like her, to forget?

'You've never been strong on brains, Susie,' she said aloud, 'but if you weren't so *tired* . . . Duchess?'

Now, if her friend were here, she'd scold, 'Get up! You can't sleep lying down. What if you're attacked?' Duchess . . .

Susie closed her eyes against the swirling white, while above her, the wolf crouched, grinning.

* * *

201

'They aren't back *yet*,' fumed Duchess. 'He's been gone for hours. Look, it's getting dark again.'

'I hear them!' Cory's triumphant barks filled the cavern, and Duchess sprang to the entrance. The Dancer came slowly across the clearing, Susie at his shoulder. The Paint's head swung low and she stumbled frequently, her progress shaking and weak. She stopped and swayed in the middle of the clearing. Cory trotted up to them, his expression grave.

'She was in a snowbank, past the creek,' said the Dancer. 'She'd spent the entire storm there. She fell into the creek as we came through and she's wet.'

'Bring her in,' said Duchess. 'We have to keep her away from the cold. Cory, go find some branches with leaves on them. She's got to eat something. I'll try and keep her warm. Susie? Susie, can you hear me?'

The three supported her into the cave. Susie's nose was hot against Duchess' withers.

'This is the fence that bites,' she said clearly. She fell heavily onto the floor, eyes closed. Cory, dragging a dried branch with a few leaves attached to its skeletal twigs, came sideways into the cave.

'Here,' he grunted. 'I'll be back with more.'

Duchess nosed the branch over to Susie and said anxiously, 'Come on, you have to eat.'

'She's very ill, Duchess,' said the Dancer softly. 'Sleep may be the best thing for her. That, and quiet.'

'Yes, yes. But she has to eat. And she has to be kept warm. Cory can curl up beside her. His coat is almost as good as a blanket. That's what they used to do with sick horses at the farm. Cover them up. We don't have a blanket, but Cory will help her, won't he?'

'Yes, I'm sure he will.'

'And the vet. They always used to call the vet, and he struck her with a needle when she coughed. Her breath was easier after that.'

The Dancer said nothing.

202

'And David would rub her chest with some strong-smelling ointment. It made it easier for her to breathe, too.'

Susie's breathing, loud and hoarse, filled the cave in an uneven cadence.

'Come outside with me, Duchess. The storm's lightened. Let her sleep.'

'Yes,' said Duchess. 'Yes.' She didn't move, but stood and looked at her herd mate unhtil the Dancer gently pushed her into the clearing.

Two days passed, then three, and the storm raged and died and raged again. In the infrequent lulls, Duchess and Cory pushed Susie to her feet and down to the creek for a drink. She remained hot, feverish, and her coat became dry and brittle. A sweetish smell came from her mouth. Duchess, remembering that scent from another time, another place, with a friend who had lain as still and quiet as the Paint, made Cory fill the cavern with dead branches and dried leaves until there was no room to move about, and the Dancer asked Cory to drag them out again.

As evening fell on the third day, Susie raised her head with a jerk. Her eyes were clear, and she looked at Duchess in sudden recognition.

'Pony,' she said. 'Where is she? Did she get lost, too?'

'I don't know where she is,' said Duchess. 'We haven't seen her.'

'Did he go to find her, like he found me? Is it still snowing?'

'It's let up a bit,' said Duchess.

'Well, then, he'll have to find her, won't he? She's part of the herd. It's not because you are all takin' care of me, is it? I can manage, like. Someone should find Pony. I have a feeling she's in trouble. She's near here, and she's in trouble.'

Duchess went to the mouth of the cave and looked out on the clearing. The moon was rising, and its bleared shadow made a grim pattern in the snow. Cory and the

Dancer stood guard in the clearing, the dog sitting up alertly, his ears pricked forward, the Dancer tense and still. Both of them gazed with concentration at the dense grove of pines.

'Susie woke up,' said Duchess. 'It's the first time she's made sense since she came in from the storm. She says she woke up because of . . .'

'Get back inside,' said the Dancer. 'Quickly, now.'

A faint, rhythmic rustling came from the pine trees. Cory growled and snapped his teeth: click-click-click. The hackles on his shoulders rose and a long, ululating howl escaped from his throat.

The Dancer shoved Duchess into the cave and turned to face the trees. Cory crouched at his feet, his growls reaching a furious pitch. The stumbling came on.

Pony came through the pine trees; she was clearly visible in the moonlight.

The Shetland's forelock was pasted flat with damp. Snow beaded her eyelashes and packed the feathers at her pasterns. The fly bites Duchess had seen on her neck – was it only three days ago? – were swollen and flushed with black.

A great rage swept over Duchess and her hindquarters clenched with the effort of remaining still. Pony approached at a steady, fumbling pace and stopped before them.

'Look at her eyes,' said the Dancer quietly. 'Look, and temper your rage with pity, Duchess.'

Cory's snarls died, and from behind them, Susie said gently, 'Come in, Pony. Out of the cold.'

Pony started, trembling as though she had been whipped. Her blank, bewildered gaze swept past them, and Duchess spoke the eerie thought that came to her.

'She doesn't see us, Dancer. Or if she does . . .'

'It is through flame and devastation. We are shadows to her,' said the stallion. 'She is trapped, locked away.'

'Come in, Pony,' said Susie, struggling to a half-seated position, her forelegs knuckled under. 'It's warm in here,

204

and you'll be safe. You're back with the herd, where you
belong.'

Pony looked back over her withers to the pine trees,
her mouth working. A guttural noise came from her
throat.

'He's coming, you bet,' she said.

The Dancer, silent, didn't move.

'He's coming, and you're gonna get it good.'

'Get out of here!' shouted Duchess. She lunged at the
Shetland, her teeth bared, and the Dancer stepped
between them. Pony blinked.

'Why, Pony?' said Susie. 'Didn't you want to be with
us? Didn't we treat you well? We didn't, Duchess,' she
said. 'And now she's gone and found another herd.'

'Get out, Pony, before I kick you bloody,' said
Duchess.

Pony, looking at something they couldn't see, listening
to a voice only she could hear, fixed her eyes on a point
above the Dancer's head.

'Oats-green-grass-always-summer,' she gabbled. 'It's
been promised, you bet. Sugar cubes. Pony is Lead Mare.
No more p-p-pony rides. No more stinkin' trucks. Sweet
grass and summer.'

'Summer,' said the Dancer. 'Poor Pony.'

'You-come-Susie,' said Pony in that guttural monotone.
'Your cough will go away. You'll run f-f-f-free again.
Come-with-me Duchess. You'll be Lead Mare, after me.
You'll carry f-f-f-fifty colts. Red like the rising sun. And
you . . .' She dropped her gaze suddenly to the Dancer's
full, dark eyes, held the look for a second, then snatched
her gaze away. A voice, raged-filled and not her own,
came from her throat like a thunderclap. 'And *you*! C-C-
C – CAST DOWN! The first to die. A trophy for the
others to see. How they will tremble. Carrion P-P-P-PIG!'
A skull's head seemed to form on her face.

The Dancer swelled with fury. His poll flexed, crest
high and proud. He struck the ground *once*! and multi-
colored sparks danced about his hoof and *twice*! the

shower grew to a bright corona and *three* times! A rainbow arced on the moonlight.

'Tomorrow! At sunrise!' he screamed.

The skull shaped in Pony's face snapped back and there was only Pony left, her expression twisted, her eyes confused. The Dancer screamed a stallion call, high and wide, that grew louder, louder, until the cave walls shook.

'Anor! Anor! A-A-A-Anor!'

Pony turned and scuttled for the trees.

'Wait!' said Susie. 'Pony, come back!' The Paint heaved herself to her feet with a grunt. Legs trembling, withers shiny with the sweat of fever, she began to stumble across the clearing.

'No, Susie!' said Duchess.

The pines rustled with a rising wind. Fingers of dark clouds scudded across the bleary moon. Pony disappeared in a gout of wind-whipped snow. The wind rose with a high, keening inspiration and a sudden, devastating cold. And, as though it had been a purposeful, living creature instead of a phenomenon born of air currents, the chill struck Susie like a fist.

The Paint mare faltered, swayed, and fell.

3

The Owl Forces a Choice

'Dawn's near,' said Cory softly. The collie, the stallion, and the buckskin mare pressed together in the cave. Susie lay at their feet, withers stirred by faint breathing. The dog looked up at the Dancer. 'Will you tell us what will happen?'

'I will fight Anor,' said the Dancer calmly. 'And I will send him back.'

Cory stretched forward, his white ruff a pale glimmer in the predawn light, and licked Susie's face. 'And what if . . .'

The Dancer glanced at Duchess. 'Come outside for a moment,' he said. 'Duchess, call us if she wakes.'

The cave seemed colder when they left, and Duchess blew softly at Susie's face, a faint hope stirring. Her breath was stronger, surely . . .

Susie opened her eyes. Their deep brown was clouded, smeared, and her voice was so faint that Duchess had to kneel to hear her.

'Who's looking after the babies?'

'What?' asked Duchess.

Susie closed her eyes and seemed to sleep. Then she murmured, 'It's nice, Duchess, summertime, I mean. Did the vet give me a shot? I had a funny dream. Sometimes I get funny dreams after a shot. I dreamed we ran away from home,' amusement shadowed her voice, 'to some mountains, like, and there was a big, spotted horse who danced.' She stirred, and Duchess smelled despair. 'I dreamed I left my job so I could have a foal. I dreamed I put myself above the herd – and that I killed a fox. I couldn't have. I couldn't have.'

Duchess, a great grief in her heart, nuzzled her friend's ear. The sweetish smell of her breath was thick.

Susie coughed. 'Summertime,' she said drowsily. 'My favorite time of year. Funny, isn't it? Cissy *hates* summer because of the flies, I guess. But you know, she doesn't like much of anything. Oh, she can't hear me, can she?'

'No,' whispered Duchess.

'Good. I don't want to be mean.' Susie sighed again, luxuriously. 'Summertime. I like it best because it's so busy. I have my job, you know. Did I tell you El Arat said I was the best Caretaker the herd's ever had? Do you think it's important – my job?'

'You have the most important job there is – protecting life.'

'I do, don't I.' Susie raised her head, joy in her face, and her eyes cleared a little. She looked doubtfully around her.

'Why – we're in a cave,' she said. 'We're not at home at all. And it isn't summertime, is it?'

'No, Susie. We're in the mountains.'

Duchess saw in Susie's eyes that her dreams were true.

'I'm sick again,' she grunted. 'Foal's movin' in my belly. I can't be sick. I'll be up and around in no time.'

'No time,' said Duchess, grieving. 'Yes.'

'Is *he* around?' said Susie. 'He hasn't been asking for me or anything, has he?'

'He's been here all the time. He's outside with Cory now, but he's been watching over you all night long. Shall I fetch him?

Susie nodded. Duchess went to the entrance and called the Dancer in.

'Well, Susie.' The big stallion bent over her, and the touch of his muzzle brought a gleam to Susie's face.

208

'I hope I haven't been much trouble,' she said. 'You found me, didn't you?'

'What? Yes, in the drift, under the trees. It was very clever to seek shelter there, Susie. It kept you from the wind.'

'Well, I never been *clever*, you might say, but I think I've been good with the babies. Except I left that job. Perhaps I shouldn't have. It wasn't the most important job that ever was, but it was important to me. Do you think I was wrong to come here? Have I betrayed my job? My herd?' She stirred sadly on the cave floor. 'The Tale of the Least Shall Be Best. I'll never be allowed to hear it again!.'

'I don't think I've *ever* heard it,' said Duchess, with an attempt at cheerfulness.

'Well, you probably wouldn't, you see,' said Susie, 'you not being a Caretaker. But Pony's supposed to be the Storyteller. If she doesn't know it, I could tell her, so she could pass it along, like. I could . . .' A furrow appeared between her eyes. 'Pony's in trouble. Pony . . .'

'I'll tell it,' said the Dancer. 'Bring Cory in, Duchess.'

'*You* will!' said Susie, pleased. 'Stallions don't bother with the Stories!'

'We do, indeed. Especially an important one like this. Cory? You and Duchess and Susie will hear The Tale of the Least Shall Be Best. It will pass the time until dawn.'

The Tale of the Least Shall Be Best

'Once upon a time,' said the Dancer, 'when horses roamed the earth free-born, and all the earth was grass, a band of mares lived in splendor by a river.

In that band were mares whose names are some of the greatest in our history. Elyn, the granddaughter of Alamain the Fair, the most beautiful mare of her time and generation. Taryn the Graceful, whose floating steps rivaled the flight of gulls. Swallow, who could race the eagles themselves.

There was one mare named Shadow – so-called because her coat was splashed with the light and dark of the moon on a misty night. She was smaller than the rest, and she was neither beautiful nor fleet, nor did she move with the grace of wild birds.

Shadow thought she was well-named, and so she told a particular friend of hers, a black beaver who lived by the river.

'It's Shadow, you know, because the others shine so brightly. Elyn is so fair, the winds hold their breath around her. And Swallow can jump the clouds – the lower-lying ones, that is. Taryn moves like a beech in a wind. Do you think there is something about me that is – oh – sort of special? You needn't say it if it isn't so. But . . .' Shadow sighed, and humbly cropped at dandelions.

The beaver, busy with a particular hole in his dam, slapped his broad tail in the water and said, 'What's special about *you* is that you take care. You take care of everyone, even those stuck-up eagles.'

Shadow sighed again. it was easy to take care, after all. That wasn't a gift. She returned to where her herd ate grass by the river, and found that the Owl had brought good news.

'It's a Council meeting,' said Elyn, her delicate nostrils wide with delight. 'We're all to go! We are all to meet Equus himself.'

Shadow leaped in the air with joy, forgetting all her trouble in the face of this great news.

'There *is* a problem, though,' said Elyn. 'What shall we do with the weanlings while we travel to the Council? It's much too far for them, and besides, it wouldn't be seemly to bring foals to a meeting.'

'They say that Equus loves foals above all,' said Shadow, with a sinking feeling. 'They say . . .'

But no one listened to her in the discussion that followed.

'I'll stay,' said Elyn. 'I've been to Council once, after all.'

'You can't,' said Shadow, shyly. 'You're the most beautiful mare of all, the granddaughter of Alamain herself. Equus would be sure to miss you.'

'I'll stay,' Taryn volunteered.

And each mare in the herd offered in turn, and for each, there was good reason why they would be missed.

'Well, look here,' said Shadow, determinedly. 'I take care of weanlings. I think they like me. And it's only right that I should do what I do best. I'll miss the Council, of course. But I don't mind, truly.' Although she did, of course, very much. For she had never seen Equus the Shining, nor the splendid Courts of the Outermost West, nor the Army of One Hundred and Five that accompanied Equus while he grazed. 'But Twyla, the Story-Teller, can tell me all about it when you get back. That'll be just as good as being there. Practically, anyway.'

And so, after a lot of discussion along the lines of 'Are you *sure*, Shadow?' and 'You *really* don't mind?' and 'Oh, not a bit, *honestly*,' the mares picked up and left with promises to tell Shadow *everything*, mind you, when they returned.

So Shadow played with the weanlings along the river bank, stood over them while they slept, and once, late at night, scared away a sly red fox by pretending to be a whole battalion of mares. She told the babies Stories and the Laws and nuzzled them when they missed their mothers, which, because Shadow loved them, and they loved her, didn't happen too often.

Then, one night, when Elyn's red-gold filly had finally fallen asleep after a slight attack of grass colic, the winds slowed and a great stillness swept the river.

Shadow was scared. She nudged the weanlings into a small huddle and stood guard, her head high, her hind feet ready.

Something was coming.

The moon rose, flooding the meadow with a white-gold light, and the stars shifted with a crystalline chime.

'Shhhadowww.' A great voice rolled against her like a wave from the river. The weanlings slept. And like the brightest sun ever seen, Equus himself rose from the river, water streaming like gold from his coat, his hooves aglow with silver, his eyes like stars come to earth.

What was said between them, only Shadow's descendants know. But from that time forward, Shadow walked with a proud, light step and all her foals, and her foal's foals, are marked with a special mark – light on shadowy dark – and they are all Caretakers of the young of each herd.

And they are all beloved.'

The Dancer's voice died away.

'It's a bit of a secret like,' said Susie anxiously. 'I hope you don't mind my not telling what was said. But my great-great-great-granddam promised Him not to say, and we all promised, too.' Susie seemed to smile. 'But it is special. An Honor. That's all we can say.'

'A Law came from it, Susie,' said the Dancer. 'You can tell them that.'

'Oh, yes. The Law of the Least Shall Be Best. It goes like this:

The Second Law is Balance
What is given to one is given to the next
In equal size and kind
Where one horse in beauty walks, the next shall fly with
*   the winds*
And where one horse Leads, the others shall follow as
*   equals.*

Susie sighed, a deep sigh that came from her center, then stretched her neck along the rocky floor. Panic flashed through Duchess. Pride had looked like that, had stretched his neck out in just that way. Cory raised his fawn muzzle and howled. The Dancer bowed his head.

212

'Do something!' Duchess shouted. 'She's dying! You have to save her. If she hadn't come with us, none of this would have happened. It's my fault. And it's your fault, too! She didn't want to come. She was shappy where she was! And we forced her choice. We made it impossible for her to refuse. We played on her feelings. It isn't right that she should die here, so far away from things that matter to her. It isn't just! You're the Rainbow Horse, you told me so! Call on your god. Call on the One! You hold powers I can't begin to guess at. Save her!'

The Dancer shook his head slowly, bewildered.

'I don't think I know how, Duchess. My task was not this one. I've taken the easy path – and she is paying for my sin.'

'You *do* know how! You must!' Duchess struck out at the cave wall and a small shiver of stones ran down, powdering the Dancer's coal-black head. 'Save her, damn you! Try!'

The Dancer's great sides shuddered. 'If I could be sure,' he muttered. 'But it's all confused now, and has been since we left the Farm. My recollections and my dreams are wrapped now in light, now in dark.'

'Call the Owl!' shrieked Duchess. 'Call the Owl.'

The Dancer raised his head, dazed.

'The Owl,' he said, softly. 'Yes, perhaps.'

Moving slowly, slowly, as if he were under water, he raised his right forefoot and *strike*! an iridescent shower of stones fell about his head and *strike*! the black hoof shone with a clear light and *strike*! the white light merged with the spinning stones in a whirling pool of light, and Duchess saw what she had seen once before at the barns of Bishop Farm.

Cory whimpered deep in his throat.

The Owl took shape in the spiralling light. His wings were folded tight, his shining head and breast bathed in light that tapered to gleaming darkness at his feet. The great gold eyes were shut. He blinked, his body motionless, then turned his head with a smooth and sudden twist.

213

The light encircled the Dancer, glancing off the spotted white on his flanks, pooling on the black of his chest and belly, casting the finely carved head in sharp relief.

'I know you,' said the Dancer.

The Owl blinked soundlessly at him, then raised his wings in a wide rush, and in the light from them, Duchess and Cory saw a serried rank of stallions, a hundred strong or more, glowing with a perfect beauty that was more than earth allowed. In the petal-soft dark around the Army, stars chimed.

They stood in grass of a deep green, starred with brilliant flowers. Duchess saw an Arabian stallion, finely made; a Quarterhorse of chestnut brilliance; a Thoroughbred with long, elegant bones and legs built for supernatural speed. All types and kinds of stallions stood there, even a small, perfectly formed Shetland with a cream-colored mane and tail.

At the forefront, shining with all the rainbow colors, stood a stallion she knew as the Dancer.

A white glow moved among the stallions like a banked and glowing moon. The stallions parted ranks, great necks arched, and Duchess saw Equus face-to-face. Her flesh prickled and she shivered. There was a sad wisdom in the silver eyes, and a grief from his long guardianship.

Equus raised his head to the Court's blue sky. A shadow fell from the sun. But the Rainbow Horse stepped from the ranks and the shadow caught him in the heart. He fell through the Courts of the Outermost West, spinning and wheeling. The Owl's wing came down with a rush. The cave went dark.

The Dancer cried out, a long, drawn ululation of pain, and Duchess screamed, 'No!'

The Owl spun suddenly and raised his wings. The darkness in the cave was replaced by an amber glow.

There, his colors touched with light from a different sun, the Dancer stood at a bridge that spanned a fiery stream. Susie stood beside him, kind eyes bewildered, her homely brown and white spots touched with reflected glory. Duchess saw with a chill that there was only room for one to pass. The bridge was swaying, shattering, into the liquid flames below.

'A choice!' the Dancer shouted. 'My thanks!'

The Rainbow Horse placed a forefoot on the crumbling bridge.

A hollow, triumphant booming filled the cave. The river's flames leaped high.

The Owl winked out, and dawn's light filled the cavern.

Susie's stertorous breathing was the only sound. Duchess quivered, her throat bound with fear. The sun inched up over the mountaintop and touched the Dancer with pale fire.

'What do we do now?' asked Cory, practically. 'What does the vision mean?'

'I have a choice,' said the Dancer. There was a wildness in him that Duchess had never seen before. 'I have a choice. I see now that I have chosen the wrong path – but there is time to turn back, and start again. And I can save you all – you, Duchess, and the foal, and Susie. Perhaps even that wretched Pony.'

'How?' said the dog.

The stallion twitched impatiently. 'Why, I must go, of course.' He stamped his forefoot at their expressions. 'I must follow Pony. There was only room for one to pass to the Black Barns, as you saw. Susie will survive, as will my foals. There is a chance now, don't you see? My life for yours. And you, Cory, I must trust you to get them back safely. I should have known there was a reason for your presence here . . .'

'You offer your life so freely?' said Cory. 'Perhaps you haven't seen what I have seen. The things that come from the belly of the earth.'

'You think I don't know? I, a Watcher at the Pool? Of course I know. But I have powers left at which you, dog, can only guess.' He bent and nuzzled the recumbent Paint. 'There isn't much time,' he said. 'I must go.'

'Yes,' said Duchess. 'We must go.'

Cory looked at her. She stood as she might have before a judge, ears pricked forward, neck arched, all four legs squared. Beneath the rough dun of her winter coat, he saw the fine lines of her heritage, the last of the true Appaloosa mares, her belly swollen slightly with the foal.

'I don't think you can, Duchess,' said the collie gently.

'What? Go with me? Of course not,' said the Dancer. He trotted to the cave entrance and into the clearing. Duchess moved blindly at his heels.

'Stay here,' the Dancer ordered. 'Cory, you must get them back to Bishop Farm. Wait for early summer when the foals are fit to travel, and take it slowly. The forage will be sufficient then to sustain you and the mares.' He lengthened his trot into an easy, purposeful canter. Duchess ran heavily behind him, her belly swaying. Cory broke into a lope to keep up.

The Dancer, becoming aware of both dog and mare, came to an abrupt halt. He tempered the wildness in his voice with obvious effort. 'Duchess,' he said. He stood close to her, and she felt the warmth of his breath, inhaled the fresh scent of thyme. 'Duchess.' His tone, filled with love and a kind of longing, dropped to a bell-like rumble. 'I should have known that this was wrong. But you, and these mountains, and the freedom of a mortal life were calls I couldn't resist. I must save what I can, now. If you follow me, there will be no true line of Appaloosas. Our breed will exist only at the whim of man, a whim that changes with each passing mortal year. Would you have it all destroyed?'

'Yes,' said Duchess. 'There is no life for me without you.'

'And the foal?'

'He'll be born to suffering, as I have suffered. Born to be sold, beaten, starved. To be pushed beyond endurance. Far better that we all go.' She spoke reasonably, although a frantic insistence fought the deliberate calm.

'You know that isn't true.'

'I know no such thing.'

'You deny the Balance? Look into your own life and see if that denial's true. You deny your own courage, and your own ability to choose. You ask me to believe that you're a coward, or worse, a youngster who denies the responsibility that I – no, that the One Himself has given you. You are more than those things, Duchess. I know, because I've seen them, I know because I would not love you as I do if all these things were true about you.'

A great sob burst from her throat. Cory thought that the agony of the sound was more than he could bear.

'It's so hard!' she cried. 'It's not fair. It isn't just! I can't. I won't, I tell you.' She knuckled forward onto the snow in grief, and Dancer groaned a little.

'Listen to me,' he whispered. 'There is nothing under heaven that is final. Nothing, do you hear me? What is sacrificed now, may be regained later.'

'It will never be the same,' said Duchess. 'Don't lie to me.'

'It will never be the same,' he said. 'But there will be love, pleasure, and happiness for you, Duchess. That cannot be destroyed. You will raise this colt. You will, by Equus' grace, have more. And you'll have the friendship of other mares, other stallions. There is no permanent loss for anything, especially for you, Breedmistress, unless you yourself choose to have it so.'

He nosed her to her feet. 'You asked me once about the Tests. This is the hardest one of all. Now, come. If you take a solemn oath not to interfere, you may walk with me to the eastern ridge. Do you swear?'

'I swear,' said Cory.

'And I,' said Duchess. 'If I must.'

The sun was rising. Spears of bloody light pierced the tree tops and an early morning mist boiled up from the westward path. The sunlight touched the white on the Dancer's quarters, turning the spots to crimson. The mare and collie followed with lowered heads, stumbling in the snow. The Dancer gained the eastern ridge and stood there, looking down.

217

It was worse than Cory had described it. The earth was churned and scalded from an unhealthy fire, and melted snow steamed in the blasted hollows. A faint howling of hounds harrying a prey was carried on the wind.

'Turn back to the cave, now, and stay with Susie,' said the Dancer. 'There will be no danger. The Balance will be restored.' He glanced sharply at Duchess and said to Cory, 'You will not interfere, no matter what. Guard her well, and ignore any sight or sound until it's over.'

'Will I know when it's finished?' asked the dog.

'You'll know.' The Dancer turned, his step high and springing, and picked his way down the ridge. The howling in the sky increased, as though hounds had drawn the scent.

Then, from around a blackened shoulder in the valley, came the forlorn and beaten shape of Pony.

4

Anor

'Pony!' said Cory.

Pony raised her head wearily and pawed at the blasted ground. She caught sight of the three figures on the hill crest and backed up a little. The unnatural lines that had disfigured her face were gone; in their place was a bewildered disgust.

The Dancer stood thoughtfully for a moment, indifferent to the rising howling and the black stink in the air that choked both Duchess and Cory.

Suddenly, the Dancer reared and screamed a challenge. The defiant cry echoed, and died. There was a sudden end to the howling, and to the wind.

He was answered by a slow, thick rumbling from the very bowels of the earth.

The ground began to split open under Pony's feet. She screamed and ran a little way up the hill toward Duchess and the Dancer. Cory growled and began to bark, filling the air with a volley that ricocheted between the hills and gullies.

The rumbling reached a crescendo. The ground shook. Pony squealed in panic, rolling a white-rimmed eye at the Dancer.

'Come, Pony,' he said. 'Join us. There is time.'

Pony whirled to face the widening split. A hot breeze struck Duchess' face; it carried the scent of Pony's fear, and a carrion sink of rotting meat.

The rumbling stopped. Before them a great rift had appeared in the blasted valley. A path lay in the center of the torn earth, pocked with holes filled with an oily liquid that smoked and smelled of blood.

From the depth of the path, Duchess saw two glowing pinpoints of yellow light. And then Scant appeared, his skull's head fixed in a grin. Behind him were Harrier Hounds, a parade of skull-headed figures with tails that trailed behind them, ratlike.

The Hounds lined each side of the path and sank to their haunches, rotten tongues lolling. Scant faced them briefly, then turned with a cringing eagerness. A cloud of August flies circled his skull's head, and he giggled.

The Dancer moved down the hill in a lengthy, ground-eating trot. Duchess forced herself to remain still, Cory at her side. Suddenly, she moved down the hill. Cory blocked her way. 'We promised not to *interfere*.'

'He said nothing about my watching over him,' she hissed. 'Let me pass!' Cory hesitated, then walked down the hill with her.

The Dancer halted a few yards from the tunnel entrance.

'Where is the dung whose Voice you claim, Scant?'

'He'sss coming. Sssoon,' crooned Scant. 'He hearss your call, spotted dung. He comesss.'

The Dancer reared and screamed his challenge.

'ANOR!'

The earth responded with a hollow, shifting groan. A trickle of steaming liquid bubbled at the tunnel mouth, snaking up from the clouds of earth. The trickle grew and became a turgid stream that puddled around the Dancer's feet.

'Duchess, Cory, get behind me,' said the Dancer. The water had a foul odor and Duchess, backing behind the stallion's hindquarters, raised her feet high to avoid its touch. Cory nosed it and leaped back with a yelp, his muzzle streaming blood. It swirled about the Dancer's feet, but wherever the liquid touched him, it turned clear.

220

'Not entirely hopeless, you see,' said the Dancer with a gleam of amusement. 'Pony, get behind me.'

Pony, a kind of hopeless muttering rising from her throat, backed up the hill and stood there.

The liquid steamed in the cold air. The trickling died away. Scant hissed.

And the earth began to tremble beneath their feet.

ONE!

A slow, dull booming sounded.

TWO!

There was a noise of an iron gate bursting.

THREE!

The Harrier Hounds cringed and whined. Scant whimpered with eagerness.

FOUR!

Anor came out of the earth.

Anor was the red of dried and crusted blood, of an unhealed wound. His hindquarters were chunky with muscle, and he moved stiff-legged, clumsy with power. A scar circled one coarse ear and trailed a spider-fine line to his jaw, peeling back a corner of his upper lip. Duchess saw, a hot weakness in her belly, her heart choked with fear, that Anor's teeth were fanged and dagger-shaped. This, more than the miasma of fear that he carried, more than the hot eyes of the Harrier Hounds, more than the peeled and scabbed earth itself, turned her bones to water.

Anor came up, out of the earth, and as he neared, the Hounds fell back, the flies buzzed frantically and fell. The Dark Lord's Executioner stopped and grunted.

'You sssee!' cowered Scant. 'My Masster hass sssent a message. Anor hasss come.'

'And so have I!' the Dancer cried. 'Equus! I face the Executioner, and I call upon the Rainbow!' The Dancer reared and screamed, and his challenge spiraled to the sky, a golden hammer that forced the Hounds against the earth. He began to glow with a splendid, many-colored light, a healing flood of crimson, blue and green. The colors were a wave that lifted the fear from Duchess' heart, and she raised her head with a joyous shout.

Scant turned his skull's head from the light and howled. Anor sprang forward, fanged mouth gaping, and a wave of bloody dark rose from his body, a terrible fountain of despair.

'No, no, no, no, no,' Scant whispered. 'You do not understand, ssspotted dung.' Both lights receded, dark and many-colored, and the Dancer's colors dimmed.

'We are *owed*, sssstallion. Because you forfeited your duty. And because of thissss.'

Scant crept nearer, his body writhing with a peculiar eagerness.

'Watch!' he said. 'You. Pony. Come here.'

Pony whimpered.

'Anor calls you. Come!'

Pony, her head outstretched, her steps dragging, stumbled nearer.

'You thought you'd descend with us, to challenge our Dark Lord himself, didn't you!' said Scant to the Dancer, as Pony neared. 'You thought you could enter our domain with all your powers intact. You thought, spotted dung, that we would open our gates to the enemy in force – all for the life of these?' He howled in laughter. Pony stumbled before the Pack Leader, whimpers coming from her throat.

'If you want the buckskin mare, her foal, the Shetland, the Paint, and yesss – that wretched dog to live, you must give up your powers as the Rainbow Horse!' hissed Scant. 'You will come to usss as what you are. A mortal stallion.' The Hound spat at Duchess. 'He may not get *that mare*, but we will have *you*. In chainsss. Hai!' he yelped.

Scant's Hounds leaped to their feet.

'Hai! Hai! Hai!'

The Hounds circled Pony, who seemed very small and helpless. They raised their skull's head to the skies and howled. 'Hai! Hai! Hai!'

'Ssshall we sssee how the Balance tips?' Scant cried.

'Ssshall we disscover how your crimess have been weighed? Call on your color now, Dancer! Asssk your gods! Call upon your rainbow power!'

The Dancer stood immobile, dark eyes turned inward. A faint soughing, a distant wind, came from the mountaintops. The wind blew stronger, wilder, sweeping down from the peaks, whipping the Dancer's mane and tail. It grew, a steady gale, and Duchess closed her eyes against the rising dust. The wind died, as suddenly as it had come, and she opened her eyes.

His colors were gone. His hindquarters were glossy black, white spots trailing his chest and barrel like ivy leaves in shadow. Pony screamed and began to run, first this way, then that. The Hounds chivvied her in a slow circle, straight to where Anor waited, mouth gaping wide. She fell with a hopeless, continuous crying. The Executioner reared, scarred belly exposed, fanged teeth glinting, and plunged his teeth into her hindquarters. He raised her up, blood staining his muzzle. He shook his head and Pony screamed, 'eeee,' like a mouse in a trap.

'Stop!' roared the Dancer. 'Let her go!'

'Then *kneel*!' hissed Scant.

Anor dropped Pony at his feet and placed one razor-sharp hoof at the soft spot beneath her jaw. The stallions faced each other. Pony lay without a whimper, her eyes squeezed shut. The Dancer surged forward. Anor pressed down, and a gout of blood rose from Pony's throat.

'Kneel!' hissed Scant.

'No, sir!' said Pony, weakly. She rolled one brown eye at the Dancer. 'You let him do what he's gonna do.'

Anor, jaws gaping, yellow eyes locked on the Dancer, pressed slowly down, and the blood turned to a steady stream.

'ON YOUR KNEES, DANCER!' The Dark Lord's voice came from everywhere and nowhere, from the oily sky, from the tunnel, from beneath the earth itself. 'KNEEL!' The voice dropped to a voracious eagerness that made Duchess' flesh creep. 'That buckskin mare is still in foal. Your own immortality is forfeit, now – but perhaps the foal's is not. You came here to fight, did you not? Your gods have abandoned you – yes? Remember that the Balance exists for me and mine, as well, Dancer – and kneel.'

Pony's blood was puddling on her chest, her flanks rose and fell with her rapid breathing. 'Don't do nothin',' she gasped. 'Don't believe him. He lies! He lies!'

The Dancer pawed the ground in frantic desperation.

Duchess' heart stopped.

The Dancer knelt. Slowly, carefully, first one knee, and then the other, finely sculptured head down, muzzle in the dirt.

'No,' screamed Duchess. 'No!' She plunged forward and Cory leaped in front of her, his furry shoulder knocking her aside.

'We swore!' he gasped. 'A sacred oath!'

Anor, with malign deliberation, removed his hooves from Pony's sides. He struck contemptuously at the Shetland, leaped over her and grabbed the base of the Dancer's neck.

Duchess felt the ground sway under her feet. The victory cry of the Hounds rose in the air. Pony's eyes blinked open. The sound of the Dancer's spent and helpless breathing filled Duchess' ears.

Anor dragged the Dancer toward the tunnel. Scant threw back his head and laughed; his pack howled in chorus. Cory snarled hopelessly, paws scrabbling in the earth.

Pony wobbled to her feet. Absurdly small against the giant stallions above her, she kicked at Anor, her hooves glancing off the Red's flanks. A black fire ran up her hindquarters and she clenched her teeth and tried to kick again. 'Run!' she shouted to the Dancer. 'I got him!'

Anor kicked out once, as if he were brushing away a fly. His right hind left a smoking, crescent-shaped wound in Pony's side. The Shetland hurtled through the air in a wide arc and landed at Duchess' feet.

Thunder rolled. Anor pulled the spotted stallion down into the tunnel's depths. The Dancer's eyes, kind, wise, filled with an infinite grief, swept over Duchess. The earth pulled together like a healing scar. The Hounds melted back to the darkness.

The tunnel slammed shut.

A desolate wind whistled across the empty valley, lifting Duchess' mane with icy fingers, stirring the collie's ruff. Pony gave a shuddering sigh. Duchess was numbed; she felt as though she had been dropped from a great height to a place with no landmarks to guide her home. Two tears slid down her cheeks and hung at the corners of her muzzle. They tasted of grimy salt.

'Come,' said Cory. 'We must leave now. There is nothing we can do.' The collie nosed Pony gently. 'Up with you,' he said. 'Susie and Duchess will lick those wounds clean. Duchess, follow the tip of my tail. One foot after the other. That's it. Up the hill, both of you. Up. Up.'

The collie urged them on. Duchess walked blindly forward, stumbling over the rocks and hollows in the snow. Pony trudged forward, teeth clenched against the pain.

They made their stumbling way across the ridge, down the other side, and when they finally reached the clearing and the cave, Susie was on her feet to welcome them, the midday sun glancing off her gaunt sides.

5

Anor Redux

Duchess didn't speak at all for two days and nights.

Pony healed rapidly, with both Cory and Susie attending to the cuts and slashes.

'I don't think that one mark is going to heal well at all,' Susie said, on the evening of Duchess' second day of silence. 'The hoof-shaped one. And if it does heal, it's going to leave an awful scar.'

Pony peered at her flank and shook herself.

Cory sighed heavily and settled onto the cave floor with a thump. 'You're both coming along well, though,' he said. 'And that's a relief. Your cough has really cleared up, Susie. You're getting stronger every day.'

'Yes,' said Susie. 'I'll be out and grazing with Pony and Duchess in no time.' She glanced at the buckskin mare standing motionless, head hanging, in the far corner of the cave. 'She hasn't said anythin' yet?' she whispered.

Cory shook his head.

'Maybe she'll talk to me,' said Pony. 'I thought she'd want to kill me after what I did, but she ignores me. Pretends I'm not there. That's almost worse.' Then, humbly, 'You aren't so mad at me, are you?'

Susie looked away from the Shetland, into the clearing. It must be late February, she thought, the way they reckon time at Bishop Farm. The snow was melting some, and the nights weren't so cold.

'Why did you do it?' said Susie. 'Was it because we

226

didn't treat you well, like? Or maybe you didn't know what was happening 'til it was too late.'

'I knew,' said Pony roughly. 'There isn't much of an excuse for me.'

'And now he's gone. The Dancer's gone,' said Susie. As if she had been waiting for a spoken confirmation, Duchess raised her head and repeated, 'He's gone. Oh, Equus. He's gone. And what shall I do now?' Moving as though she carried a great weight, she went out to the clearing and apathetically began to graze.

Late winter moved slowly on, and they lived on what forage they could find. Pony's crescent-shaped wound finally closed, leaving a jagged scar that must have pained her in the cold and damp. She didn't complain, and in fact, was subdued much of the time, moving nervously out of the way for the others when a patch of grass was found under the snow, automatically taking the last place in line when they went to the stream for a drink. Pony seemed to walk in shadows, waking the others at night with muttered dreams, jumping at sudden sounds. She had a haunted look, and she would stand for hours gazing at the sickle scar on her hip.

Duchess, recovering slowly from her loss, thought dimly now and again that the issue of Pony's loyalty must be settled at a Herd Meeting. But grass had no taste, and water didn't slake her thirst, and nothing much seemed to matter anymore except the birth of the foals in the spring. She clung to that with desperation. He'd called her Breedmistress. Perhaps, through them, there was hope for her line.

'There's only the three of us,' she said to Susie once. 'I will have to judge, and Pony's the one on trial, and that just leaves you, Susie, to vote about what should be done.'

'There's Cory, too,' said Susie practically. 'He took the Oath, remember?'

'You're right. So he did. But nothing seems to matter

227

now. Not even what Pony did. And I, all I want is to be with the Dancer. Pony can rot or run free for all I care.'

'He wouldn't have liked that at all, Duchess,' said Susie. 'You're still Lead Mare, and Pony's crime has got to be settled one way or the other. There are the Laws to be thought of. And it isn't fair to her.'

So that afternoon, with the promise of a late winter storm in the air, Duchess convened a Herd Meeting. Pony, who seemed relieved, stood in front of Duchess, Susie, and the willing, although confused, Cory.

'Just follow along,' said Susie in response to Cory's question about protocol. Duchess stamped her feet, and Susie squared up, head tucked in, four feet aligned, tail slightly plumed. After a moment, Cory assumed the same position.

'Pony,' said Duchess, 'you are charged with endangering the herd, and with contributing to the . . .' she choked, '. . . the disappearance of the herd stallion. This is a serious charge – a charge that can result in expulsion from the herd – which, in these mountains, is a death sentence – or in the Silence. If we invoke the Silence, you will be here and not here, never to be spoken to by any member of the herd. Ignored, and none will move to protect you if such protection is needed. Do you have a response to this charge of treachery?'

'Yes,' said Pony, firmly. 'I did it. I did what you said.'

'How did it start, Pony?' said Susie. 'Can you tell us?'

Pony, head down, looked up at them through the fringe of her creamy forelock. 'From the beginning?'

'From the beginning,' said Susie.

'I was walking in the woods one afternoon, trying to find some good grass. It was some time after Cory came, and told you about the . . . about the circus.'

'Pony ride,' said Duchess.

'Yeah, that. Anyway, the snows had come, and we weren't getting enough to eat. And this hound showed up, see? That Scant, only he didn't look like he did that day when the Dan . . . when he went away. He looked

228

like a dog. "Green grass," he said. "You look a little thin to me. I know where you can find green grass just for you, and not for anyone else. Green and thick and sweet, it is," he said.'

'Sure!' I said back.

'So he took me down to that place where It came out of the ground. But that was later. This place was great, then. Like spring. I ate and ate some more. I haven't been that full since I was little. It was good. And this Scant said, "Eat all you want, ma'am." See, he called me ma'am, like I was a show horse or something. "And there's more where that comes from," he said. So I ate, and next day, I went back and ate some more, and there wasn't any! So I waited around, wondering, and pretty soon this Scant comes crawling out of the bushes. "Well, ma'am," he said, "There'll be grass tomorrow, all you can eat. We just want you to do one little thing for us. Just one."

'Who's we?' I asked.

'My Master,' he said, hissin', like. 'Just this one thing, then there will be grass, and even better things. Oats, sugar.'

Pony ducked her head and stared at the ground.

'You can be Lead Mare, too,' he said. 'Tell the others what to do. You'd like that, wouldn't you?'

'Sure!' I said. 'But what's this one little thing you want me to do?'

'He wriggled along the ground like a snake. "Bring me to *him*," he says, and I know right away what he means by "him". It's the Dancer, see. "My master must be brought to him by one of his own," said Scant.

'I start to say, No. You never treated me very well, but *he* always did. No, I said, forget it. Beat it, dog. He wriggled again, and as he's wriggling, the grass is growing up behind him, right out of the snow. And I took a mouthful, sort of absentminded, and it's good.'

'Lead Mare,' said the Hound. 'And you'll be close in your stallion's regard. For he wants this, too. He has been

229

seeking this, too. Haven't you seen how he watches and waits? Haven't you seen how he searches every day? He wants to see my Master as much as my Master needs to see him. And if you do this, think, why, you'll be close in my Master's regard, too. Chief among my Master's mares. Just take me to *him* and all this can be yours.'

'"What does this Master of yours want?" I said, eatin' and oh, that grass was good, the best I ever ate.'

'My Master wants to talk, that's all. Just talk.'

'So I think about it, and all the while I'm eating that grass and remembering that you really didn't believe me about the circus, and maybe things would be different if I was Lead Mare, and I showed you this grass and you'd all say, you know, "Good work, Pony," and "We're glad you're Lead Mare; we should have done it before."

'Okay,' I said. 'I'll do it. But only if everyone gets this grass, and I'm Lead Mare.'

'Agreed!' said the Hound. 'And I will call my Master.'

'And the ground opened up, and It came out. I knew right away nothing would ever be the same again. I knew I should run, but I couldn't. It looked at me, and It got inside of me, and sleeping and waking I saw It and I couldn't see or hear anything except what It was saying to me, showing to me.

'So I brought It to the cave that night. You remember, It was with me and I thought, now I've shown you, go away, things will be better now. Go away. Go away. And It went. But when It did, It took the Dancer with It.'

Pony huddled within herself.

'Poor Pony,' said Susie. 'But at the end, you were very brave. Cory told me all about it.'

'I would have killed It if I could,' said Pony passionately. 'I tried, but It hit me like I was no more than a fly.'

'The Dancer said,' said Duchess. 'He said, "Poor Pony. Look in her eyes and see that she is to be pitied."' Her tone was dull, indifferent.

'So what are you going to do?' asked Pony. 'I'm ready. You do what you have to. I did it.'

'Can we, any of us, say that we would not have listened to such a voice, such a power?' said Cory soberly. 'The Dark Lord would have offered what each of us most wanted in our deepest hearts. Would any of us have been strong enough to resist?'

Cory looked at Duchess. The buckskin's eyes were sunken, and there were gaunt hollows behind her withers.

'Perhaps not,' said Duchess. 'I know what the Dancer would have asked me to do, and I'll do it.'

Pony braced herself, her head up.

'OK. I'm ready. What're you going to do?'

'Nothing,' said Duchess. A brief glow of anger flared in her eyes. 'If it were up to me alone,' she hissed suddenly, 'I might kill you myself. I might . . .' She struggled with herself, then said in a composed and lifeless tone, 'But it's not just me, alone here. It's Susie, Cory, and the foals. So I am going to do nothing.'

'Nothing?' said Susie. 'No punishment? I like that, Duchess. I think Pony's punishing herself, and that we don't have to do it for her.'

'Nothing?' said Pony. 'But . . .'

'Nothing,' said Duchess. 'And I hope – from a purely personal standpoint, you understand – that you rot in the Final Death.'

The buckskin turned and walked into the cave. Pony groaned with relief or despair, it was hard for the others to tell.

'Well,' sighed Susie. 'We're all together again, except for the Dancer. Maybe there'll be no more trouble now.'

'We should get back into the herd routine,' agreed Cory. 'As a matter of fact, it's time for evening graze. Do you think you can make it past the stream today, Suze? We're going to have to go farther and farther afield now.'

'Oh, yes, I can go wherever the herd goes now.'

Cory looked at her a little doubtfully. Her ribs sprang out from her flanks, and the swell of her pregnant belly was pathetically unwieldy on her shrunken frame.

'We ought to think about moving to that new cave – the

231

one by the waterfall,' said Cory. 'The forage was good there and it's bigger.'

So Cory, Duchess, Susie, and Pony began the walk to the new cave by the waterfall.

By the time they reached their new home, Susie was gasping for breath in deep, hoarse coughs. Cory checked the cave thoroughly before allowing the mares to enter; then Susie stumbled in and fell heavily asleep.

The evening graze was late, and by the time Pony and Duchess had finished, the wind was up, and snow was on the way. As Cory urged Duchess inside the cave, he cast Pony a significant look.

Duchess stumbled into the cave and stood over the sleeping Susie. 'She's better,' she said, dully.

'Yes,' said Cory, simply. 'The bargain's been kept. Pony and I are going outside for a moment, Duchess. Will you be all right?'

She didn't answer, but stood over Susie, her eyes tragic.

'Why should we go outside?' asked Pony, reasonably. 'It's cold out there, wind's coming up.'

'I want to check the water supply,' said Cory, giving her a warning nudge with his paw.

'The water supply?' said Pony. 'Break some ice up or something? Oh! The *water* supply.' The wind gusted as they stepped out of the cave, snapping the barren treetops like whips. 'What's up?'

'I think we should stand guard duty. I smell wolves.'

'So, tell Duchess. She's Lead Mare.'

'I'm telling you. Duchess has had just about all she can take.'

'Duchess? She's as tough as they come. Besides, what could wolves pull anyhow? Against three horses and a dog.'

'Susie's in pretty bad shape. And when meat-eaters are hungry . . .'

'Maybe you're right. I guess we can protect the entrance to the cave. There's no other way in.'

'That's what I was thinking. Duchess isn't in any shape

to pull guard duty. I thought perhaps you and I could take turns keeping an eye out.' The dog hesitated, his eyes resting briefly on the sickle-shaped scar disfiguring Pony's hip. 'I can count on you, can't I?'

Pony followed his gaze, said nothing for a short while, then spoke with difficulty, looking over the dog's shoulder as if to avoid his steady gaze.

'I'm sorry that that stuff with It happened. I've always had a pretty strange idea of what herd life is like. My dam died when I was born – at least, I don't remember her at all. I do recall being fed with a bottle by a little girl. I was at my home farm for a good while, you know, maybe five seasons. I'm not too sure. It was a good place, a ways from here, where the winters were mostly warm. I didn't see snow until I moved with the circus – I mean the pony ride.'

'How did that happen?'

'Got sold.' Pony's tone was a little too careless. 'She got too big for me, or something.' She paused, then said, low-voiced, 'I didn't like moving much.'

'What was your new farm like?'

'It wasn't a *farm*,' said Pony. 'It was that – you know.'

Cory began to say 'circus,' thought of Pony's new honesty, and said casually, 'Pony ride.'

'Yeah. Pony ride. You know what those are don't you? I guess Duchess filled you in. You're tied to this big wheel, and little kids get on your back and you go around and around. Every day, just like the one before, only sometimes it was better, and the ride was in the shade, and sometimes it wasn't and the sun was real hot. Sometimes the man that ran it would let big kids, adults, get on, and we'd get smacked around if we bucked because they were too heavy. I kicked and bucked a lot, you bet. It wasn't a bad life, though. We saw a lot of places. We were on the move in a great big truck all the time. There were usually about six of us, although most of the ponies got traded off, or got sent to, well – never mind – or got old. You had to be pretty good with your hooves to get

233

your share of hay. And if you looked like this on the ride,' Pony hunched over, her eyes half-closed, head drooping, belly sagging, 'some of the kids wouldn't get on you because they felt sorry for you. I could go a whole morning doing that. And the nights we didn't work weren't too bad. Some places we stayed would have a pasture to be turned out in, and we'd get to run around a bit. That's where the Dancer found me, as a matter of fact.

'Sometimes they'd turn us out with the circus horses, if we worked the Big Top, with a circus that was, say, in town for a while. Those circus horses were big! And shiny! I remember one called Legs. Huge Thoroughbred who did dressage work – you know, fancy steps in the ring – and people used to come around and watch him eating, just *eating*, because he was such a star.'

'Did you have any stable mates?' asked Cory.

'Who needs 'em?'

'So you were never really part of a herd – until now, that is.'

'So what?' demanded Pony. 'I was a lot better off on my own. Say – did I ever tell you that Story of how Ponies came into the world?'

Cory cocked a quizzical eye at Pony. 'Susie told me the Story,' he admitted. 'Is it a true Tale?'

'Well, maybe it was a made-up Story.'

'I think it's very clever,' said Cory.

'You do?'

'I do. It takes a very clever brain to make up a Story. Susie was quite impressed.'

'Ah. She's a good old sort, is Susie.'

'Yes. Why don't you check on her, and then get some sleep. I'll take the first shift of guard duty.'

'Oh, I'll stay awake and watch. You can depend on me. You sleep right next to her. It'll keep her warm.'

If Cory had any doubts about Pony's loyalty, he kept them to himself, but he made a point of waking periodically through the night, only to see Pony, her sturdy form bulked against the cave's entrance, ears up, and to Cory's anxious eye, alert.

At that time of night when the moon is down and the sun is not yet rising, Cory lay curled in a snug ball at Susie's back, and Duchess had fallen to sleep. Susie slept deeply, the rattle in her throat gone, the fever down, a healing sleep.

Pony, humming under her breath to keep herself awake, stopped humming abruptly. Two pinpoints of orange light flickered at the back of the cave, hovering in mid-air. Pony peered into the darkness. The orange pinpoints were joined by two more. Pony caught a familiar lupine smell. Two wolves crept into the cave.

"Ware!' she shouted. ''Ware!' The animals snapped awake. Pony half-reared and shouted, 'Everybody out!' The big dog growled and leaped over the recumbent Paint. Susie fumbled halfway to her feet and dropped back.

'Get out!' shouted Cory. 'I need room to fight!'

Pony and Duchess fled into the deadly winter cold. The wind racketed in the trees with an intensity that whipped the snow like sheets of solid water. The battle in the cave raged, the collie's growls and snarls mingled with wolfish howls. A grey body came hurtling from the cave, Cory racing after it. Pony backed around for a kick that landed in the wolf's ribs with a solid 'whack.' Cory skidded to a halt. The wolf ran limping for the trees. The collie's white ruff was bloodstained, his right jowl gouged and scratched. But he was on all four legs, and from the little the mares could see in the dim light, he had no major wounds.

'Where's the other one?' asked Pony.

'Back through the ledge,' Cory gasped. 'There's a tunnel there. That's how they got through.' The dog grinned, his white teeth smeared with blood. 'Easy food storage. Like a hay barn.'

'Hilarious,' said Pony. 'Look, we have to get outa here.'

'You're right. What about the Dancer's cave, the one that was too small. Do you think Susie can make it?'

Pony shook her head doubtfully. 'The wind's coming up again something fierce.' Cory and Pony beat their way into the cave with an effort, past Duchess standing dazed at the entrance.

'Can Susie move at all?' Cory asked her.

'How did they get in?' She glared at Pony. 'I suppose you fell asleep, damn you. Or did you invite them in?'

'Hold up!' Cory's tone was sharp. 'Pony didn't have anything to do with this. They got in through a tunnel at the back of the cave.' He led Duchess to the ledge. Susie sat with her head up and her forelegs knuckled under her chest. 'Wolves,' she said. 'I thought I heard wolves.' She was shivering like the branches of the trees in the wind. 'Did I have a bad dream, Pony?'

'Ask Herself, the High and Mighty Duchess,' said Pony bitterly.

Duchess carefully examined the tunnel entrance. 'I was wrong, wrong,' she muttered. 'I apologize.'

'Well – thanks,' drawled Pony.

Duchess blinked at her. 'What should we do, Cory? I'm so tired, I can't think straight.'

The collie glanced significantly at Susie, slumped in exhaustion. 'Yes. I know.'

Duchess was silent, then said, 'Let's wait here until the wind dies down. Give Susie a chance to get some strength back. Then . . .'

'We move to the Dancer's cave,' said the dog.

'Yes. That is, what do you think, Pony?'

'I should have a say in this? Me, the Prime Sneak?'

'I said I was sorry,' said Duchess, humbly. 'Please forgive me, Pony.'

'Pony,' said Cory, with the barest wink at Duchess, 'just about saved our lives, as far as I can tell. Gave the alarm as the wolves crept into the cave with murder in their hearts. I myself saw her kick the great, grey wolf squarely in the ribs. She may have cracked two ribs, possibly three. Certainly one, and that right over the heart. It was one of the bravest things I've ever seen anyone do, Horse or Dog.'

'It was wonderful,' said Duchess, promptly. 'You're a real star, Pony. Just like the mares in the legends.'

'Like what mares?' said Pony, suspicious, but more than willing to listen.

'The greatest ones. Alindar, for example,' said Duchess. 'I'm deadly serious, Pony, you saved our lives, mine and Susie's. She's much too weak to fight. They must have thought we would run away and leave her.'

'You mean mares like Afreet, or Elador, too, I expect,' said Pony, carelessly. 'Those mares?'

'We do,' said Cory. 'Without a doubt.'

'Well!' Pony arched her neck and threw her chest out a little. 'Ah. As far as the plan to get to the Dancer's cave goes, I think it's a good idea. But we ought to wait 'til the storm's over. I'll stand guard.'

'No,' said Duchess, gently. 'You deserve some sleep, Pony. Cory and I will stand watch. Truly. You settle down in the corner. Let's move Susie over by you, so you can protect her in her sleep.'

'Good idea,' said Cory. 'The farther away she is from that tunnel, the better off we'll all be.'

Duchess nudged Susie away from the ledge. Pony settled at the entrance, where wind-whipped snow quickly powdered her fuzzy coat. Cory sat facing the tunnel, Duchess towering above him.

All through the rest of that long night, with the wind howling, the two kept their eyes steadily on the dark mouth of the tunnel. Once, Duchess thought she saw the glow of a wolf's yellow eye, but Cory growled a warning and the glow disappeared.

The wind dropped as morning came, and when they stumbled into daylight it was to a world piled high with cold, wet snow. The deep sleep seemed to have done Susie good, and she joined the others in their search for grass with a semblance of her former cheerfulness. 'That hot feeling's gone,' she informed the others. 'And that cough just isn't there. For a while there, Duchess, I could tell it was just sitting there, at the bottom of my throat. Just waiting, like.'

Duchess nibbled gently at her ears. 'You'll still too thin. Try and eat. There's a patch of grass here, where these branches are piled up.'

Susie grazed for a while, then stopped and stood with her head down. 'He's gone, isn't he?'

'Yes,' said Duchess. 'He is. When I think of him now, it's with the feeling that he's very far away.'

Susie raised her head, and the grief in her eyes shocked Duchess. 'Is he dead?'

'I don't know. I think so. I hope not.'

'It's my fault,' said Susie. 'I was willing to go. I should have gone.'

'It wouldn't have worked that way. I wanted to go, too, you know. At least, I wanted to want to go. I would have been terribly afraid. And he knew that.'

'I know what you mean. I did and I didn't.'

The two mares shared a moment of silence. 'But he couldn't have wanted to go, either,' said Susie. 'What made it different for him?'

'I think he tipped the Balance, somehow, to let It and Scant out. He brought us here, and it was a great wrong. A terrible wrong for him to do this. Oh – I wanted to go. I would have gone anywhere with him. Even to a Final Death, if it would have helped, if he'd led me.'

Susie blinked. 'I see, a little. Is he in Summer, do you suppose? Not there, in the Black Barns, not with . . . Him.'

Duchess shuddered. 'The Twisted Horn? No. I won't believe that. I can't believe that. He must have gotten free. There is a Balance, Susie. And maybe, somewhere, he's alive and well. You're better, aren't you? That was the bargain, that he should leave us and we all survive. We have to have faith in the Balance.'

238

'The bargain. The bargain was for death,' said Susie. But Duchess shook her head in denial.

'How are you doing?' Cory, emerging from the stand of pines, and back from his morning hunt, made his way to Susie and Duchess, and sat at their feet, licking his paws free of snow. Pony, pawing irritably at a recalcitrant branch nearby, whinnied briefly in greeting and returned to her digging.

'I feel excellent this morning,' said Susie, firmly.

'Good. Look. I think we're standing in all the sunshine we're ever likely to get today. And it's too dangerous to hang around here long. Let's go back to the Dancer's cave while the weather holds. That is, if you ladies have had enough to eat.'

'I don't think we'll ever get enough to eat,' said Pony. She shook a leaf off her upper lip, watched it drift to the ground, and ate it.

'I'm ready,' said Duchess. 'Susie?'

'I'm ready, too. The wolves can't get in *this* cave, can they, Cory?'

'We'll check it out very carefully,' he promised. 'Come now. We'll take it slowly and eat along the way.'

The way was slippery, the snow light and powdery due to the cold, and the mares lost their footing more than once.

They stopped twice to eat, finding scant forage under the deep winter cover. By the time they reached the tall pine, the sun was going down in a pale imitation of its summer splendor.

'Here we are!' Pony said in relief. 'I see the entrance, behind that drift.' The mares broke into a chancy trot, slipping occasionally on hidden rocks.

Cory stopped, stiff-legged, the hair on his neck raised and bristling.

'What is it?' asked Duchess.

'A smell. Funny, I don't know what kind of smell.'

'A good smell, or a bad smell?' Susie asked.

'Just a smell. Like a henhouse with rotten eggs.'

239

'Chickens?' asked Susie. 'What would chickens be doing here?'

'Is it safe?' asked Duchess.

Cory circled the small clearing in front of the cave. He pawed rapidly at the mound in the snow, then backed off, a growl in his throat.

'What is it?' said Duchess. 'Let me see. Oh!'

The torn and raddled body of a vixen grinned up at them.

'It wasn't killed for food,' said Cory. 'It was just – killed.'

Duchess, trembling, sprang away from the corpse. 'Cover it up,' said Pony, sharply. 'Was it the wolves?'

'No. Even they kill only for food.' Cory walked around the bloodstained snow.

'What was it, then?' said Pony. 'What kills for no reason and just leaves it there? Even man takes the bodies away. Unless she was trapped. Was she trapped? Then why would she be so ripped up?' There was only one answer to this, and it was Susie who finally voiced it.

'Scant.'

'It couldn't be,' Duchess said. 'They're gone.'

'It's pretty old,' Cory agreed, gravely examining the body. 'It's possible this was done before the battle.'

'Do you know for certain?' asked Pony.

'Nothing's certain, Pony. But this isn't recent.'

'Is it safe to stay here, then?' asked Duchess. 'Pony, Susie, what do you think?'

'We should stand guard, at least,' said Pony.

'The Dancer wouldn't have let us stay here if there'd been any danger,' said Susie. 'If Cory thinks that thing is old, why, I'll bet this is just left over. Scary, but that's it.'

'I don't think he would have left us if we were all in danger, either,' said Duchess. 'I vote to stay.'

'Me, too,' said Susie.

'What else are we going to do?' asked Pony, practically.

The collie, who had been searching the clearing in ever-widening circles, came back to the mares. 'What scent there is, is old and fading. But Pony's right. We don't have much of an alternative, and we should be sure and keep a watch going at all times. We'll take turns – Pony, Duchess, and I.'

'Me, too,' Susie protested. 'I'm feeling much better, and it's part of my job as a herd member.'

'Very well, Susie, you too,' said Duchess. 'Now, let's find a place to break the ice in the stream, and then we should find what we can to eat.'

Dark came early, and the four settled into the cave after a mildly successful effort at finding food and water. The night was cold and clear, and the moon sailed high and white among the stars, flooding the sky with chill, silvery light.

'Do you remember that song, Susie, the one you sing to the foals about the moon?' asked Duchess.

'The-Horse-in-the-Moon,' said Susie. 'Oh, yes. I've always thought the Dancer was like the Horse-in-the-Moon, with his black and white colors.'

'And the way he would run in the dark,' agreed Duchess. 'Sure-footed and shining.'

'I never heard it,' said Pony. 'Sing it, Susie, will you?'

Cory, settled at the front of the cave with his eyes watchfully on the pines and boulders – familiar objects made misshapen by the dark – thumped his tail encouragingly. 'I've never heard it either. Try it.'

'I don't know if I remember it all,' said Susie, shyly. 'But I'll think of the Dancer, and that might bring it back to me.'

'Start from the beginning,' said Pony. 'Just like with the foals.'

'Well,' said Susie, 'I usually tell the babies a story before they sleep. Most times, it's one of the gentler ones – 'When Clover First Sprang in Summer's Meadow,' or 'Alinda's Foal Learns About Porcupines.' I save the 'Eight Immortals' and 'The Race of Enidor' for morning lessons, because they get all excited and want to play at being Silver Star or Enidor racing to save the herd from

241

the lion pride. But at night, one or the other of them will look up at the moon, and they'll ask, 'Why?' or 'What is it?' and then I sing the moon song, to tell them. It goes like this.' Susie cleared her throat and her voice rang out clear and sweet.

The-Horse-In-the-Moon

Joachim, the Silver, the Horse-in-the-Moon
Looked down from a nighttime sky
To a ribbon of dark that was river
With his Moon's unwinking eye.
'Come down!' The beech trees whispered
With a dried-leaf rattle and hiss.
'Come down,' they sang with a breezy snarl,
'Come down for a beech tree's kiss.'
Joachim, the Ageless, the Horse-in-the-Moon
Whose heart beat ardent with time
Looked past to the forest's dark secrets
Where his shadow lay pooled in the pines.
'Come dance,' the meat-eaters invited,
Hiding their hunger in song,
'Come dance in the forest among us,'
'We'll spin as we play to your song.'
Joachim, the Waxing, the Horse-in-the-Moon
Looked deep in the farmlands to see
Men with their whips and their bridles,
'We'll ride on your back – you'll be free.'
Joachim, the Waning, wise and aloof
Remained where he was in the sky.
Like a spider, slow spinning,
A web's end to beginning,
Watching the mortals pass by.

Susie sang the Moon song twice, and by the time the second round was finished both Duchess and Pony were asleep. 'That was a beautiful song,' said Cory. 'Both light and dark like the night itself. Pups wouldn't find that song very comforting, though.'

Susie snorted in amusement. 'Foals don't either, I guess. But it's tough, you know, bein' a horse in the world of men. Duchess isn't the only one who knows that.'

Cory looked at the Paint more thoughtfully. 'You've changed a little, Suze.'

'Have I? I suppose we all have, Cory.'

'Yes, I suppose we have.'

The sun was up when they went out on the morning search for food. Meeting later at the cave, Cory called them all together. 'I have something to say, and since an agreement among us all is necessary, we should discuss it. I think we should start back.'

'What!' exclaimed Duchess. 'Start back, where?'

'Bishop Farm,' said the collie. 'We have to start home sometime, and better now than later.'

'Absolutely not,' said Duchess. 'This is our home. The Dancer brought us here. And I'm not leaving. It's out of the question.'

'We can't stay here,' said Cory. 'I came after you in the first place to bring you home. That's where we all belong. We don't have a real home here in the wild. Look at us. We're all thin and scrawny. I look like a junkyard dog. My fur's so matted with burrs and dirt, they'll shave me like a poodle when I get back. And if you could see yourselves . . .'

'I don't know about me, but you all look pretty disgusting,' said Pony. 'Duchess is so grimy you can't tell what color she is. And Susie isn't a Paint anymore. She's one color and the color's mud.'

'Really?' Susie tried without success to look at her chest.

'The weather's much too chancy,' said Duchess, desperately. 'We'll wait until spring to talk about it.'

'We should talk now,' Cory said firmly, 'before we get too weak to travel. Now, there's two ways out of the

243

valley. I checked this morning, and the easy way, the way you and I came in, is blocked with drifts higher than the flagpole at home. The second way is slippery, dangerous, but we can get out if we take our time.'

'Why should we get out at all?' shouted Duchess. 'We have to stay here. What if . . .' She bucked in wordless rage.

'You think he's coming back!' said Pony, suddenly. 'You think the Dancer's still alive!'

'Shut up!' screamed Duchess.

'Is that true?' asked Cory. 'We all know in our hearts what happened.'

'My fault,' whispered Susie, like a leaf falling on a breeze. 'It was because of me.'

'No. No. No. No!' cried Duchess. And it was unclear whether she was denying the Dancer's death or Susie's words.

'No. No. No . . .' mocked an echo. Cory wheeled, snarling. 'No. No. No.' The pine trees rustled and the smell of dead and rotting flesh washed over the four like a fetid wave. 'Yes. Yes. Yesss.'

'Scant!' said Cory.

The Hound, thinner than ever, his yellow teeth stained and sharp, slunk to the edge of the clearing.

'Back for another thrashing?' challenged Cory. 'I'll kill you, this time.'

'I think not, Dog.'

'My hip!' sobbed Pony suddenly. 'Oh, Duchess. NO!'

Duchess turned wildly and saw that Anor's scar, faded to a jagged white line this past month, was glowing a furious red. And from the surrounding cliffs and stones, a dull, resounding thudding filled the sky, shook the trees, like a giant muffled drum. 'My Massster ssent uss,' hissed Scant. 'We've been waiting. Waiting.' He crouched on the ground and wriggled horribly in the snow. 'And now . . . *we're here*!'

Anor broke through the trees, his yellow eyes flaming,

244

his fanged mouth opened in a lifeless gape. The slow thudding of his hooves beat like a giant heart.

The mares stood frozen, and Susie's wheezing was the only sound that stirred the air.

Cory leaped at Scant and snapped with lucky ferocity at the Hound's foreleg. The bone snapped. Cory sprang back, whirled, and cried, 'Run! Follow me!' The collie dashed through the pines, and the mares ran after him.

'This way!' shouted Cory. 'We'll leave them in the twists and turns.' Fear made their feet effortless and even Susie raced along like a whirlwind. They scrambled over rocks, slipped over the frozen stream, and still Cory urged them on, circling now in front, now behind, to make sure they stayed together.

'Too ssslow!' Scant, his broken foreleg dangling, the white ends of the bones protruding through the skin, leaped at Pony from behind a boulder. Cory sprang at him a second time and the Hound's yellow eyetooth left a smoking wound in the collie's muscular shoulder. Anor's booming hooffalls sounded below and Pony screamed as the scar flamed on her hip. Cory's strangled snarls buried themselves in Scant's throat. At the drum-like pounding, he broke free.

'Up that way. To the cliff. Run! I'll hold them off!'

'We won't leave you,' said Duchess. She whirled and kicked. Scant howled dismally, his back broken, and scrabbled with his forepaws. Pony squealed and charged the Hound, and still Anor came, and the Hound grinned up at them through shattered teeth.

'My Masster calls you! We've come to bring you to Him!'

Cory and the mares turned and raced up the twisting path. The dog's pads held, but the mares slipped and slid.

'Susie's down!' shouted Pony. The Shetland stopped, stood over the fallen Paint, then turned and faced what was coming.

Scant crawled up the torturous path, and far below him, Anor came slowly, like a mindless rolling mountain.

'She's up! Pony, save yourself!' called Duchess. Susie struggled to her feet, and the mares resumed their frantic race in single file.

'The top. Just get to the top!' Cory cried. And they reached the top in a scramble of flying hooves and turned, all four, to look down the mountainside. The path they had followed was a mere toehold in the giant flanks of the mountain. Pony shook her head, catching her breath.

'How did we get up here?'

'How are *they* getting up?' asked Susie, her voice trembling. As shattered as Scant was, he was picking his slow, bloody way up the steep trail. And Anor followed.

'Wait.' Cory limped heavily to a fallen pine tree. Blood marked his once magnificent gold and white coat, and one tulip ear hung torn.

'If we can get this pine in the path, we'll block them. The other ways are snowed in. They'll be locked here until spring.'

He grabbed a protruding root and tugged. The tree shifted and a small cascade of snow rolled down the mountainside. 'PULL!' shrieked Duchess, and they grabbed roots between their teeth. The pine tree rocked, then wedged firmly between the rocks.

'We can't budge it!' said Pony, desperately.

'Try again,' said Duchess. 'It has to move. Try again.'

'Oh, Owl,' said Susie. 'Oh, Dancer. Help us.'

And it may have been that their senses, heightened through fear and desperation, felt the brush of a shadowy wing that wasn't there. And it may have been a trick of the pale sun, or the flicker of light on the crystal minerals in the granite wall, but it seemed to both mares and dog that time stopped for a breathless moment, that a bright and fearless glow touched the trunk of the fallen tree. The pine tree moved and fell with a crash, and an avalanche of rocks, snow and boulders gathered with the tree as it tumbled down the path. The snow rose high and powdery, shutting out the sun.

The way was blocked.

6

A Meeting in the Forest

Cory led them down the mountainside, navigating by sight and smell and the position of the sun in the sky. He was nimble over rocks and through gullies, and the mares followed the white tip of his tail with increasing difficulty.

'We'll have to stop awhile,' said Duchess. Susie was stumbling with fatigue. 'She's walking without thinking at all. Look at her. Do you think we're safe enough here? Have we gotten far enough away?'

Cory stopped and lay in the snow, his sides heaving. The mares stood with their heads down. Susie felt her way blindly to Duchess' side, and they rested without speaking until the darkening sky alerted them to oncoming night.

Too exhausted to look for more than basic shelter, they found a place out of the wind, behind the rocks and boulders littering the mountainside.

Pony and Susie slept almost instantly. Cory lay with his head on his forepaws, looking into the night. Finally, he spoke.

'We have to know why they came back,' he said. 'Something is very wrong.'

Duchess nodded dully. 'Yes. Something is very wrong.'

The dog rolled over onto his side with a grunt, then said, 'The Balance is the same for all who live by the grace of the One. The Dancer's . . .' He paused. 'The Dancer's act should have righted the Balance. Yes, he left

Bishop Farm and his task, to run away with you, and this was a crime of no small order . . .'

'It was not,' said Duchess. 'Don't say that.'

'Duchess, he abandoned his duty to his gods. Whether it was out of pride or whatever, it was still a grave injustice. And the Dark Lord did have a right to demand Pony's life, if not all of ours as well.'

Duchess, miserable, bent her head. The dog looked at her sympathetically. 'I'm sorry. These are hard words. But I'm lost, I don't know what to do next.'

He lay back with a thump and gazed up at the grave-gray night. 'I don't understand why Anor was let loose again. The Dancer's sacrifice should have kept Anor barred behind the Third Gate. I thought that that was part of the Agreement. And no matter how evil the Dark Lord is, he wouldn't be allowed to get away with a lie. The Owl would see to that, if the Dark Lord bargained in bad faith.'

Duchess stood absolutely still for a moment, then sprang to vivid life.

'He'd come back! The Dancer would come back to me!' She tensed, ready to bolt. 'We've got to go back there. He could have been anywhere in the mountains. He'd go back to the cave, I know he would.' Her eyes shining, her whole body eager, she made to move out into the night.

Cory jumped to his feet and blocked her way.

'No, Duchess. I can't let you go back.'

She looked at him, and her expression reminded Cory briefly of the attacking wolves. 'You won't let me?' she said softly. 'Since when has a meat-eater your size been able to prevent a horse from any action at all?'

'You could trample me, I guess,' said Cory. 'And kick me. You could kill me if you wanted to, Duchess. But that's what you'd have to do to leave. I can't let you go back there. It's foolish. And I promised the Dancer to get you home to Bishop Farm.'

His voice softened, and a small keening sorrow under-lay the sternness of his words. 'You are carrying the last

248

of the Dancer's line, Duchess. You've never asked, and I often wondered why. But you've never wanted to know what your Tests were for. Why the Dancer chose you and not some other mare, more beautiful, such as El Arat. Tell me, why haven't you wanted to know?'

Duchess, breathing hard, stamped her right fore in despair.

'Look at what's happened to you in the past few months,' said Cory. 'You passed the Test of Courage in the show ring. You were elected Lead Mare by Susie and Pony . . . and yes, me, too, which means you passed the Test of Pride. There are two more, if you remember El Arat's words to you. Don't you want to know why these Tests are important? Do you want to know how important the foal you are carrying is to the Appaloosa line?'

Duchess shook her head. Grief made her muzzle seem gaunt in the half light. 'I just wanted to be with him,' she said. 'I don't want anything else. I don't want to be anything else. If I am being tested to replace the Breed-mistress, Cory, don't think I haven't recognized the signs. I'm not such a fool as that. I don't want to do it. I just wanted to live out my days with the Dancer. Bear the foals. And that's all. I don't want to be great. I don't want to live in the Courts. I'm afraid of it. I don't want anything more than I've got.'

Cory looked at the rock that barely sheltered them from the biting wind, then at the ice and snow beneath his feet, and chuckled. 'I can see that,' he said. 'I mean, this is ideal. This is what every dog dreams of after he's passed from the world of men. Ah, me.' He rubbed his muzzle wearily along his forepaws. 'Duchess, we can't give up now. We must get on with it, back to Bishop Farm.' He glanced at her sharply. 'Agreed?'

Duchess nosed Susie's flank. The Paint mare stirred and groaned a little in her sleep. She could feel the heaviness in her own belly from the foal.

'Agreed,' said Duchess. 'At least until we get off the mountain, to a place safer for them.'

'Good.' Cory got to his feet and stood in front of her. His expression was both sad and grim. Duchess swiveled her ears at him inquiringly.

'There's more?' she asked dully. 'Haven't we been through enough?'

'Canis knows we've been through enough,' said Cory. 'And yes, there's one thing more. I'm afraid it's important. We can't go too much farther without knowing why Anor and Scant are loose in the valley back there. I need to know why. And I need to be on the alert for whatever may be in front of us.'

Duchess shivered. She was frightened, and tired, and she didn't want to hear any more. 'Let's talk about it in the morning. Maybe we can send you ahead to do some scouting, while we wait here. As long as the grass doesn't run out too quickly.'

'No. There's no time. If we wait until tomorrow night, the moon will be past its height. It's full now, and I want you to find the Path to the Moon. There's a stream near here; I think it's part of that whole system of waterfalls that runs through the valley. That will have to do for water.'

'You've got the madness,' said Duchess flatly. 'I'm not a Dreamspeaker. I wouldn't know where to begin. I'm not even a Story-Teller. How could someone like me call on Jehanna to open the Path to the Moon?'

Cory cocked his head. 'Four Tests,' he said. 'The Test of Courage, the Test of Pride, the Test of Heart and the Test of Knowledge. I don't know when the Test of Heart is going to come around, but I can smell a rabbit trail under my nose. You've got to try. You have to pass the Test of Knowledge. I have to know what's happened.'

'You want me to stand in icy water, in the middle of the third month of the year, and try to walk the Path to the Moon,' said Duchess. 'After all we've been through?'

'You were scared, we all were,' said Cory. 'But it's not as though we've been starved or had no sleep for weeks on end, or you have stealsbreath. And Duchess,' he paused, and an expression came into his eyes, almost, Duchess would have said, of self-loathing, 'You may find out what's happened to the Dancer.'

She brought her head up. 'Yes,' she whispered. 'Yes. Very well, Cory. I'll try. Where's the stream?'

'Follow me. And quietly.'

'Wait.' Duchess nudged Pony awake. 'Quiet, Pony. Don't say anything. Just stand here and keep watch. Cory and I will be back soon.' She hesitated. 'If we don't come back, find your way home as best you can. Just follow the sun as it travels across the sky every day.'

'Where are you goin'?' Pony demanded.

'Never mind. Just do as I ask, please.'

'Can I come?' said Pony. Her shrewd little eyes took in Cory's wretched look of self-disgust and Duchess' air of excitement.

'Susie needs you,' said Duchess simply. 'And I do, Pony, here.'

'Oh, all right. Look, wherever it is you're going, be as careful as you can. Not that it's much,' she grumbled.

Cory picked his way down the slope of the mountain, Duchess right behind him. Soon, she heard the distinctive trickle of water through ice. She lifted her head eagerly to the sky. 'It's dark and cloudy,' she said. 'How do you know the moon is full?'

'Oh, I can tell by the way the light comes through the clouds. Here. The water's collected into a bit of a puddle.' He stopped and looked at her anxiously. 'How far do you have to be in?'

'I don't know. And I don't know what to say, either.'

'I was with El Arat once,' said Cory. 'She said Jehanna was to send her a dream that she had to hear, so we went down together to the duck pond. It seems a long time ago, now, but I remember what she said. She just called on the goddess mare to open the Path.'

'And then what happened?' said Duchess a little nervously.

The collie flattened his ears. 'I don't know. I closed my eyes.'

'Well, we're a pair, aren't we,' said Duchess tiredly. 'Come on.'

She walked forward until the icy waters stung her pasterns like the needles from the vet. Almost immediately, she became numb up to her hocks. She looked up at the sky. 'It's still clouded over.'

'Wait,' said the dog.

She waited, her feet and ankles getting colder, and then finally, strangely warm. She sighed and shifted her feet, looking down at the dark water. A brush of moonlight touched its surface. Both dog and mare looked up as the moon emerged through the chilly clouds. It had a shadowy quality to it, as though whatever made the light was tired or weak.

'O Jehanna,' said Duchess, feeling a little foolish. 'O Jehanna, goddess mare of our lord Equus. Dreamspeaker to the One Hundred and Five. Open the Path.'

Duchess became warm all over, as though she was standing in August sunlight. The moonlight brightened to a clear white glow, so that she no longer saw the wintery side of the mountain. A mist rose – perhaps it was from the warmth meeting the snow – and when her vision cleared, she was in a misty land, soft with green, swelling with the beginnings of flowers. It was a no-place – she didn't recognize the sky, the sun, or the very air she breathed. It was a place, she knew, without knowing how she knew, where the sun remained half-risen, where rain was hinted at, but never came. It was Summer, the place of Judgment.

Duchess walked forward in the meadow, the grass hock-high and sweet. She stood there, and with the wide-angle vision that the One had given to the horse, she saw the meadow in its wholeness. There were two gates at either end: one, a softly pulsing white, like the moon itself; the other, a scabby red that held something of Anor's color and despair.

252

A golden mare came out of the mist by the white and shining gate. She dipped her head to Duchess in greeting, and the buckskin trembled a little at the knees. Jehanna, Goddess Mare of the Courts of the Outermost West.

'Welcome, Breedmistress,' said Jehanna. Her voice was like a lark's song at Longlight.

Duchess was afraid her own whinny would sound like rusty hinges, so she whispered, 'Thank you.' Jehanna turned and the white gate opened before her.

'Come,' she said. And Duchess followed her into the Courts of the Outermost West.

On each side of the Courts were meadows of a soft and brilliant green. Small flowers of red, blue and white starred the grass, their colors of an intensity Duchess had never seen before.

Linden trees with straight white branches grew in a circular grove at one end of the longest meadow. Around it and through it was a serene, still river. The meadow grass ran straight to the clear water, where brightly colored fish darted among silver stones. Through the trees Duchess caught the flash of a brilliant chestnut hide.

'That is Miler, the Eighty-third,' said Jehanna in her soft voice. 'It is his Watch today.'

The way was smooth and level, as though she were walking in an arena made of the finest sand. Duchess glanced down at her hooves, and almost bolted at the way their scarred and chipped surface looked against the sand.

'They will grow back,' said Jehanna, without looking around. 'And they are scars of honor, Duchess. Don't be ashamed.'

They passed through the outer ring of linden trees, their cool shade a haven and a delight. The path wound around, twisting, and then they stood before the Watching Pool.

The mighty stallion standing Watch was the most beautiful Quarterhorse Duchess had ever seen. She glanced shyly at him once, and bent her head to the Path again.

Reflected at her feet was a gaunt and roughcoated buckskin mare. Startled, Duchess realized she was gazing at her own reflection, and that she looked as beaten, or worse, than she had looked in the scum-filled pond when she and Pride had been imprisoned in the shed. She squared up, raised her head, and looked Jehanna in the eye.

The Dreamspeaker's look gleamed gold, and she breathed out lightly, once, twice and once again, on Duchess' shoulder, the greeting of a Story-Teller to a Lead Mare.

'We must Watch,' said Jehanna simply. And she turned and breathed once on the water.

Duchess' reflection disappeared and she looked into the Vision in the Pool. She thought her heart would break. . . .

The Vision in the Pool

They dragged the Dancer into the earth, the tunnel walls around him pulsing like a great slow heart.

The Executioner was immensely strong. His teeth dug into the Dancer's neck like blacksmith's pincers, iron hard and hot.

The Hounds trailed their Pack Leader, wormlike tails leaving a faint oily sheen in the dirt.

The Dancer knew in his heart that he would never see the sky again, or hear the crow's sly call, or feel Duchess beneath him on a bright spring morning.

The tunnel ended in a dull red light. Anor drew the Dancer to the edge and the Hounds milled about the Dancer's flanks.

'Up! Up! Get Up!' said Scant. The Hound giggled and licked his lips. 'We don't like to wait for our evening feed, me and mine.'

The Dancer rolled to his side, splayed his forelegs into the muck and rose to all four feet. A Hound behind him

254

sank his teeth into his quarters, and he kicked out. The Hound howled and Anor turned with a snarl.

'You promised!' Scant shrilled. 'You swore a sssacred oath to my massster! Now, walk, walk, walk!'

Anor moved out of the tunnel into sullen light. The Dancer followed, head up, legs moving in an insolent dance. Behind him, Scant growled and kept his place.

They walked through the pastures of the Dark Barns. What grass grew there was sparse, unwilling. The rest was waste and shadow. Misshapen figures moved wormlike in the sands as they approached the First Gate. It was guarded by the skeletal remains of men mounted on horses with dull eyes and the pointed teeth of carnivores. The scent of the Dancer's wounds reached them as they passed, and the horses opened their mouths like blind birds seeking food.

Anor struck the First Gate once with an iron hoof, and it opened and swung wide.

They traveled on. The Second Gate circled a black and oily Pool. The grass that grew there was shot with yellow like an infected wound and blood-red flowers gaped beneath the rusted Gate. The Gate was open and Sycha stood there. Her eyes briefly met the Dancer's. The Dancer nodded in arrogant greeting, as if to a well-known competitor in the ring.

'Sssycha,' said Scant. 'A chance to redeem yourself.' He turned almost gaily to Dancer, 'She's in trouble at the moment. She thought *she* knew besst – better than my Massster. Now I,' his skinny chest swelled slightly, 'now I and Anor are the ones who'll please my Massster best. You watch how you walk this path, my girl, or you'll reap the Final Death. And *I* will become the Sssoultaker!'

The Hounds began to yowl, 'Hai! Hai! Hai!' and mill around Sycha's feet. She turned as the Dancer passed, and fell in behind him. 'You have a competitor, Sycha? You – who had no equal among mares, now scrabble for position with such as this?'

'I stand accused of *losing heart*,' said Sycha. 'Of failing

255

to pursue my duties with sufficient – ' she paused, ' – sufficient enthusiasm. They say I lack a true sense of the cause.' She glanced at him, sidelong. 'Could this be true, Dancer? Tell me what you think.'

He could feel her cool breath on his withers. She breathed out lightly, twice, as a mare will when she meets a favored stallion.

The Path twisted on. In the distance, the Third Gate appeared, set in an iron wall that filled the horizon, from sky's edge to edge. There was a darker fog behind the Gate. At first, the Dancer saw nothing but its tendrils, shot with yellow-green. Then the fog darkened, grew, and filled the Gate, and with a blow, the Gate swung open. The Hounds settled. Sycha came to a halt. Anor stood immobile. Only the Dancer moved, carelessly switching his tail, as if to rid himself of flies.

In the dense, unhealthy silence came the sound of a horse walking.

Click. The scrape of hoof on stone.

Click. The gait was easy, almost light.

Click.

The Dark Horse came out of the Gate.

The Voice that came from the darkness was calm, almost ordinary in its tones.

'The Rainbow Horse. At last.'

The Dancer stamped his right fore, idly.

'My herd has waited for you, Dancer. Even now they wait, and their hunger has grown fiercer for the waiting.'

'I am here,' said the Dancer courteously.

The silence grew. The dark cloud swelled, then receded.

'I had considered,' said the Voice. 'I had considered asking you if you might join us. It's a good life, Dancer. I offer you a vaster herd than you have ever had before. You would rule much more than mere spotted horses. You would be, could be, First in my regard. Not Second, as you are with the White Fool. I need little, if anything at all, for myself, you see. Just your willing soul. You would be First, called First by your subjects. I would ask little else of you except your allegiance, and perhaps, a foal or two of your loins. And you – you would rule as you never have before.'

The dense cloud shifted with the Dark Lord's breath. The Dancer saw the shape of a giant horse within the cloud – the mightiest, the largest, he had ever seen before. Its eyes glowed like banked coals.

'Sycha may not be here to welcome you. No. I may have another to take her place. A fine Soul-Taker – beautiful – who would please you. I have decided to turn Sycha over to Scant and his fellows for sport. She runs fast, do you not, my Sycha? But perhaps not fast enough. To escape the Final Death.'

The grey mare jerked a little, then subsided.

The Black Horse spoke again. 'The Black bargain Sycha made, so many seasons ago – it has not been kept. No. It has not been kept. Sycha wavers in her faith. My plans have not gone well. Your Duchess carries renewal of your line – and that was not in my plans at all. Far better, Dancer, to join your forces to mine, to abandon your colors and your breed. What use are they to you?

'The new Soul-Taker would welcome you as mate. She is a mare, of course, and we are in the middle of – shall we say – negotiations. The price is yet to be determined. And, of course, I have not yet given up on Sycha.' The fiery gaze burned through the clouds. 'What do you think, stallion?'

'You took advantage of Sycha in her grief,' said the Dancer harshly.

'Did I? Then I must be more careful in my next choice.'

The Dancer looked at the Hounds, at the scarred earth, at Anor's sharpened teeth, and snorted. The Voice paused, and dropped to a silken whisper.

'You know, your Lord Equus cares nothing for you or your kind. You yourself would not be here, except that you were abandoned by the Light. Left in the mountains to die as a mortal stallion, by your fellows. And all for

257

what? Because you wished to spend time with that buckskin mare and taste the pleasures of earth, free from the rule of men. Was that such a crime, Dancer? What did you do that was so wrong, after all?'

'I broke the Law,' said the Dancer mildly. 'I forsook my position as Second. My punishment is just. I am responsible for it.'

'Indeed. And for all your wish to be free from the Law – a desire to be commended, stallion – for that one wish, that buckskin mare of yours lies dying on a mountainside, the foal dying with her. Just waiting for Scant and his pack to find her and bring them here. For if you are outside the protection of your Laws, so is she, since she joined you in your folly.'

'Which will not happen,' said the Dancer. 'That is why I am here. And I am ready.'

'For the Final Death?' asked the Dark Lord, a terrible amusement in the Voice. 'Are you truly? When Sycha calls you,' the gaze turned fiercely on the grey mare, 'as she will, as SHE WILL, your soul becomes mine anyway, spotted horse. Give it to me now, of your own free will, and you shall live here, and perhaps, if you rule my Army well, out there, as well. You might even get that buckskin mare to agree to come with you.'

The Dancer lifted his head. The fetid stink of the Black Barns was in his muzzle, and he wanted to spit the smell from his throat. He said, 'I've moved too quickly in my life. Been too hasty. I have learned to wait and judge according to my Law. I will consider now, and then answer you.' He lifted his head and called out. 'I remember the Courts and the taste of the meadows there. I remember my Lord, his silver shining in battle.

'And I remember Duchess – the color of her coat like wild grasses at the end of autumn and the scent of her coal-black mane. I recall how she spun on the hillside on that first day out from Bishop Farm, singing "Featherlight."'

He turned, deliberately, so that his back was to the Gate.

He lifted his tail and staled in the Dark Lord's face.

The Dark Horse shrieked. The sky trembled.

'SYCHA! CALL HIM!'

But Sycha stood mute. She glanced at the Dancer out of her age-old eyes and shook her head a little. She seemed to speak to the Dancer alone, although Scant, Anor, and the Hounds all heard her clearly.

'I remember, too,' she said. 'And I would like to leave this place. Shall we walk together?'

'TAKE THEM!' screamed the Dark Horse. 'TAKE THEM!'

Anor, dull eyes glittering in anticipation of death, charged like a boulder rolling from a height.

Sycha whirled and kicked out at the Executioner. Her hooves slammed into Anor's jaw, and the red horse staggered. The Dancer leaped forward and shouldered the grey mare away from the gaping teeth. As he sprang, his coat came to vivid-colored light under the sullen sky and the Rainbow Horse shone brightly against the Dark Lord's Gate.

The Vision faded.

Duchess looked into the Pool, a great hope and fear in her heart.

Jehanna said, 'It is strange, is it not? We all know here that Sycha regretted the choice that she made, that long ago day by the river. I still miss her, although I shall not see her as Breedmistress again. I do not know if she has been redeemed.'

'But what's happened?' Duchess whispered. 'Where is the Dancer?'

Jehanna shook her head. 'I don't know. This is all we have been allowed to see. The Balance cannot exist without a Soul-Taker and the Black Horse is now owed. And this I know, that Sycha must be very soon replaced. But who – or what – will replace her must be a terrible loss for the Courts. Soon after what you have just

Watched occurred, Anor was let loose, and attacked you in the mountain. For how long he may run free, I don't know. What concessions were made to allow this, I cannot tell. I haven't seen the Owl, and of course, no one controls the Owl's Flight. But I do know that the times aren't good, and that the Balance must be restored.' The gold mare stepped close to Duchess. 'Return, Breedmistress, Dreamspeaker, to Bishop Farm. And wait for the Final Test.'

Duchess stared into the Pool, eyes straining for the Dancer.

'Breedmistress,' said Jehanna. 'Do you hear me?'

'I can't go back. I won't go back.' Duchess' voice was low, vibrant, and her lips drew away from her teeth. She raised her head suddenly, 'If he's on the mountain, in the woods or near the river – I'll find him. I won't go back to men, to their fences and their walls. I'll search until I find him, and we'll run. We'll run to a place where there are no Tests, no Laws, no evils to destroy me and mine.'

'It's your choice, Breedmistress – no one can force it.' Jehanna stepped nearer, and her muzzle brushed Duchess' poll. 'There is no such place. You know that in your heart. But it is your choice.' A sad, quiet smile wrinkled the corners of Jehanna's golden eyes. She blew out softly, once . . . twice . . .'

She was passing through warmth, such warmth as she loved in summer.

'Duchess.'

Who was it calling to her, just when she felt most comfortable? Jehanna would want to know . . .

'Duchess!' Cory's teeth grazed her ankle, and she jerked away. Winter greeted her with cold and dark.

'Well?' the dog said. 'Something must have happened. The light grew too bright for me to see. I closed my eyes for a moment, and the light went away. I was afraid your hocks would freeze in that water. Come out. We should keep moving as you dry off so you don't catch a sickness.

260

Come on.' He bumped her side with his head. 'Are you awake? Did you dream?'

'Yes,' said Duchess. 'I'll tell you on the way back to Susie and Pony. The most wonderful thing is this, Cory. I believe the Dancer's free, and that we can find him, somewhere in the woods.' Her eyes were shining with an unnatural glow. 'Not in these mountains, though. Farther down in the woods. He may be waiting for us there.'

The dog sighed, wisely kept silent, and padded after her as they returned to the others. After a look at Cory's grim expression and the light in Duchess' eyes, Pony asked no questions when they got back.

'How long do you think it'll be before we reach safety?' Duchess asked, as they set out again in the late morning.

Cory looked at the sky, and the trees bare from winter. 'I don't know. You can see that the grass is showing through the snow already, and the forage should get better as we go on down the mountain. It's hard to tell how close we are to spring up here, although from the time the sun comes up and goes down each day, I'd say a month, maybe more. And the weather has a lot to do with how fast we can travel. But don't worry, we'll make it.'

'Before the foals are born?' asked Duchess.

Cory looked at her, startled. 'Are *all* of you in foal? Pony, too? When will the foals come?'

'I'm not certain about Pony, but the two of us will foal just after Longlight, for sure.'

'Well, that's a good three months away,' Cory said, flatly. 'If Susie can keep up, we'll make it home far before that.'

'Or to the Dancer,' whispered Duchess.

'Mm,' said Cory. 'Come, now. Keep an eye on Susie, you two.'

As the journey wore on, they became less certain that Susie could keep up. The race up the mountainside seemed to have set her back; she swayed from fatigue when they stopped to rest, and although her cough didn't

261

come back, she spoke little, and Duchess had to urge her to eat.

Spring came hard to the mountains, but as they made their slow way down, the first pale-green tinge flushed through the snow and the forage improved. One morning, four days into the journey home, Cory approached Duchess again, a worried line between his eyes.

'We've got to find a safe place for a few days. There's another storm coming; I can smell it. This side of the mountain is exposed to the north.'

'What other way was there to get out?' asked Pony.

'None,' said Cory. 'But that doesn't help us now. What we need is a place away from the wind and the snow. Look at those clouds.' There was a flutter of fawn-colored movement in a nearby copse of trees. Cory suddenly turned his glance from the sky, and his ears pricked forward, giving him a slightly comical, puzzled look.

'What is it?' asked Duchess.

A stag stepped out from the trees and Cory charged forward, his barks splitting the air. The stag scraped one foreleg fiercely in the snow, and he snorted once, in challenge.

'Who does he think he is?' grumbled Pony. 'Hey, you – you think you own the land around here? We have as much right here as you do!'

The stag bellowed and lowered his head, sharp antlers aimed at the collie's chest. 'This is my territory,' rumbled the stag. 'You have no rights here. Get out!'

'We can understand him,' said Susie in astonishment. 'Why do you suppose that is? They're wild deer, aren't they?'

'Maybe they escaped from somewhere,' said Pony.

'I doubt it,' said Cory.

'There must be some explanation,' said Duchess.

Behind the stag, Duchess caught a glimpse of soft black noses and white tails.

'He has a doe back there, Cory,' whispered Duchess. 'Maybe we should go.'

Susie lifted her head and called out to the females behind the stag. 'Howdy! We feel a storm coming on. Do you think you could help us? Is there a safe place to stay, out of the wind and snow? We'd surely be grateful.'

The stag advanced, a threat. 'Out! You have a carrion eater, a meat-eater with you.'

'Quill. Wait.' The mares stood frozen with hope. A delicate, sloe-eyed doe with a gentle face picked her way around a pine tree. Her silvered muzzle and gaunt withers proclaimed her age, but her coat was smooth and healthy, and her eyes were bright.

'Hello,' she said. 'I'm Butternut. And this is our Lead Stag, Quill.' Cory wagged his tail briefly, without taking his eyes from the stag.

'Ma'am,' he said courteously. 'What Quill has said is true. I am a meat-eater. But I've travelled for nearly half a year with these mares . . . and they have been safe with me, as would your fawns and yearlings. We're not looking for anything but shelter, and perhaps a bit of grass or root for the mares.' He hesitated. 'Are you . . . free deer?'

Butternut wrinkled her eyes interrogatively. 'To what god do you give your allegiance?' Cory asked.

'Oh, why, the Great White Stag, of course.'

'And – excuse me if it seems impertinent – but you don't speak the language of the wild. Are you allied with men?'

'With the Willow Warden, yes.'

This name, or part of it, struck a vague recollection in Cory's memory of a vast place, wire-fenced, where food was placed out in the winter and animals allowed to roam free with no fear of traps.

He relaxed a little, and his plumey tail lowered.

'I promise that all we seek is a temporary refuge. We offer no challenge to your rights here. Could you show us the way to a thick stand of trees – or even a cave?'

Quill looked at Butternut and she dipped her head slightly.

263

'Very well,' said Quill. 'But one false move on your part . . .' and he lowered his antlers threateningly.

'Strange things have happened in our forest,' said Butternut, as she turned to show them the way. 'I am our herd's Dreamspeaker, and I'd like to ask you about it. But it can wait until you've found food and water.'

The deers' sure hoofsteps led them past the edge of the trees to a great forest. From the size and thickness of the pines, it must have been very old. The band of four came from a world of dizzying white and harsh wind into a green silence that shut out the noise and confusion of the storm. The trees were tall, and the branches of their beginning were far above the horses' heads. The snow had penetrated even this thick fortress, and it lay in piles that sparkled in the dim light.

'It's like a big green barn,' Susie whispered. Quill pawed the ground several times in a signal. Suddenly, the woods seemed alive with does and yearling fawns, and the twitter of their soft voices. A large doe, almost as large as Quill himself, stepped forward from their midst.

'Butternut has explained the circumstances of your arrival here,' she said. 'I'm Bayberry, Quill's mate, and Lead Doe.'

Duchess introduced her own band and said, 'And this is Cory, also a member of my herd.'

'A meat-eater?' Bayberry's ear twitched. 'There are strange things in the woods these days. How can this be?'

'We'll tell you later,' said Duchess. 'I don't mean to be rude, but if you could share some water and food we'd be grateful.'

'Oh, we've more than enough to eat. There are branches and buds of all sorts. Despite the fact that there is a storm outside, spring has come to this part of the mountain, at least.' She looked at Cory with distaste. 'What will he eat? Quill and Butternut have given their words . . .'

'I'll just leave you for a moment,' said Cory. 'I'll find early berries, grain. Tubers. I can exist on these things if

I have to. Better yet, if there are weasels in the woods . . .'

Bayberry's frown cleared.

'Actually, that would be a favor,' she admitted. 'The weasels have been known to attack our young ones. The water's here.' She led them to a small, rock-lined creek. 'And there are plenty of branches, although I guess you'd prefer grass. There's quite a bit of that. And when you're through, Butternut would like to see you.'

Presently, after they had eaten, Quill and Butternut appeared and stood gravely watching them.

'Where's the dog?' demanded the stag.

'Here!' Cory sat up. Joined by Duchess, Pony, and Susie, they faced the two deer.

'What is it that you wanted to ask us about?' asked Duchess.

'You are the Lead Doe?' asked Butternut.

'Yes . . . that is, I'm the Lead Mare.'

'Two or three suntimes ago, a strange light passed through the woods,' said the deers' Dreamspeaker. 'It was as though the moon had come down from the sky and walked among our pine trees. We were afraid. There was no noise, no sound of this thing's coming, and so most of our herd fled. We deer are meant to leap and run, you know, not to stand and fight.'

'Except for me,' said Quill.

'Except for you, dear Quill. Bayberry and I crept up on this thing. We smelled no danger; indeed, the smells and feelings from these things were almost as if we were in the presence of the Great White Stag. Almost, but not the same. In this light moved one such as you. A horse.'

'A spotted horse!' said Duchess. 'Yes!'

Butternut shook her head. 'No. A horse of many colors, like a rainbow, glinting in a waterfall. I hailed this thing . . .'

'That was brave,' remarked Cory.

'Thank you. I hailed this thing. Softly, you understand.'

'The Dancer,' said Susie joyfully. 'It must have been the Dancer.'

'Hush, let her go on,' said Pony.

'. . . and it turned and looked at me, so.' The doe gazed at the mares with a great sorrow in her eyes. I said, 'What can we do for you, shining one?'

'And what was the answer?' asked Cory.

'The Horse said, "Watch, and take care of my own when there is need." That was all.'

'Nothing else?' said Duchess. 'This shining one had no name?'

The doe shook her head.

'None that he told me. But my question is this. Are you a member of this horse's herd? You are so strange to see in the wild. We can tell that you are not truly one of us . . . your scent, the way you walk in the woods.' She looked at Cory. 'The fact that there is a meat-eater with you.' She said again, her eyes wondering, 'Are you of this shining one? Was this message for you?'

'It may have been,' said Cory, a wary eye on Duchess.

'Your Lead Mare's eyes shine with that same light,' observed the doe. 'Well. Whatever the answer is, we have fulfilled our obligation to this Horse-in-the-Moon. Now, although your company has been most interesting, we will have to ask you to leave our grounds in the morning. You will be rested, the storm over, and you can find your way to – wherever it is that you journey.'

'Very well.' Duchess inclined her head, and the deer, after one last look, melted into the brush.

Duchess looked deep into the woods, her eyes eager, her head up.

'He *did* pass this way. I can feel it.'

'Take it easy,' advised Cory. 'The storm may be dying down, but we have a long way to go yet, and none of us is in the best of shape to travel.'

By the morning the snow and high winds had gone, and the sun pushed through the clouds.

'It seems a little warmer,' said Susie doubtfully, as they

stood ready to leave the deers' haven. 'But not much. Do you think they might let us stay a little while more?'

'Come.' Quill appeared noiselessly before them, and Pony jumped in surprise. 'I will show you the way out.'

The stag turned, and the mares had to move quickly to keep up with him. When he got too far ahead he disappeared, his mottled back and light cream coat melting into the trees and leaves as though he were one with them.

'Here is a path,' said Quill, pointing with outthrust muzzle. 'My Dreamspeaker asked me to tell you that this trail will take you to the edge of the wood closest to the bottom of the mountain. There is a friend who lives at the end of the trail. One whom we seek when we are in need and our own cannot help us.'

'What kind of friend?' asked Pony, suspiciously.

'A friend to all. Not just to deer, but to any forest creature who is sick,' he glanced at Susie, 'or dying.'

'She's *not*!' said Duchess, furiously.

'His name is Willow Warden, and he can help such as you.' He moved quietly away, and Cory called, 'Wait! How long will it take to get there?'

'Five suntimes, perhaps. It depends on how well you travel . . . and what you meet.' And with that, Quill was gone.

The forest was thick. Lighter and more agile than the horses, the deer had made a trail that wound over rocks and boulders, skirted stream beds, and jumped over narrow chasms, shouldering through close-growing trees. On occasion, the trail disappeared altogether, and if it hadn't been for Cory's unerring nose, they would have been hopelessly lost.

They nibbled bark, and the new buds off branches, and when streams and ice-covered ponds eluded them, they ate snow to slake their thirst. Cory slipped off to hunt on his own, and the cry of a captured rabbit would reach the mares and make them shiver. But, as Pony philosophically pointed out, the collie had to survive, and if he couldn't leave them long enough to get completely out of their hearing, well, that was part of the Balance, too.

In a way, he was better off than the mares, and perhaps because food was plentiful for him, or because his thick coat protected him from the fatiguing chill, he was the first to find Willow Warden.

7

Willow Warden

The morning of the fifth day out from the deers' haven found Susie almost too weary to rise. Cory, who had gone ahead to scout the trail while Duchess and Pony tried to encourage Susie to eat the sparse grass, returned in a flash of gold and white excitement.

'It's a man!'

'What?' Duchess jerked her head up in alarm.

'In a little house. In the middle of the forest. Come on.' Cory dashed away, his barking rousing even the lethargic Susie. The mares surged after him. In a clearing in the midst of the thickly growing pines sat a small log house with a straw-thatched roof. A plume of woodsmoke rose thinly in the air.

'How do you know this is safe?' Duchess called to Cory.

'Look,' said Pony. A great willow tree stood in the center of a good-sized paddock filled with peeled branches and the trunks of small trees. In the paddock were a doe and a yearling fawn, and beside them, a pile of hay and branches. To the side of the house, in a series of open pens, were other wild animals – a fox, a snowshoe rabbit, a family of skunks, and a bear cub.

'Meat-eaters and grass-eaters together,' said Susie.

'Oats,' said Pony. 'I smell oats.'

Cory ran eagerly to the paddock with the willow tree.

'This is it! This is a safe place. And these deer are from the herd we tracked. This yearling has a broken leg and

269

his dam is with him. The man is called Willow Warden and he fixed the leg.'

'Is he a vet, like?' asked Susie, hopefully.

The door of the cabin opened up. Duchess turned to run.

'Hold on,' said Pony. Cory stood in the clearing, head up, ears cocked forward. The bearded man in the doorway bent down and slapped his knee. Cory took two forward steps, his tail wagging furiously.

'Let's run,' said Duchess.

'I can't,' said Susie, sadly, and Duchess, knowing this was true, turned her attention back to the clearing. The man was kneeling by Cory, rumpling the dog's ears, running his fingers through the collie's burred and tangled coat. Cory broke away and ran to the mares, who were half-concealed from Willow Warden's sight by the pines at the edge of the clearing.

'Come on,' he said, imperatively.

'What if he decides to keep us here?' asked Duchess. 'What if we decide we want to get back, and he won't let us go?'

'We'll get back to Bishop Farm. Trust me. But right now, this is what we all need. Help. We need the help, Duchess.'

'*I'm* going,' said Pony.

'Duchess, what are you going to do?' asked Susie. 'I'll do whatever you think is right. That's why you're Lead Mare. You have to make decisions for us if we can't decide ourselves. What are you going to do?'

'Go,' said Duchess. 'If we have to break up the band now – well, maybe it's the only way. I can't do it. I won't do it. You and Pony go. I'll wait here for you – if you need me, call. I'll be around. But I can't come with you. I remember Pride starving to death in that shed. I remember how they trapped the Dancer and tried to pen him in. All that we've suffered has been because of man. If they'd just leave us alone, we'd be fine, and free. Go on, go!'

270

'I don't think Cory would rein us wrong, Duchess.'

'Cory's a dog. It's different with them, Pony. Take Susie with you and get her the help she needs.'

'You won't leave us, Duchess, will you?' asked Susie. 'You'll stay in the woods. Maybe we can sneak you some of that hay. And when we're all better, when spring is really here, we can start back to Bishop Farm again.'

'I need time to think,' said Duchess. 'We left the valley so fast, I don't know what to do. You haven't seen what I've seen!' she said, suddenly desperate. 'The Dancer's here, somewhere in these woods! You heard the doe! I haven't actually *agreed* to go back to Bishop Farm with you! Maybe I should go back to the mountains.'

'And become one of Anor's herd?' said Pony, bluntly. 'Take it from me, Duchess. That's crazy talk. And don't think you could escape him – you can't. I know what I'm talking about.'

The little Shetland's tone was grim.

'It's death and destruction, Duchess. I know that you and Susie are carrying the Dancer's foals . . .'

'To be born in men's barns,' said Duchess. 'It's better to be free, no matter what the cost. I could hide from him. The valley's big enough.'

'You can't be serious,' said Pony, with chilling quiet. 'You've seen It – you can't imagine what It's like. I dream at night, you know. I never used to. But I dream at night, wondering just what kind of foal I'm carrying. Will I have the Dancer's foal or Its monster? And if you think you can hide from It, you're a fool – a criminal fool.'

'All right, then . . . but there must be somewhere else to go!' said Duchess, desperately. 'There are other horses that live in the wild. Other stallions, other herds. I can find them – and I won't have to give in to this.' She jerked her head at the little house and barn.

'If Anor wasn't after the foals when he came for us that last day – I don't know what else it was he wanted. I'm not stupid enough to think it was me,' Pony said quietly.

271

'I won't believe that. It can't be true,' said Duchess in an appalled whisper.

'You don't know like I do. Like I wish I didn't. But I've been thinking on this, while we were headed here. Trying to figure out what brought It out of the dark to get us. Other horses never even dream about these things. We're living 'em. Men can protect us from the dark. It's that simple. We don't have a choice – about Willow, or about Bishop Farm.'

'And even if we did,' said Susie, 'remember what the doe said. We don't belong in the wild. We're part of Man's world, like.'

'Go into the woods, then!' said Pony, suddenly angry. 'Hang around here, waiting for us, or go off and look for another set of horses crazy enough to live like we lived this winter. But I'm telling you, keep an eye on your backside, because Something is always gonna be around the corner waiting for you!'

'The Dancer may be here,' said Duchess softly, turning to the pines.

'All right. You want to think about that, we'll think about that. WHAT IF HE IS? You ever think about *that*? What if he is! What's he going to be like? What's your job now? To find the safest place to take care of the foal? Or to go off chasing magic horses? Go on – get caught up in things that aren't your business and weren't in the first place. What're you buckin' for – to be one of the Eight Immortals? *You*, Duchess, you're chasing in the wrong race. You're Lead Mare. You're due to foal. Susie, and you, and me, and that walkin' furball dog tried livin' in the wild and couldn't do it, through no fault of our own. So you got a choice. You go with what's right, and maybe harder, or you go into the woods, looking for trouble, because you're too selfish and thinking about what *you* want over what's good and what's needed.'

'Leave me alone.'

'All right. But Suze and I are stayin' right here until you decide one way or the other.'

272

'Oh no, you don't. Don't push, Pony. Go into that paddock. Leave me alone. I need to think.'

Susie shifted her feet, and Pony grumbled, 'Oh, damn.' Furtively, she and Susie stepped into the clearing.

The bearded man had been standing patiently in the circle in front of the log house. He headed straight for Susie as she came to him, running quiet fingers over her ears, pressing gently at her sides. Slipping a lead rope over the Paint mare's neck, he led her to the weathered shed that stood against the far side of the paddock. He placed a large pile of timothy in front of her and was almost knocked over by Pony's rush to join her.

'Saa, saa,' he said, and making a halter out of bailing twine, he pulled the reluctant Shetland away from the hay and put her into the paddock with the deer. He tossed a large bale of clover-alfalfa into the paddock, and Pony plunged her entire head into the center. Duchess could hear her chewing.

Willow continued to ignore Duchess. He propped the paddock gate open with a block of wood and returned to Susie, who was making slow but steady progress through the timothy.

Pony lifted her head and called, 'Come on, Duchess, there's enough here for all of us. And see? The gate's open, you can walk out any time.'

Cory, sitting patiently by Susie's feet, thumped his tail on the ground encouragingly. Willow paused, then disappeared into his little cabin, reappearing moments later with a large, steaming, wooden bowl which he placed before the collie.

'Stew!' said Cory, with a grateful bark.

Duchess was pulled two ways at once. The woods and the winter waited for her. She thought that the Dancer – still – could be somewhere, somehow. These things waited, and the freedom she had sacrificed so much to win. Pony's practical advice, despite the fact that it had been delivered at fever pitch, at the height of anger, made a peculiar kind of sense. But Duchess knew that something was missing. If she took Pony's view of things, where was the poetry in life? How could the Stories ever have been written, or horses inspired to do great things, if the path they followed was always the safe one? But what if Pony were right, and she was being selfish? Was she being arrogant and thinking only of herself and not of the herd? That had been Alamain's sin, she remembered, and perhaps the Dancer's sin, too. She swung her head to the trees as if an answer lay in their skeleton branches.

'Duchess!' shouted Pony. 'These deer are gonna eat your share!' Willow Warden, his back to Duchess, was patiently combing the burrs and tangles out of Susie's coat, treating the scratches and wounds on her legs and sides with yellow salve. How long had it been since any of them had felt the hand of man in kindness? For Pony, too long. For Duchess herself – she had met kindness at Bishop Farm, and had the Dancer not come with his promise of freedom, how would she have felt about man at this moment? How would she feel about men if she'd been at Bishop Farm all this long, despairing winter? A faint wind stirred, lifted Duchess' mane, and a whisper was carried to her, an echo, 'Go in. Rest.'

Duchess walked slowly through the paddock gate and joined Pony at the hay.

Late that night, together in the wooden shed, they agreed that it was wonderful. The wind whipped sharply outside the snug wooden walls; inside, they were warm and dry. There was fresh water, and hay in the long wooden troughs. Best of all, after months of snow and the harsh cave floor, was the sweet, yellow straw. They all looked better, although once they were combed, brushed and fed, their gauntness was even more apparent to each other.

'I didn't realize how itchy I was until I got brushed out,' said Pony contentedly.

'Do you think the deer are all right out there in the

open paddock?' asked Susie. 'They wouldn't come in with us. Do you think we took their place? Are they cold?'

'Have you ever met a wild animal who wouldn't rather spend the night outside?' asked Cory. 'The trees will shelter them and the straw is piled up so they're protected from the north wind. It's what they want.'

'Straw!' said Pony, in immense satisfaction. 'Clean, crackly, beautiful straw. Piled so deep I can sink in.' She rolled luxuriously. 'Things are definitely lookin' up.'

Susie nudged Duchess affectionately. 'Aren't you glad that we're warm and full, Duchess? Don't you feel good?'

'I want to know why he's doing this,' said Duchess. 'Why should he help? There's something wrong here.'

Cory, curled into the thickest part of the straw so that only his tulip ears and fawn-colored nose were visible, yawned sleepily, and said, 'It's natural for man and animal to be together. You've had some bad experiences, Duchess, but not all men can be judged by what was done by a few.'

'What do *you* know about it?' she asked. 'What do you know about what happened to me before we met?'

'We know all about it,' said Pony. 'At least, Cory and Susie told me, and they heard about it from – where *did* you two hear about it?'

'We've always known,' admitted Susie, 'ever since you came to the Farm, Duchess. There wasn't anything anyone else talked about after you got there. News travels fast. We know the men who left you in that shed were taken away. And we know that Pride died of thirst and starvation and tried to chew the walls down. We know all of that. It was a truly terrible thing. But Duchess, although men starved you, didn't they save you, too?'

Duchess, who had thought that the only other being in the world who had completely understood her bitterness was the Dancer, was silenced.

'You knew all the time,' she said finally. 'About Pride.'

'Didn't you want us to know?' asked Susie. 'We're your friends and we wouldn't have said anything, except that

275

you don't feel safe even now. You've got to forget about that sometime, and go on. Say, do you want to hear the Story of Featherlight? I could tell it. It's about Horses' First Man.'

'I remember that Story – it's Equus-be-damned.'

There was a shocked silence, Duchess rarely swore and never blasphemed. 'Well?' Duchess demanded. 'What have the Stories ever done for us, when you think about it?'

'You aren't yourself,' said Cory. 'Too much has happened in the past few days.'

'Tell me,' insisted Duchess. 'You tell me. The Stories. The Balance, Equus. That Owl. Those things snatch happiness away, give you excuses for accepting grief.'

'For one thing,' said Cory, 'the Stories help keep you mares together. Teach you to watch out for one another, keep the herd going now and years from now when your sons and daughters will be members of the herds of the future. But most important is that the Stories teach the Law. You have a choice, after you've heard them as to which path you will travel, which way you will go. If we didn't have the Stories, we'd have to learn about life all over again, each time an animal is born.'

'Do dogs have Stories, too?' asked Susie. 'Really, Cory, I didn't know that. Have you got a Dog Story you can tell us?'

'Of course Dogs learn the Stories,' said Cory. 'And yes, I have a favorite one that I learned as a pup. It's highly appropriate for Duchess at the moment.' Sitting up, his expression serious but not grave, Cory began. 'This is the Story of Dog's First Man. There's a chorus, by the way,' he interrupted himself. 'Can you ladies howl? No? I thought not.'

'We would whicker, like,' said Susie.

'I can howl,' said Pony. 'Listen. EEEeeeee. EEEerrree.'

'We'll forego the chorus,' said Cory.

Dog's First Man

In the very beginning of things, before the Sun was set in the Great Kennel to rule the seasons, before the Moon was harnessed to draw night across the earth, the One convened a Council to give animals a choice. This choice was special, for the animals would be allowed to choose one thing that would distinguish them from one another.

All the animals tried to get to Council as fast as possible. There was a limit of things to choose from, and each wanted first choice. So Canis, after playing one last game with his pups, and making sure his mate had enough to eat and drink for the period he would be gone, set off on his long journey. He trotted forward for a day and a night, and then another, only stopping to drink from the river or catch a fish to eat. And one afternoon, as he passed through the Twilight Grasslands, he heard a faint, despairing howl.

'What's this?' he asked himself. 'I suppose I should stop and see what manner of creature is in trouble. But if I do, I'll be late, and I'll have fewer things from which to choose. Well, whatever it is, someone else will stop. I'll go on ahead.'

And he trotted forward a little faster, so he could get away from the cry more quickly.

'Ooooh.' The cry followed him, heartfelt and sad, and Canis, plagued by his conscience, turned from the path and followed the cry. And then, after what seemed a very long way, he found a man trapped in a pit, unable to get out.

Canis heaved a sigh, for this was going to take a little thought. He pulled a vine from an overhanging tree with his teeth, and dropped it into the pit. The man grabbed the vine and tried to move, but Canis saw that his arm was broken and it was useless to expect the man to pull himself out with a broken arm.

277

Canis was getting exasperated. If he spent much more time near this pit, he'd miss the Council meeting altogether, and he'd come back to his pups and mate with leftover choices, such as gills or pinfeathers. But there was a man, alive and sobbing and broken and in the pit, and there was Canis, healthy and whole and out of the pit, and with a resigned sigh, Canis set out to find help.

It took him all afternoon to find the man's village, and another long time to convince the man's people, by barking and picking up an extra pair of the man's shoes and then running a little way in the direction of the pit, to follow him. But follow him they did, and by the time the man with the broken arm was out of the pit and Canis could be on his way again, it was another day and a half and the Council was due to be over.

When Canis arrived at the Council, breathless, tongue lolling, hot and thirsty, all the animals had come and gone again – all but a little ancient, crinkly turtle, and the turtle himself seemed to be making his slow and methodical way home.

'Turtle!' said Canis, by way of greeting.

'Dog,' responded the Turtle, courteously.

'The Council is over?' asked Canis, looking at the empty seats and the ground packed and littered with the comings and going of many hooves, paws, and feet.

'Yes,' said the Turtle. 'Why were you late?'

'Oh, a small chore. It was nothing, really. Tell me, are there any choices left at all?'

'A few,' said the Turtle. 'But to get back to why you missed the Council . . . ?'

'A small thing. It had to be done, I guess. And now that it is, it isn't important. Rats. I wonder what I should tell my mate.'

'NOTHING!' said the Turtle, in a voice that resounded among the hills and plains. 'NOTHING!'

And before Canis' astonished eyes, the sky darkened, the winds grew fierce, and the Turtle's shell grew and

278

grew until it seemed that all the world was under a vast, sea-smelling tent of green.

'DOG!' said the Turtle, and although it was the Turtle's voice (at least around the edges), there was a deep, dark, demanding tone in the middle of the sound, and Canis knew that he was in the presence of the Voice of the One.

Obediently, he dropped to a crouch and placed his head humbly between his paws.

'YOU WERE LATE BECAUSE YOU STOPPED TO SAVE A MAN,' said the Voice. 'AND THERE IS ONE CHOICE LEFT, DOG, WILL YOU TAKE IT?'

Canis nodded.

'WHAT IS LEFT IS A LOVING HEART. AND BECAUSE YOU STOPPED TO SAVE A NEEDIER BEING THAN YOURSELF, THERE IS A GIFT THAT ACCOMPANIES IT. YOU, OF ALL ANIMALS, SHALL BE A BRIDGE, A LINK BETWEEN THE WORLD OF MAN AND THE WORLD OF ANI-MALS. BOTH YOU AND MAN SHALL RECEIVE MUCH JOY FROM THIS PARTNERSHIP. BUT BECAUSE THERE IS A BALANCE IN ALL THINGS THAT NOT EVEN I CAN OVERSET, YOUR DARK TASK WILL BE TO FORGIVE. FOR THERE IS MUCH IN MAN, AND ANIMALS, TOO, THAT COMES FROM THE DARK – THAT CAN NEVER SEE THE LIGHT.'

And with a soft, soundless explosion of weedy fire, the One was gone, and Canis was left to marvel.

He returned to his home and, taking his mate and his pups, he went to the village of the man he had saved, and lived there in much happiness, and only a little sorrow, until the end of his days.

'We are given a choice,' said Cory. 'That is our control over the Light and the Dark.'

Duchess remained awake long after the others fell asleep, then dozed uneasily, images of the Dancer making slow turns with a giant turtle on a wide and sandy plain flickering through her dreams. She woke abruptly, her heart aching for the sound of the Dancer's voice, for the sight of his stippled coat, and she braced herself for the familiar wave of grief.

The wind howled. A sudden gust blew the door of the shed open. A green mist veiled the outdoors, shading the moon and tingeing the scudding clouds. Duchess peered fearfully out, the hair on her neck and withers prickling. The green light poured in over her sleeping friends – on Cory's fawn muzzle; on Pony's belly, round with hay; on Susie's coat, blotched with chestnut and white. They slept on, and Duchess, fearful, was wide awake. The shadows beyond the open door swirled, moved, and in the dim green light, the muscular form of a spotted horse took shape. In a flood of slow-green radiance, the Dancer beckoned to her from the doorway.

Duchess trembled. Moving slowly, wonderingly, she passed through the door and into the circle of light.

'You're here. Dancer!'

'I'm neither back nor gone,' said the Dancer. His voice was as deep and resonant as Duchess remembered, and the scent of wild thyme rose with him in the mist. 'Where have you been? Let me join you! Just show me how!'

'One of the healthy living, passing into Summer before its time? No, Duchess. That will come soon enough.'

'And so you *are* gone.' Grief closed her heart.

'I passed into Summer, yes,' said the Dancer. 'But now, I'm on the move again, toward an end that confuses me a little. I, who have been so sure what was right and wrong. I don't know where I'm going.'

'There are so many things to tell you, Dancer,' said Duchess. 'The foals. Our journey back. And that Hound,. . . he. . . .'

The Dancer stopped her, his breath on her cheek, his eyes alight with a deep tenderness. 'I stopped to tell you this. You must get back to Bishop Farm and bear the foal. If you choose the wild, you'll be lost. Anor waits there, and the Hounds. Go back to the Farm. Go back.'

The green light began to fade like a sinking sun and Duchess cried out, 'Wait!'

'We'll meet again, before my journey ends. Before the spring is over.' He turned and walked slowly up a long green tunnel that ended in the sky.

The light died.

The wind rose.

The cold was back.

Duchess stood there until she began to shake from the cold, then went back to the shed to wait for daylight. As she entered, Cory woke and asked, 'Are you all right?'

'Yes. Yes. We'll stay here a while, Cory, and get strong enough to travel. And then we'll go home.'

The dog cocked an eye quizzically at her. 'Home?'

'Bishop Farm. By spring.'

'You seem in a chipper mood,' said Pony at morning feed. 'You've lost that droopy look, if you know what I mean. And you seemed to like Willow Warden groomin' you this morning. 'What's up?'

'Nothing,' said Duchess casually. 'Do you feel spring in the air, Pony? We should be able to move on home soon, to Bishop Farm.'

'Well, I'll be a donkey,' said Pony. 'So it's "home to Bishop Farm" now, is it? Hooray.'

8

Home, Again

The woods surrounding Willow Warden's clearing turned green as full spring arrived with a slow turn of the season's wheel. The snow melted into the rush of the brook, and rain puddled under the willow tree in the paddock, making a miniature pond surrounded by sweet new grass.

Ladyslippers unfolded in the shade of aspen and birch; purple and white phlox lined the edges of the small pasture behind Willow Warden's cabin. The winds held the fresh, astringent scent of wild mint and the clear-water smell of daffodils. The grass flourished under a strengthening sun.

Willow Warden brushed the mares twice a day. Under his gentle hands they settled, no longer springing to the alert at the rustle of wild creatures in the brush, or jibbing at the soughing wind. As the days grew longer and the night retreated before distant summer, they shed their long winter hair and their coats grew supple with good health. The man groomed Cory, too, and the soft-spun white of the collie's undercoat littered the cabin yard like grounded clouds.

'Isn't this somethin',' sighed Pony in content one afternoon. The grey skies were soft with rain and the trees were veiled with fine drops of water that made a faint music in the breeze. 'I *love* days like this. When I was with the pony ride, I was always looking for rain. Cancelled things out. Besides, I like the way it feels. It shuts things in, makes the pasture seem littler.'

'Cozy,' agreed Susie.

Cory, waking from a light dognap, emerged from the little shed that stabled them at night and yawned heartily. 'Where's Willow Warden?'

'In the woods,' said Duchess, 'collecting berries and leaves. He puts them in a pot over a fire and then drinks them. I've seen it through the window.'

'He usually stays out until twilight,' said Cory. 'Good.'

'Why?' asked Duchess.

'It's time to move on.'

'Back to Bishop Farm?' Susie exclaimed. 'You mean it?'

'Oh, no,' groaned Pony, 'on the trail again? Sleeping outdoors on the rocks? Through the woods with branches that poke you in the guts and just being able to find little crummy patches of grass to eat? Nuts to that. Why don't we stay right here?'

'Oh, no,' said Duchess softly. She gazed at the woods, her eyes soft.

'You want to leave now, don't you?' said Pony. 'Look, let's at least wait until tonight, after the oats.'

'No, he'll be in the cabin, sitting by the window as he always does,' said Duchess. 'We can't count on his letting us go. I've watched you with him, Cory. You like him. You go for walks together, and I've seen you sneak in and sit by the fire with him, with your head on his knee just like you used to do with David. Maybe he'll keep you.'

'He's not like that,' said the collie, bristling a little. 'He's not a . . . a . . . *keeper*. He's like Susie, in a way.'

'Me?' said Susie. 'Like me? He's a man. I'm a horse. How could he be like me?'

'He's kind. And he helps without holding. No – Willow won't stop us. He'll be sad to see us go, and I'll be sad to leave him. But we must go sometime. And now's the time. Susie, do you feel up to the trip back?'

'Sure. I'm feelin' better and better all the time.'

'No cough or anything?' asked Pony skeptically.

'No. Well, a bit of a one, like. But no more than usual.'

'We'll take it slow and easy,' said Cory. 'Are you all ready?'

'Just let me say goodbye to the bearcub,' said Susie. 'He misses his mother something awful. I'd sure like to know what happened to her,' she muttered. 'Said she went out for berries and never came back.' She ambled over to the pen that held the cub. He was playing with a red rubber ball Willow had left him, and he shambled eagerly to the little gate as Susie approached. She bent her head and whispered. Duchess took a last look at the shed, the neat stacks of hay and straw, the cabin with its wooden door lashed with twine.

With his teeth, Cory untied the knotted rope that held the gate. It swung free, and bumped gently against their sides as they filed out one by one into the forest.

'Farewell, Willow Warden,' murmured Cory.

'Farewell,' echoed Duchess, 'and thanks.'

'Goodbye, reg'lar feed. Goodbye roof. Goodbye straw,' said Pony. 'Hello cold and damp.'

They travelled through the woods for the remainder of the afternoon, only stopping when the moon poked its silver crescent through the twilight sky.

'I smell water up ahead,' said Cory. 'A few furlongs, maybe more. Let's stop there for the night.'

They proceeded through the dark, nose to tail, until they heard the faint splashing of a stream.

'Ummf,' said Pony indistinctly. 'I can't see a damn thing. It's as black as the Dancer's butt around here.'

'Pony!' said Susie in reproof.

'There's grass over there. Smell it?' said Cory. 'Let's drink, graze, and settle down. You won't mind if I leave you for a short while? I'm going hunting.'

'We'll be fine,' said Susie happily. 'You're goin' hunting and we're all goin' home.'

'Grass isn't bad,' Pony admitted, taking a mouthful. 'Not as good as oats, but it isn't bad.'

The mares grazed, Susie humming a little under her

breath, 'Cory's going hunting, we're all goin' home.' Pony joined in, making a little chant, and finally, they all sang together.

> *'Cory's gone a hunting*
> *and we're all going home*
> *To a place that we've been wanting*
> *No matter where we roam*
> *Our adventures have been . . .'*

'What *have* they been?' said Susie. 'Haunting? Baunting? No, that doesn't mean anything.'

'Daunting,' said Duchess firmly. 'That's what they've been.'

'What's that mean?' asked Pony.

'Scary,' said Duchess. 'Fearful.'

'That's for sure,' said Susie.

They sang . . .

> *'Our adventures have been daunting*
> *Although bravery we have shown . . .*
> *Oh, Cory's gone a hunting*
> *and we're all going HOME!'*

'Home, home, HOME!' said Susie.

'What exactly is this Farm like,' asked Pony, a little too casually. 'Who lives there, anyway?'

'Well,' said Susie comfortably, 'there's Fancy, the Lead Mare. You know, I never thought of this until now, but what are we goin' to do with *two* Lead Mares? Now, that'll be a little problem, although I guess after everyone hears about all our travels, they'll want Duchess to be Lead Mare, just out of respect.'

'No thanks,' said Duchess. 'I'm retiring to brood mare, thank you very much, although I expect to get a little jumping in now and then.'

'Jumping, hey?' said Pony. 'So who else is there at this-here Farm?'

285

'Well, there are Feather and Snip, two real good friends of mine and of Duchess,' said Susie. 'And there's Cissy, who is, well, you'll meet her. And, of course, there's El Arat.'

'Who's that?'

'Our Story-Teller and Dreamspeaker,' said Duchess. 'She is of an ancient and honorable line – an Egyptian Arabian – and she is very beautiful.'

'And there's David, and Mr Bishop, and Bunkie the barn cat, and the weanlings, and Stillmeadow, the Farm stallion . . . You'll have lots of horses and people and animals to meet, Pony.'

'They have ponies at this Farm?'

'Not a one,' said Duchess. 'Which means that you will be one of a kind, Pony, and very important because of it.'

'You said everyone has something to do,' said Pony. 'Like brood mares, and you, Duchess, with the jumping, and Susie as a Caretaker, and this El Arat as the Story-Teller. If you don't have any ponies, you must not have pony rides. I could do that, I expect, if they wanted.'

'No pony rides,' said Susie firmly. 'I'll tell you what they might do, Pony, is have you teach little kids to ride. The little ones that are scared of bigger horses. That'd be a good thing for you to do.'

Pony brightened, 'And I have experience. They could tell that right away, I suppose, that I knew what I was doing.'

'I expect they could,' said Duchess.

'I'm full and kind of sleepy. Is it okay if I guard after somebody else?' said Susie, yawning.

'Sure,' said Pony. 'I'm not sleepy. You snooze away. I'll wake you up later. Besides, Cory should be back soon.'

In the dark of the night, as the moon went down, Cory padded out of the woods and awakened Duchess with a light touch on her flanks.

'You sleeping?' he hissed.

'I *was*,' said Duchess crossly, who was never at her best

when awakened from a sound sleep. 'What is it? Pony – you're up, too. Are you all right?'

'No,' the Shetland said. 'Come over here, away from Susie. Cory's got something to tell you.'

They went down to the stream and Duchess bent her head to Cory's muzzle.

'Well?'

Cory hesitated, his breath smelling of some meaty creature.

'Back up a little, will you?' said Duchess. 'Thanks. Now, what is it?'

'It's that place,' said Pony, somewhat incomprehensibly.

'What place? Where you were standing guard? Move, then.'

'Naw. That place – on my hip.'

Duchess snapped fully awake, a cold, stealing fear on her heart. The night sky settled heavily around them; no stars shone in the sky and the moon was obscured by clouds.

'That scar! Not that scar!'

Pony sniffed miserably. 'It thumps.'

'It may be from all that walking we did today,' said Duchess. 'I'm sure that's it.' She whispered, 'How badly does it hurt? Is It near?'

Pony shuddered with revulsion. 'It can't be. We locked It in the valley. The way was blocked, I tell you. It couldn't have gotten out.'

'Snow's melted,' said Cory briefly.

Duchess, feeling the foal move under her heart, forced herself to stand still and think, not to run chasing through the black surrounding them. 'What's the thumping *like*?' she asked desperately. 'Can you tell anything at all?'

'It's just an ache, sort of a reminder. I don't think anything's too near here. But I want to get out of here, Duchess. Can we leave, now?'

'What about it, Cory?'

287

'I don't know what to do,' he said. 'Please,' said Pony. 'We gotta leave.'

Pony had never begged before, and Duchess nuzzled her ears gently. 'Of course we'll leave. We'll wake Susie.'

They stole quietly back to Susie. The Paint was heavily asleep and Duchess looked lovingly at her, then nosed her gently awake. She told Susie what was happening. The mare rose to her feet and said, 'I agree, we should leave. Right now. We've got the foals to think of, Duchess. I think we should get as far away from here as we can.'

'Me too,' said Pony. 'Come on. Let's GO.' Pony trotted off toward the woods, then stopped. 'Which *way* are we going?' she demanded. 'I hope one of us knows.'

'Finding the way back is the easy part,' said Cory. 'It's the getting there that's going to be a problem.'

Cory led them through the darkness at a rapid, ground-eating trot, a pace that was to eat up the miles between them and Bishop Farm for many days. They made infrequent stops to gaze and drink, and slept during the warmest part of the day, when the sun left no shadows anywhere, when they could be sure that nothing was concealed. The rest of the days and nights were taken up with running, now at a trot, now at a rapid walk, as fast as they could go. They splashed through streams and rivers, stumbled over rocks and boulders, the mares' hooves splitting with the constant travel, Cory's paws splaying with wear.

A week passed, then two.

'How's the hip?' asked Duchess as they stopped at high noon for a brief rest.

'Okay,' said Pony. 'The same – It isn't any nearer, and It isn't any farther away. But It's back there, somewhere. How close are we to this Bishop Farm?'

Duchess raised her head consideringly. 'Another week, perhaps less. This is the end of the wilderness, as you can see. Those fields ahead are cultivated. We'll be running across farms and houses now, and men, too. We'll have to move even more carefully.'

'You've been this way before,' said Pony.

'Yes,' said Duchess briefly. A memory came to her, of the Dancer running on the hillside. 'Whirling, feather-light,' she sang aloud. 'You should remember this, too, Pony – it's where we picked you up.'

Pony blinked her little eyes, and looked around. 'So it is!' she said. 'I should have seen it. But that sun makes everything red-like. I don't know how you all can tell where you are.'

An echo of the Dancer's voice sounded in Duchess' ear. 'She sees through flame,' he had said. 'Pony, are you *sure* It's no nearer?'

'I'm sure,' said Pony. 'I'll tell you. Look.' She scraped at the ground with one stubby foreleg. 'I don't know what's really happening here. I mean to say, if I start acting funny. If I start talking funny . . .'

'You're going to be all right,' said Susie softly. 'You've been through the worst already. You're going to be fine.'

'Well, if I'm not, you do something about it. Not you Suze, you're too soft. But you Duchess, and you Cory – you have to promise.'

'Promise what?' said Duchess. 'We're all in this together, Pony. We're a herd, and I'm the Lead Mare, and nothing's going to happen to you. Let's rest now, and move out as soon as we can. We're getting closer to home.'

The days and nights of running had taken their toll; finally, late that night, Susie stumbled over a log hidden in the brush and didn't get up again.

'You go on ahead,' she said. 'I'll be up again in a little while and catch up with you. I just need to rest.'

Duchess examined her flanks and saw how they heaved in and out. 'We're not leaving anyone,' she said firmly. 'You take your time and rest, Susie. Cory, Pony and I will stand guard. Just close your eyes and sleep.'

Susie closed her eyes obediently, and soon slipped into

a deep sleep. Duchess gazed out into the night. The odor of man and his work was in the air. They had crossed cultivated land for the first time in many months that day, and the way was easier on their feet.

Susie woke refreshed after her sleep, and they continued on.

They moved now as a united band with a common purpose. The events of the past year had knit them closely together, and they communicated without speaking in many ways: stopping automatically when Susie's cough caused her to stumble; taking turns to watch at noon when they rested. They all dozed on their feet, the lesson of instant readiness hard-learned, and so it was that the mares moved instinctively together one afternoon when they heard the faint rattle of rock. They ranged themselves into a circle, hindquarters out, ready to attack.

'Whatever it is,' said Susie, low-voiced, 'it's in that clump of ash over there.'

'Pony' said Duchess tersely, 'your scar?'

'It's okay,' said Pony. 'As a matter of fact, I can't feel it at all. That's strange.'

'Where's Cory?' Duchess demanded.

'Out gettin' food, I expect,' said Pony.

The brush shivered with movement.

'Come out,' said Duchess with authority. 'Show yourself.'

The brush parted and a graceful black mare stepped through.

'El Arat!' said Susie. 'Why, it's El Arat.'

Duchess greeted her with a joyful nicker. The delicate Arabian stepped lightly toward them, the sunlight glancing off the black sheen of her coat.

'Welcome back, Duchess and Susie,' she said. 'You have been missed.'

'Why, we must be close to home!' said Susie. 'What are you doing out here, El Arat? How did you know where to find us? How did you know we were back? This is amazing!'

'I was sent a message, of course, and early this morning, I left to find you and welcome you back.'

'Who from?' said Pony belligerently. 'Who told you . . .'

'El Arat's our Story-Teller and Dreamspeaker, Pony,' said Susie. 'She knows lots of stuff ordinary mares don't know.'

'Ah, but you are not ordinary, are you?' said El Arat. 'The messages from my god have been scattered and few, and I have not seen all clearly. But I have seen enough to know that you, Susie, will never be ordinary, as you put it, again – and you, Duchess.' She turned to the buckskin mare. 'It turns out that you were never ordinary at all. The last of the true Appaloosas. And carrying a foal with a destiny. How wonderful your times must have been.' Her face sobered, 'and how terrible, too. Come, I will escort you to safety – it is no more than a few hours' easy trot from here. And you will all sleep protected tonight. You, Susie, and you, Duchess, and . . .' She hesitated, looking at Pony in polite inquiry.

'This is Pony,' said Susie. 'Pony, this is El Arat. Pony's a member of our herd now. They'll take her on at the Farm, won't they? David wouldn't turn a mare in need away.'

'Certainly not,' said El Arat, with peculiar intensity. 'Well. Please. Follow me. And do not be surprised if we appear to go out of our way. There are strange things abroad in these days. You must be guided by me if you are to be safe.'

El Arat turned and the mares fell into single file behind her: first Susie, then Pony, Duchess bringing up the rear.

'She knows what she's doin'?' Pony muttered to Duchess.

'El Arat knows many things,' said Duchess, 'and the mares at home have told me that she is sent messages through dreams by Equus and those who live in the Heavenly Courts.' The buckskin's own eyes were alight with excitement. 'She is probably protecting you, Pony, and Susie and me, too. She might even be able to find out . . .'

'What's happened to the Dancer?' said Pony shrewdly. 'Hmm. Maybe. I wonder how long a way we've got to get there; I'm about worn out with this walking.'

'It'll go real fast,' said Susie. 'When you're happy, time just flies.'

'Stop,' said El Arat suddenly. She held her head up, muzzle questing the air. 'We are being followed, I think.' She swung her fine head towards Duchess. 'Have you sensed anything behind you? Have you had a feeling of being followed?'

'We have,' said Duchess grimly. 'Hindquarters out.' The three travel-weary mares swung into kicking position, as El Arat watched in bewilderment.

'Great gods,' she said, 'you have been through some very disturbing times, have you not? To take the battle formation so quickly, without thought.'

'We're ready for whatever it is,' said Duchess. 'Pony?'

'Nah. I'm okay.' Pony shook her head violently. 'That red mist's gone. I can see real clear now.'

'Perhaps it's a stray dog? I can't scent it properly – it's upwind,' said Duchess. 'We're back in man's country now. Maybe it's a man hunting birds.'

'You were right the first time,' said a familiar voice.

'Cory!' said Duchess. 'Where have you been?'

'Hunting,' he said. 'Where do you think you're going, anyway. You're headed back toward the mountain. The Farm's in the direction of . . .' He broke off suddenly, dropping to the ground in an attack crouch, his lips pulled back over his eye teeth, a snarl rising from his throat.

'Cory!' said Duchess. 'That's El Arat. Don't you remember her? What's the matter with you?'

Cory barked and scraped his forepaws into the earth.

El Arat looked at him imperturbably.

'Cory,' she said imperatively. 'Cory. It is I, El Arat. Story-Teller and Dreamspeaker for the Bishop Farm herd. Do you not know me, dog? We used to talk together in the pastures, under the moon, at home.'

Cory's snarls died away. He rose to his feet, sniffing hard, then he said in an apologetic tone, 'El Arat, of course. I'm sorry.' He shook his head violently, as if to clear it. 'I have the stink of that Hound up my nose yet, I'm afraid. Please excuse me.'

'Of course,' said El Arat kindly. 'You, too, have been through the terrors, have you not? You must tell me of your adventures as we walk.'

'Yes, but it's *this* way, El Arat – you must have been turned around,' said Cory. 'Here – follow me.'

So they told El Arat their adventures, finishing just as they were walking up a slow rise to the past. The sun was going down in a burst of cherry pink, blazing orange, triumphant yellow behind them. The smell of spring full blown was in the air: violets, Sweet William, early honeysuckle, mingled with the rich scent of oiled leather, oats, and drying alfalfa hay.

They reached the top of the rise. Below them was Bishop Farm: white fences turned to gold by the setting sun, pastures flooded with new grass, the barns mellow, rich and dark.

'We're home!' said Duchess.

'We're home, El Arat!' shouted Susie. 'Home!' She looked around for the black mare and said in a puzzled way, 'El Arat?'

'She's gone!' said Pony in surprise.

'Maybe she went ahead of us,' said Duchess, gazing at the Farm.

'I don't see her,' said Pony. 'She just disappeared.'

Cory circled the top of the rise, his nose low to the ground. 'I can't find any scent indication at all,' the dog finally said. 'It's as though she wasn't here at all.'

'Who cares,' said Pony. 'Let's just get down there. I smell oats.'

'All right,' said Duchess happily, 'but let's make it a

real procession. Pony, show us how those circus horses walked in the parade.'

'Me?' said Pony. 'Sure!' Pony tucked her nose to her chest, raised her tail, and pranced a few steps forward.

'You all see that?' said Duchess. 'Okay, now, everyone line up. Susie, you get right behind me. Cory, you stay at my side, and, Pony, you bring up the rear. Cory? A few loud barks would be appropriate, so they know we're coming. Ready? Go!'

Accompanied by the noise of Cory's barks, the four companions stepped high, stepped light. The mares' tails floated out behind them as they trotted proudly down the slope to Bishop Farm, away from the setting sun.

9

From End to Beginning

Feather, the bay brood mare, was dreamily cropping grass under the oak tree at the top of the pasture when the sounds of Cory's barks filled the valley. She raised her head abruptly, a dandelion sticking out at one side of her muzzle.

She snorted in disbelief.

'Fancy!' she shouted. 'Lilly! Snip! Come here, quick!'

The Bishop Farm brood mares, each heavy with foal, clustered at the paddock gate.

'It's *Cory*!' Snip screamed with excitement. 'And it's *Susie*! And *Duchess*! I remember Duchess – she run away last year. But I don't remember that little short one. Now I seen it *all*, I have! Fance, I bet *you* seen it all now, too!'

'This is absolutely incredible,' muttered Cissy. 'That little short one's a pony, Snip.' Cissy turned to the grey mare at her side. 'Wouldn't you call that a pony, Lilly? You came after these animals ran away from the Farm, but I can assure you, we had no ponies here, *ever*.'

Lilly, a grey Arabian mare, stood quietly at attention, her large eyes fixed on the little procession coming toward them.

Duchess, Susie and Pony came down the drive to the Big Barn, heads proudly held, their feet stepping daintily.

The door to the farmhouse slammed wide open and David Bishop raced down the drive, his arms flung wide. Cory leaped on his master with a sound very like a sob.

Emmanuel and the barn hands came running, and until the sun had been set for many hours, the fields of Bishop Farm rocked with joyful celebration.

'I'm 'mazed,' said Snip that night. 'I'm just 'mazed.'

The mares were all bedded down in the Big Barn. Duchess, Susie and Pony had been bathed, brushed and groomed as if for a horse show. The vet had come and gone, and Susie had had a shot that cleared up her cough like magic. The farrier had come to trim their feet, and David had given them each a dose of wormer. After an evening feed of bran mash, oats, and several flakes of timothy, they settled into their stalls clean, warm and well-fed. Cory, exhausted by delight, had sleepily gone up to the farmhouse with David, and the mares were alone in the dark, the sounds of home familiar all about them.

'Well,' sighed Duchess happily.

'Well, indeed,' said Fancy. 'This is the most incredible event, Duchess. You must tell us everything that happened to you. It sounds as though there is a new Story in the making.'

'Oh, Pony will do that,' said Duchess. 'She is our herd Story-Teller, you know. And she has a very vivid imagination – so you can all be assured of a well-told tale.'

'We thought we never would see home again,' said Susie. 'It's so good to be back! You'll have to tell us everything that happened while we were gone. About the babies and all. And about this new mare, Lilly. She sure is beautiful! And about El Arat. We met her early this morning and it was the funniest thing. She led us *away* from the Farm.'

'You met El Arat?' said Fancy, astounded. 'Are you sure?'

'Of course we are,' said Duchess. 'Why isn't she here with us?'

'So many things to find out,' said Snip. 'So many things to tell. El Arat's been gone – oh, a while, hasn't she, Fance?'

'Sold, was she?' said Pony with passionate interest. The little Shetland had to stand with her neck stretched up in order to see over the oak boards of her box stall, which was built for a horse-sized mare.

'No, Pony,' said Fancy gravely. 'A terrible thing happened. Her colt, El Riadam, died a senseless death. He was sold to men who foundered him through overwork. And El Arat was never the same after that. She became solitary, and kept very much to herself. She started stallwalking. El Arat, mind you! That's a stable vice we've never had here. And she would walk up and down, up and down, all winter long.'

'I didn't get *no* sleep,' said Snip indignantly. 'Not a wink, I tell you. I was just as glad when she left!'

'My,' said Susie. 'El Arat stallwalking. Of all mares!'

'And weaving, *and* cribbing,' said Cissy. 'The Bishops were quite upset.'

'At any rate,' said Fancy, 'she wandered off during Turn Out time one afternoon. Just didn't show up for evening feed. And we were not only without a Farm collie, and our best babysitter and our best Open Jumper, but without our Story-Teller and Dreamspeaker, too.'

'And then Lilly came,' said Cissy. 'And she's a better Story-Teller than El Arat ever was.'

'Lilly,' said Duchess. 'Where are you from, Lilly?'

The grey mare, whose coat was the color of clouds before sunrise, whose clear, liquid eyes looked older than her youthful coat and delicate head, paused a long moment, then said in a soft voice, 'I have been many places, Duchess. Seen many things. I hope I've found a permanent home here at the Farm. It's the most peaceful place I've ever been.'

'She's going to be bred to Stillmeadow in a few weeks,' said Cissy, 'probably after our foals have dropped. She's an Arabian, Duchess, in case you were wondering what the tone of the herd has become.'

'Duchess,' Susie burst out, 'is an Appaloosa. The last of the true line! So don't you say anything about her being

297

a Grade anymore, Cissy. She's from an older line than most of us!'

'You bet,' said Pony loyally.

'An Appaloosa,' said Cissy. 'Well. And a Shetland. Even better. Now we *are* going to have interesting babies around here. What're you carrying, Duchess? A genuine brightly colored Appaloosa colt, perhaps? One destined to become a foundation sire, I'm sure, famous all over.'

'As a matter of fact,' said Pony, 'she is. So you shut up, bran face.'

'Oh,' said Cissy politely. 'I see. And, of course, you are carrying the registration papers, Duchess. Tucked under your scraggly mane, perhaps? Or maybe Cory has them for you wound around his excuse for a collie's ruff?'

Duchess stood stricken. 'Well, I – '

'Appaloosas are a color registry, Cissy,' said Lilly. 'All that's needed for papers is that the colt be brightly marked. And it will be a colt, as brightly colored as his sire.'

'What do you know about his sire?' Duchess said softly. 'You weren't here when he came.'

'We told her all about it,' said Feather. 'Tell me, Lilly, how can Duchess be an Appaloosa when she's a buckskin?'

'Yes!' said Cissy. 'Tell us that. I'd be very interested in finding out.'

Lilly shifted lightly on her feet and her eyes grew dark with memory.

'The Appaloosa carried sturdiness of purpose and high courage. But once, a long while ago, this courage failed when it was needed most. A terrible betrayal, by a mare whose name horses know and curse, punished all the breed. Since the Palouse time, Appaloosas born and bred to color see that color die.'

'What does that mean?' asked Pony anxiously.

'Duchess was born as brightly colored as any App we have ever seen. But the Black Bargain meant that her color died when she reached the age of maiden mares.

298

This greying out will happen to many Appaloosas, more and more, unless . . .' She paused, eyes dark, then said abruptly. 'No matter. This is no matter for me anymore. Your Duchess carries the color within her and will pass it on. Her colt will pass true color, strong color on to his own offspring. And the Appaloosa breed will continue.' She swung her finely shaped head toward Duchess and an odd expression crossed her face. 'If the foal is healthy and survives.'

'Hmmf,' said Cissy.

Susie pawed at her stall floor and Duchess was briefly reminded of the rabid fox and the single blow that killed it. Pony snorted as if about to charge. Duchess herself felt her powerful hindquarters clench to strike.

Duchess, her breath coming short, met Pony's glance and said, 'How do you know this, Lilly? Who are you?'

'Should I get Cory?' asked Pony in an undertone. 'You think she knows something? He'll get it out of her if we can't.'

'What are you doing?' exclaimed Fancy. 'You're all behaving like warrior mares. Stop it, right now.'

'You, Lilly, *how do you know about this*?' said Duchess. She curled her lips back over her teeth.

'From what is sent to me,' said Lilly serenely. 'I am a Story-Teller and Dreamspeaker both, you know.'

Fancy rubbed her muzzle nervously against the mesh of her stall.

'I think we all ought to settle down and get some sleep. We'll discuss this at the morning turnout, if it has to be discussed. The foals will be coming soon, for all of us, and it's important that we remain calm and obey herd Law. Is it agreed?'

'I don't agree to anything,' said Pony flatly. 'You aren't my Lead Mare, Duchess is.'

'We aren't going to go through this again, are we?' said Feather plaintively. 'Fancy's Lead Mare.'

'I think,' said Duchess reflectively, 'that we'll have to wait on that. For now, at least until the foals are born, we will assume that we have two herds here . . . mine, Fancy, and yours. After things have settled down a bit, we'll look to having things the way they once were. But I can't agree to give up my position yet.' She looked for a long moment at Lilly, who returned her regard impassively. 'Not yet.'

'A wise decision,' said Lilly.

The barn quieted as the mares dropped off to sleep. Duchess remained awake; she felt an uneasy need to watch the grey mare as she slept. El Arat's disappearance, the mystery of this mare who took her place, and the constant fear that she, Duchess, was being stalked, that the Dancer's unborn foal might be in danger, that Pony might be carrying the unthinkable, kept her awake and restless.

'Hey!' whispered Pony in the dark.

'Yes, Pony.' Duchess moved to the front of her stall and peered across the concrete aisle at the Shetland.

'You think we have trouble here?'

'I don't know. Your hip – how does it feel?'

'Not a twinge.'

'I wish we knew more,' sighed Duchess. 'This is what the Dancer told us to do. To come back to Bishop Farm and bear the foals in safety.'

'He's probably right,' said Pony. 'I think we should just take it easy. You know, eat good, rest up and all of that. We'll worry about things when they happen.'

'And this one?' said Duchess, with a nod toward sleeping Lilly.

'I don't have any bad feelin's about her.' Pony chewed on a bit of straw, then mumbled, 'It's me we have to worry about.'

'What?' said Duchess.

'Nothing. Lilly's a little – remote, if you get my drift. Not too interested in the day-to-day stuff. Nothing wrong with that. Most of the Dreamspeakers I met in my time are like that. Weird.'

'Except for you,' said Duchess. 'You're a Story-Teller,

Pony, by vote of the herd. And you may be Dream-speaker eventually – who knows? And there's nothing weird about you.' She repeated fiercely, 'Nothing!'

'Right,' said Pony with a noticeable lack of enthusiasm. 'Say, should we keep watch? I'll take first round.'

'Not here, Pony. No. If we aren't safe at Bishop Farm, we aren't safe anywhere.'

''Night, then.'

'Good night.'

They all slept.

While on the crest of the hill overlooking Bishop Farm, a delicate black Arabian mare stood grazing down, her eyes glowing yellow-green in the dark.

Spring stepped through the next few weeks with fresh scents and infant color; one by one, the Bishop Farm brood mares dropped their foals. Fancy delivered a healthy, bright-eyed bay colt called Bucky; Feather and Cissy each had a filly, and Lilly was sent to Stillmeadow for breeding. This last event relieved Duchess' anxiety about the grey – for Fancy had told them all of the Herd Law demanding allegiance to the Herd Stallion. 'And besides,' she said to Susie, one morning out at pasture, 'if there were anything funny about her, she would have done something to Stillmeadow, don't you think? And Bunkie would have let us know if anything had occurred that was out of the way or unusual. No, Susie, I think everything's going to be just fine.'

'I hope so,' said the Paint. She yawned widely, and Duchess looked a little anxiously at her.

'Will you listen to that Pony?' said Susie. 'Cissy's about ready to have fits over the way she's tellin' stories about us.'

Duchess pricked her ears forward with interest. 'And *then*,' she heard Pony say to the disgusted Cissy, 'the Dancer slammed him a good one right in the chops.'

'She was pretty direct about what she did,' said Fancy thoughtfully.

'She's paid for it, over and over again,' said Duchess, a

little gruffly. 'And she's fitting in just fine, don't you think so, Suze? Susie,' said Duchess. 'You're asleep on your feet again.' She nudged the Paint, and Susie yawned again.

'Can't help it, like,' she said.

'They say that you sleep a lot before a birth,' said Duchess. 'Isn't that right, Fancy?'

'Oh, yes.' The Lead Mare swallowed a mouthful of grass, and glanced briefly at Bucky, playing in the sunshine near the fence. 'It's a very tiring business. This is your first, isn't it?'

'Yes.' Duchess shifted uncomfortably on her feet. 'I feel fat and sluggish. Tell me, what's it really like?'

Fancy considered a patch of clover and chewed off a few leaves.

'It hurts some. Both when they're born, and then later when they're nursing and get teeth. But by and large, it's wonderful. It's a kind of magic – not the magic you've encountered, but magic all the same. You've felt the baby, moving and kicking and paddling around inside, haven't you? It doesn't actually become real until there it is on the straw, new and little and damp. A whole new horse to add to the herd. They're little slippery things at first, with all kinds of silly ideas. Grass tickles their feet. They love the sunshine, drink it in like water. They chase cabbage flies, trip over pebbles, have to be taught about fences. And the *endless* questions! Why can't they play in the water bucket? Why do men have two feet instead of the proper four? Where does the moon come from and where does it go during the daytime? They like little songs, like One-two is a Trot, a Trot, Three-four is not, is not.

'Weaning is hard on everyone. You miss their little muzzles at your side, and your bag aches with wanting them. And they cry like anything, the first couple of days. But Susie knows what to do with them, don't you Suze?'

'My job,' Susie agreed sleepily.

'All in all,' said Fancy, 'you'll like it.'

'What if there's trouble?' said Duchess. 'What if something goes wrong?'

'Then the vet comes,' said Fancy. 'And if, with all the help that David and Emmanuel and the vet have to give, the foal doesn't make it – why, it wasn't meant to be, that's the way I look at it. I wouldn't worry, though – you're young and strong, and so is Pony.'

Duchess looked at Susie dozing in the sunshine, and Fancy, following her glance, said softly, 'And Susie's time will be Susie's time, Duchess. I wouldn't worry about her.' She looked at Duchess with an experienced eye. 'How's your belly feel?'

'Tight, swollen.'

'Has the foal dropped yet?'

'Dropped?'

'Well, it's an expression more than anything else. Do you suddenly feel fuller? Sort of a pressure underneath? I noticed you didn't eat all your grain this morning.' Fancy chuckled a little. 'That's unusual for you.'

Duchess thought a moment. 'Yes, I do feel full, like something's pushing on my stomach.'

Fancy pricked up her ears. 'Now *that's* an encouraging sign. How's the base of your tail?'

'The base of my tail?' said Duchess in astonishment. 'To tell you the truth, I don't spend a lot of my time thinking about the base of my tail.'

Fancy rubbed her muzzle along the top of Duchess' black tail. 'It feels soft, like a stone bruise.'

'But it doesn't hurt,' said Duchess, trying to stretch her neck around to see.

'It's not supposed to. That's an excellent sign, that softness. If I had a guess, I'd guess that you'd deliver tonight.'

Susie made a soft snort of agreement. Duchess, spending the rest of the day under the oak tree, too full to graze, felt a growing excitement mixed with unease. As David came to put them inside for the night, Lilly

303

wandered casually over to Duchess and said, 'Duchess? I know you've been worried about this birthing . . .'

'Not at all,' said Duchess, pointedly turning her hind-quarters toward the grey mare.

'I just wanted to tell you that we're *all* here to help you if you need it. There's the herd and Cory, and the Bishops. If the foal is – something special – it will be protected. And I will tell you something else that you may not know. Of all creatures under the rule of the One, animal and man, mares are the only ones that can stop labor once it begins. Do you understand? If there is any threat – just *hold it*, until we get help.'

Duchess nodded a muttered thanks, and followed the mares into the barn for the night.

She was dozing lighty when she knew it was time. She began to pant in heavy, regular breaths, and she felt a tremendous surge of joy, a certainty that events would turn out all right. She felt, somehow, the Dancer's presence in the air she breathed, in the touch of the evening shadows on her withers.

Fancy caroled a high, shrill whinny, and Cory came racing into the Barn.

'It's Duchess,' said Fancy. 'Get the Bishops.'

Cory, barking loudly, whirled and raced to the Farm house. The lights in the Barn snapped on in a few moments, and David was there, Emmanuel right behind him, the younger Bishop running careful, experienced hands over her sides, rubbing a pungent ointment on her teats to ease the tightness from the milk.

And suddenly, in a rush of pain and joy, Duchess forgot all the questions she had ever had – the answer lay, a small, brightly colored colt, on the fresh sweet straw of her stall. Perfectly formed, he lay in the straw, his hooves and ears absurdly small, the damp from the afterbirth darkening his coat. Duchess turned with a soft, low whicker, and nosed the baby to his feet. He scrabbled like a mouse, four hooves churning up tiny mounds of straw, and got to his feet, swaying a little with the uncertainty of this new and sudden height.

'He is an Appaloosa!' cried Lilly, from the stall next to Duchess.

'Black chest and white hindquarters,' reported Fancy from the other side. 'And Duchess, he is beautiful.'

Duchess, warming the baby with her tongue, saw that white trailed across the colt's hindquarters like ivy leaves.

A new language came to Duchess, a language of soft whickers, gentle puffs of breath, and low-voiced whinnies. Nudging the foal to her teats, she watched with a brimming heart as he nosed eagerly for the first suckings of milk, the small, feathery tail flipping in circles as he drank. His eyes, milky blue at first, cleared gradually, and as the hours wore on, he took in his mother's shape, the stall itself, the stiff, scratchy feeling of the straw, with a look of delighted wonder.

David left them alone all through the night, and when dawn came, came back again, accompanied by Cory.

'Finally,' said the dog with a relieved grin.

'Finally,' said Duchess. She looked at the collie with shining eyes. 'He looks just like his sire, Cory. The markings are exactly the same.'

Cory cocked his head in pretended criticism.

'Actually, I think he looks more like you. He has your head, and he definitely has your legs and pasterns, Duchess. He's going to be a super mover – and I'll bet he'll be a terrific jumper.'

'I wonder what the Bishops will name him,' said Fancy.

The baby gave a tiny cry, like a piping bird, high and sweet. David slid the stall door open, and the foal, startled by this invasion of a large, curiously shaped object into his new world, gave a miniature buck, then advanced his nose to David's outstretched hand. David ruffled Cory's ears with one free hand, and stroked the foal with the other. The boy said something to the dog and Duchess said, 'What? Is he saying something about a name, Cory?'

David ran gentle fingers over the colt's ears, left the

stall for a moment, then returned with a small box. He swabbed the foal's eyes and ears with a bit of cotton, then carefully cleaned the navel. He spoke aloud, and again Duchess asked the collie, 'A name? Has the baby got a name?'

The foal, a crystalline spark of light deep in his eyes that recalled the Dancer's gaze, piped the clear, birdlike call once more.

'Piper,' said David clearly.

'Piper,' Duchess whispered to herself. 'You are The Piper.'

Piper, unimpressed, settled abruptly into the straw and went suddenly to sleep.

10

Winter's End

'Will you listen to that Pony?' said Susie with a chuckle. 'Tellin' the babies about the Journey from the Mountain? I never heard such a Story in all my life. Doesn't sound like what happened at all.'

The mares were grazing peacefully in the early summer sun. In the far corner of the pasture, the babies, The Piper and Susie's own spotted Daisy among them, were gathered in a circle around Pony, whose stout sides were swollen with her own unborn foal.

'The day the wolves came, it was as dark as Dancer's butt,' Duchess heard Pony say dramatically.

'Pony!' protested Lilly. 'This is *not* the way one should refer to the herd stallion, much less the Dancer himself. The Stories are Tales born in beauty, and they come out of the words of Equus.'

'You bet,' said Pony. She lowered her head and whispered, 'They snuck up on us from behind, with murder in their eyes.'

'Good grief,' snorted Cissy. 'Some Lead Mares would feel a greater responsibility towards the education of the foals. Fancy would, I'm sure, put a stop to that kind of language. Wouldn't you, Fance?'

'I think they like it,' said Susie mildly. 'And it's *our* herd, after all, isn't it, Duchess?'

'Yes,' Duchess rubbed her nose thoughtfully along one foreleg. 'But I'm wondering if it isn't time for us to become one herd again, instead of two. What do you think, Fancy?'

The chestnut mare hesitated, then said, 'It's up to you, of course. It is very unusual to have us all grazing together, being together . . . perhaps, if you are ready, I should call a Herd Council Meeting.'

'I'm ready,' said Cissy. 'It's about time that she gave this ridiculous stuff up, if you ask me.'

'I didn't hear anyone ask you,' said Snip. 'Did you ask her, Feather? Maybe Susie asked her, and I didn't hear. Did you, Suze? Ask Cissy if it was time for Duchess to give up bein' Lead Mare of her herd?'

'Nope,' said Susie. 'But I think it's time. I know it's time for me to give up my job.'

'What do you mean?' said Feather in astonishment.

'You've always been the Caretaker. Who else would do it? Don't you like the babies anymore? Is my Beecher being a pain in the tail? He's a rowdy little guy, I'll admit.'

'Rowdy, rowdy, rowdy,' hummed Snip. 'Say, if any of them babies is too rowdy, it's that Cissy's Blackwatch. Now *there's* a row-row-rowdy colt for you. He kicked the stuffin' out of Susie's Daisy the other day.'

'He did *not*,' said Cissy indignantly. 'And even if he did kick a little, it was because he was provoked.'

'The stuffin',' said Snip firmly. 'I seen him.'

'Susie, you can't give up your job,' said Duchess. She looked at her stablemate with concern, seeing the dark shadows around the mare's large brown eyes and the hollow behind her withers.

Susie yawned. 'It's just that I'm so sleepy all the time, like. I need to rest some.'

'You deserve all the rest you want,' said Fancy softly. 'Perhaps I should call a Council right here, and we can settle some of these issues.'

'Okay by row-row-rowdy me,' said Snip cheerfully.

Fancy whistled to Pony, who left the foals capering in the grass and joined the other mares in a circle beneath the oak tree.

'This Council has been called to settle the issue of Two-Herds-in-One,' said Fancy. 'When Duchess, Susie and Pony returned from the Dancer's mountain, they had formed a herd of their own and elected Duchess Lead Mare. Pony was voted in as Story-Teller, and Susie, of course, was Caretaker. Now that we are all together – and with two new mares – it's time that we became one herd, as the law decrees.'

'I never did get straight why we had two herds in the first place,' said Cissy, 'but some mares think they're a little more special than the rest of us, I guess. So I never said anything.'

'You're *always* saying something, Cissy,' said Feather. 'And I know why Duchess wanted to stay separate. She wanted to be sure that she didn't bring any danger with her. And I, for one, appreciate that.'

'So do I,' said Lilly. 'It was a generous thing to do.'

'Oh, *that* was the reason,' said Cissy. 'Pardon me. I should have guessed. Duchess, old Grab-the-Hay-While-It's-Green Duchess, had *our* interests at heart.'

'That's not fair,' said Feather heatedly. 'Duchess has changed, any mare can see that. She's the best brood mare I've ever seen – excuse me, Fancy – and her sense of responsibility makes her one of the wisest.'

'I don't believe this,' said Cissy.

'I agree with Fancy and Feather,' said Lilly. 'Duchess led the mares home from great danger. She has earned the right to be Lead Mare.'

'I think so, too,' said Snip. 'Duchess'll be great at the job. And I'll bet she'll see to it that my ugh list stays short. You know, she'll keep us away from black flies, stomp on Cissy once in a while, that kind of stuff.'

'This is silly,' protested Duchess. 'Cory was the one who led us home.'

'Cory was away most times,' said Pony. 'And who was it who decided not to kick me out of the herd when I should have been? And who was it made the Dancer call the Owl . . .'

'Praises,' murmured Fancy, Feather and Snip. '. . . when Susie was dying? And who was it that decided to come home from Willow's? And who was it kept her word to the Dancer when she would have rather gone with him down *There*?'

'Duchess, that's who,' said Snip. 'I vote for Duchess.'

'And I,' said Fancy.

'And I,' said Lilly.

Feather, nodding acceptance, gently nudged Susie, who had fallen asleep in the sun.

'Ask her,' said the Paint mare drowsily, 'if she *wants* to be Lead Mare.' Susie chuckled, and the chuckle turned into a cough. A spasm shook her that almost brought her to her knees. She snorted her throat clear and mucus tinged with blood came from her muzzle.

'Let's wait a while,' said Duchess. 'Pony, would you call Cory, please? Tell him to bring David. Susie needs the vet. Honestly, Susie, your withers are going to look like nettle rash if these shots keep up. It's sure taking a long time to cure this.'

'I don't like nettles,' said Susie. When Cory came with David to lead her to the barn she stepped carefully, as though avoiding great patches of imaginary weed beneath her hooves.

Daisy followed her mother to the gate and stood looking forlornly after her as she disappeared into the barn.

'Which one of us will take over Daisy's care?' said Fancy after a long moment. 'Snip, you always have a lot of milk – what about it?'

'Sure,' said Snip.

'Don't be absurd!' snapped Duchess. 'If Daisy misses her afternoon feed, she'll nurse right alongside the Piper!'

'You aren't quite recovered from your journey,' said Fancy gently. 'And a growing foal needs a lot of milk. Snip would be the ideal choice; she's the biggest mare in the herd, and her bag is always full.'

'Susie will be back in pasture as soon as the vet comes,'

said Duchess. 'We aren't talking about an orphan foal here, for Equus' sake.'

Even Cissy avoided looking at Duchess. The buckskin looked from mare to mare, then went suddenly cold, her heart constricting in her chest. She ran to the paddock gate and reared, striking at the latch, calling loudly for Cory. When there was no response from the barn, she screamed again, and the collie ran out from the open doors.

'Open this gate!' ordered Duchess.

'The vet's here,' said Cory. 'He's taking care of her, doing the best he can.'

'Open this *gate*. Or I'll jump the fence.'

'I can't,' said Cory. 'I can untie a rope, but I don't know how this works.'

'*Won't*, you mean,' said Duchess furiously. She backed up, circled, then came at the gate in a gallop.

'Don't,' shouted Cory. Duchess skidded to a halt. 'You know you can't make it over. It's too soon after the Piper.'

'Let me out!' Duchess struck the gate with her forefeet. Cory began to bark, running back and forth from the gate to the barn doors, until David came out. Cory ran up to Duchess, and pawed at the gate latch, whining. Duchess reared and called out to Susie.

'Duchess,' said David. He took a lead line that had been looped over the fence and unlatched the gate. As soon as it swung open, Duchess brushed past him and ran into the barn.

'Whoa!' David shouted.

Duchess trotted down the concrete aisle, her eyes adjusting to the electric light inside. Far down toward the end of the barn she saw Emmanuel Bishop and the vet. She heard the labored sounds of Susie's breathing.

'Whoa, WHOA!' said David. He wound the lead line around her neck, and drew her into the stall next to Susie's. Duchess peered anxiously through the mesh that separated them.

The Paint mare lay on her side, stretched out in the straw. Her eyes were closed. The area in front of her stifle heaved in and out, in and out, and her breath whistled in her throat.

'Susie!' said Duchess urgently. 'Get up!' She moved restlessly back and forth in front of the mesh. From outside her stall Cory said, 'Take it easy, Duchess.'

'She hasn't eaten her grain! Look, her bucket's full! Susie, get up! You have to eat, you hear me? Get up!'

Susie's coarse, kindly head jerked up, and she said, 'Are we home yet? I thought I heard a storm coming. The wind whistling something fierce.'

'We're home,' said Duchess desperately. 'And Susie, you have to get on your feet. Look, here's some alfalfa in my stall. You get up and we'll share it.'

Susie chuckled. 'You remember when you first came here, Duchess? There was times when I was sure you'd never share with anyone.' She coughed. 'And now look at you. You're going to be Lead Mare to us all. Even Fancy . . .' She closed her eyes and seemed to doze. 'Oh! I was asleep! The Dancer . . . where's the Dancer? He's gone, isn't he?' Her eyes opened wide. 'He's back.'

Susie drifted into a fitful doze that veered between sleep and wakefulness. She heard Duchess telling her to get up over and over again. She scented Mr Bishop and the boy and felt their hands on her neck, stroking with lingering warmth in a world gone cold. Cory was there, too, in and out of her dreams, with worried eyes and a high keening in his voice.

Toward the end, her vision cleared. Duchess was there in the next stall and she raised her head to say, 'Howdy, howdy,' but the sound buried itself in her chest and she knew Duchess wouldn't hear.

Summer! She could feel it coming, and before she went to welcome it, she stopped, looked back, and saw the babies – countless knobbly-legged foals, their small muzzles raised and ears pricked forward in salute. Then, one after the other, like birds in flight, the babies grew: mares

312

with foals of their own at their side; geldings racing free along wooded paths, red-coated riders on their backs; her babies, all her babies, jumping splendidly high and wide before a cheering crowd of people; and finally, she saw Duchess and The Piper sharing a stack of glittering hay by a crystal river.

Then Summer came with a sweet rush, with a scent like clover, and a great, golden silence.

Cory threw back his head and howled.

'She's gone,' the collie cried. 'And I-I-I-I send her in peace with my song. She's gone!'

Answering howls came from the farms beyond the Bishop's and echoed through the hills, the farewell cry taken up by all the dogs within the sound of Cory's voice.

'She's gone!' the collie keened. 'Peace to this friend of the pack.'

'Gone,' came the faint chorus. 'Gone.'

Duchess heard Daisy's plaintive whinny from the pasture. The brood mares called out:

'O, Equus, with mane and tail shining like the moon.

O, Equus, with eyes like stars when there is no moon.

Take this member of our company into the Courts of the Outermost West.

And guard her well, Equus!'

David, his face damp with tears, put Duchess back into the paddock with the other mares. They were gathered under the oak tree, and Fancy led the funeral lament:

'Who stands the dead mare's friend?' the chestnut mare asked.

'I do,' said Duchess, grieving.

'And what shall be spoken at Summer's Gate?'

'That her heart was true, and kind,' said Duchess in a whisper. 'That she never hurt another, except once, and that was to protect the herd – a killing so that others might live.

'Say also that she inspired love from those around her, and that she was my friend, my stable mate.'

313

'Who stands the dead mare's friend?' said Fancy.

'I do,' said Pony, weeping.

'And what shall be spoken at Summer's Gate?'

'That she made friends with an outcast, and that she never turned her back on a mare in need. That she had guts, without havin' to be boss.'

'Courage without arrogance. A true heart, a kind and loving soul,' said Fancy. 'Who stands the dead mare's friend?'

'We do,' said Snip, Feather, and Cissy.

'She was a member of our company.

She was one with us.

May she live in the Courts of the Outermost West.

And may those who went before know her worth.'

Duchess stood with her head down and a dull ache in her heart.

The Piper moved quietly through the grass and up to Duchess' flank. It seemed to Duchess that a rainbow lightly touched his hooves, and she felt the puff of his breath against her bag.

'Feed now,' he said, in his high, sweet voice. 'Daisy, too?'

'Yes,' muttered Duchess. 'Yes, of course. Daisy, come here. You'll feed with the Piper now. You'll be with me now, and the other mares.'

'Where's my dam?' said Daisy. 'I want her.'

'I'm your dam, now,' said Duchess.

'And I,' said Fancy. 'And Snip and Cissy, and Pony and Feather, too, Daisy. You belong to all of us.'

'I want my dam,' said Daisy. 'I want her.'

'She is in a great and glorious place,' said Fancy. 'And you miss her, Daisy – I know. But she is watching over you – as we all will. You just can't see her, smell her, play with her as you once did. But she is very much with you.'

Fancy raised her head and looked at the herd. 'She is here, too, in us all.'

11

The Soul-Taker

The golden wheel of summer moved slowly on. The foals grew and thrived on the rich new grass, and as the Piper grew, the grief that Duchess felt at Susie's loss lifted day by day. She pushed aside the fears she held for Pony and the future of the Dancer's get. What would come would come.

The foals were weaned and placed in a separate paddock, with Snip taking over Caretaking duties.

'And the Bishop's aren't happy about it, oh, no!' said Bunkie on a late afternoon visit to pick through the mares' grain. 'Snip's just too slow to be any good at it.'

The cat stretched out lazily on the barn beam over Duchess' head, one forepaw dangling down. 'Something's going to be done, and soon, or you'll have the weanlings getting stuck in the fence or falling into chuck holes and I don't know what all.'

'You're always so full of good news,' said Feather. 'I think that's what I like about you best, Bunkie, your good cheer.'

The cat narrowed her green eyes at Feather, then caught sight of her own tail switching on the beam. She rolled suddenly to pounce on it, and fell yowling onto the hay bales piled by the tack box. She clawed her way straight up the door of Duchess' stall, then flattened out on the beam, scowling.

'Good cheer,' she spat. 'I'll give you good cheer.

You've got a perfectly good candidate for the caretaking job right here in the barn. Perfectly good.'

'Who?' asked Feather.

Bunkie crouched, eyes shut, purring loudly.

'Who!' demanded Feather, exasperated.

'Wouldn't *you* like to know? I'll give you a few hints. It's a real short mare. And, if you ask me, a real *vulgar* mare. And a real pregnant mare that should have dropped her foal way before this.' Bunkie shot to her feet and stared intently at nothing in particular. 'And,' she said relaxing suddenly and busily cleaning her paws, 'if you want to know that, ask your Lead Mare – she knows ALL.'

'Duchess?' said Feather. 'Does Bunkie mean Pony?'

'I'm *not* your Lead Mare,' said Duchess, abruptly. She flicked an ear in apparent unconcern, but the flesh on her withers prickled. 'I don't know what I'm carryin',' Pony had said to her that day at Willow Warden's. 'The Dancer's foal, or Anor's. . . .' Duchess stopped and refused to let her thoughts go forward. A foal's life was precious – the most important thing in life, next to the survival of the herd itself. She sighed heavily, a sigh that came from her very center, and saw Fancy give her a startled look.

'Strange,' said Cissy. "Of course, one never knows with ponies, does one?'

'We're the same as you guys, only shorter,' said Pony crossly. 'Just let me alone.'

'This is your first, isn't it, Pony? You be sure and let us know if you need help,' said Fancy, after a long pause.

'Yeah, yeah,' muttered Pony. 'Where's David? I want to go out.'

'He's coming now,' said Duchess. 'Pony, the Bishops should be there, for the foaling. They'll be able to help if anything goes wrong. Don't try to fool them like you fooled the people at the pony ride. Too much can go wrong.'

'Uh huh,' said Pony. 'Nothing's going to happen for a while yet. Let's just go out, okay?'

David came down the concrete aisle, opening the stall doors for the mares to proceed to evening pasture. He came into Pony's stall, ran his hands over her hindquarters, felt her bag, then stepped back to look at her belly. He hesitated, inspected the half-eaten bucket of oats, and started out the stall door. Pony thrust her nose into the grain bucket and began to eat, rapidly cleaning up the remaining grain. David snapped her halter on, and let her get in line with the other mares. They went slowly out to pasture.

It had been a clear and golden afternoon, but as night approached, lightning appeared at the edges of the sky, and the heat pressed down like a woolen blanket. In their strongly built paddock, the weanlings were restless, and Duchess could hear poor Snip trying to keep them grazing quietly.

The moon rose late and red. The sullen atmosphere increased.

'If there is going to be a storm,' Fancy observed, 'I wish it'd hurry up. At least we'd cool off a little.'

Duchess flicked an ear in agreement. It was almost too hot to talk or move. The mares grazed in a lethargic way in the dark.

Then deep into the hot and heavy night, Pony went into labor.

Duchess heard her in the dark, the Shetland's groans coming in deep, painful bursts, and she called to the others. As was the custom with pasture births, the whole herd gathered in a protective circle around Pony as she lay on her side in the meadow grass. Her withers and flanks were patched with sweat, and her eyes rolled in her head.

'It's about time,' said Fancy. 'We were beginning to worry, Pony. Do you want us to call Cory? A pasture birth is most unusual for us here. You'd be better off with the Bishops being present.'

317

'Call Cory,' grunted Pony. 'But just bring him here. No men. And everyone else – go away.'

A flash of heat lightning briefly illuminated her face. Duchess backed away in shock. Pony's lips drew back in a horrific grin, her eyes glazed red. Her sides shook with heavy, rhythmic contractions that were like blows from the inside.

'What's the matter with her?' said Feather in a hushed tone. 'She looks . . .'

'Get *away* from me!' shouted Pony. 'Get out of here, quick! But bring that dog!'

'Why?' said Duchess. 'Why do you want Cory and not me, or the others?'

'I've seen things,' Pony muttered. 'I've seen black crows in the oak tree. I've seen bodies by the fence . . . I need Cory!'

'What's she talking about?' said Fancy. 'Perhaps she has birthing fever. We've got to get the Bishops right away.'

'They don't know,' Pony said to Duchess. 'I can't let them find out. Help me.'

'Yes,' said Duchess. 'Yes.' Her breath coming short with fear, Duchess turned to the mares and said as calmly as she could, 'I know it's unusual – but perhaps you could leave us alone. I'll stay with Pony. And Fancy, I guess we do need Cory.'

'You go away, too,' screamed Pony. 'Just the dog.'

'You must tell me why you want him, Pony,' said Duchess gently. 'I can't leave you here like this. It's wrong to send away the herd, too, but I can do that much for you, because of what we've been through.'

'It hurts, Duchess.' Pony spoke in a ragged whisper. 'I can't tell you how much it hurts. It hurts like that place on my hip, and I can't tell you how scared I am.'

'Cory can't help,' said Duchess, swallowing panic. 'The herd can. The Bishops can. What could Cory do?'

Pony's look was stark. Her eyes darkened, her expression changed, and she looked beyond Duchess in the night.

318

'He can kill it,' said a familiar voice. 'That's what the dog can do.'

El Arat stepped out from behind the oak tree.

She shone with a lucid, incandescent light that rivalled the last rays of the sun as it set behind the hills of Bishop Farm. She moved within the light as a bird flies in the air – lightly, with assurance and a curious familiarity. There was something terrible in her beauty. Her eyes were flat, obsidian, and there was no reflection in them, like a pool of water with a bottom too far to be reached. Beside her, the silver of Lilly's coat dulled to iron grey, and Lilly herself seemed stiff and clumsy.

El Arat rose slowly to her hind legs, her body a graceful arc.

Lilly turned and gazed directly into the splendor that was El Arat, her gaze curiously wistful, her withers slumped with something close to regret.

'El Arat!' said Fancy, 'El Arat! Where have you been? How could you leave the herd without a Dreamspeaker?'

'I want to go in now,' said Feather suddenly. 'I don't want to see this. I don't want to hear this.'

El Arat settled onto four legs, and regarded the brood mares with a cold, unblinking gaze. She swiveled her head once, took in Lilly with a brief, dismissive glance, and pointed her muzzle at Pony. 'That foal. It is mine. I claim it. And it must die.'

'What did you say?' cried Fancy. 'Kill a foal? Have you lost your wits? What's going on here? What's happening to us?'

'You tell them,' Pony begged El Arat. 'You tell them what we have to do.' The shadows from the red moon, from the flickering lightning, played tricks with Pony's agonized face, and for a moment, Duchess thought she saw the Shetland's teeth gleam fanglike.

'Anor's foal. You are carrying Anor's foal, after all,' said Duchess. She shook with cold in the oppressive heat.

'It is an *afreet*, a demon,' said El Arat gravely. 'It must

319

be killed before it sees the light of dawn. Or we will have chaos, disaster.'

'You lie!' said Duchess. 'The most basic Law of all is to protect the young.'

'Tell them,' Pony said hoarsely. 'Tell them what will happen.'

El Arat curled her lips. 'There will be another such as Anor the Red. The Balance will be tipped. Destruction will reign, and terror. The foal must be killed, and at once. Call the dog. He will do it for your sake, and for the sake of the herd. Is he not a member of the herd? Does not his oath bind him to you? Does not the First Law demand that he accomplish this? I tell you, by all that I hold holy, that I know of things you mares can only dream of. This must be done.'

'Ask her,' said Lilly softly, 'just what it is that she holds holy. Ask her who her god might be. Ask her what light she carries with her – and what sort of glories she has seen that drive to the murder of the young. Ask her,' said Lilly, stepping close to El Arat, and gazing deep into the black mare's eyes, 'who I once was – and what *she* has become.'

The ground trembled beneath their feet, and Pony squealed in pain. The two mares, one dark, one silver, challenged one another with a look.

And it was El Arat who backed away.

El Arat who snarled, her breath a stream of smoke in the night. 'So you were the mare the Black Horse described to the Dancer,' said Duchess unevenly. 'And you,' she turned to Lilly, 'you helped save the Dancer. You are Sycha.'

A squeal escaped from Feather's throat.

'I was,' said Lilly. 'I renounced my name. My place. And because I repented, I was offered a choice. I could dwell forever in Summer – that place of Judgment between the Courts and the Black Barns – or I could come here and live out my days as a mortal mare, and take a chance that when I passed again to Summer, as all mortal horses must, that how I lived my life here at Bishop Farm would redeem my soul.' She looked away from Duchess and swallowed hard. 'There was just one thing I asked – that I lose my name. A name that all horses, your breed in particular, would find so terrible that I would never have a chance to clear away my betrayal. Lord Equus granted that, and named me Lilly – a name he took, he said, from men, whose own history began with a female's betrayal of her kind.' She turned, squared up and faced El Arat directly. 'And now you have fallen to my former place, El Arat. Do you know what you have done?'

'What *I* have done?' mocked El Arat. 'I have had the courage to make a choice and follow through. I will not fail the task that's been set before me – nor will I make your mistake, *Sycha*, and take the coward's way. He was right, you know, my Dark Lord – you were weak, afraid, cowardly. He was wrong to choose you to stand at his shoulder. And he will not regret that he chose me!!'

'This is wrong. This is the worst kind of madness,' said Duchess desperately. 'Why did you do it, El Arat? Why?'

'She hasn't done it yet,' said Lilly. 'There is a price for her entry to the Black Barns – a price she must get us to pay. The death of Pony's foal – whoever its sire might be. As to why, Duchess – can't you guess? She is proud. She couldn't stand to see you – a mare she believed to be a Grade, a mare who lineage was nowhere near her own – the new Lead Mare in the Courts. She desired to be Breedmistress and she knew she could not. She is an Arabian; no Appaloosa blood runs in her veins. And she could never have the Dancer. Pride and jealousy, Duchess. Because of those two things, she is ready to kill. To take Pony's foal and use it as her pledge to the Dark Lord. She's lost her own foal. She's lost her place in the world of men. And she seeks revenge – as I once did.'

Pony shrieked once, twice, her sides heaving.

Duchess stood protectively over Pony and called desperately, 'Cory! To me! Cory!' She heard his deep barks in the distance, the heavy thud of his racing feet.

321

The collie leaped the fence, his gold and silver coat awash with reflected moonlight. He landed next to Pony, and stood in front of them both.

'It's come, then,' he said. 'Pony's foal?'

'It's mine!' shrieked El Arat. 'If it's Anor's or the Dancer's it is mine! And I will kill it! Kill it!'

With a tearing groan Pony stiffened, heaved once and the dark shape of a newborn foal lay at her hindquarters.

Duchess reared, her hooves ready to attack the black mare.

'Don't you move!' she cried. 'Don't you come near it. No matter what this foal is, it will live, do you hear me? It will live!'

Cory snarled, standing at Duchess' side. El Arat plunged up and down, then backed away. Fancy, Feather and Cissy huddled together in soundless fear. Pony and the newborn foal were very still.

Cautiously, Duchess nosed the baby. In the light from the sullen moon, its coat was dark red, damp with the afterbirth. It stumbled to its feet, and Duchess expelled her breath in an explosive sigh.

'It's a filly. And her eyes are brown – not yellow, not like – not yellow.'

Pony grunted, rolled to her feet, and nosed the foal to her side. Her voice was a hoarse whisper. 'Duchess?'

'Yes, Pony?'

'I don't know who the sire is. It could be either.' Duchess began to help Pony clean the foal with rough licks of her tongue.

'It is *mine*,' hissed El Arat. 'It belongs to me.'

Duchess spun, hindquarters out, steel-hard hind feet ready to plunge into El Arat's chest. 'Fancy! Do I stand alone?'

'No,' said Fancy suddenly. 'We stand by you.'

She joined Duchess, side by side, her hindquarters out. Feather and Cissy completed a half circle around Pony and the foal.

'I have a claim,' screamed El Arat.

The moon broke through the lowering clouds, bathing El Arat in a sickly light. Her eyes were red-rimmed, fierce, and she began to breath out in sharp, explosive sounds, as a stallion breathes before a kill.

The black mare loomed large, triumphant. Duchess was afraid.

12

The Beginning

'Come with me, all of you,' said Lilly. 'It's time for us to gather at Summer's Gate.'

El Arat scraped the ground, first one forefoot, then the other. Her eyes rolled to half moons.

'You haven't quite struck your bargain, yet,' said Lilly to the black mare. 'Are you regretting what you've put in motion? Until your agreement has been fulfilled by the death of this foal, Scant continues to Take Souls. There is time, El Arat, for you to change your course.' She stepped closer to the black and said, low-voiced, 'You will regret your choice, as I have done. Who knows if a chance to redeem yourself will come along for you as it did for me? I saved the Dancer, and redeemed my own soul. I must live my days out here, at Bishop Farm, and pass into Summer as any mortal mare, there to be finally judged. There is no place for you in the Courts, El Arat, as there is for Duchess. But there was a life of honor, which you abandoned. There was a life of good – which would have been rewarded at its end. I understand your pride. I understand your grief. I had it once myself. But it isn't worth it. Will you turn back now, and join us?'

El Arat rolled her teeth back from her lips in answer.

'Let Pony's foal go,' urged Lilly.

'My Lord demands its life. I offer it in forfeit. We shall see who stands by whom in the Courts, when this final battle's over.' El Arat backed up. The muscles in her chest and withers clenched and unclenched so that her hide rippled like a snake's.

Lilly sighed and turned to the dog. 'Cory. The pasture gate. Would you open it? We must all go now, to the pond.'

Cory wriggled under the fence and worked the gravity latch free. Lilly led the huddled band of mares, Pony's foal stumbling within their protective circle, out of the pasture and over the rise to the duck pond. Snip, in the weanling paddock, called out to them and was ignored.

'I don't like this,' Feather muttered. 'What's going to happen? I'm worried about the foal.'

'We'll have to trust in Equus,' said Fancy, soberly. 'But I wish I were in my stall.'

They reached the duck pond. The moon was round, full and pulsed a little in the heavy heat. To the brood mares, the safety of the barn and paddocks seemed very far away.

Lilly waded into the pond, grey and ghostlike. Just beyond the bank, she turned in the water and faced the mares.

'I, Lilly, once Sycha, Lead Mare to the mares of Equus in the Courts of the Outermost West, call Duchess to my shoulder.'

Duchess walked into the pond. The water was warm around her hocks and splashed a little on her belly. She stood at Lilly's near side.

'I, Lilly, once Sycha the Soul Taker, Dreamspeaker to he who should not be named, call El Arat Al Hakimer to my side.'

El Arat splashed into the water in an ugly, ungainly trot. Her coat glowed coal-like and her eyes were fierce and arrogant.

'I, Lilly, now Story-Teller and Dreamspeaker to the Bishop Farm herd, call these mares to my side: Fancy, Lead Mare; Feather, Second-in Command; Cissy, unranked, and Pony, unranked; and the foal at her side.'

The brood mares stepped carefully into the pond,

nudging the gawky foal before them. Cissy was so close to Fancy that she bumped her muzzle into the chestnut's withers with a thump.

Cory settled on the bank, forepaws extended, and waited for the white light.

Lilly reared to her hind legs and called on Jehanna, the Goddess Mare.

And for the last time in their mortal lives, the mares found themselves in the Meadows of Summer.

Lilly and Duchess stepped through the soft grass with easy familiarity. Jehanna, glowing like the sun, waited at the white gate. At the red gate stood Scant, his matted hair a darker dun than when Duchess had seen him last, his hide unscarred. The red eyes rolled back in the skull-like head and he grinned at Duchess. 'Sssweet mare,' he said. 'We have a score to settle.'

The red gate burst open with a crack that made the brood mares jump. The Path behind the gate smoked, and in the distance came a slow, dull booming.

ONE!

TWO!

THREE!

FOUR!

'Anor,' said El Arat, with a mixture of desire and fright. 'Anor comes.'

Anor emerged from the Black Barn's depths unchanged. His iron jaws gaped wide; his hot and mindless gaze swept over the mares like a scythe in a wheatfield. His clawed hooves worked the ground, as a great cat's will when it's about to spring. Then, a faint howling came from the bottom of the earth, 'Hai! Hai! Hai!' and the Harrier Hounds came up and arranged themselves around Anor's feet.

Jehanna struck the ground. A white light sprang from her hooves and a rainbow arced over her head. There was a sound of many horses walking, and the moon itself seemed to move behind the gate.

The Army of One Hundred and Five walked proudly

into the meadow. Equus, a bright sphere of silver, moved among them. At his near side stepped the Dancer, The Rainbow Horse, Breedmaster of the Appaloosas and Second to Equus, Lord, his Appaloosa coat brilliant with many colors.

Anor snorted and belched fire.

Equus stopped and the Army flowed into formation around him, except for the Dancer, who stood aloof, gazing toward the red gate.

Duchess' breath came a little faster.

'Scant,' said Equus in deep, rolling tones, 'call your master. Tell him to come before me.'

Scant crawled. 'He comesss,' he said. 'My masster comesss.'

The air around Anor shivered, then quieted. And they all heard the four beats of a walking horse in the silence.

'Click,' The scrape of hoof on stone. 'Click!' One of the stallions in the Army lifted his voice in a brief, fierce battle cry. 'Click!' El Arat laughed, eagerly. 'Click!'

Darkness came out of the ground.

He was a black deep enough to swallow any moon, a sable shadow that carried an iron spear where its brow would be. Two red coals glimmered briefly in that cloud, and Duchess fixed her eyes on Equus to avoid the fiery gaze. She felt the brief brush of feathers on her cheek, a reassurance. And she saw the Owl from the corner of her eye. He settled in the air over all their heads, and floated there, wings folded.

The giant shadow rolled to a halt, darkness flowing in a malignant halo about its head.

'We have been given much,' said the Dark Lord reasonably. 'And it is just one more thing we are owed, and then – why, we will return from where we came.'

'You have taken much,' said Equus. 'And are owed nothing.'

'We have El Arat Al Hakimer,' said the Dark Lord. 'One who has seen the dark, and knows it for what it is: the Truth, the way to follow. The price of her admission

327

to our ranks was a small thing, a little thing. Just that foal.'

'The foal's life is its own,' said Equus. 'It is you who owe us.'

'It was *agreed*!' the Dark Lord hissed. 'This piece of dung *here*,' and a spear of flame leaped toward the shrinking El Arat, 'struck the bargain. And that spotted fool – the Rainbow Horse – he breached his word. He tipped the Balance by giving up his task. He stole my Soul-Taker and our bargain has not been fulfilled! And he has not been punished yet! I demand the life of this foal, here, and I demand the life of the Dancer. And I will take it!'

'We will let the Owl decide!' said Equus.

The Hounds howled 'Hai! Hai! Hai!' The Stallions of the Army screamed 'War!' in a ringing chorus.

The Owl brought his wings up with a great rush and held them level in the air. The right wing dipped slightly, as with an invisible weight. The left wing curved down and from tip to tip the two hung equally Balanced.

A great cry rose from the Army's ranks. 'A Tournament! A Challenge!'

'Hai! Hai! Hai!' the Harriers wailed.

The Dancer paced forward and the light from his god threw the colors of his coat in bright relief. He struck at the ground, then reared up and shouted 'ANOR! ANOR! A – a-a-anor!'

The Red Destroyer shifted his weight and his jaws gaped wide. Greed and hunger flickered in his dull eyes and he walked heavily forward, clawed hooves striking sparks from the rocks in his path.

'Clear the way!' shouted the Percheron. 'A Tournament! A Challenge! Clear the way.' The Army backed into a half-circle and the Harrier Hounds came out of the steaming gate and completed it.

Duchess moved involuntarily forward, then stopped, shaking.

The Dancer reared, hooves cleaving the air, then

charged, ears pinned back, head snaked low to the ground. He hit Anor full against his fiery side. The red fell with the sound of thunder. The Dancer bit deeply into Anor's neck. The red stallion shook the Dancer free and struck out with his claws; a thin red line of blood welled along the Dancer's flanks. The spotted stallion whirled and kicked out with both hind legs in a blow to Anor's chest. Anor staggered to his knees, twisted his head, then sank his fangs deep into the Dancer's belly. The Dancer grunted deep, tore free, and bit at a coarse red ear. Black blood steamed, and Anor screeched.

The Dancer raced around the red stallion, charged once and shoved his shoulder deep into Anor's chest. The red stumbled, went down, and the Dancer dived for the nape of his neck and missed. Anor rolled, scrambling to his feet.

'Hai! Hai! Hai!' A Harrier Hound, skull's head ghostly white, ducked out from the circle and snapped at the Dancer's pastern.

The Morgan stallion broke from the Army's ranks, and herded the Hound back to its grinning fellows.

The Dancer's breath sounded like a bellows in the brilliant air.

He faced the Red, chest heaving.

Anor belched dark flame and oily smoke. The Dancer reared and feinted to Anor's near side. Anor swung, and sank his fangs into the Dancer's withers. The spotted stallion twisted away, whirled and drove his teeth deep into Anor's jugular vein. The Red stallion screamed again, then fell with the sound of rolling rocks.

The Dancer stood over him, muzzle dripping black blood, his eye glowing with white light. He placed a razor-sharp hoof at Anor's throat and looked at his god.

Anor writhed; with each agonized movement, the Dancer's hoof pressed deeper into his vulnerable underthroat.

'Sire,' gasped the Dancer.

'It is your choice,' said Equus gravely.

The Dark Lord snarled and the Harrier Hounds bayed.

'Kill him, then. Take him to the Final Death,' the Dark Lord sneered. 'He is of no use to me if such as *that* can beat him. Kill him, and his body will, I swear, be left to rot in the plains before my Barns.'

The Dancer, his gaze never wavering from his god's, said, 'I have tipped the Balance once, through pride, through the failings of my own will, through a choice that was for me alone. I jeopardized my own line through selfishness, did I not?' He looked down at the scarred stallion beneath his feet. 'Pah! If I kill – if they demand a life for a life? It will never end.' He raised his hoof from Anor's throat, and the Hounds hissed.

Anor rolled over, then clumsily got to his feet.

'Coward!' screamed the Dark Horse.

'Go back!' thundered Equus. 'Return to the foulness that bred you! Go back!'

'Back! Back! Back!' shouted the Army. They advanced in a shining wave, and Anor roared in fury.

'Back! Back! Back!' cried the Army, moving toward the gaping earth as one mighty force. Equus walked at the Army's head, his steps high and proud.

'Down!' ordered the Dark Horse.

The Hounds milled restlessly about the path, their tails whipping back and forth. The Dark Horse stamped his foot and one by one they slunk into the earth. Anor trailed after them and as he passed his Lord, the darkness shifted and the Twisted Horn struck at the Red, piercing Anor's yellow eye.

'Carrion!' hissed the Dark Lord.

Anor howled in pain, the empty eye socket dripping blood. He leaped into a heavy gallop and followed the pack into the bowels of the earth. El Arat, standing as though frozen, made a sudden bolt for the brood mares. The Dark Horse snapped and struck out. With a frightened scream El Arat fled below.

The brilliant red and yellow flames died. The smoke cleared from the path. The Dark Lord turned and faced the Army. His banked-coal gaze swept the god, the Army, and stopped at the clutch of frightened mares. For a brief and terrible moment, the world turned red for Duchess. She saw leaping flames, and in the center, a black stallion, a giant of his kind, the very heart of evil in his look and breath.

The red flames died away. Her vision cleared.

And the darkness moved down the now-silent, now-dimly lighted path.

Click! And the hoof hit no stone. Click! And there was no call of challenge from the Army. Click! And the red gate closed. Click!

'Well, Dancer,' said Equus. 'You've done much to redeem yourself.' The god turned to the Army. 'The Dancer has fulfilled his task! He has rescued the buckskin mare, the last true mare of his line, and she has given him a foal!'

'Thanks be to the One!' cried the stallions.

'He has defeated the Executioner in battle, and his crime is redeemed.'

'Thanks be to the One!'

Equus looked at Duchess with a silver shining. She stood quietly under the fierce gaze.

'The Mare Duchess has passed through the Tests. She is a true Second in Courage, in War, and the games of War. She is Lead Mare, putting the welfare of her herd before her own. She is Dreamspeaker and Story-Teller, having been to the Courts and Watched, and She is Caretaker, defending the life of the young.'

'Thanks be to the One!'

'Welcome, Breedmistress. Your task is this: You will live out your days at Bishop Farm. At the close of your mortal days you will take your place as Lead Mare to the mares of Equus, to become Breedmistress to the Appaloosa.'

'Thanks be to the One!' cried Jehanna, her voice a golden song. 'Welcome, Breedmistress!'

'And now, Dancer,' said Equus. 'There is the matter of this new Soul-Taker, of El Arat's loss. If you had

331

remained at Bishop Farm as you were charged to do, the black might have remained there in safety. She is lost to us now, and you bear no small responsibility.' He mused for a moment, his eyes on the grey mare, Lilly. 'Sycha's redemption shall count in the Balance, Dancer, but I must consult the One as to your final fate.'

The god turned as if to go.

'Wait,' said Duchess. Her legs felt weak, and she moved hesitantly out from the huddle of the mares. A whinny failed her, and as she approached her god, she walked more and more slowly, until she crept like a small and frightened bird toward the pool of crystal.

'Duchess,' said the Dancer, his voice deep and tender, 'wait.' He moved toward her, his breath on her withers, the warmth of his body like a fiery sun against her side. She saw the open wounds, the streaming blood, and she whickered deep in her throat, and nosed his shoulders wistfully.

'Do not approach too close,' the Dancer said. 'He is kind and good, but he is of such great strength that his power flows from him like water from a pool. That is the light you see. Too close, and it will consume you.'

Gently, he placed himself in front of her, shielding her from the god's bright glow.

'May I ask him something?' said Duchess in a whisper.

'Ask,' said the god, his voice like distant thunder. 'She is a mare of courage, Dancer, and worthy of your line. Ask, mare. But expect no answer.'

'He is still to be judged, Sire. The Dancer?'

The light brightened, then dimmed, as if the god had nodded.

'Please, Sire, Remember that I chose to go with him. That if he failed in his task because of pride, I failed, too. If he is to be judged, will you not judge us both? Will you not take into your accounting the love I have for him, and the love I think he has for me?'

'I might,' said the god. 'And then again – I might not. Remember that there is a new Sycha now. That El Arat,

332

who was a worthy mare, has been lost forever because the Dancer broke his vow.'

'Sire,' said Duchess, taking encouragement from the kindly tone. 'He failed partly because of pride – but mostly from love and the desire to right a wrong in my own past.'

'Enough,' said Equus impatiently. 'It is time to go. Return to your Herd, Mare, and ask no more.'

'But you *will* remember,' Duchess said. 'Sire.'

The bright glow flared, and the Dancer whispered. 'Go back, now. And do not grieve. If I return to you, you will know that all has turned out for the best. If he decides in my favor, I too will live out my mortal days at Bishop Farm, and return to the Courts through Summer.'

'Come!' said Equus. 'We must return. I must consult the One.'

The light faded. The warmth of Summer's half risen sun turned to the warmth of the water of the duck pond. The mares walked out of the water, Pony's foal in front of them, and greeted Cory in subdued voices.

'It went well, then,' the collie said. His eyes were deep and grieving. 'Yes,' said Fancy, softly, 'but how do you know? And why are you sad, Cory?'

The dog rose and sniffed at a dim shape huddled in the water.

El Arat.

And she was dead.

'I missed it *all*?' said Snip the next morning in the barn. 'Every little bit? I was in the pasture with them babies and I didn't see *nothin'*. I didn't hear nothin', 'cept Cory barkin' like a fool.'

The mares, their excited discussion of the night's events past, were settling in to sleep. But for Snip, whose obvious disappointment touched them a little, they would have been asleep hours before.

'I'd be just as glad if I'd missed it,' said Feather. 'It was the scariest thing I've ever seen.'

'I will tell you everything in detail,' promised Lilly,

'when we have a Herd meeting tonight. It will be almost as good as if you'd been there.'

'Ummm – that's okey-dokey with me if you don't,' said Snip, a little nervously. Feather had told her that Lilly had been the Soul-Taker, and Snip was of the opinion that the more space between her and the grey mare, the better. 'I'd just as soon *not* get snatched by you-know-who,' she said in a loud whisper to Feather, in the mistaken belief that she wouldn't be overheard. 'My ugh list is gettin' longer by the day. Now *she's* on it.'

'I'm just glad that everything turned out all right,' said Feather. 'Isn't Pony's foal beautiful? I wonder what they'll name her.'

'Fox,' said Pony. 'Her name is Fox. 'Cause she's fox-colored.'

Duchess, a great weariness in her body and soul, realized that she had forgotten to check the color of the baby's eyes.

She looked, and her heart leaped. 'A good clear brown,' she murmured, the vision of Anor's violent yellow eye before her. 'Oh, Equus, thanks.'

'And Duchess just walked right over and talked to Equus!' marvelled Snip. 'Oh, I shoulda been there.'

'It would have scared you right out of your hide, Snip,' said Cissy, not unkindly. 'Duchess, shouldn't we all go to sleep now? I'm really exhausted and I know you must be. Oh, good grief, here comes that nosey cat.'

'Hello-alo-alo-alo,' said Bunkie, sauntering down the concrete aisle. 'How are you ladies this morning? That dog is slung out on the kitchen floor like a half-empty grain sack. What happened last night to you guys?' She jumped onto the tack box and gazed at them inquisitively. 'So what's new?'

'What's new with you, Bunkie?' said Snip. 'There's nothin' new with me. But there's *lots* new with them. You got news?'

'Yep,' Bunkie yawned, her pink tongue curled like an

oddly colored caterpillar. 'That spotted horse? The one that snatched Duchess and poor old Susie?'

'What about him?' asked Lilly.

Duchess pressed her nose to the wire mesh, her heart pounding.

'He's back.'

'He's back?' said Duchess, stunned. 'He's back?'

'That's what I said, didn't I,' snapped the cat. 'The Bishops found him in the back pasture this morning. He was clawed up pretty good, let me tell you. And you know what? They found El Arat's bo. . . .'

Duchess flung herself into her stall's paddock. David was coming up the drive, and with him was the Dancer.

His head, neck and chest were as coal black as when she'd known him first. White trailed across the glossy hindquarters like ivy leaves. Fresh wounds, weeping blood, crisscrossed the glossy hide. But his step was light, his eye proud, and he called out to her – a long whistle.

Bunkie jumped on the fence post near Duchess and gave her the barest wink. 'He's back for good this time,' she said. 'Or that's what they tell me. Gonna start a whole new line of those little spotted foals with all the mares in the herd. That's what the boss says. And he ought to know. Well, for Bast's sake – *you* sure look happy about it.'

EPILOGUE

Equus moved with quiet majesty through the Courts of the Outermost West. The river ran clear and sweet, scarlet flowers bloomed in the thick green grass, and the sun cast a rich radiance over the grazing Army of the One Hundred and Five.

The god paced slowly to the Watching Pool, and addressed the patient Miler.

'He returned safely?' said the god.

'Yes, Sire, he was welcomed. And he is happy – not as though it was a punishment at all.'

Equus may have smiled to himself – Miler was uncertain.

'Sometimes,' the god observed, 'the burdens of our guardianship may be given up for other, more rewarding things. Who is to say what makes each of us the happiest?'

'Sire?' said Miler timidly. 'When will the Story be finished? The mare who is now Lilly must have a Story to tell.'

Equus gazed thoughtfully into the Pool.

'See how the Piper dances, beneath the oak tree on the hill. His colors glow as brightly as the Dancer's ever did. And watch how he plays with the dog – a brave colt. A worthy successor to his sire. Perhaps. We shall have to see. I should think the Army will not remain diminished for long.'

Equus turned to continue his rounds, disappearing into a grove of silver beech.

Miler resumed his Watch by the Pool, and waited for the end of the Tale.

The Army of One Hundred and Five

The Army of One Hundred and Five

1. Appaloosa/The Spotted Horse
2. Arabian
3. Akha-Teke
4. Alter-Real
5. Andalusian
6. Anglo-Arab
7. Ardennes
8. Avelignese
9. Bahr-el-gazel
10. Basuto
11. Bavarian Warm-Blood
12. Bofian
13. Boulonnais
14. Borny
15. Barband
16. Breton
17. Budenny
18. Cleveland Bay
19. Clydesdale
20. Connemara
21. Criollo
22. Dale
23. Dartmoor
24. Døle
25. Don
26. Dutch Draft
27. Einseidler
28. Exmoor
29. Falabella
30. Feanches-Montagnes
31. Fell
32. Finnish Draft
33. Fjord
34. Fredericksbörg
35. French Trotter
36. Friesian
37. Fulani
38. Furioso
39. Garrano
40. Gelderlander
41. Hackney
42. Haflinger
43. Hanoverian
44. Highland
45. Hispano-Breton
46. Hokaido
47. Holsteiner
48. Hucul
49. Icelandic Pony
50. Irish Draught
51. Jutland
52. Kladruber
53. Knasbstrup
54. Knoik
55. Lithuanian Heavy Draught
56. Lipizzaner
57. Llanero
58. Lokai
59. Lusitano
60. Lyngen
61. Malopolski
62. Mangalarga

63.	Morgan	85.	Salteno
64.	Murakosi	86.	Schleswiger
65.	Murgese	87.	Serkano
66.	Mur-Insulan	88.	Shetland
67.	New Forest Pony	89.	Shire
68.	Noric	90.	Sorraia
69.	Northland	91.	Standardbred
70.	North Swedish Horse	92.	Suffolk Punch
71.	Novokhirghiz	93.	Swedish Warm Blood
72.	Oldenburg	94.	Tennessee Walking Horse
73.	Orlov Trotter		
74.	Paint, Overo and Tobiano	95.	Tersk
		96.	Thoroughbred
75.	Palomino	97.	Toric
76.	Percheron	98.	Trakehner
77.	Peruvian Paso Fino	99.	Vladimir Heavy Draught
78.	Pinto		
79.	Pony of the Americas (P.O.A.)	100.	Weilkopolski
		101.	Welsh Cob
80.	Quarter Horse	102.	Welsh Mountain Pony
81.	Renish Warm Blood	103.	Wurttemberg
82.	Saddlebred	104.	Yakut
83.	Sadecki	105.	Zweibrucker
84.	Sandlewood/Sumba		

A complete listing of *all* breeds registered in the World of Men would number over 200. However, the fact that Brazil and Argentina claim that the Crioulo and the Criollo are two separate breeds, for example, doesn't cut any ice at the Watching Pool. In all instances where the same breed has been claimed as separate by two countries, there is only one listing.

– Mary Stanton
Puddle Jumper Farm
Walworth, NY
1988

Appendices

A Note About Time, the Seasons, and the Weather

The hrunn base their understanding of natural phenomena on their observations and needs of their biology. Unlike the calendar year which humans use, the hrunn divide the year into the four seasons, using summer, the period when births are at their highest, as a focal point. Therefore, a year-old colt would be a one-summer colt or four seasons old; an aged hrunn would be a ten-summers mare or 40 seasons old.

Each day is divided into periods of sunlight and darkness. From dawn to sunset is the time for moving from one place to another, and the period when the major portion for grazing is done – although hrunn, having small stomachs for their size, tend to graze whenever and wherever they get the chance.

* * *

From sunset to moonrise is the period for herd activities such as Council meetings, settling the foals for the night, and accomplishing all the major and minor necessities of herd business. In times when there is no moon, the hrunn tend to be quieter and not argue and discuss among themselves so much.

From moonset to dawn is the time when births are most frequent; the hrunn feel that this is the safest time, the darkest part of the night. They are frequently wrong about this, but no one I know has ever been able to convince them it isn't true.

Language

Translating the language of the hrunn is a difficult task. Hrunn communicate through body posture and vocalizations which do not lend themselves to the static, less flexible languages of human beings. In short, talking, to hurnn, is almost impossible.

This vocabulary, therefore, is merely an approximation of the language of the hrunn – and a pale approximation, at that. (The Ya-O Himself only knows how accurate my efforts are.)

But there is a small test, if you readers would like to attempt it: some moonwashed night, when the great wheel of summer itself is felt in the turning of the earth, slip into your local stable (and mind the *feh-hi*; a good watch dog will alert his master to your presence!) and whisper 'shu-pah!' making sure that the hrunn feels the soft explosions of the your breath against a cheek or muzzle. This means 'Welcome-I-am-a-friend-of-the-herd' and you should get, if not a wise and tender smile, at least an acknowledging whicker.

NOUNS

hrunn – the horse
suhn – herd or pack
hi – an advisor to a leader
ma – she/her, the feminine
ma – he/him, the masculine
prrip! – a young foal; the young of any species
feh – dog/hound
saf – evil; the dark
ya – a divinity; the divine
bāo – line or breed, as in the Appaloosa bāo
nehma – a weanling; prepubescent filly
nehmo – a weanling; prepubescent colt
seh – a meat-eater
nruh – a grass-eater
ba – flank
rebah – left or near side
reboh – right or off side
haugh – war
eehaugh! – challenge/a formal invitation to fight
hanhaugh – a pivot to kick; an extrememly aggressive action designed to main or kill
haihaugh! – teeth-bared-to-bite; an action designed to maim or kill
hē – barren, dry
nehē – sickness
brahn – an old or broken-spirited hrunn
aĥ – an aged horse, over the age of ten years
ahseh – death
hrunnmahe – a barren mare
nemahi – a maiden mare; one who has not been bred to a stallion
hrunnama – a maiden mare; one who has had a foal
nemohe – a gelding

344

hrunnmago – Lead Mare
hrrunn-hi – Second-in-Command
hrrunma-sai – the Story-Teller
hrunnhema – the Caretaker
ry – obedience to the law; to man
ayn – man; an omnivore; a two-legged creature
shu-pah! – welcome
hrrunomo-ya – the Herd Stallion
Mo-hail! – the Celestial Army of One Hundred and Five
Mo-Ya! – Equus, the Horse God
Yo-hun – the Heavenly Courts of the Outermost West
Sehhun – The Black Barns
Anor-Saf – the red destroyer
Mo-Saf – the Dark Horse
He-Ya – the messenger; the Great White Owl
yohunme – good forage; literally, heavenly food
hunme – feed, especially oàts and other grains
sehunme – barren pastures
ry-ayn – performance, as in a horse show; also work, as in
    pulling a cart
sai – a story or tale
sai-ya – Tales of the Law
Nehun – stable mate or close friend

VERBS

mirah – to kick out with both hind feet
mir – to kick out with one hind leg; a cow kick
mir-re – to kick with the left hind
mir-ro – to kick with the right hind; usually more powerful in a
    'right-handed' horse
sen – to strike out with the forefoot; *sen–re* with the right; *sen-
ro* with the left
senrah – to rear and strike out with both forefeet; an action
    usually limited to the stallions or hrunnmo-ya
hai-shun – to herd mares; snaking; performed with the head
    low to the ground and the teeth bared
syn-shun – to travel in a herd in formation: Lead Mare, second
    in command, Storyteller, brood mares and foals, caretaker,
    geldings or sexually immature colts

345

synmih – a travelling gallop

synprrip! – to play, as in the foal's game of Tag-Tail

syn-dah – to canter or lope; a slow, easy gallop

tah-tah – a trot; this gait is not comfortable for the hurnn, and this term is their understanding of what man demands

nesyn – walk

pahnin – the act of breeding

pahnin-ya – to give birth to a live foal

pahnin-seh – to abort, or deliver a dead foal

pahnin-ma – top come into heat; in mares, this usually occurs eight times a year

nuph – to drink

rhruhn – top graze

hira – to guard

PIERS ANTHONY

VALE OF THE VOLE

The first of a new Xanth trilogy

It all started when Metria, the shape-shifting demo-
ness, took up residence in Esk's secret tree house.

Esk *needed* his hideaway. When your mother's a
nymph and father part-ogre, you have to be able to
get away from it all now and again. But Metria was
determined to force him out. She tried violence,
threats, wheedling and seduction. Seduction nearly
did it.

So it was that he set out through the Kingdom of
Xanth, to find and ask help from the Good Magician.
Travelling the enchanted pathways, first he saved
Chex, winged she-centaur, from the overheated atten-
tions of a small but nasty dragon.

And then they met Volney the Vole, who had a real
problem. And so one thing just kept on leading to
another . . . and another . . .

POST A LITTLE HAPPINESS

Post·A·Book

A Royal Mail service in association with the Book Marketing Council & The Booksellers Association.
Post-A-Book is a Post Office trademark.

MARION BRADLEY

WEB OF DARKNESS

Atlantis lived and flourished in the Time of Fable —
that Time that is no more, yet lives still in the true
and ancient world of the imagination.

Atlantis fell, betrayed, to slip beneath the seas of
forgetfulness. Yet sometimes can even now be dimly
discerned beneath the surface of our waking life, a
looming memory of a great empire.

This is the story of Atlantis and of the forces that,
magically unleashed, led to her downfall. And it is the
story of two sisters, priestesses of a high and age-old
cult, who, by love, were fated to let loose those
forces . . .

HODDER AND STOUGHTON PAPERBACKS

DIANA L. PAXSON

WHITE MARE, RED STALLION

The Lady of the Ravens.

Maira lived in the land that someday would be called Scotland, in the time when magic hung heavy on the hills and the Old Gods were revered with pageantry – and with blood.

The soldiers of Rome had claimed the island for thier own, but the Celts would never surrender their homeland for they were a fierce and warlike people. When they were not warring against mighty Caesar, they warred against each other.

Daughter of a chieftain, Maira was as fierce and proud as any Celt, trained in the arts of war as well as the mysteries of women. She was of the White Horse clan and her beauty shone like the sun itself. Carric had loved her since he'd first seen her. Even though she was of an enemy tribe. Even though she had vowed to kill him . . .

HODDER AND STOUGHTON PAPERBACKS

FREDA WARRINGTON

A BLACKBIRD IN AMBER

The great serpent M'gulfn was dead, its power dispersed and all save one of its demon-servants destroyed.

Now was the time when the power of sorcery might be harnessed for good or for evil.

Journeying disguised to Gorethria came Mellorn, daughter of Silvern and Ashurek, by training and by will eager to use that latent power for good.

But to Gorethria, summoned by the usurper Duke Xaedrek, there came also the demon Ahag-Ga in the guise of an old woman. Together they plan to use the power: he to rebuild the terrible authority of the old empire; she, silently vengeful, determined to unleash the dark forces of Chaos on a world that, saved, is yet in peril.

A Blackbird in Amber, sequel to *A Blackbird in Darkness*, is the third in the series which began with *A Blackbird in Silver*.

HODDER AND STOUGHTON PAPERBACKS

FREDA WARRINGTON

A BLACKBIRD IN TWILIGHT

Unnoticed, urgent, the blackbird Miril flew headlong toward Earth.

She had risen up, singing and joyous when the Serpent had died. Through the stars and through other times, she had flown free. But now, insistently, she was being called back.

Some part of the Serpent was not dead. Its evil, coiled and deadly, lived on in the guise of the old woman Ah'garith. She had wormed her way into the court and the counsels of the Emperor Xaedrek, ruler of Gorethria.

Now she urged him to strike at the exiled sorceress Melkavesh, and to make war on the last of his enemies. Still he was wary, for he knew of the dreadful power that lived within Ah'garith. But the temptations were great. Both his advisors and his own instincts demanded war. Yet by the very action that should ensure the Empire's safety, an Evil could be released that would destroy everything . . .

The blackbird who was the world's Hope, winged her way desperately through the void.

A Blackbird in Twilight is the fourth in the spellbinding series that began with *A Blackbird in Silver*.

HODDER AND STOUGHTON PAPERBACKS